Love Unconventional

The Fredericks Family Series

Lala B.

ISBN-13: 979-8-9994181-0-4

Cover design by: Art Painter

Library of Congress Control Number: 2018675309

Contents

Contents Continued

Trigger Warnings

I'm going to hold your hand while I say this baby love if any of these things listed below bothers or triggers you in anyway, please exit stage right now and I promise I won't be offended. Now for the rest buckle up *smooches*

★ Explicit language

★ Graphic sex scenes

★ Various sex kink/fetish content

★ Rape

★ Child loss

★ Mild stalking

★ Kidnapping

★ Graphic violence

★ Pregnancy

★ Sex trafficking

★ Drug use

★ Poly relationships

★ Orgies (Multiple sex partners at once)

Some characters in this book suffer from mental disorders such as antisocial personality disorder, psychopath, and sociopath.

Prologue

The countryside was supposed to be her sanctuary. After years of heartache and chaos, La'Meira Jennings craved the simplicity of open skies and quiet mornings. Her life had been anything but simple—a mother of three teenagers, one of whom she inherited under tragic circumstances. Adopting Mariah after her best friend's Jameia's murder wasn't a choice; it was a calling. Leaving the city was her chance to give her family peace, a fresh start in a world untouched by the shadows of their past.

But as La'Meira works on what was supposed to be a simple divorce case for her other best friend Dean, she couldn't shake the feeling that danger would be waiting around the corner. The small-town smiles seemed too warm, the woods too silent, the nights too long. Her best friend Dean wanted to be her protection but as usual she was too stubborn to open up.

Montavius Fredericks sat in his office overlooking the city he grew up in as it surrounded his family's security firm. Retired from the Marines but far from retired in life, he spent his days managing operations with his for all intents and purposes partner and five brothers, each of them as formidable and loyal as he was. But the nights were different. Montavius had a secret—a craving for connection that defied convention, a yearning for a partner who could embrace his intensity, accept him as he was and indulge in his fantasies while creating memories.

He had resigned himself to waiting until fate brought her to him. Yet, when his brother Dean finally reveals his mysterious best friend La'Meira Jennings, with her thick short frame, guarded eyes and an air of strength, something stirred deep within him. He didn't know if she was ready for him—or if he was ready for her and everything that came with her but they both might as well get ready because he was coming for his woman.

As the days turned into weeks, of Montavius keeping an eye on La'Meira for her own protection it became unbearable to not to claim her as his. But the ghosts of her past and the enemies she's gained from helping his little brother may be too much for her, but he is determined and so is his other brother Jax. Their worlds collided in a storm of passion, danger, and trust that would force them both to confront what it meant to truly love someone, even when love itself was anything but conventional.

Chapter One

La'Meira "Meira" Jennings

Who would have thought my big ass would be riding a horse on a ranch watching the sunset with my babies at the ripe age of thirty-five. Well, I am because the city girl has turned into a country woman, and I am loving every bit of it chile. Moving from Miami, Florida, to Ashford, Alabama was the hardest decision I have ever made since taking over custody of my god daughter Mariah over two years ago. Raising 3 kids alone was never in my plans but after losing Jameia, my best friend, to a murder that has yet to be solved there was no way I would leave her with her sorry ass father. You would think the man she knew as her father would have put up a fight in trying to keep her but no, the moment he received the paperwork for custody he signed over his rights completely. At first, I could not believe just how easy it was but then quickly realized it was definitely for the best. So here I am living in a small town raising my twins Za'Meir and Za'Mara and now Mariah. Unfortunately, before I knew it my five am alarm was going off getting louder and louder, I purposely set it that way so I could force myself to get up earlier and have more time for me before waking the kids up for school. I have developed a routine, and it is working for me as well as the kids, which made these past six months transition here so much smoother. "Ugh" I could not help but groan while tapping my alarm clock to turn it off and stretching out in the bed. "Alright Meira let's get this day started" I coach myself while heading to the bathroom to relieve myself and start part of my hygiene routine. Once I am done, I grab my yoga mat and head out the double doors attached to my master bedroom that leads to my large backyard. Getting my prayer and stretch time done in the morning was essential to getting the day started. After a good thirty minutes of my routine, I head back in to start breakfast for the kids, which I only did a few times out of the week. Since moving here, the kids love the country style breakfast they get at school, it tastes like real food. It was Monday so I decided to go with their favorite pancakes, sausage and scrambled eggs with cheese of course and some fresh fruits. While letting the batter for the pancakes sit for a few minutes and after putting the sausage in the oven I started my kettle for my morning tea. I take a look over my spacious kitchen, dining room and living room space still in awe that the little hood girl from Opa Locka, Florida could afford such a big, beautiful home she always dreamed of, well close to it. We still have some remolding that needs to be done but with my uncle Tones help we have already finished the major parts like the kitchen, all the flooring in the house, and upgraded the windows. I started on my bathroom and the kids have transformed their rooms. The kettle going off for my tea dragged me from my thoughts and long to do list right back into reality.

"Morning mama." Za'Mara sang as she skipped over to me in the kitchen giving me my morning kiss on the cheek. Za'Mara was always the first to get up, she was like me, not a morning person but getting in a routine made it much more enjoyable for us both. Soon Mariah and Za'Meir came out of their rooms joining us in the kitchen.

"Oooh something smells good Ma." Za'Meir sniffs the air walking over to give me a kiss too. He was my greedy baby but, in his defense, he does play football and run track during the off season but even before that he always loved to work out so him always being hungry was nothing new.

"I'll do the eggs if you want Ma." He offers grabbing what he needed out the fridge and the mixing bowl from the cabinet while I started on the pancakes on the griddle pan that I have on the island. We move in unison finishing up breakfast in no time. The girls grabbed the orange juice pitcher, milk, fruit bowl, and syrup to set the table at our little breakfast nook in the left side of the kitchen. The built-in bench in the bay window next to the kitchen was one of our favorite spots to sit and eat because it looked out on the cleared two-acre size backyard with the best view of the sun rising and the beautiful trees on the remaining two-acres.

"Alright Meir it's your turn to say grace baby." We grab each other's hand and lower our heads for prayer.

"Thank you, heavenly Father, for this delicious meal laid out in front of us let it be a nourishment to our bodies, thank you for the roof over our heads and the clothes on our backs. Be our guiding light today and give us the strength physically and mentally as we go about our day and block the enemies attack on our minds body and spirit, Amen."

"Amen." we say in unison then pass the food platters around the table filling our plates and ate in silence for a bit.

"So, what's on the agenda today kids?"

"Well, you know I have football practice today, but we have this social studies test today that I am hoping I pass." Za'Meir says first with his mouth half filled with eggs.

"Boy what have I told you about talking with food in your mouth? We did your study sessions twice this week so I am sure you will do great. Just take a few deep breaths before you start and don't over think it, okay." I encourage him and he nods his head. Out of the three he is the least confident in school but great at athletics and handling money.

"I'm riding with Bell today after school to martial art class, so you don't have to come get me today, Mama." Za'Mara chips in next making sure she finishes chewing her food first. She was diagnosed with ADHD a few years ago and I tried multiple different techniques to help her with being able to focus for longer periods of time but martial arts was the only thing that stuck, probably because she just liked to beat up on boys without getting into trouble and I can't help but have an internal laugh at that thought because that was me in Jiu Jitsu as well as boxing growing up. Putting me in those classes was about the only thing my sperm donor did right for me as a kid.

"Ma did you sign my field trip form? Oh, and I have girls scouts meeting today right after school, but cheerleading tryouts are tomorrow." Mariah finally stops eating long enough to speak.

"Yes, baby it's already in your folder in ya book bag, but that's cool I'm sure it's time to get ready for the first fundraiser of the year. I can't wait for my box of Tagalongs and don't start Papa, I know you want your s'mores cookies." I say before Za'Meir could even start up about his favorite cookies.

"Alright y'all it's time to get ready for school. Ya don't wanna miss the bus." I announce to the kids after noticing the time on the clock that is hanging on the wall across from the kitchen. The girls loaded the dishwasher and cleaned the table while Za'Meir headed to the bathroom to start on his hygiene routine. In this home a strict hygiene routine was not up for debate to the point I made all their soaps and moisturizers by hand. Mariah and Za'Meir both were born with eczema, and I tried to use all those steroid creams or ointments the doctors prescribed them but only the ointment worked but still left them super grease. Za'Mara was lucky though she only had a bit of dry skin because she tended to be the lazy one out of the three of my babies, but she was beginning to get better as she started smelling herself as the old folks would say. By the time the girls were done in the kitchen and grabbing their snacks for school Za'Meir was heading to his room to get dressed. I was happy for the mornings that went by smoothly with the kids because lord knows it wasn't always this peaceful. I walk to my office in the front of the house, it was supposed to be a formal dining room, but we had no need for it that way. I yelled out to the kids that they had 15 minutes before the bus came. It was one of the other things I loved about living in a small town, the kids caught the bus to school, and their stop was right on the corner of our street, I could literally sit in my office chair and watch them get on the bus. I sat at my desk to load up my emails to see if I had any new clients and to see my agenda for the day. I make money fixing phones and computers whether it be a broken screen, unlocking phones, or any repair or upgrades their devices may need. I have my own store front in a plaza downtown, but some days I choose to work from home since I could get request through my website or app I have for my business. Before I had to call for the kids to get outside for the bus, they were all headed towards my office.

"Later mom, love you!" They all shout and wave at me through my open door as they head out.

"I love y'all too, have a great day." I smile, looking out the window at them greeting their cousins coming from next door, another perk moving here provided. Once they were on the bus and off to school, I headed to my room to take a shower before starting work. Once I was feeling fresh and back at my desk I noticed an email from Dean Fredericks my male best friend, I outsourced my computer skills to his private investigator firm and others from time to time. Apparently, he needed help with a case where the wife thought her husband was cheating on her and she wanted to gather as much evidence before filing for divorce. Seeing as I only had two cell phone screens to fix and one computer to do a hard drive upgrade on, I accepted the job. He paid the job invoice right away as he always does and sent me the basic case information. I sent the husband a bogus promotional email and billing text message with links he would click that allows me full access to his devices and of course he clicked on both within the hour. I sit at my desk for the next few hours replacing screens on two cell phones then upgrading a hard drive on my graphic designer client's laptop while my program collected information from my unsuspecting targets devices. Whatever firewalls he had installed were pretty good but not good enough. Dean knows I like a challenge, so he sends me all the good cases. He has really become a best friend I did not think I would get after Jameia left me, but he has and is one fine ass man on top of being the sweetest. He stands at about six foot five with a thick muscular frame, broad shoulders, skin the shade of dark chocolate, full face soft beard wrapped around his heart shaped chocolate toned juicy lips, almond shaped hazel grey eyes, lashes most women pay for and four c hair in 360 waves that I know have women swooning over. As fine as he was though he is my friend, and I needed that more than his dick which I know is large. Let's just say the print be printing and he don't need grey sweatpants for it either. His damn big brother though holy mother of pearls that man was absolutely delicious and even though I figured he would not be interested in a woman like me it did not stop me from checking him out on social media from time to time. I know I am a good-looking woman don't get it twisted and nowhere near ashamed of my thick curvaceous body but being a thirty-five year old woman not all there in the head with 3 kids the likelihood of a multimillionaire bachelor with no kids being interested was slim to none. My alert for my program goes off pulling me from my thoughts. I opened the program and looked through the first few folders which weren't much of anything but standard work information. I thought for a moment it was all work stuff until I opened the fourth folder which turned out to be encrypted so that piqued my interest. It took me another thirty minutes to unlock the folder but when I did dammit, I wish I would have left it closed. Hundreds of videos and photos appeared of young girls even young boys tied up in filthy settings. I became so engrossed with opening file after file filled with more photos, others that look like bookkeeping pages, property records, and so much more than I expected to find on a simple cheating husband case and before I knew it my phone was ringing with Za'Meir calling me.

"Yes baby."

"Um ma, do you not know what time it is?" He questions me and I finally looked to the clock in my room smacking myself on the forehead because it was after five pm and his practice was over ten minutes ago.

"I am so sorry baby I am on my way now." I apologize picking up my wallet and keys, walking out of my office and heading for the garage to hop in my two thousand Chevy Impala. Thankfully, the kids' school is barely ten minutes away from our home by car, so it did not take me long to grab both Za'Meir and I was just in time to grab Mariah too from her girl scouts meeting.

"So, babies mommy didn't get to prep dinner today, so it's either eat what's at home or if y'all have a taste for something we can pick up fine with me."

"Why are you running so behind anyways mom, that's not like you?" Za'Meir's voice was full of concern.

"He's right ma, is it another bad case?" Mariah chimed in from the back seat also sounding concerned.

"Yes, an unexpected one though, but don't worry I am not going to handle this one. It's a case for Uncle Dean so I will be handing it over to him." I try to relieve some of their concern. I have another side job well not job because there is no pay, but I track down trafficking rings and the kids discovered me patching up my wounds one night and me not wanting to hide things from them or lie I gave them a highlighted version of what I do sometimes. I haven't been out since we moved here over six months ago, I wanted to get the kids settled first but life has been so peaceful a part of me doesn't want to go back and start them worrying about me again. The kids decided on Chinese food once we called Za'Mara to take her vote on dinner for tonight. While waiting for the food to be done we walked over to the grocery store to grab our favorite fruit bowls, I sent Dean an email that we needed to talk securely asap about this case. By the time we checked out of the grocery store our food was done and we were headed back home. I tried focusing on the small talk we made over dinner, but my mind was still on all those photos and videos of those poor kids being forced to do unspeakable things to those disgusting old men and women. Once we finished with dinner the kids went to their respective rooms to get ready for bed and I headed back to my office with a much-needed glass of wine. I went through more file folders I collected and complied everything to send over to Dean with the secure link we usually used, then took myself to my room to shower than run me a bath with some of my sativa infused Epson salt to relax my body, also lit me a few candles with lavender and chamomile. I had to have been in the tub for maybe ten minutes when a knock on my bathroom door came.

"Come in." I shout knowing it was one of my babies and sure enough in came Za'Mara. "Mom Mariah told me about the case, are you really not taking it?"

"I'm really not taking it on myself."

"Why momma? I thought you liked rescuing those kids. You were doing good." She probed me.

"Well mainly because the info came to me working on a case for uncle Dean but if he doesn't do anything about it maybe I will check into it further, but I honestly don't want you guys worrying about me while I'm out there doing what I must do to rescue those kids." I explained feeling a little proud that my baby thinks I was doing something good.

"Ok well mommy we are good those kids don't have anyone, and we hope you're not giving up on them just for us. You're our hero and it's okay for you to be theirs too." My kids never cease to blow my mind completely.

"Baby mommy is no hero because I'd burn every city in this God forsaken country to the ground to save you guys over anyone, but I haven't given up on them, I am just taking a break yes for you guys but also for myself, besides even if I don't physically do something myself you know mommy has her online friends that help in getting to those kids as well, do you understand that." I tried explaining to her my reasoning for stepping back from killing off the scum of the world.

"Yes, ma'am I do. I am going to go to bed now, love you ma." She leans down giving me a kiss on the cheek and leaving me in my thoughts even more than I was before. My kids think that I am a hero should make me feel good, but it doesn't because I truly don't feel like a hero. If it came down to my kids or those that I use to go out and save with help from some of my dark web friends, I would choose my kids every time and I am not sorry about that. I rescued those kids simply because I had the ability to access the information needed to find them and the knowledge of weapons and hand to hand fighting to get them out. I have been doing it for the past eight years and have rescued over two hundred kids. Those first few years were brutal on my body simply due to inexperience but the more I went out the more efficient I became plus adding in a few online friends to watch my back during the process helped. I definitely felt better after that bath and rubbing myself down with my lavender body butter I made last week, laying down in my bed in my birthday suit on my silk sheets had me asleep in no time.

Chapter Two

Montavius "Monty" Fredericks

After my morning workout I head to my large
modern style kitchen to grab my yogurt, oatmeal, and fruit
parfait from the fridge. My chef often prepped my breakfast
bowls for the week, but he was on vacation this week, so I
was on my own. After getting my fill, I head upstairs into my
large master bedroom to get my hygiene together then get
dressed. Once I was all dressed, I stood in front of my floor
length mirror inside my walk-in closet to admire how good I
looked in my tailored three-piece navy-blue suit. With my
six-foot six muscular frame I have all my suits tailored and in
my business first impressions were everything. I checked
around to make sure I had everything and nothing was left
on then headed to my attached garage deciding to drive my
black 2024 Range Rover. Before I could fully get out of my
driveway, I was getting a call from my business partner in my
security firm Titan Security Group.

"Yo what's up Justin?" I answer through the Bluetooth in the
truck.

"Morning Monty. Look I'm going to get right into it I have to
head out for maybe a few days that job we sent Brent and his
team on hit a major bump." Justin rushes out sounding
frustrated.

"What's a major bump Justin they were on a simple job securing that social media influencer Drea for a few days?"

"Well instead of one of the dudes securing her home he decided it was a good idea to secure some pussy instead and ended up getting shot in the leg by some crazed fan that broke in through her bedroom window." He practically shouted through the phone.

"This stupid ass nigga. Let me guess it was Chance?" I start squeezing my steering wheel so tight it hurt a bit. Thankfully the traffic is minimal, and my home is about twenty minutes from the office otherwise I'd have to end my day torturing somebody to ease my frustration. "Yup it was him and before you say I already drew up the paperwork to fire his ass and had HR issue a severance check." Justin sighs with pure irritation in his voice.

"I told you not to hire his young dumb ass anyways, I don't care that he's army, the boy is way to young minded. Whatever though get that mess handled I'll be pulling into the office in a few." I hang up and soon reach the office garage gate tapping my fingers on my steering wheel as it starts to rise reacting to the sensor in my truck then I head up to the fourth floor. I do not like having to deal with people the moment I walk into my building, therefore having my building designed in a way that provides me the space to get in and out without being bothered was paramount to my mental. The building is four levels above ground that consist of the main level for the receptionist desk, lunchroom to the right, an office supply room behind the reception desk, and the to the left ultramodern gym. The second level is where the offices for the security agents are and two conference rooms for larger meetings, third level is for the apartments for clients as well as agents that needed to stay overnight on one side then on the other a well-equipped medical wing for any injured agents or clients to treat everything from a minor cut all the way to deadly gunshot or stab wounds and the fourth floor was split between Justin and I office along with a medium sized kitchen as well as both of our assistants desk, who were nestled right in the middle. Now the basement of the building was the crown jewel that held the building's security armory along with the ops center and the offices of the IT team that I was able to cultivate of some of the best white hat hacker's money could buy. After about fifteen minutes of checking over things I hear three knocks on my door and in walked my assistant Whitney carrying her tablet that held everything, she needed to get her work done from her desk in one hand then the other my morning coffee.

"Good morning, Mr. Fredericks, here's your morning coffee. Are you ready to go over your schedule?" She sits in the leather armchair in front of my desk crossing her legs wearing a skirt that was almost too short for the workplace. She's subtle with her flirting but I notice and don't care main as I am not one to mix business with pleasure plus she is just not my type. Don't get me wrong she's beautiful but the skinny model figure, always long nails, and weave was a no for me.

"Yes, let's get to it because after this email I just read my day is probably going to need to be rearranged." I run my hand over my beard frustrated with one of my more pompous clients that I just received an email from. We went over my schedule for the next thirty minutes making changes where they were needed to accommodate Justin possibly being gone for the next few days and for the issues sure to arise from the earlier email.

"I will send Mr. Benemy in when he arrives in about 20 minutes."

"By the way sir your brothers just walked in." She informs me before fully strutting out of my office. I run my hands through my beard taking a deep breath because if my brothers are here this early it was more than likely not good. Being the oldest of 6 and raised by a single mother I often had to wear the father figure hat even though our mother was very present and loving but still handling six boys was a lot for anyone. My brothers were Jax, Dean, Chase, Demetrius, and Marshall from the oldest to the youngest man. Even though I felt like something may be wrong I still looked at all my brothers with pride because to all be black successful men in their own professions, no records, mentally and physically healthy, with no personal drama was rare.

"So, what do I owe the pleasure of your appearances this morning?"

"We can't come visit our big brother na?" Dean the third oldest who ran our PI business, asked sitting in one of the dark brown leather armchairs in front of my desk. While Jax sat next to him and Chase, Demetrius, and Marshall sat in the matching leather sofa up against the wall to the right kicking their feet up on the coffee table in front of them.

"Don't make me kick y'all asses this early in the morning, getcha damn feet off my table." I look over at them with my right eyebrow raised and hands folded on my desk. They quickly moved, knowing even if I did not look mad, I was serious about kicking their asses.

"Sooooo." I say looking at each of them in the eye waiting for one of them to speak up.

"Ok fine we may have a bit of a problem." Dean finally speaks up first.

"A bit bro you know he's about to blow a gasket, and I told you this." Jax, my brother that's a year younger than me and practically my twin groans.

"Dean speak quickly nigga."

"Ok so the PI firm took on this cheating husband case last week and you know sometimes I outsource the online proof gathering, while I do my thang. Well, I didn't notice that the husband of the client is one of the security firms' clients and I out sourced it to La'Meira to handle and she's started her work." Now I get why Jax thought I'd blow a gasket.

"Which client Dean?" Reeling in my frustration since it's not his fault.

"Mr. Sinclair." He responds bracing himself for the tongue lashing he was about to receive.

"You gotta be fucking kidding me, he's one of our biggest private clients Dean. Wait that explains his email of needing to speak to me right away." I let out a deep sigh and lean back into my chair. I knew they were going to come in here with some bull today, but this mess is going to take some serious cleaning up. The thing is I don't have any grounds to force Dean to withdraw from the case, for one he's already started and taken payment, and besides the PI company is not directly owned by the security firm therefore he can take on whatever clients he wants.

"So, what do you want to do about it Monty?" Dean inquires.

"Ya already took on the case at this point. This friend La'Meira, she must be pretty good to get through our firewalls on his devices." I ask thoroughly intrigued about his best friend which he has never introduced us to, but I figured he has his reasons, so I've never pushed.

"La'Meira is one of the best I've ever met or dealt with not to mention she's beautiful and my peaceful place." He says with a big grin on his face.

"Beautiful huh, let me see." I test to see if he will finally let us see the mysterious La'Meira. Dean pulls up La'Meira's Instagram while all of us surround him sitting in the chair.

"DAMNNNN!!!" We all say while looking at a photo of her at the beach with a black tropical two-piece bathing suit and long black and blue braids hanging down to her voluptuous ass, her wet dark honey colored skin glistening in the sun light while she strikes a pose looking to her right over her shoulder.

"She is thick as hell, just like I like em. So, this is the mysterious best friend you never let any of us meet and I see why. Is she more than a best friend, though?" I question walking back to my desk and pulling out my phone to check out her page on my own.

"Nah we have flirted with each other but real shit like I said she's my peace, so I don't want to ruin that. I met her at a tech convention about four years ago as you already know. She mainly fixes computers and cell phones, but she is a damn good hacker, one of the best I've worked with. She just opened a little shop of her own in Ashford, Alabama trying to get a fresh start for her family. I did some work for her tracking down her best friend, that died a while back, deadbeat husband to get physical proof he was mistreating her god daughter Mariah so she could take custody of her. She has my babies Za'Meir and Za'Mara they're twins and the coolest kids to be around." Dean finally tells us more about her and I see the genuine smile on his face. He really cares about them.

"Oop that's my que." Marshall says walking back to his seat.

"Facts she fine and all but I'm not ready to playhouse." Demetrius chuckles walking back to sit down as well.

"How old is she?" Chase asks as he's walking to sit back down.

"She's 35."

"Wait for real. Damn that just made her even finer cause I thought you were going to say about mid to late 20's." Chase says taking out his phone to text back someone, his fiancé Kenya more than likely.

"Nigga aren't you engaged, why you worried about her." Marshall says smacking him on the shoulder.

"Put ya hand on me again and I'm going to break it. I was just asking a question. I'm engaged not blind plus my girl likes girls." Chase says with a grin, and I remember him telling us Kenya was bi sexual but we haven't seen her in action yet.

"Mr. Frederick your nine fifteen is here." Whitney comes over my office intercom.

"Alright fellas we will chop it up more later, it is time to make this money." I tell them standing from my seat then putting my suit jacket back on and buttoning it in the middle.

"Aight we still having drinks and dinner at the Fredericks tonight?" Jax finally speaks, standing up to dap me up on the way out of my office.

"Fa sho." I confirm giving him dap and side hugging my brothers one by one as they leave. The next few hours went by in a flash of meetings with possible clients and meetings with my agents' getting updates on current clients. During my lunch break I found myself completely forgetting my food to scroll through the beauties Insta that has been on my mind all morning. To me having kids was a plus, that meant when we had our own, she would already know what to do and could teach me. I paused over a picture of her and her kids at a theme park and shook my head at the fact that I was even thinking about future kids with a woman I haven't even met yet. I placed the phone down and went about to finish my workday.

"Heading out Mr. Fredericks, do you need anything else before I go?" Whitney came over the intercom asking.

"No, you're fine Whitney, have a great night, and I'll see you tomorrow." I replied looking at my watch as I didn't realize how late it was after digging back into to research on some potential clients. I was definitely going to be late meeting up with my brothers at our restaurant. Sending a text message to let them know to order my usual and that I'd be there in about fifteen minutes. On my way out of my office one of my IT reps stopped me before I could get to my private exit.

"Mr. Fredericks, sorry to catch you this late but we have a problem with Mr. Sinclair's devices, he's being hacked." The IT rep rushed out as I was closing my office door.

"Yes, I know. Continue to block as much as you can. He's under investigation by Dean's PI firm as the wife has contracted his services. The only thing we can do is our jobs at this point. I've already let him know to contact a lawyer to settle with his wife before anything he doesn't want to get out does because this hacker my brother hired seems to be beyond good." I inform him while opening my private entrance door. The rep turned to walk over to the main elevator as he knew that was all he needed to know. I made it over to my car, turning on some old school Eminem. A call comes in through my speakers and of course it's my mother doing her nightly check in.

"Hi Iya." I greet her in our native tongue we discovered a while back.

"Hi baby, I didn't catch you still at work, did I?" She asks just making sure I'm not still at work.

"No ma'am. I am headed to meet with the guys at the restaurant."

"Ok good, you're always working so hard. I missed you at Sunday dinner by the way." I hear a little sass in her voice, and I knew that was coming.

"Look Ma I love our Sunday family dinners, but I will not fake the funk with this boyfriend of yours. Something about him not sitting right with me." For whatever reason I didn't like that old head at all, but I couldn't quite put my finger on why. She didn't date much while we were growing up but since she retired, she decided to dip her toes in the dating pool, and this is the first man she has introduced to us, and she could've kept him to herself as far as I'm concerned.

"Really Monty? I haven't dated in years, and I really like Frank."

"Yes ma'am. I'm not going to make you choose or anything like that but if he's there I'm good on coming over there until I figure out what's up with him."

"You only met the man once Monty. Can you just come over this Sunday and give him another chance please?" She pleads with me because she knows if I don't start showing up my brothers will stop showing up eventually. They only went this last Sunday because I told them to.

"Ugh fine mama. I'll give him one more chance for you but if something still not setting right with me, he is getting out and you go have to try again." I tell her as I pull into the valet at our restaurant getting ready to hop out my truck.

"But mama I'm pulling up to the Fredericks now, I'll talk to you later." I say finally getting out and handing the valet my keys.

"Ok baby mo nife re."

"Mo nife lati, Iya." I end the call as I walk past the host nodding at her as I head to our private area in the back left side of our restaurant. We liked to sit where we can see every part of the restaurant at once.

"What were you fools talking about before I walked up?" I ask dapping everyone at the table then taking my usual seat.

"Man, the incident that happened at Euphoria last night, I didn't get to tell you this morning but some fool at the club thought he knew what he was doing with the Saint Andrews cross that we have with automatic neck collar attached to it. Somehow, he was able to bypass the safety protocols on it and damn near choked a girl to death. Luckily it alerted Bree in the control room eventually and she went down to the room to get her out of it because this fool was too busy screwing another chick right in front of her while she was apparently eating the dying chick pussy. These fools were high as hell." Jax informs me sitting to my right blowing out a hard breath clearly frustrated by the whole situation.

"How the fuck did they even get drugs into the club or bypass the damn safety protocols?" I whispered yell at him.

"We are still figuring that out. We have him at the cage sobering up because whatever they were high on had them buggin out heavy. We sent the girls to the Care room to sober up and get treatment for the other's injuries to her neck." Jax explains.

"So basically, somebody trying to sell drugs in our damn clubs because there was a supposed accidental overdose in Passion's night before last." Marshall, my youngest brothers, spoke with an increasingly irritated look on his face. We sat in silence for a long minute because we never had these issues before with how tight we keep security and screen all of our employees to avoid this exact thing. We grew up in a nice neighborhood, but we were no strangers to addiction after how our doctor father died of an overdose when I was just 8 years old and my brothers were just 7, 5, 3 and 2 years old. We wanted no parts of the drug life growing up so instead I used my brain to help our mom pay bills by doing rich kids' homework or projects at the private school we all went to plus tutoring those that wanted to actually earn their grades. The only drug we ever partake in is weed, so much so that it was infused in a lot of dishes at Fredericks. Demetrius well we like to call him Meech, loved to create his own strands of weed and cooking was his passion, so he came up with most of the recipes for the THC infused dishes.

"So, wait one almost overdose at Passion's, high club members at Euphoria, anything else y'all need to tell me?" They knew better than to wait until all this mess is happening at once.

"Well, there was something I didn't quite register as a big deal before but with these two problems with drugs, now I'm starting to think the robbery at one of the empty houses I am selling for an international customer wasn't a random event. They found drugs there when the cops investigated last week Monday." Chase fills us in rubbing his tongue ring along his lips something he does when he's deep in thought or irritated.

"Nah there is no way in hell that's a coincidence. What the fuck is going on and if y'all don't know we have a big fucking problem to figure out quickly because three out of nine of our businesses being hit with a drug problem and security systems being overridden is a cluster fuck." I down the rest of my Jack Daniels Sinatra cause at this point something needed to calm my damn thoughts. There are only a few things on this earth I care about five sitting this room, my mother, and my money at least until I'm blessed with my wife and kids. I have a feeling I might've found them though. Before I can waive our server down, she's already coming over and we all order another round.

"Aight so it sounds like all of us have some work to get done tomorrow but tonight we need to eat and chill cuz nothing we can do right now." Jax is always being my right hand in calming us down when I'm the hot one.

"Jax is right, I will see about rearranging my schedule tomorrow and we can meet at my office to start going through everything we might've thought was nothing and video footage from every property." Our drinks show up then food comes right behind it. We sat there for an hour or so talking and we all decided to blow off much needed steam so to Euphoria we were going.

Chapter Three

Dean Fredericks

We all pulled into the above ground garage to our designated parking spots right behind each other and went through our private entrance. We entered Jax's office that looked over the open playroom area. Down below we could see those that were hanging at the bar watching others taking part in voyeurism and exhibitionism, which are two of my favorites to take part in. On the first floor besides the bar, there were beds, sofas, and then on the surrounding walls were the rooms for beginners they all had the standard beds and different sex toys. The second floor are the rooms for experts which contains different contraptions like the Andrew Cross with the neck collar the girl was hurt in last night. The third floor housed our four theater rooms, two of them played different porn videos that you could pick from, the other two played live footage from different rooms, all of them hold twenty custom two seater chairs that can lay flat like a bed if things get a little heated. The basement level is strictly our place that has six private rooms with attached bathrooms, and one room with a bar different toys as well as contraptions but in the middle on a platform is a customized large bed with restraints all around it and then across from all the rooms is an open space designed for hunting. I walked away from the tinted panoramic window to the office bar and made me a drink, which looking at my brothers they had the same idea.

"So, what we getting into tonight fellas?" I ask taking a seat on the black leather loveseat in the middle of the office next to Jax and Chase while Monty, Demetrius, and Marshall sat on the sofa across from us.

"Well, my sub-Blossom is meeting me in our usual room in about ten minutes, but I think tonight will be the last night with her she's getting clingy." Demetrius shakes his head. It's his third sub this year. Some women just don't understand how this lifestyle works. That's why we run by contract only or don't play with the same person consistently. By Jax's rules all members must be tested by the on-sight doctor regularly so the risk of STD's was slim to none.

"Stop slow deep stroking those damn women like you do, and you wouldn't have that problem nigga." Marshall laughs teasing Demetrius.

"Fuck you bru." Demetrius curses Marshall.

"Well, he does have a point nigga. We've all seen how you get down on live display. I told you; you can't be giving those love strokes to them cause that's exactly what they go do fall in love." Monty points out and Meech just shakes his head again then takes a sip of his drink. We all liked to watch and be watched, so it was nothing for us to see each other have sex with the women here that had the same kink. Hell on singles night sometimes full-on orgies happen on the first floor.

"Kenya will be her in a few minutes she wants to try out the sex swing I had added to my room." Chase tells us about his fiancé that we were all shocked he had, not that Chase wasn't a lover because he was but to find a woman truly okay with our lifestyle was one thing but to find one that actually wanted to participate and understand it was rare, it was why the rest of us were still single well except for Marshall now baby boy was just a hoe. I had to laugh at that thought because you could say the same for me a few years ago.

"I'm just observing tonight but y'all have fun." Monty lets us know after sipping on his cognac. I side eyed him because I know that look, he had earlier when I showed him La'Meria. Monty didn't like many women well people in general, but I swear I saw a light pop on in his eyes seeing her and I wouldn't stand in his way because my big brother definitely deserves happiness after everything, he's done for us, but I will fuck him up if he hurts her. I am mildly worried about our unconventional methods scaring her off especially with this fool. See we were all required to visit a psychiatrist due to unfortunate events back in high school and well most of us were diagnosed with anti-social personality disorder, but Montavius was diagnosed as dissociative identity disorder with psychopathic tendencies and the doctor tried to have him committed so he can study him but mom was completely against it and decided to manage his differences on her own. I never thought of my brother as crazy as some people have called him because he doesn't respond to things like they do, well none of us did but him more so. He showed earlier signs of being different like when I father died and at the funeral an 8-year-old Monty sat next to our mom with a blank look on his face and that apparently pissed off our aunt, my dad's sister, who slapped him telling our mom she needed to lock his crazy ass up because what child doesn't cry at their own father's funeral or ever for that matter. That caused a big fight that day between my mom and dad's side of the family because my mom knocked our aunt out and she fell inside the grave where they were lowering our father, and my brothers and I busted out into a fit of laughter, which did not make the situation any better, so suffice it to say we never saw them again.

"Yo Dean, where'd you go bro?" Chase says snapping his fingers in my face.

"Nowhere but my Sub is here, so I'm bout to go blow off some steam. These past two weeks have been annoying to say the damn least." I tell them tossing back the rest of my drink placing the glass on the table and standing.

"Don't forget we need to get on this drug situation full force tomorrow and I'll need you here with me to talk to the couple from last night and the bartenders to figure shit out." Jax reminds me as he's standing clearly still pissed.

"Gotcha, we will get this shit figured out." I place my hand on his shoulder and squeeze it. Jax loves this club, he came up with the idea after visiting a similar one in Atlanta, but we all agreed that it was the right business so we could all be free and closer to home. There was a knock at his office door and in walked Briana well we all called her Bree his second manager.

"Hey boss." She says and then noticed all of us and speaks to everyone. Bree is a beautiful woman with a chocolate skin tone, pink full lips, big doe eyes, probably about C cup breast, she had a little fupa, with wide hips, an ass you can sit your drink on, thick thighs as well as calf's. She was only about five foot six inches, so she forever wore heels around us even if it didn't help much in the height department with us all being over six feet tall. She was also very deadly with an any type of blade. She helped keep us all balanced by calling us on our bullshit since she handled her anti-social disorder better than we handled our so call issue. I grabbed her by the waist and kissed her on top of the head walking out Jax's office and heading to my private room in the basement. My room was decorated with a deep red color on every wall and black on the ceiling as well as the floors with gold grout lines. The walls had a 3D woodwork effect on them to give the walls some depth. On the back wall sat a California king size four post bed covered in black and red silk sheets. My favorite toys were lined up in a dark cherry wood cabinet with glass doors on the right of the room, next to that was my Andrew cross, sex bench with opening and holder for a dildo, a swing on the other side of the room, next to large sex chair with removal pieces for the legs and arms. I entered the ensuite bathroom to freshen up, change into my sweats, and one of my favorite

Ghost face mask, it glowed in the dark, and made hunting my sub just that much more fun. I go to my cabinet and grab my hunting knife and unsheathed it admiring the sharp knife with jagged edges in the dim light of the room. I heard the code being put in on the door panel signaling my sub-Candy as she called herself entered the room wearing a dark colored trench coat and I couldn't wait to see what was underneath. She has become my longest running sub to date as most started to either catch feelings or agreed to things just to please me but were a hard pass in reality for them, which was something I really hated and why all my subs signed a contract that included an NDA. Candy was an exception though; she truly liked every one of my kinks, even consent non consent play or I like to call predatory play, I prefer to do it outside, but we had our own way of doing it inside as well. We designed the open area across from the rooms as somewhat a maze or obstacle course in a sense with partial walls led lights, tall and short potted plants, and mirrors strategically placed for a fun house feel. I watched Candy walk through the room after placing her trench coat in the armoire next to the room door and I felt my dick getting hard in my sweats looking at her slim thick frame, caramel skin covered in a white lace lingerie body suit with matching garter attached to fish nets stocking leading down her long legs to six-inch blood red pumps, which I am still shocked she can actually run in. Tonight, she is also wearing a white lace butterfly mask that only covered the top half of her face and calling out to me were her luscious heart shaped lips covered in red lipstick that I could not help but to imagine wrapped around my dick by the end of our play time. "Hmmm you're looking extra good tonight, Candy." Licking my lips as I slowly walk towards her with my knife in hand. Through her mask I could still see her eyes and they just gave this dilated look and not out of fear but arousal which made me even harder. I wish I could have met her outside of here, I'd love to make her mines completely. Once I get close, I run my left fingertips down her arm and her skin feels so warm under my touch.

"Someone has some new artwork." She traces her fingers over the intricate design of a large roaring lion head with his wavy mane connecting with the sun setting on the Sahara on the right side of my chest that also connects to the sleeve going down that arm. Her soft fingers felt so damn good against my skin. I closed my eyes reveling in that feeling for a few more moments then grab her wrist and kissed the top of her hand.

"Ready to play sweetness." I rub my thumb over the hand I'm still holding.

"Yes sir." She lets out a low moan. I use her hand to lead her out of my room over to the open play area.

"Tonight is going to be a bit rough my sweetness, you may want to remove the heels." I stand behind her leaning over her right shoulder speaking directly into her ear and rubbing my beard lightly against her cheek. She nods her head in response then bends over to remove each heel giving me full feel of her plump round ass. While she was bent over still, I grabbed her by the waist with one hand and smacked her on her right ass cheek because she knew what she was doing and dammit it was almost working, as much as she liked to play, she loved to just have sex too.

"Ok sweetness here's how tonight is going to go, I am going to give you a thirty second head start to find you a place to hide wherever I find you is where I fuck you and please fight back, you know I love it when you fight back baby." I whisper in her ear rubbing my knife up and down the left side of her arm feeling the shiver run down her spine. The room span twenty feet long and thirty feet deep and with all those half walls, plants and small closets she had a few places she could get away to.

"Run sweetness." I whisper then look to my right as I hear the elevator door open and knowing it could only be one of my brothers as only our codes worked to get down to this level. Sure enough, stepping off was Monty, Chase and his fiancé, and Meech with his sub-Blossom. I nod my head at them and notice the shocked look on the ladies' faces, seeing me with my Ghost face mask and knife in hand but only Chase's fiancé had a look of intrigue in her eyes.

"I'm coming for you, my sweetness." My voice sounds menacing through the mask and added to the atmosphere. I start walking into the room listening out for her heavy breathing while noticing Monty leaned up against his room door watching me. Knowing him he would go into his room and watch the television inside as this room had cameras throughout the space for enjoyment later or to watch live. I slowly walked through the room dragging my knife against different surfaces making a scraping sound causing the air in the room to feel even thicker with anticipation and pure lust. Opening the door to the first closet in the room, which she's hidden in there before but clearly wants to make the chase a little long tonight since she's not there. I hear a noise a few feet in front of me to my right and see her dart out and run to the other side of the room near a bed in the corner. I take off running towards her grabbing her leg as she tries to slide under the bed. I drag her from under the bed kicking and screaming but she slips one of her legs loose and kicks me in the chest, momentarily causing me to fall backwards and allowing her to get up and run off again.

"Oh, my little Sweetness wants to really have fun tonight." I say out loud while rubbing my chest and standing up to run after her. I feel my dick getting harder with the way she decides to fight tonight. I hear a door close to my right and take off towards it twisting my blade in my hand. I slowly push open the door revealing my Sweetness standing in the small shower inside the bathroom behind it. I stalk towards her looking from her to my blade and tilting my head to the side.

"Tsk... Tsk my Sweetness. You have nowhere to go now. Do you still have any fight left in you, baby?" I get closer and closer to her until I am mere inches away. She is leaned against the shower wall breathing hard and I watch her triple

D breast rise and fall keeping me in a trance for a few seconds. I slide my knife from the middle of her collarbone down and in between her breast watching as her breath hitches and goosebumps start to rise on her arms from the coldness of the metal blade. She pushes against my chest, but I don't budge and grab both her small hands in one of mine then swiftly moving closer while placing her hands above her head.

"Get away from me you psycho." She shouts twisting in my grip causing her breast covered in that thin white lace to rub against my chest and I can feel how hard her nipples are. Feeling that turned me on even more so I rubbed my blade from her left nipple over to her right then back to the left again, watching as she bites down on her bottom lip and closes her eyes. After tonight she won't be hiding from me any longer, I don't care what I have to do, she will be mine. I take my blade sharp end down and begin cutting the thin lace right down the middle.

"Stop moving Sweetness or you might just get cut. We wouldn't want any blemishes on this delicious looking caramel skin now, would we?" I say stopping my movement since she wants to still fight me and while I'm looking in her eyes, I notice she actually may like that.

"Wait my Sweetness would you like for me to cut this pretty skin of yours?" I turn my blade around and rub the handle across her love box. She clinches her thighs together and lets out a low moan.

"Use your words baby. Do you want me to mark this beautiful skin of yours?" I raise my mask just enough for me to lick her essence off the handle of my knife and then rub it against her clit inciting another moan from her pretty lips.

"Yesss... yes my Ghost face mark me as yours." She moans out causing my breath to hitch this time because I can't believe just how perfect for me, she is. I can't contain myself after her confirmation, I put my knife in my pocket, release her hands, and rip the rest of the thin lace from her body letting it fall down her arms then to the floor. I lift her by her arms making her wrap her legs around my waist pushing her flat against the wall and snatching off my mask because I want her to look into my eyes as I ruin her for any man that dares to come close to what is mine. I grab my knife from my pocket placing it between my teeth then pulling my pants down and letting them fall to the floor. Placing my dick at her entrance and rubbing it through her fat lips covering it in her sweet essence causing a low growl in my throat. I couldn't tease her any longer placing my dick back at her entrance and pushing straight in to the hilt and holding there for a moment. I pressed the knife against her chest causing it to break her skin just slightly and small pricks of blood appear, and she bites her bottom lip.

"Breathe baby, there you go. Damn this pussy has my dick in a chokehold, shit. This shit wet, you really like me marking you." I moan sliding out to the tip then giving her slow deep strokes allowing her to adjust to my size and me to catch myself. Her pussy always makes me feel like a high school boy getting his first nut, the shit is crazy. Every time I'm in her it feels like home, it's just so damn warm, tight, and boy this pussy is gushy wet. Dropping my knife then bracing myself with one hand on the wall behind her and the other still firmly holding her by her waist as I speed up my strokes while keeping them deep and she meets me stroke for stroke bracing her hands on my shoulders.

"That's it sweetness take every inch of this dick, mm." I moan in her ear, pumping into her harder.

"Fuck Ghost, fuuuccck." She screams as her eyes roll in the back of her head.

"That's right take this dick, take it. This pussy is mines." I grunt out feeling like I'm about to cum but no way I'm coming yet.

"Shi... Shittt. I'm... I'm about to cum." I can feel her walls tightening around me.

"You better hold that shit. I didn't say you could cum yet Sweetness."

"Oooh fuck, I... I don't think I can hold it, ple... pleassee Ghost." She starts begging me as her eyes flutter and roll in the back of her head. I stopped moving to step out of my pants and turn to walk to my room still holding her in place on my dick. She tries to bounce and rock to give herself the friction or pressure she needs to cum, but I hold firm on her waist. I smirk at her while inputting the code to my room and kicking it open with my foot then closing it the same way. Finally lifting her from my dick and laying her on the bed to lock her arms in place over her head with the restraints on the bed. Going to my cabinet to grab my spreader bar and my smooth-edged blade since I left the other behind. I place each ankle in place, pull them tightly, and pull the spreader as far as it can go.

"Mmm sweetness you haven't fed me in a while. I told you not to stay away from me for so long, I get withdrawals." I say gliding the blade up her left leg while holding the spreader and pushing her legs towards her head.

"I'm sorry Ghost, I was busy with work, please forgive me." She pleads only trying to get me to end her punishment.

"Hmm maybe I should visit your job because they will not keep you from me." I glide the knife down the back of her leg and then press it firmly on her clit. Watching her twitch from the contact made me moan in satisfaction.

"I've tried to give you time to accept that you are mines here and outside Sweetness. Either open up to me on your own or you may not like my methods of finding what I need to know about you. Either way you're mine." I press the blade to her lower abdomen and cutting ever so lightly drawing blood.

"Ghost, I like you I really do but this could never work on the outside and you know it. You're just sexually attracted to me. You do realize it takes more than that to make a healthy relationship." She says panting clearly turned on by me cutting her and the position I have her in. She's really starting to piss me off with that rant she was on about us not working. It wouldn't be the first time we had this conversation but it damn sure as hell was the last, I'd be putting my detective skills to use after dealing with this email from La'Meria in the morning.

Chapter Four

Montavius "Monty" Fredericks

Sitting here watching my brother play with his sub usually would give me a rise, I loved the chase myself but tonight all I could think about was that beauty La'Meria and hoping she would let me chase her soon. I turn the TV to our open room upstairs to see if anything would catch my eye because a nigga was way past horny and just needed a quick release at this point. I notice one of the women I've been with in the past at the bar, she had some good head game so I decide she will do for tonight. I send a message to Bree to have her sent to my room and watch as one of our security guards approached her then they start walking her to the elevator. I grab the tablet out of my nightstand to pull up her test results and find she was retested this morning with all negative results, we had all of our members regularly tested to protect those that took part, plus all women were recommended to be on birth control, men were given information on vasectomies and condoms were strictly enforced otherwise. After the two attempted lawsuits, one for child support paternity and the other for a sexually transmitted disease, we shortened the time frame between testing and added on staff medical teams to process results. I put the tablet back in the nightstand then went to my large cabinet and grabbed my white Phantom half mask, took my shirt and shoes off, switched into my sweats, then made my way to my armchair in the right corner of the room next to the bed. After a couple of minutes, I heard a knock on my door, and I pressed the unlock button in the security app on my phone only my brothers and I had access to. I trusted only my brothers and soon my wife to have the code to my door, too many people have been taken down by being too trusting and I be damned if it was me or my brothers. Soon in walked a beautiful dark chocolate woman that I knew by the name Coco, we didn't use real names and only looked at the real information of a member if it was absolutely necessary. Thus far none of us have felt the need to investigate anyone at the club but I have a feeling Dean is going to want to if his sub doesn't give into him willingly. He can tell she feels the same as he does but something is holding her back, but I know my brother he's at the end of his patience. Besides me, only Jax knows how he feels about the beauty he's had as his sub for the past six months or so. I looked up coming out of my thoughts to see Coco kneeling with her palms resting on her knees face up. I rarely found the need to have a sub, but I do occasionally play but I always wear one of my mask.

"Crawl to me, slowly Coco." I command her and she obeys at once, going to her hands and knees slowly crawling towards me swaying her thick hips side to side. I love my women thick even bbw size if proportioned like I like them which is curvy. I am an ass, hip, and thigh man.

"Pull my pants down." I lift my hips so she could pull them all the way down and watch her expression when my third leg as the ladies liked to call it sprang from my sweats hitting my stomach then just standing straight up. The arousal in her eyes tells me exactly what I need to know.

"Are you going to keep looking at it or are you going to wrap those pretty lips around it?" I ask, looking her in the eyes and making him bounce. She licks from the tip of dick down to my balls then back up, swirling her tongue around my head then taking me as deep as she could down her throat and wrapping her hand around the rest and squeezing. "FUUCCCKKK!!" I moan low when she hollows out her cheeks then swallows around my dick taking me even further down that deep throat of hers. Her not gagging yet damn near took me out. I grab the back of her head by the root of her hair moving her faster up and down my dick enjoying the scene before me of her juicy lips wrapped around me and tears sliding down her face. She takes her other hand and starts playing with her pussy and it sounded so fucking wet. I released her hair then she slowly lifts up off my dick with a pop sound and licks from the tip to the underside along my thick vein down to my balls sucking on them both then taking her tongue around the back of them hitting that sensitive spot right behind my nuts.

"Shiii...shiiittt." I moan as cum shoots from my dick landing on her back and some in her hair. I snatch her up by her hair, turning her away from me and pushing her head towards the floor while keeping her on her knees. I grab a condom from the bowl filled with them on the table next to me ripping the gold wrapper in half with my teeth while rubbing my fingers in between her slick lips. The moment I was fully sheathed, I spread her legs further apart placing my hand on her lower back arching it just how I like and enter her in one long deep stroke holding it for a few seconds allowing her to adjust to my girth and length. I give her quick deep strokes in between rotating my hips in a circular motion and soon as she catches my rhythm, she begins throwing that juicy ass back. I have to remind her who she was fucking with though grabbing her by the back of her neck pushing her head into the plush carpet and getting into a squatting position stroking that shit even deeper.

"FUCCCK, ye... yesss E." She screams as she squirts at the same time, she creamed all over me as she's still screaming out the middle initial of my middle name Ekon which means strong. Hmm I hope wifey knows how to squirt if she doesn't, I'll teach her. I cum a few pumps later pulling out. This was pure fucking, and she knows that, so I stand up after smacking her on the ass and go to take a shower. Once the shower reaches the temperature, I wanted I step in and hear the bathroom door opening, figuring she was going to clean herself up at the sink before leaving but instead she steps into the shower with me placing her hands on my back.

"What do ya think ya doing shawty?" I turn my back to the water, and it sprays my back as I grab her hands in mines as I tilt my head looking at her with a curious frown on my face, thankfully I forgot to take my mask off but in this light, she could see my face now and that's another thing ha ass know I didn't play.

"Coming to take a shower with you, is that such a problem?"
She questions me with this sad look in her eyes like I give a
damn, I had rules for a reason. I did not have sex without a
condom and no intimate acts like kissing, holding each other
afterwards, especially no showering together amongst other
things, all those things are reserved for my woman/ wife and
now that I'm sure I've found her I definitely was not in the
mood for this shit.

"You know the rules and don't act like you don't. If you want
to take a shower dats cool but you can wait till I get out or go
to the hall bathroom, na leave my shower Coco." I remind
her while dropping her hands with a bit of venom in my
voice because she really irritated me just now touching me.

"Really E, we've being doing this for months now and you
still treating me like I'm just anybody and you won't even
take off that damn mask, are you kindin me right now?" She
screams at me like I really give a damn about the stupid shit
she was spitting out the side of ha neck right now.

"I'm really trying to stay respectful but you really pissing me
off. I never gave you any idea that we were going to do
anything outside of fucking. Ya talking about the past few
months like we have had sex with each otha every day or
communicated outside of this damn club. Na unless you
want your access to said club revoked completely, I'd
recommend that you get the fuck out like I said before and if
you haven't gotten it already this will be the last time I fuck
you." I am seething inside but I convey to her calmly with a

deadpan look on my face. This bitch was really trying my patience. I purposely have my rules in place to avoid having problems like this but clearly some broads just see what the hell they want. She finally got the hint and walked out of the shower, but I no longer trusted her, so I stepped out of the shower to watch her get her shit and leave. Once I see the lock click in place I turn and walk back in the shower. Once I got out moisturized my skin and redressed, I sat back in my chair sending a text to Jax and Bree to make sure her ass is not allowed to come to my room again and restrict her access to just the beginners level since she doesn't know how to act. I sent a text in my group chat with my brothers letting them know I was out since my mood is ruined for the night. Grabbing my keys and heading out, I had more important things to deal with tomorrow and at the top of the list was getting my woman.

Chapter Five

Jax Fredericks

After my brothers all went their separate ways to enjoy the night, I stayed in my office looking down at all the members involved in sexual acts while others watched from the bar with drinks in hand just like me. I had a lot on my mind with this pop up of drugs in our businesses and I won't lie it's also on the beauty Dean showed us earlier. She seems so familiar to me, but I can't figure out why or where I would've seen her. One things for sure I want to know, and I will, I am just hoping Monty isn't a problem. We shall see though.

"Jax you good?" Bree asks, placing her hand on my back. After rescuing her a few years ago from a sex trafficking ring Dean worked to dismantle she became a part of the family and my sub. She needed the safe space to regain her confidence in herself after all the shit they put her through. We started having sex occasionally outside of when she needed an attitude adjustment about six months ago and only because she had needs but didn't trust anyone but us.

"Just thinking about all the mess going on. Drugs popped up at one of our realty spots and Passion's." I turn around and walk towards the couch to sit down.

"What the hell is going on? Y'all have never had this problem before." Bree sounds just as frustrated as we were when we talked over dinner.

"Not sure but clearly somebody fuckn wit us and we will get to the bottom of it." I declare taking the rest of my drink to the head and watching as she picked up the glass to make me another drink.

"Well, let me know if you need me to handle anything, you know I got y'all at all times." She says handing me my drink.

"I know, thanks Bree." Taking a sip of my drink while she walks behind me then starts to massage my shoulders.

"Damn that feels good woman." I groan out so thankful for what she was doing because damn I was stressed the fuck out at this point.

"Hmm damn Bree as good as that feels, I need you to come bounce that big ass on this dick." I moan out reaching around to grab her juicy ass. I'm glad she doesn't want anything more than sex because I am not in the mood for anything tender and she tends to like it rough anyways. She walks around the chair sliding her dress up over them thick but toned thighs and wide hips. Even if just fucking I still like my women thick, some may say BBW size, but I didn't care plus I am a big dude all around and a thin chick was just not for me. As she stood in front of me, she bent over rubbing circles around her clit then sliding her fingers through her fat pussy lips, pushing them into her essence causing a growl deep in my throat. I smacked her once on each ass check loving the sight of the ripples it caused.

"Grab ya fucking ankles Bree." I scoot to the edge of the chair placing her in between my legs and grabbing her by her thighs keeping her in place as I bury my face in her fat pussy. I didn't eat ha pussy often but Bree doing that sexy shit just now all in my face was cause for this session. I flatten out my tongue licking her from her clit to her entrance and back again swirling my tongue around her clit sucking it in with my lips and using my teeth to nibble on it just enough to boarder between pain and pleasure. The way she gasped for air then moans my name lets me know just how much she enjoyed what I did to her. I slurp on her clit for a few more seconds then licking with the tip of my tongue flicking it against her clit side to side a repeatedly. Licking back to her entrance dipping my tongue in her juicy pussy as deep as I could going in a circular motion.

"Shiiiit Ja... Jax." She moans out my name again as she cums all over my tongue and beard. I flattened my tongue once more licking up her juices then sitting back unbuckling my pants sliding them down along with my boxer briefs. I feel her legs shake as I pull her back towards me to slide her down my dick as she sits upright then arches her back just a bit before she begins twerking on my shit then sitting completely down on it till, I was pushing at her damn cervix.

"Fuuuck! I swear this dick is going to be the death of me with that damn curve and the way it's stretching my shit." She moans out bouncing on my dick making that curve she was talking about hit one of her spots in the back side of her pussy. When she starts rotating her hips in a circle, I lose it and start pounding into her from under her causing a slur of curse words.

"You taking this dick good baby girl but I need you to breath for me." I smack each ass cheek as she's bent over slightly with her hands resting on my knees then I feel her walls clinching my dick, I knew she was cumming for the second time tonight and I was not far behind her.

"Come suck this nut out." I say after I feel her shakes subside and she immediately stands up and turns around taking me to the back of her throat then pulling me out licking all her juices off my dick and balls. Bree wrapped one hand around the base of my shaft putting my dick back in her mouth while flattening her tongue on the underside as she bobbed up and down using that hand at my base in a twist and squeeze motion. I swear this woman tried to suck the soul from my body every time she did this.

"Damn gurl just like that, fuuuucckkk I'm... I'm about to cum." I growl right before rope after rope of my cum shoots down her throat and she swallow every drop sucking until I was completely empty and start to soften. She leans to the side opening the arm of the chair, grabbing some wipes that we kept there for these times to clean ourselves up.

"Feeling a bit better boss man?" She asks after wiping me clean for some reason she enjoys doing that and I wasn't one to complain then she stood to clean herself with the rest of the wipes she pulled out.

"Yea a bit, I may actually get some sleep when I get home." I say closing the arm of the chair, then stuffing myself back into my pants buckling them back up and then reaching for my drink.

"Go home Jax it's been a hectic couple of weeks, I got the club tonight." She always bosses me around while calling me boss man. She pulls down her dress then walks to dump the wipes in the garbage. I was definitely contemplating it because a brother was tired as hell after being at my gym all morning since my morning manager is on maternity leave for a few more weeks.

"You sure, Flex not coming in tonight dealing with his mom being sick." I check with her and remind her about Flex one of my boys from the Marines whose moms was just diagnosed with early on set Alzheimer a few weeks ago. He served his required time and started online courses as well as pursued his MMA career but made some smart investments one being the gym with me and retired early to have some sense of a normal life physically, it's crazy how some of them stay in too long and end up with life altering injuries.

"I'm good, I promise, and I dropped off a pan of lasagna to them before I came into work to give em one less thing to worry about." She tells me making me give her a closed lip smile, one thing I love about our lil family is we all take care of each other.

"Aight then call or text me if anything pops off." I stand grabbing her and kissing her on the forehead then going to my desk to grab my wallet and keys to head out. I check my phone to see a text from Monty crazy ass about this chick he messed around with from time to time and shaking my head.

"Already on it gone on nah." She tells me before I can even say anything causing me to chuckle then I see what she did in our brother group chat and that made me shake my head again because of all my brothers Monty was the most rigid about his damn rules in our club, hell he didn't like us bending ours either. We had some issues arise when we first opened from accidental pregnancies, std's, pissed off spouses, and stalkers to name a few but once he implemented the rules, we have been good ever since. I am hoping this dumb ass broad don't cause no problems cause if she does, I have no quips about dropping her ass off at the Hunting Lodge messing with my brother. When I made it to the garage the cool night air hit me right in the face and sobered me up quite a bit but then I spot Monty leaning on his truck looking at his phone. I walk up on him quietly and look over his shoulder to see him looking at La'Meira's Insta again.

"You know I don't like when you try to sneak up on me J." He says not even looking back at me and still scrolling through her pictures.

"I didn't even make a damn sound, how the hell do you always hear me?" I swear I can never sneak up on this man it's like he has eyes behind his damn head or something even as kids he always heard us coming.

"Just call it big brother intuition." He says shrugging his shoulders, finally looking up and giving me a left sided smile.

"Wateva, so what's up with this chick we just put on restricted access and apparently you snapped on which you never do?"

"Bruuu this dumb as broad thought it was a good idea to come get in the shower with me then touch me. Talking about I'm treating her like she just anybody even after fucking around for the past few months together then got even more pissed cause I still had my mask on."

"Wait so she thought just because y'all had sex a few times over the past what six months or so she could break the rule you clearly laid out for her, plus you gave her no type of affection or signs period that it was anything more than fucking." I reiterated everything I knew already and what he told me shaking my damn head because these females can be nuts, then they want to blame us for leading them on.

"Pretty fucking much. I'm going to get my family she bet not cause any fucking problems when I get back, I'll put ha stupid ass in the Wax Museum." He says calmly which meant he was way past pissed off at this point.

"Wait nigga what family?" I ask looking at the side of my brother's head cause I just knew he wasn't talking about who I think he was talking about.

"Look I'm not going to try and explain it to you, but I know she's mine and the kids come with her so their mines too simple." He tells me like we were talking about going shopping or some shit like it's normal to say he has a family before even meeting them in person. What if the kids don't like him, hell what if she doesn't like him or can't get down with our lifestyle.

"Look bru you know I trust you with my life and if you say it so then it is. I just don't want to see you hurt by this woman no matter how damn fine she is." I say placing my hand on his shoulder to convey what I was saying and not saying, like the fact that you could see the love she has for those kids, her strength in raising them alone, and the pain in her eyes from what we don't know yet at least.

"I know and I won't. What I'm sure you saw in her eyes like I did is pulling me to hear something fierce. I don't care how crazy it sounds but if I have to tie their asses up and put em in my trunk, they're coming home with me or I'm making a home with them there." He says looking me dead in my eyes and I knew he was serious, and I hope she can handle this crazy band of brothers. Honestly if he didn't, I would try my damn self because it's something special about her and we need her in this family as much as she probably needs to be in it.

"Look I know that look in ya eye J, you like her, don't you?" I knew he would see it, but we hide nothing, so I tell him the truth that I am and it's something familiar about her that I can't put my finger on. How we are isn't accepted by everyone, but we don't care whether you do, or don't we will not hide or change who we are, no acting normal around here.

"So, what's the plan Monty cause I know you just as well and I know you have one?"

"I'm coming up with one but we need to deal with the drug problem first but I'll be leaving in a day or two, so we need to come up with a plan in the morning well in six hours rather." He says looking at his watch then grabbing me for a hug and saying goodnight. I turn and head for my 69' Chevy Chevelle SS in all chrome black gloss, I don't bring her out often, but I need to clear my head so it's open road type of night which means I'm going out to my Hunting Lodge about an hour outside the city.

Chapter Six

La'Meria "Meira" Jennings

Waking up this morning I felt a bit more at peace with my decision to not go out and track down more traffickers on my own physically at least but I'll let God lead me on how to go about it going forward. Today the kids were on their own for breakfast since I have to open the shop this morning and I have quite a few devices to fix that are coming early delivery this morning plus more drop offs scheduled later. I've already had my heart to heart with God, meditated and stretched these thick limbs out.

"Alright babies it's time to get going." I yell walking out my room, book bag in hand, tea in my thermal in the other hand. I decided to dress cute comfy today with my black sweater tights, tan off the shoulder oversized cashmere sweater, and black knee-high leather boots, which I was glad to find some that fit because even my calves are thick being a curvy two-hundred-and-ten-pound woman is a headache sometimes. Checking the kitchen to make sure the kids cleaned their mess, and everything was turned off because no matter how much I teach them independence they're still kids.

"Coming mama." I hear Mariah and Za'Mara yelling from their rooms and Za'Meir walking down the hall. He reached me first giving me a side hug and kiss on the cheek, then heads for the door. The girls came running out right behind each other giving me a kiss on the cheek each and out the door they went. I head to my office to grab my laptop then out the door myself to take my ten-minute drive to my store front in downtown. My store front is maybe the size of a decent two-bedroom apartment with an office in the back left corner that I have lined with shelves to hold devices to be repaired, already repaired, equipment to fix devices and a medium sized cherry wood desk, bathroom to the right, and up front is another small desk, glass display counter for devices I've purchased and fixed for sale, then each wall lined with phone accessories. Once inside I lock the door behind me since it's not open time then I head to my humidifier on my front desk and choose Lavender as my scent for the day and hit play on my morning gospel playlist. By the time I made it to my office to set my things down my phone was ringing with a video call from Dean.

"Morning Dean."

"Morning Lil Dove." That nickname always caused the warm and fuzzes for me. I fought with him for a while about it until, he explained why he called me that along with the fact I knew he wouldn't stop.

"Did you read the file I sent you?"

"Not yet I am actually waiting for it to open right now, but what's going?"

"I'll just sum it up for you. Your client's husband is doing a lot more then cheating the man is a part of a damn sex trafficking ring D. What the hell did you get me into?" I rush out annoyed again just thinking about the damn land mine I just stepped on. He was sitting relaxed until I said that.

"What the fuck did you just say Lil Dove? Sorry baby I'm looking through the file now. I cannot believe this shit." He says in a low growl, and he already has a deep Luther Vandross voice with a look that could kill the more he read on his screen.

"You covered your bases like normal right Lil Dove?"

"Yes, I did."

"Ok I am going to have my brother double check, I need you protected completely from this. If I had any idea that he was into some shit like this, I would have never exposed you to the risk."

"It's ok, you couldn't have known. It took hours to go through the encryption on those hidden files, so whoever did it for him is good just not me." I boasted getting a half smile from him which is exactly what I wanted because I could tell he was beating himself up and I did not want my best friend stressing out about something he would have never known about without me looking.

"Fuck but this is dangerous Lil Dove. I can't even turn this over to my client or she's going to be put in the line of fire as well. Don't worry, I am going to do whatever I need to make sure you and the kids are safe." He declares running his fingers through his thick beard getting more agitated, but I've always found sexy when he does that.

"I know you will, and you know how I move anyways."

"Yes, I know my Lil sexy mama bear, but I'd feel a lot better if you let a couple agents from my brother security firm come ova and watch you as well as the kids, please." He tries batting those long ass lashes most women pay for at me.

"No D we will be good and if anything, I will call you but keep looking into the file because there are some things you can share with your client since he is also cheating. That fool has no damn chill."

"That's cool and all but Lil Dove, if you don't let me send someone, I'll come myself dammit, I haven't seen my babies in a while anyways."

"D love how about this give it a few days and if any of my alarms that I have set go off for someone trying to track me you will receive an alert when I do, I promise and besides you know you can come see the babies whenever you want." I walk back to my front desk after unlocking the door and grabbing the delivery I was waiting for.

"Ughhh fine set me up for the alerts now woman. I have to go and meet with my brothers though, clearly today is for putting out fires. Please be safe Lil Dove." He's still visibly annoyed and worried about us but he doesn't need to worry. The only thing my father did right was make sure I knew how to defend myself.

"I just set your email and text alerts, and I promise." I tell him while sitting the boxes down and getting to work opening them up.

"Ok I got the alert for setup. I'll be texting you later Lil Dove and everyday till I know you're safe and I want you to share your location wit me too no fussing or I'm on the jet." He says pining me in place with a seriousness and worry I've never seen in his eyes before maybe even a little fear.

"If it will keep you in Kansas City and not standing in my kitchen when I wake up I will." I agree after a few seconds of thinking it over. In all honesty, I am cool with him having it because as tough as I am having someone else look out for me feels good.

"As long as you know but I'm walking into my brother's office, talk to ya later beautiful." He says ending the video call. I place my phone down and grab the phone out of the first box. As soon as I get my tools laid out the alarm chimes with someone at the front door and I look up to see one of the teachers from the kid's school.

"Morning Mr. James, how can I help you?"

"Call me Drew, Ms. Jennings and I need a screen
protector as well as a case for this new phone I had to get."

"You can call me Meira. What type of phone did you
get?" I ask taking a moment to look him over and he's a
good-looking man but a bit on the short and thin side for my
taste. He's maybe five eight or nine, caramel skin, small
pouty lips, almond shaped brown eyes, tone but small, bald,
and thin beard. I also noticed him eyeing me a few times at
Za'Meir's games being he's one of the football coaches.

"S22 plus."

"Ok so all Samsung cases and glass screen protectors
are on that wall to the right. All heavy-duty cases are in the
middle and bottom." I point to where everything is for him
to look over. I am really not feeling how he's looking at me
now and I'm getting the feeling he's about to say something I
am not going to like soon.

"Ok this Otter Box is going to be my best bet with the
way I drop phones." He tells me picking up the case then
grabbing the glass screen protector for his model phone next
to it and handing them both to me.

"Yup when in doubt Otter box is the way to go. So,
with the teachers discount your total is $44.82 you can tap,
swipe or insert, while I put your screen protector on." I
inform as I ring up his purchase on the small register on the
right side of my glass display counter while taking his phone

from him and starting the process of cleaning then applying the screen protector and case.

"Ok perfect. So, I wanted to ask you, are you seeing anyone because I'd love to take you out to dinner sometime?" Great, I knew that damn question was coming and now I have to figure out how to let him down nicely which is not my forte.

"That's nice but I am not in the dating scene right now. I'll keep your offer in mind if I change my mind." I tell him the only thing I could come up with trying to be nice and hopefully he takes the damn hint. I finish with his phone and hand it back to him along with his receipt.

"Ok I'll hold you to that Meira and thank you it's real convenient having your shop right here." He says pocketing his receipt and giving me a wink then walking out the door. I have a feeling that won't be the last time he tries to ask me on a date. Well, it's time to get to work on these phones and I have two computer drops with another cellphone.

Chapter Seven

Montavius "Monty" Fredericks

Getting in my office this morning with coffee in hand and two of my brothers already waiting for me outside of their cars let me know this Tuesday is definitely about to be eventful and I already feel a headache coming on.

"Chase, Jax." I fist bump the both of them while walking to my private entrance then I hear another two cars roll up. By the time I type in the code then do the retinal scan Meech and Marsh are getting out of their cars heading towards us. We walk in speaking to Whitney and head straight to my office to wait on Dean and thankfully my first two meetings rescheduled last night so we're free to talk the next hour and a half. I sit all my things down while the guys take their seats on the couch and Jax in one of the chairs in front of my desk as he usually does and leaves the one next to him for Dean. He comes in still on the phone with someone.

"Ok I'm walking into my brother's office, talk to ya later beautiful." He says and the moment he ends the call he snaps.

"Man, we got a fucking problem!" He roars slamming the door behind him which put all of us on high alert because Dean is just as calm as I am so him yelling and slamming shit right now has me on edge.

"What the hell is the problem that has you slamming my damn door like that Dean." I stand and round my desk to lean in front of it.

"That piece of shit client of yours is a part of damn sex trafficking ring and I put La'Meira in his cross hairs if he figures out his computer and or phone has been hacked by her."

"You gotta be fucking kidding me." I question as I rub my hand down my face trying to calm my nerves because I am literally on the verge of snapping if my woman is danger from a sex trafficker of all people.

"This some bullshit, Monty how the hell you do not know one of your damn clients is into sex trafficking, some shit we been working on shutting down in our damn city?" Jax snaps but I only know he's snapping because his voice is calm and even like mines gets with some extra base.

"He didn't disclose anything to us in the onboarding process and you know we have a clause in our contracts with clients so that's on him." I say shrugging my shoulders because it really was on him. When starting this company and creating our contracts for clients I entered a clause where all illegal activity needs to be reported in advance, we have the right to refuse any client with NDA agreements for both sides if that happens, and if any illegal activity is discovered after the fact we reserve the right to cancel contract without refund and no NDA, which means for him this voids his contract with us.

"And that stubborn ass woman won't let me send anyone to watch out for her. I mean she is pretty bad ass with a gun and even fighting but still these are damn sex traffickers who knows who the head of this damn ring is, but I did make her constantly share her location with me."

"You really think that's enough?" Jax ask the same question on my mind because in my mind I have already decided to cancel all my meetings or have Justin take them for a bit since he made it back early. Our client Drea was fine, and agent fired will be good.

"Same thing I want to know bru. She's a beautiful woman with two teenage girls, I don't care how bad ass she is she can't be everywhere at once." Chase jumps in from his seat on the couch. The thought of women and kids in danger in my brothers and I mind take priority which means this drug issue unless something new pops up is going to take a back seat for now.

"Hey Whitney I need you to cancel all meetings that can't be taken over video call or add to Justin's schedule what he can take on I am going to be out of the office for a few weeks. Call the pilot and have wheels ready to roll in the next few hours with the nearest private landing strip to Dothan, Alabama as the destination." I instruct her while pressing the intercom button on my desk phone. I'll be leaving here to go pack my camping gear and finding me a RV to buy while I am there.

"Ok Monty what's going on in that head of yours, you have clearly made a plan already?" Dean asks me with his head tilted to the left, which he always does when he's reading me.

"I may or may not have looked up her home info and found out she lives on about four acres of land, two of which is still forest and same for her neighbors on both sides as well as behind. The lot next to her neighbor on the right of her, well when you're facing the house, is vacant and closes to the road, I'm going to take an RV up there and park it on the lot to keep an eye on her. I also kinda sent a message to the realtor selling the plot that I want to buy it cash. I will take some of our surveillance equipment with me to place around to keep an eye on things when I'm not out watching things." I explain to them the jest of the plan but not everything at least. I am at some point getting my woman. I know it might sound crazy to some but those can kiss my ass.

"Well sounds like a solid plan to me. I was going to show up to her door with my bags and tell her I was moving in till we found out if anybody knew what she uncovered." Dean says shrugging his shoulders.

"Hell, either that or we go down there make her and the kids pack up for a few weeks to come back here. I'm not opposed to putting her in the trunk if she acts to stubborn."

Jax puts his two cents in making me chuckle because everyone always thinks I'm the one that goes completely off left field but he's worse sometimes.

"Uh Jax no we're not trying to scare the shit out of the woman and her kids, I mean dude ease the crazy on them sheesh. How we know if she's into being kidnapped by a bunch of handsome men." Meech says causing all of us to laugh at this point and Jax gives us a half smile bunching his eye brows like he was actually contemplating if she would.

"Alright crazy crew. We clearly have a lot of shit to do. As much as I want us to drop everything and only focus on this we can't. So, Chase, Meech, and Marsh handle this drug problem, I know y'all are tech savvy but go down stairs and grab Jace and Jude, y'all already know if it's a camera nearby Jace can get into it and Jude can get a nigga to tell him any damn thing." I direct them getting down to business. Jace and Jude are two brothers I hired from a veterans only job fair we had six years ago, and they quickly became some of my most highly sought after agents and friends, they definitely matched a niggas crazy.

"Ok yea this may even get fun with Jace and Jude helping out." Meech says standing while rubbing his hands together looking like he's about to start some damn trouble and knowing him he will, but Marsh and Chase will keep him in line.

"Well let's go get this shit started, I have to meet Kenya in a couple hours hopefully she will finally pick a damn date." Chase mutters as he stands clearly still bothered, she hasn't agreed on a date yet. Then he starts dapping each of us then heading for the door with Meech and Marsh right behind him.

"Let me guess while ya out there protecting Lil Dove you're going to let her know she belongs to you huh?" Dean questions me finally sitting down in his usual spot leaned back in his chair while running his hand through his beard.

"What did you just call my woman nigga?"

"I gave her the nickname Lil Dove a few years ago when her best friend was killed. I flew to Miami to be there for her, it was right before Dad's memorial, and you know how my head gets around that time but being around her that day even with all the pain she was in I felt at peace hence the name." I just sat there and looked at him because I wasn't trying to be in a competition with my brother for my woman.

"Don't worry bru we're just friends but I won't act like I don't care about her deeply besides I'm about to be on Candy's ass. She thinks she can keep hiding from me. Well, she did give me her real name last night after rearranging her insides to only fit me." He tells me so casually and shrugging his shoulders.

"Ok bet. Well while I'm gone get ya girl but go check with Jace too and see just how deep Mr. Sinclair is in this trafficking ring."

"Bet, I need him to check if Lil Dove covered her tracks as well as she thinks she did anyways. I need to go meet with my client and her lawyer in about an hour to give her the cheating file and let her know she may be in danger with this fool since she leaving him."

"Damn that's true. I was going to ask you if she ever had any issues with him being violent towards her." Jax asks Dean but I notice the look in his eye when I said I was getting my woman.

"Yea apparently they had an issue where he pretty much raped her because she told him she was in pain and not in the mood, but he pinned her to the bed, and you can figure out the rest I'm not repeating that shit."

"Damn." Jax and I say at the same time.

"Ok well don't tell her everything, she clearly knows she not safe with that nigga anyways no need to paint a target on her back for whomever is in charge. Let her know we can do her protection and relocation. I'll be sending an email sighting violation of contract for him before I leave, so send me over those files." I say as I sit at my desk starting to draft the email as the files come through and I attach a few of them then send it off.

"Ok, well let me hit up my contacts and see who the ring leader is. If he or she doesn't come for La'Meria I'll hand it off to my contact in the FBI but if they do, we're burning that shit to the ground." Jax starts texting on his phone, but I see the seriousness in his eyes.

"Best believe we will." Dean adds in as a knock comes on my office door.

"Come in."

"What's this email I just received a copy of Monty?" Justin questions me walking into my office nodding at my brothers as he comes up to stand next to where they're sitting. I typed up the email while we were laying out our plans and Dean sent me the file as soon as I requested it.

"What he violated contract, so it's voided."

"He's one of our top clients Monty. He isn't the only one involved in illegal shit that we protect." Justin tries defending Mr. Sinclair.

"Which he did not disclose upon contract signing and you know how I feel about sex traffickers, so I'm not even understanding why the hell we having this conversation, Justin." I tilt my head to the right with a deadpan look because he has me looking at him funny now.

"Look I'm just saying that's a multi-million dollar contract you just ended with no replacement and you leaving for a few weeks. What the hell is that about you never take vacations?"

"Just something I have to deal with. Besides, did you not get the government contract email since you're so worried about money. We will be the exclusive security for four different government buildings downtown by the end of the year. So, what the fuck are you really worried about?" I ask standing from behind my desk.

"Look I didn't see the email for the government contract otherwise I wouldn't have mentioned it. We're good then." He confirms turning to leave.

"I never liked that white boy." Jax says shaking his head.

"Never did understand why you kept him around after high school." Dean adds in.

"Listen he's cool when he wants to be and smart, but I've never totally trusted him anyway. You know like I do we needed the extra funding when we started this ten years ago but it's also why we're majority owners so if anything, his ass can go at any time."

"Bet well let me get out of here." Jax says standing to leave dapping us on his way out.

"Same, let me know when you board the jet." Dean says standing to leave as well. I spend a few minutes checking a few emails then head to our ops center equipment room to gather about two duffel bags full of sensors, cameras, perimeter alarms, satellite phone, hot spot device, and all the cables I need for them. Once I make sure I signed everything out I head out to pack up my guns from home amongst other things and get on this jet to my woman.

Chapter Eight

Dean Fredericks

After leaving my brothers office and meeting with Jude I head straight to mines to meet with Mrs. Sinclair and her lawyer. At least I know Lil Dove will be taken care of with Monty out there watching her back, she may not be my woman, but she is special to me, and I need her safe. Pulling into the side garage of my two-story building that houses Precision PI firm, I noticed Mrs. Sinclair's car in the guest parking lot and head inside. My office doesn't look like the PI firm you may expect it. I had it modernized with white marble floors with black and gold veining, ten-foot ceilings, mostly black and white decor from the front receptionist desk to waiting area couches, coffee tables but all with blue and gold accents. I head to my private entrance on the second floor of the garage and come into my office walk-in closet then enter my office. Once I make it to my desk, I use the intercom to have my assistant send Mrs. Sinclair in.

"Good morning Mrs. Sinclair and Mr. Fern." I stand to shake both of their hands and sitting back down.

"What have I told you call me Shamaya. I have decided to change to my maiden name after the divorce as well, I want no ties to that man."

"So, what have you found Mr. Fredericks?" Mr. Fern asks.

"Well first off, I need you to understand that I can't give you all the information I found and that is for your protection. Secondly, he's definitely been cheating on you and this folder contains all photos as well as digital evidence along with where he's hiding all his money." Her lawyer grabs the folder holding it open for the both of them to go through it and I see as her pretty caramel face gets redder and redder as he turns the pages for her to see everything.

"This is great information. I don't see his lawyer letting him take you in front of a judge with this, great job Mr. Fredericks, I will need to put your firm on regular rotation for all of our cases." Mr. Fern informs me, and I am happy to hear that. Having four law firms as clients has been my goal and I already have one, so this gets me closer to that.

"But this thing you won't tell me, should I be worried?" "Yes, you should, and I recommend you plan for a safe place to be until this is all over. My brother owns a security firm, and he is willing to help with one of his safe houses and round the clock security team."

"Wait it's that serious? Why not take the information you found to the cops then?"

"With the info my tech pulled up if anybody is going to be informed it will be the Feds. So, no more questions about it. Just let me know what you want to do so I know what arrangements to make, and I recommend not seeing or speaking to Mr. Sinclair unless it's with your lawyer or someone else present." I inform her and I see when the color leaves her face as she starts to grasp without definitive details how in danger she is.

"Ok your brother's company is Titans Security firm?" Mr. Fern asks me with a concerned look on his face.

"Yes, it is. If you are worried about conflict of interest or anyone selling her out to her husband because he's done business with my brother, there is no need to worry since he has been dropped as a client. There is no one better to protect you then Titans security firm. If you decide to use my brother's firm you will be taken on off the books and secured by only men, he trusts but it is up to."

"I trust you Dean and if you trust you brothers' firm then I trust them as well, set everything up."

"Ok making the call right now." I say pulling out my cell to call my brother. I may have just discovered that Mr. Sinclair was Monty's Sinclair, but I have secretly been working for Shamaya for about a week and a half having my agents following him around. La'Meira's finds actually made some of the other things they found make sense.

"Hey Monty, I need you to send the agents you trust to my office to guard Mrs. Sinclair, yes of course off the books. Ok perfect I'll see them soon and I'll talk to you later."

"Ok so your security detail will be Ramon and Fin.
They will be with you at all times and only they will have the
address of your safe house and don't worry they will be
proper accommodations. When they get here, which should
be in about ten minutes, they will also secure your phone and
give you a burner until everything is over with your case. I
will keep your phone here in a secure lock box and check it
regularly and pass any important messages along. You are to
only contact me and your lawyer. Do you understand, I
know this is a lot?"

"I will admit I am scared because this is a lot of
precautions to go through for a divorce and it makes me
wonder what he's into but at the same time I don't want to
know then it has me thinking to myself who the hell did I
marry six years ago. I'm really glad he never wanted kids and
had a vasectomy. I can't imagine still being attached to him.

"So, what's next?" She asks looking at Mr. Fern.

"Now that I have all this evidence of his breach of the
Prenup he won't get any of your money in the divorce and I
will write it up exactly as you requested even though I think
you should ask for alimony or at least part of the company
you helped him build but I can respect that decision after our
findings today. So, I will be going to my office to write up the
dissolution of marriage and he will be served by the end of
the week." As he finishes my assistant comes across the
intercom, letting me know that Ramon and Fin had arrived.
A few moments later they walk in. Ramon and Fin were both

pretty big dudes standing at about six three or six four and clearly never missed a day in the gym with broad shoulders thick muscular build, I mean the men were swole. They could be in those body builder competitions.

"Dean long time brother." Ramon says as I stand to give them a handshake and one arm hug.

"It has been a while, when this is all over you guys need to stop by the club and restaurant sometimes. This here is Mrs. Sinclair and who you'll be protecting until her divorce is over but possibly longer if she chooses to."

"Dean what have I told you about that, It's Shamaya and damn you are some beautiful men." She says standing and holding out her hand to shake theirs which they oblige with smirks on their faces. She is a beautiful woman, so I get the look on their faces, but they better keep it professional.

"Well fellas she is all yours and I'm sure you have things to go over with her, you can use the conference room downstairs, I have a few more meetings today and Shamaya your phone." I tell her while opening the metal phone safe I use. She places it inside then turns to leave the room with her new guards.

"Mr. Fredericks I will be in touch with you once the partners and I have drawn up a contract for your continued services."

"I look forward to it." I tell him while reaching out to shake his hand. He leaves my office, and I head back to my desk to get ready for my next client meeting.

Chapter Nine

La'Meira "Meira" Jennings

Damn today ended up being busier than I could have ever imagined. Some of the kid's friends' parents stopped by with screens to fix for cellphones, computers needing upgrades or virus protection, then the kids got out of school buying cellphone cases, chargers, I even sold six cell phones that I bought and repaired. Looks like I'll need to open the store more days out of the week. The kids walked over or were dropped off to the store after practice and helped me close up shop. Thankfully on my lunch break I went up and put the roast I took out the night before then seasoned this morning in the crook pot and all I need to do is put the carrots and potatoes into the crock pot to cook with the meat for a bit. Turning down our street I notice the for sale sign on the lot on the corner was gone. My realtor actually showed me that lot first, but we wanted a home that was already built even if we had to renovate it and I'm glad this one became available. After dinner with the kids, they retired to their rooms, and I headed out to the deck off my bedroom with a glass of wine the moment I sit down my phone rings with a video call from Dean.

"Hi Lil Dove, how was your day?" He asks the moment the video comes through.

"Hi D, it was good the store was really busy today. How was yours?"

"Ugh these crazy clients stressed me out a bit but nothin I can't handle. I did get closer to my goal on having four law firms on contract." He says taking a sip of a brown liquid and knowing him it was some top shelf whiskey.

"That's what up friend, I know how important that is for your business."

"Don't think it's going to keep me too busy to check on you Lil Dove." He says a matter of fact giving me a knowing smile and I can't stand that he has come to know me so well.

"I don't know what you're talking about and besides you know when ya get ya girl you will have to stop checking on me so much. No woman wants her man checking up on another woman as much as you do me." I say looking at him over my wine glass as I take a sip.

"Why do you want to get rid of me so bad woman and any woman I'm with will know her place and yours no changing that."

"I'm not D. Ok I'm just not that use to people genuinely caring about me after my Jameia. You can admit I have gotten better though." I tell him looking away from the phone as its propped up on the patio table. Everybody I thought was my friend turned on me when she died.

Everyone who called themselves auntie or uncle to Mariah disappeared leaving me to raise her on my own.

"Well, I got you baby so stop tripping please and yes you have gotten better somewhat."

"I'm trying. So, what happened with Mrs. Sinclair?" "Well, I got her squared away this morning. Her lawyer filed the divorce papers so he should be served by the end of the week, and she set up with my brother's security team at a safe house till everything is done."

"That's good at least she will be able to get out of that marriage and safe away from that sick fuck. I read up on your brothers business he's built a really good team there."

"Yea if only someone else would let me protect them but yes, he has. He hires a lot of veterans because he has a soft spot for them, being one himself along with Jax and I. He also does ex law enforcement officers, so it gives his security team an edge over other companies that just train them to be agents."

"I can definitely see that as a plus for him and those veterans feel useful again. What the hell?" I say looking out at the tree line on the back end of my property because I swear, I saw a light moving in between the trees.

"What's wrong Lil Dove and don't lie to me woman?"

"I thought I saw a light moving through the trees on the back end of my property."

"Get ya ass in the house. I knew I should've just came down there and I am." He says standing walking into his home.

"Love can you chill out please. It was probably the new neighbors exploring the woods in between all of our properties. Someone bought the empty lot next to my cousins house. Dean Jamel Fredericks stop." I demand watching him walk through his home and going straight to his walk-in closet in his room grabbing a duffle bag.

"Lil Dove look you possibly being in danger is driving me nuts, you've become one of the most important people outside of my brothers and mom."

"Look at me Dean. The light didn't even stay still, it literally kept moving. Please relax I am ok the kids are safe in their beds." I tell him and he finally looks at me and I see the worry in his eyes. I realize just how genuine a friend he's become and that warms my heart. I didn't think that was possible with how sexually attracted to each other we've been since meeting even though we've never crossed that line.

"Ok... ok I'm calm. Can you at least go in the house for me though and make sure everything is locked up?" He asks me sitting in the chair in his closet. I swear I love his closet.

"Ok fine love I'll go inside. It's getting a lil chilly anyways and I don't feel like turning those heat lamps on right now." I tell him going inside, locking my patio door then setting my wine glass down on my nightstand and I continue to talk with him as I walk through the house checking all the locks and making sure the kids are in bed asleep. Heading back to my room to get in bed.

"Alright all locked up and in bed love."

"You need to get a security system and cameras Lil Dove like asap."

"Yes, that is on my list of things but it's still so much to renovate. I do have my ring doorbell camera though."

"That's something, I guess. Well, you look tired get some rest Lil Dove. I will call you in the morning."

"You get some too D stop worrying so much." I tell him getting comfortable taking off my nightgown and settling under my covers.

"One of these days woman I'm going to get you for teasing me so. Love ya Lil Dove."

"Love ya too D." I reply giggling at his comment and hanging up the phone. I say a quick prayer then roll over and go to bed.

Chapter Ten

Montavius "Monty" Fredericks

The flight here was quick and smooth. I was able to get the property paid for along with my pickup truck, I decided on a GMC Sierra this time around, and a RV before landing. Thankfully the RV company had delivery so all I had to pick up was the truck and some groceries. Once the RV arrives, I unpack my things and get to setting up the surveillance equipment around my property and behind La'Meira's. I've been here a week and a half now and have been alternating between exploring the small town, watching her work at her store, taking meetings through video, to watching her and the kids out in the yard working out together or out by the fire pit even when they were throwing a small party in the backyard for our daughter Mariah's sixteenth birthday. When she's doing her yoga in the yard she moves so gracefully, and I can see myself folding her thick ass up in some of those positions then fucking the shit out her. I feel like I have been watching my family have fun without me but as long as they're safe I will be good for now at least. I ordered me a new Kawasaki Ninja ZX-4RR since I left my Yamaha and old 2018 Ninja at home because I need to hit these open roads out here. My brothers would love this shit we have open roads in KC, but these are smooth, barely any cops, and barely any traffic. After making sure her and the kids were inside safe, I headed out on my bike. It was the perfect time of day, not quite dark out yet but still sun out the sky different shades of pink, red, orange and blue plus the air smells so fresh with the occasional hints of farm animals. Half way through my ride I revved my engine popping up my front wheel for a few seconds just loving the feeling of being on the road. I stop in Dothan to grab some necessities then head back home but before I make it a call comes in from Dean.

"What's good arakunrin?" I answer the call on my headphones.

"Hey bru, how are things out there, really?"

"Things are quiet. If she's been telling you she's good she hasn't been lying. I have had eyes on her physically or on camera since I've been here, and no one has had eyes on her but me."

"Ok good. She's stubborn as hell. She's not use to people taking care of her just because they care."

"I can see that. I've been here over a week and the only people I ever see come over is the lady and kids from next door and some old dude. Her and the kids were out fight training this morning with pads on. Hey why didn't she do a bigger party for Mariah's birthday? I noticed they just had something small in the backyard."

"Yea that sounds about right the chick next door is her cousin and the old dude is her uncle. He helped her remodel the kitchen. She won't accept much help from anyone so she does what she can, and the kids are as anti-social as she is, so they don't like many people either. You sound like you in a hole though."

"My new bike came in yesterday. I'm out breaking it in. These roads are perfect out here. I mean I really get to open my bike up."

"You sound like you're falling in love with that place not just the woman you went out there for."

"Maybe so bru. I never thought I'd like the small-town life but I'm definitely starting to see the appeal of it. Hey, I need you to convince her to allow my team to come put in a security system. I've already booked them for next week on Monday at eight am. They will have outdoor cameras, sensors for all the windows, 2 panels, and motion lights for the perimeter." I inform him while pulling into the driveway I laid a few days ago.

"Bru I've told you how stubborn she is, but she needs it, and we've actually touched bases on it so maybe it won't be too hard."

"Just tell her it's a gift for the job she did, and I've already scheduled for them to come out for her. Did you send any gifts for Mariah though?" I question him while entering my RV, putting the few things I grabbed up, and then opening my laptop to check my cameras. Seeing her sitting on the patio with her glass of wine already lets me know she's had a rough day it's only seven pm and she's usually out around nine and only for maybe twenty minutes. "Monty... Monty!"

"Huh."

"Dang bru where did you go?"

"She's on the patio with her glass of wine and the bottle. I've never seen her out this early."

"Somethings wrong, I'll call her and see what's going on but yea I have their cashapp so I secretly send them money that way from time to time."

"Ok send it to me and make sure you let me know what's going on wit her, fucckk." I curse.

"I know bru but soon you'll be telling me what's going on instead just give it time and it's sent."

"Ugh aight man it's hard being this close to her and not being able to just go to her when she clearly needs me even if she doesn't know it's me she needs yet."

"I know how you feel. I've been watching Kelia well you know her as Candy since you've been gone, and I figured out why she's been so secretive she works in the mayor's office and her family are the typical church going conservative family."

"Oh, shit what's her position."

"His damn assistant."

"You gotta be fucking kidding me. I wonder does she know he comes in the club too." I chuckle lightly.

"Wait I knew that was him coming in a few months ago but I shrugged it off thinking it was someone else especially being the person he was going in with that night was a dude and if I'm not mistaken, he's married to a woman."

"Ahhh shit I didn't even think about that. That's not the first dude or maybe it's the same one not sure but when I saw him, he was with a dude and a chick."

"Mannnn this nigga wile. As long as he keeps those sausage fingers away from my woman, we good."

"Speaking of women go head and check on my baby. I'll talk to you later arakunrin."

"Later arakunrin be good." He says hanging up the phone. I decide to go out and take a walk as I do every night now to watch the house my family is sleeping in. I've been getting closer and closer.

Chapter Eleven

Dean Fredericks

After talking to Monty, I make the call to Lil Dove to see what's wrong with her. Her phone rings a few times which is odd but then she finally answers

"Hi Dean."

"What's wrong Lil Dove." She lets out a heavy sigh.

"Just the kids nothing crazy but I did have one of my migraines last night."

"Aww Baby how are you feeling today? I know the after effects last a few days for you."

"I'm still a bit out of it but not as bad as its been in the past. I swear you have ESP or cameras in my house I don't know about watching me. How did you even know something was wrong?"

"It's cause I know you so well Baby. Now what's going on with the kids."

"Za'Meir got into a fight with some kid at school and beat him up pretty bad and his grades have been dropping. Mariah got caught kissing some boy by the locker room. Ughhhh these kids have been driving me nuts. I knew it wouldn't be easy raising three kids on my own but shit it's hard keeping up with all this sometimes. I can't even remember the last time I went on a date or did anything just for me with all the activities, the business, doctor's appointments it's just." She lets out another heavy sigh.

"Damn Lil Dove I thought your fam was helping you with the kids but if I know you like I know I do you're probably not asking for help as much as you need. Baby if you are walking around like everything is good no one's going to step in to help so you have to ask or at least express how you feel." I tell her texting Monty what's going on with her while realizing I'll be making moves to Alabama soon cause my baby is not about to be stressed out if I can help it.

"I know I should. I am still learning when and how to. I promise I'll try harder because I really am stressed the hell out."

"Well, my brother and I are taking one thing off of your list next week. He's scheduled one of his teams to come down and install a full security system for you. They will be there Monday at eight am sharp and will take about two hours maybe three to get everything done for you."

"Dean I can't afford the type of security system your brother provides, trust me I checked. I'll get it done next month hopefully."

"Nope not on you and you're not turning this down. My brother already has paid for them, I covered the equipment, and he put them on schedule. You have nothin to worry about when it comes to this. All you do is let them in when they get there and go in your office to work. Well video call me when they get there so I can make sure it's them showing up, no arguing Lil Dove."

"Ok love bug fine, thank you and tell your brother I said thank you as well. I really appreciate y'all taking that off my plate because it definitely is something needed." She tells me and I can't help but smile big cause she hasn't called me that in a while. She first called me that after her best friend died and I stayed with her for a week. We were laid up talking and she told me for someone who looks like I'd break someone in half I show her love even when she doesn't want it like no other man she's been around. I may not be in love with this woman, but I love the shit out of her and those kids even if I have only been around them a few times over the years I've known her and that's about to change.

"No thanks needed Lil Dove, but I will pass along the message. You look tired baby go take you a bubble bath, light ya candle, play those sounds you love or some 90's R&B and relax please. I haven't called Za'Meir in a couple weeks to talk, I will start calling him more and chat with him to see what's going on. He still has a Samsung, right?"

"You're right I will. Yes, he does, and I think he would like that. He likes you and Mariah told me about the birthday gift sir."

"He's a cool lil dude and crazy on that football field. When is their season over? Don't bite my head off about that though it was her big sixteenth birthday."

"They have four more games. One every other week and next game is next Friday and fine I won't. She was so excited when she received the notification. She paid for her cart on this website we like to shop on."

"Ok I'll make sure I'm free and come show lil man some love. I'll probably bring all my brothers. Let em know he has a lot more people rooting for him. They all do after I finally told them all about you guys a few weeks back."

"Love bug don't make me get emotional cause I know you if you say you're doing something you do it. I could kiss you right now." She tells me with a big ass smile on her face, this right here is why I usually video call her. I just love to see her smile.

"I always got you and them. No more keeping me in the dark on what's going on, you are my best friend hell I tell you shit I don't tell my brothers or at least tell you first. Come to think about telling you something here's something light. I'm going for Kelia tomorrow."

"It's about damn time bighead. I can't wait to meet her."

"I can't wait for you to meet her either. I think you will like her, she's just as feisty and determined to be independent as you are."

"Well, I guess she is about to get the rude awakening I got dealing with your pushy ass." She laughs as she starts the water for her bubble bath, sprinkling some of her Epsom salt in, then bubbles, she also lights one of her many candles, and turns on some Erykah Badu.

"I am not pushy. I just know what I want and won't stand by if I see someone, I care about need help and not give it whether they want to admit it or not." I say looking at her with a smirk on my face.

"Yea... yea. Well, my bath is ready."

"That I see, go ahead and get your thick ass in the tub Lil Dove. I'm going to go ahead and video chat with lil man for a bit."

"Ok talk to you later love bug." She ends the call, and I call lil man who picks up right away. We talk for about twenty minutes, digging into what's going on with his grades to me coming down to watch his games. It sounds like some classes are becoming difficult for him and he may need a tutor and I'll be handling that shit in the morning actually I know exactly who to call.

Chapter Twelve

Jax Fredericks

Trying to find out who is behind this damn trafficking ring is getting on my last damn nerve. I'll never understand why muthafuckas want to sleep with children, forcefully fuck people who don't even want them, or selling another muthafucka's body like what the hell. I swear I'm shooting each one I finds dick off better yet I'm tying their asses up in the woods at the lodge my wolves are hungry. My phone starts ringing breaking me from my thoughts, which is probably a good thing and of course it's Dean's ass.

"Yo bru what's up."

"Yo, I need ya help with something."

"Sure, lil brother what is it."

"Nigga you not that much older than chill the hell out but it's about La'Meira and I already texted Monty crazy ass to make sure he's cool." He says getting my attention instantly.

"I was about to say I'm in but I'm not about to fight with his big ass."

"That nigga is big and yo ass is too but it's really more about her son Za'Meir, he's struggling in math as well as science and stressing ha ass out. He got into a fight at school because some lil dickhead in his class was picking on him and he beat the shit outta shorty." He starts laughing his ass off.

"Mannn you not supposed to be laughing at that shit dummy." I say laughing my damn self-cause that's what his ass gets picking on our boy and I don't give a shit if I haven't met him yet.

"Dats what his punk ass gets messing with my son, I fight kids too. I don't even know why the hell lil dude thought it was a good idea to fight him anyway. Za'Meir is fourteen and five foot nine inches, a hundred sixty something pounds of muscle, and works out regularly with his mama who's a damn black belt in Jiu Jitsu the last I checked. She trains all her kids."

"Well damn she was already fine ass fuck but that is the sexiest shit I've ever heard."

"Tell me about it but anyway before your Esp having ass brother hear us talking about her. I need you to tutor him and maybe go check out some of his games with me. I'm going down next week for one of his games and plan on going to the remaining of them."

"Ok bet I'm down for both. We barely have kids in the family so this will be cool." It makes sense he would come to me to tutor our lil man seeing as I'm the numbers man in the family. Graduating from West Point at the top of my class majoring in Economics and minored in mathematics which is why even though we have an estate manager and accountant I still double check to make sure they're not fucking with our money.

"Ok perfect, I'm about to text Chase n' em about going too. She's barely has any damn body. I mean her cousin is next door, but she just divorced ha cheating ass husband and has four kids of her own, I can't stand ha lazy ass brother, her uncle is getting up there in age, and she's paying for her mom to be in this nice ass retirement home because she's partially disabled. She's about to have Monty but she's still my best friend." He informs me shocking the shit outta of me cause that's a lot on one damn person. Yup I'm clearing my Fridays and whatever days I need to help her out. We all have soft spots for single mothers growing up with one ourselves, even though our father died when me and Monty were at ages to remember him, it's not like he was around much.

"Bet, wateva ha and the kids need we got em going forward."

"Fa sho. Well let me get my ass on. You goin to the club tonight?"

"Ya I'm headed there now actually."

"Oh, and I was meaning to tell yo ass stop fuckin Bree nigga we're supposed to be protecting ha especially you as her Dom."

"How the fuck you know what don't even matter she is not some fragile ass woman, and you have to stop treating ha like that. It's the whole point of me being her Dom to give her power back and besides she was the one who wanted the arrangement we have not me. She actually wanted any of us but more so Marsh because she felt safe with us, and has a real crush on him, it just so happened to be me since we're always together at the club."

"Wait what sounds like we need to have a night on The Stage soon."

"Sounds like fun to me but let me get in this damn club, I gave Flex the night off since his mom in the hospital she almost burned down the man kitchen yesterday." I say as my driver opens the door to my Tahoe. I hate driving on nights I'm running the club.

"Damn we need to figure out something with that but bet see you in a bit." He says ending the call. Getting off my private elevator to my office the first thing I do is text my head of security to my office to check in and then text Bree because I know she was floating around here somewhere even if she wasn't working. I noticed the text in the group chat of all the boys agreeing to be there for La'Meira and the kids. I hope she ready for six men to show up on her door step next Friday and I'm sure Monty will be showing face soon too that nigga impatient. I chuckle at that thought seeing as I probably just described myself too. While waiting on them I checked my emails from Chase about the lead I gave them, which I received from the dumb ass who almost killed the chick about over two weeks ago now. Dumb ass did something right by telling me who he bought the drugs from. I may or may not have given him no other choice but to tell me. It was either me or his wife and the cops which in all honesty I may anonymously tell his rich ass wife anyway, I hate fucking cheaters. I hear the elevator door ding open, and I know who was entering you had to enter a code to even get the elevator to work, my brothers did not play about security.

"Boss man." Ace greets me standing in front of my desk as Bree comes over and sits in the chair across from it, I swear that girl needs to get a life.

"Jax." She says looking at her phone probably at a new outfit for our dominatrix room she works every now and then.

"What's up Ace and Bree seriously."

"Quiet day and night thus far boss. Well one person in the drunk tank but that's about it." He responds getting to the point which is why he's head of security apart from him being my brother in arms.

"What I didn't have much to do once I got off earlier and where better to hang out." She defends herself shrugging her shoulders and going back to her phone.

"Anyway, so let's keep it that way, send Mika ass up here so I can see what's going on because she knows over serving should not be happening, we have a system for a reason." I tell him and he's already heading to the elevator. Truly a man of not so many words.

"You know since you over there shopping anyways can you order some stuff a fourteen- and sixteen-year-old girl would like. My girls need to look fly so clothes, shoes, purses, jewelry wateva." I direct her texting my shoe guy to cop whatever new Nikes out right now and some nice dress shoes, lil man has to be fly in every fit.

"Your girls when da hell you got kids?"

"Oh, damn that's right things moved so quick this past week and a half. Monty is out stalking his soon to be wife who happens to be Dean's best friend apparently and she has two teen girls and teen boy who is the twin to one of the girls. Dean says she's pretty much raising them alone stressed and a bit struggling but won't ask for help, so we all adopted the kids as ours since their fathers aren't in the picture." I sum everything up also checking out some clothes for my big dude.

"Damn so I'm auntie Bree now I like that, it's about time we got some kids in this dysfunctional ass family we have. Do you have any pics of them?"

"I just sent you her insta."

"Oh my gosh these are some beautiful babies but damn they're big. They all look about eighteen sheesh, I'm go need a new gun for these niggas and hoes asap. Well, got damn Mama fine as fuck too." She says making me chuckle cause she sure as hell wasn't lying.

"Well, you can tell they have different fathers the other lil girl looks completely different from them even though she's still beautiful."

"Ya must be talking about Mariah, she's technically not hers. She took over custody after her best friend died and ha stupid ass husband wasn't doing shit for the girl since she isn't his." I give her the run down Dean gave us in our group chat since Monty and I wouldn't stop asking questions.

"That dick but ok I got them covered. When do we get to meet them?"

"Hey age-appropriate shit Bree, but if you want you can come with us next Friday for Za'Meir's football game, all of us are going."

"Ok I'm in and of course I don't want nobody looking at my babies crazy. So, it's Za'Meir, Za'Mara and Mariah, right?"

"Yup that's right-" Before I could say anything else the elevator was dinging letting me know Ace was back with Mika.

"Mika I'm going to give you one chance to tell me how this happened again on your shift, and you are supposed to be the bar shift manager." I look at her sideways cause she is really testing my damn patience.

"No explanation needs to be given boss man, I've already fired Trish and sent her to The Dark room for her exit interview. I will be looking for a bartender to take her shift until then I posted OT in the bartender chat." She lets me know reminding me why I hired her. She followed the rules with human compassion and didn't take bullshit from anyone.

"Well looks like you need me after all." Bree says standing to head to The Dark Room. I will head down there in a minute.

"Sounds like you also need to do some retraining for your current bartenders. We don't need this type of issue, especially after the accident. I paid enough to my lawyers this month."

"Yes, sir I will put it on the schedule. Anything else sir?"

"No that's it Mika." She walks out. I decide to let Bree handle the exit interview for Trisha dumb ass in my mood who knows how I would handle her especially after the email that popped from Jace about a lead on the traffickers and then the text from Chase saying they were headed to The Lab which only meant one thing. I sent Bree a

text to tell her she was in charge for a few hours while I went
to meet them.

Chapter Thirteen

La'Meira "Meira" Jennings

After opening up to Dean a few nights ago I can say I feel even lighter this morning. I can't say that I was completely shocked that he was paying for the security system, but I wasn't expecting his brother to be involved too. Lawd knows that man is fine as hell and it's something about a man in uniform and a tailored suit, but I wouldn't be surprised if he only liked those fake bbw women. You know the ones I'm talking about with the lipo flat stomachs, fake asses, but thick thighs with perky tits. I'm not body shaming anyone but those aren't bbw's those are just thick women to me but because they may still be in the two hundreds they call themselves or people call them bbw. Listen don't get it twisted I know I look good no matter my damn size, but you know how some of those pretty boys can be about how their women look. Montavius does have a slight rugged look to him though which probably came from being in the Marines, but he clearly takes very good care of himself. Anyway, I'm glad they are coming to install that security system in a couple of days because I swear someone has been watching us when we're outside, I even thought someone was in my room last night but when I got up no one was there but I know I felt someone. I haven't told Dean and don't plan on to, I can handle whomever thinks I'm someone to fuck with on my own besides I don't feel like the person is here to hurt me their energy feels warm, strong, intoxicating. Honestly it feels like what I imagine Montavius energy would feel like, I even ended up pleasuring myself while imagining what sex with him would be like and I actually had an orgasm. I haven't had sex with anyone for over a year, the last man to touch me turned me every way but loose in a great way but I never can see him again. I don't know how I'm going to handle these men in my space on Friday because the fact of the matter is Dean and all his damn brothers are fine as hell, it just Montavius does something deeper for me and his twin shit that man there. Today at the store was a blur of customer after customer so a sister is tired once I make it home to the kids, we order pizza which we usually do on a Friday anyway and gather on the couch for a movie.

"So, it's my turn to pick our movie and since we are heading into fall season, I chose Haunted Mansion the second part." Mariah announces plopping down on the sectional that finally got delivered yesterday. I splurged getting this huge interchangeable plush sectional from this custom furniture store in a navy-blue color cause no light colors with these sloppy ass kids, but I have to admit this damn thing is comfortable and don't think I'm going to last long watching this movie.

"Ooh yay I love that movie." Za'Mara says bouncing in her seat so giddy because she really does love this movie and the first version too, I swear we've watched it twenty times.

"Of course you do. You could've chosen anything but this Riah." Za'Meir complains from the other side of the sectional to my right while the girls sit to my left. I'm sure she chose the movie for Mara anyways, she loves seeing her little sister smile and annoying Meir is a plus. I chuckle to myself while munching on my cheese sticks as the movie starts and as predicted I didn't last long. I think I nodded off probably three times before just giving in and going to sleep. I woke up in my bed confused as hell as to how I got there, I know I was tired but not so much that I didn't remember walking to my bedroom on the other side of the house. I don't open my eyes straight away because I swear, I feel the same energy in my room again and I want to pinpoint where it is before I move. I sense it in the corner of my room where I have a black tuft oversized armchair for when I want to read. I decide to tempt the asshole into showing themselves since I know the last time they somehow left by the time I turned my light on. Slowly pulling my shirt over my head then sliding my Pj shorts off I pull my covers back reaching for my dildo in my nightstand and the warming massage oil I use from time to time then rub some on it and turn it on high. I bend my knees then let them fall to either side of me placing my toy over my right nipple first then my left. I take it to rub between my already slick lips and up to my clit applying pressure then rubbing up and down. I let out a low moan as I use my right hand to pinch my nipple and bring it to my mouth to flick it with my tongue. I hear a low moan so low I almost didn't catch it coming from the chair and I know I got him.

"You know if you're going to watch me cum you might as well cum too." I quickly reach to turn on the light on before whoever this creep is gathers himself from the show I just started. When the nightstand light comes on, I can't believe who's sitting in my armchair with his eyes trained on where the dildo once was cause I've dropped it at this point in pure shock but at the same time not.

"Ife mi it's not good to tempt a beast." He says to me in his deep baritone voice turning me all the fucking way on. I can't believe this man is in my room right now and what the hell did he just say to me.

"So let me guess Dean sent you after I told him I didn't need protection and what the heck did you just call me." I say pulling the cover over my naked body all of a sudden feeling self-conscious.

"Dean did not send me, and you clearly need protection if you think it's smart masturbating with a stranger in your room. I could've killed you by now."

"First off, I knew you were here for the past two weeks creeping around in the woods. Let me guess you bought the lot on the corner?"

"Yes, I did. I hate corner lots, but I needed to be close to you." He tells me standing and walking to my side of the bed. This man is doing something to my body, and he hasn't even touched me, shit.

"Why would you need to be close to me I'm sure your woman wouldn't be happy about you creeping around another's home or watching her masturbate either?" I say pulling the covers up to my neck but wanting to snatch them away because the way this man was staring at me and the heat radiating from him standing so close to me has my nipples rock hard and my body feeling like it's about to overheat. I'm sure if I was lighter, he would be able to see my skin turning red.

"Are you not happy to see me? I mean you were moaning my name the other night as you played with that fat pussy of yours." He says snatching the covers from my hands and off my body then kneeling on the floor still towering over me as my velvet cream colored Queen size tufted platform bed sat low and this man was every bit of six foot five or better. Once the covers left me I wrapped my arms around my breast still feeling self-conscious around him.

"I would ask how did you know but I sensed you coming closer a few days ago." I state turning my head unable to keep eye contact with him the way he is staring at me like he's trying to talk to my soul with those beautiful brownish grey eyes of his.

"You didn't answer my question Ife mi. Are you not happy to see me? You said my woman wouldn't be happy about me creeping around another woman but what about me creeping around her, huh?" He asks, placing his long pointer finger under my chin and turning my head towards him, staring into my eyes so intensely.

"I'm not your woman." I say trying to turn my head, but he grabs my chin firmly by using his thumb on the other side of my chin.

"Oh, but you are. I know it's quick, but you will get used to the idea soon enough and move these damn arms hiding my breast from me." He says releasing my chin to grab my arms and move them out the way.

"Hmm looks like these hard ass nipples answered my question since you are in denial." He says pinching my right nipple causing me to moan softly.

"Look I'm not some low self-esteem chick you can toy with or add to your rooster of women so keep ya hands to ya self and leave. You can tell Dean you saw me and I'm fine." I fuss while turning towards the edge of the bed where he's kneeling to get up and grab a robe from my closet, but he grabs me by the chin again tilting my head back and stands then bends over with this angry look in his eyes almost scaring me.

"Why the fuck would I want anyone but you? You're going to be my wife and the mother of my kids." He informs me with a look in his eyes so intense that almost has me believing him.

"I am not your type of chick and that's cool it's no need to play with me. The way Dean speaks so highly of you I didn't think you would be a liar or just plain crazy."

"How my brother speaks of me should tell you I'm far from a liar and I'll let that crazy comment slide this time but don't test me Ife mi." He releases my chin.

"What the hell does that even mean?"

"Since you think I'm a liar you're not ready to know what it means." He says heading to my bathroom then I hear water running and he comes out with a wet rag. He places his big ass hand in the middle of my chest pushing me back on the bed then spreads my legs and cleans me using the wet warm rag putting me in complete fucking shock. Once he's done wiping off my nipples and then my love box but what gets me even more is him grabbing my toy turning it off using a tissue out the box, I keep on my nightstand to wipe it off and place it back in my nightstand drawer. This man then goes ahead to throw the tissue in the garbage can I keep next to my bed, takes the rag to the bathroom rinses it out, and hangs it on the rack to dry then comes back in the room. He starts taking off his clothes and throwing them in my hamper in the closet.

"Take ya ass to bed La'Meira I'm going to shower, and you can stop looking at me like that I'm not going to fuck you not until you beg me for it at least." He states walking towards me but turning off the light on my nightstand and then walking into the bathroom partially closing the door. Did this nigga just tell me to go to bed like I'm some fucking child and why the hell am I listening to him. Stopping myself from grabbing the covers, I get out the bed and tip toe over to my bathroom door. I peep through the crack and look in the mirror over the vanity to see him standing in my shower with soap bubbles sliding down his beautiful chocolate skin covered in tattoos, and I swear the song by *August Alsina Kissin on my tattoos* started playing in my head because I would definitely kiss all of his tattoos. I especially wanted to run my tongue over every part of the big ass eagle with the globe that has an anchor through it across his back which I now recognize as the Marines symbol. This man was too damn fine from his medium sized long dreads tied in a bun on top of his head, to his broad shoulders, arms almost the size of my thick ass thighs but pure sculpted muscle, covered in more intricately placed tattoos, nice round plump ass, thick toned thighs, nice calves, and that's just the back of him. Now the front sweet baby Jesus damn near made my knees buckle and I got full view as he turns to rinse off his back. His chest had more tattoos, one being a big cross with intricate angel wings on each side then a ribbon going around it with what looks like to be names on it in the middle of his sculpted chest. He had what it looked like to be lips tatted on his neck I wanted to cut them off of him for having the audacity to have another woman lips on him but talking about lips those juicy heart shaped pussy eaters he has with a nicely trimmed full face short beard mannnnn. While cleaning himself in the front he lowered his hands to that third leg he called a penis. I mean it was average size maybe six or seven inches but thick but as he began to stroke that sucker it grew, and it grew, and I was stuck wondering how in the hell did that shit fit in anybody pussy. I mean the shit was almost as thick as a sixteen-ounce water bottle and probably grew at least two more inches as he got hard, and that bitch had the audacity to have a slight curve upwards. He turned, placing his back on the shower wall and began stroking himself faster. I couldn't take it, so I lean against the door frame placing my right hand between my legs rubbing my clit for a second then sliding my fingers through my soaked lips, dipping them inside my juices. Swirling two of my fingers around in my juices then bringing them back to my clit rubbing in circles then flicking it a few times and repeating that process as I watched him stroke himself until he was shooting streams of cum all on the shower floor. I came seconds later letting out a low moan catching his eyes in the slightly foggy mirror winking at me then he turns to rinse off and I walk to my nightstand grab a few tissues to clean myself then get in bed. A few minutes later I feel the covers move and then the bed dips on the other side. He wraps one of his arms around my waist pulling me towards his chest then kissing me on the side of my head telling me goodnight like we were an actual long time couple getting ready for a normal nights rest. I had to admit though I got some of the best sleep in years wrapped in his arms which was crazy in itself.

Chapter Fourteen

Montavius Fredericks

Waking up with my wife in my arms was the most peaceful thing I've ever experienced in my life. I lay there just holding her even after I wake up not wanting to wake her yet, especially since I was shocked, she let me hold her after her denial of me wanting her. I am going to fix that and quick. After laying there for a few more minutes I hear her room door open, and I know it's probably one of the kids coming to wake her up and I was glad we were fully under the covers otherwise the kids would have seen their mama and dad naked. After a minute or so I feel my baby stir awake in my arms.

"What the hell kids, you know you're supposed to knock before you come in my room." She whispers yell at them, pulling the covers up to her neck and looking over at me then back at the kids.

"Well mom who is he?" Za'Mara inquires pointing to me.

"Yea mom and you were supposed to make breakfast." Za'Meir asks his mom staring at me then back at her.

"I'm your mom's boyfriend Montavius I definitely did not want to meet you kids like this. Can y'all give us a few minutes to get decent and we will be right out."

"Yes, sir come on y'all." Mariah says, grabbing her sister's hand and pushing Za'Meir out of the room at the same time. I roll her over and move to hover over her once I confirm they closed the door completely when I hear the latch click in place.

"Before you say anything crazy out yo mouf again. Like I told you last night you are my woman, and I am ya man. I don't need or want anybody else but don't worry I'll prove that to you soon enough." I let her know sitting back on my calves looking down at her and admiring her natural morning beauty. My morning wood is resting on the bed in between us pointing right at her opening that's glistening wet already and just begging me to taste and enter my home.

"Why are you looking at me like that?"

"Cause you look absolutely beautiful right now and because -" I say stopping mid-sentence scooting closer to her then taking my dick in my hand and rubbing it against her slick folds. She lets out a low moan damn near making me want to lose control and slide into my home. I rub up and down against her clit making her moan and buck against me almost making me slide in.

"Hmm I thought you weren't going to fuck me yet?" She asks moaning since I'm still rubbing my dick against her clit.

"I'm not." I say letting go of my dick then leaning over to kiss her on the forehead smack her on the thigh and then getting out the bed.

"Are you serious right now?"

"Yes, now get up and come brush ya teeth ya need to get that death off ya breath before ya cook breakfast for our kids." I laugh catching a pillow in my hand that she threw at my head.

"I don't think I bought any extra toothbrushes yet; I don't have much company." She says entering the bathroom with a black silk robe on. I'm sure she was looking for her clothes she had on last night, but I put them in the dirty clothes basket she has.

"No worries I have my own." I bend over to grab my toiletry bag from under the sink I placed there before getting her off the couch last night and bringing her to bed.

"What the actual fuck Montavius? You just been setting up in my house."

"It's just my bag I use for my toothbrush and other hygiene stuff relax Ife mi." I smack her on the ass while she brushes her teeth trying to smooth things over and loving the feel of her ass in my hand. She gives me that side eye only a mother can give making me smile as I put my toothpaste on my toothbrush.

"Ok fine I might've put a few shirts and shorts in the empty drawer you have in the closet."

"Montavius." She says rolling her eyes and leaning her head back. She starts washing her face with this orange-looking soap with white pieces in it.

"What is that you're washing your face with? You have some soaps I've never seen before."

"That's because I make all of our soaps, lotions, body butters, and scrubs. This one is turmeric, lemon and oatmeal soap and the one you used in the shower last night is my lavender and chamomile soap. I make them all with shea butter, coconut oil, tea tree oil, and some other oils. Mariah and Za'Meir both have eczema, and I didn't like how the steroid ointments made their skin look or feel."

"Damn for real that's cool as hell baby. That does explain this soft ass skin you have. I need my own soap from you." I say walking up behind her after getting my hygiene situated then placing one hand on either side of her moving her robe slightly off her shoulder and placing a kiss there then doing the same to the other shoulder.

"You are really making it hard to be suspicious about you sir." She leans her head back on the top end of my stomach. Her head barely reaching my chest my baby so short. I wrap my arms around her loving the way she feels in my arms like she's molding to my body. I look up at us in the mirror and I have to admit we look damn good together.

"Question where is the twins father?" I didn't find his name searching for their birth certificate. The only evidence of him is an old apartment lease they shared before the twins were even born. I notice she looks hesitant to tell me, so I turn her towards me to look in my eyes.

"He's dead." She tells me trying to put her head down, but I grab her by the chin to lift her head up and I read the look in her eyes. It registers to me quickly that she killed him and that's why it seems like he just disappeared off the face of the earth.

"Cool one less man I have to kill. Come on let's go feed our babies and I need to put some clothes on." She just smiles then shakes her head at me.

"That you do sir." We both walk out the bathroom. She heads to the dresser that sits in-between the bathroom door and closet door decorated with pictures, her body butters, and perfumes. She grabs her a moomoo that I can't wait to lift up one day and fuck her where she stands in. Walking in the kitchen the kids have everything laid out ready for her to cook.

"Ok so clearly we're making pancakes, eggs, bacon, and I see y'all took out the strawberries and blueberries." She says looking at everything spread out and prepped to cook. I mean they had the pancake dough mixed, eggs seasoned with cheese added in the mix, and fruit cut up.

"Anything I can do?" I ask as Mariah heads to the larger table setting it up then lighting a pumpkin spice scented candle which smells amazing and really gives the room a warm cozy feel.

"You can make mama one of her mimosa's she likes having on the weekends, the wine fridge is on the other side of the island." Za'Mara says from her seat next to me. I get up walking behind La'Meira who's using a griddle to make the pancakes and bacon while Za'Meir was making the eggs on the stove behind her.

"You want a mimosa baby." I lean down and say in her ear while placing my hand on her hip and rubbing up and down with my thumb then placing a kiss on her cheek when she nods yes. We all sit down at the table once all the food is done, and I never felt more at home just sitting at the table with conversation and laughter just flowing with all of us. The kids warmed up to me even more once they discover I am Dean's big brother. I'm learning about Za'Mara's martial arts class to help with her ADHD, Mariah's girl scouts and she was considering cheerleading, and Za'Meir will be starting track and field once football season is over. Mariah's birthday was August first, and I missed the twins birthday on June tenth.

"Hey ma can we go over to Aunt Myra's?" Za'Meir asks.

"Yea once y'all rooms clean." She informs them and they all run off to their rooms. They were done in no time and coming outside to let us know they were out. I look over at my wife while she sits in the patio chair next to me and after waiting for a few minutes just to make sure the kids didn't come right back for anything I stand then pick her up by the waist and place her on the rail in front of us with me standing in between her legs.

"Now tell me what the hell has the thoughts in your head that you're not a woman I'd be with and give me the real cause I don't have patience for fuckery." I say grabbing her chin and lifting her head to look me right in my eyes. I've been trained to work the problem in front of me and not to put it off.

"Look I don't have the perkiest breast after breastfeeding two kids or a flat stomach and men like you usually go for those fake bbw chicks and don't look at me like that you know what I mean. The chicks with thick thighs butt jobs and liposuction or tummy tuck flat stomach plus I'm not normal and nor are my kids well Mariah is more normal than us all."

"I don't give a damn about all that shit man. I prefer my women natural and those breast of yours not being stuck to ya chest keeps me from having neck pains trying to keep one in my mouth while you ride this dick baby. You can ride dick, right?" I say giving her a right-side smile and she does exactly what I want her to do which was smile too.

"Maybe you'll find out just how good I can soon enough. I like attention from my man, honesty even if you think it will hurt my feelings, I am into women but only sexually, I don't play wit bitches either. I'm not fighting over a nigga who can't keep his dick to himself, but I will throw a bitch in my damn wood chipper or drop ha ass in some battery acid if she thinks playing with me and mines is something safe to do and I guess I'll have to show you the rest." She pushes at my chest to get down off the rail to head inside and I follow right behind her as we enter her bedroom then her closet.

"Close the door." I do as she says and then she pushes the bit of clothes she does have back towards the wall then twists and pulls the bar apart. She pushes the bars in and then presses a button in the middle of the wall that makes two cabinets pop out about four inches from the wall which she turns each of them and pushes them back into the wall. I was damn near floored seeing what was in her secret compartment. I walk up running my hands over the riding crop, spreader bar, hand cuffs, a box that has panties with a vibrator attached and a remote which we will definitely be putting to use soon, and so many more toys that I cannot wait to use on my woman.

"Wait you were worried about me not being into all this. I guess we were worried about the same thing."

"Hol up you don't think I'm some sort of freak or weirdo being into this stuff?"

"Baby we own a damn sex club back in KC that has all types of BDSM activities and toys. Ugh baby you don't know the weight you've lifted off my shoulders or just how much you have solidified that I was right about you being mines." I walk up to her, and I push her against the wall with my hand around her neck then bend down to kiss her in the most passionate kiss I've ever had in my life. Licking her lips and then sucking her bottom lip in between my teeth biting down seeing just how much she likes pain. When she let's out a moan then grabs my dick through my sweat pants and lifting her left leg wrapping it around me to pull me closer sent me over the edge.

"I'll take that as your begging Ife mi." I say letting go of her lip, grabbing her by the waist lifting her up making her wrap both legs around my waist, using one of my hands to pull my pants down not wasting any movement and going in for another soul sucking kiss from my baby.

"We will have time for the slow, long, me tying you to the bed love making later but let me know now if this is not what you want cause once, I enter my home it's no leaving me EVER woman. I'm yours all of me and the same goes for you, understand?" I ask, looking her right in the eyes and seeing the moment she agrees but I need to hear it.

"Words La'Meira."

"I'm all yours Montavius, now fuck me, please." She pleads as she uses her right hand to pull her dress up then reaches between us placing my dick at her entrance and I can already feel her juices coating it making me thrust my hips upward entering to the hilt but pausing to let her adjust to my size.

"Mmmm fuck Monty." I start thrusting my hips up into her slowly feeling her tight pussy squeezing the shit of my dick already.

"Fuck baby this pussy so tight. Open it up for me. Yesss that's it let daddy in his pussy." I grunt out in her ear pounding into her harder. Damn this shit so wet and I knew it would feel like home her walls were made for me.

"Fu...Fuc... Fuuuckkk." She stutters as my curve has my tip hitting her g spot with every stroke. Looking down at where we met and the veins, she was causing to pop outta my dick and her creamy juices covering it was going to be the end of me.

"Mm La'Meria I'm about to paint these walls baby, cum for me." I command making my strokes deep and slow then grabbing her by the neck going between squeezing tight then letting her get a breath in then squeezing again and I swear my baby pussy just gushes like she is loving that shit.

"Oooh yesss daddy don't stop please." She moans and that shit unleashes the beast in me. I squeeze tighter around her neck and engraving my name on her pussy.

"I... I'm cummingggg." She screams her juices gushing all over my dick and she fucking squirts all over my stomach. I followed right behind her pushing in to the hilt painting her cervix with my seed.

"Fuck woman." Is all I can get out leaning my forehead against hers breathing heavy. I finally let her down kissing her forehead.

"Let's go get cleaned up baby." I lean down picking her up bridal style, she rest her head on my chest as I open the closet door and go straight to the bathroom to shower.

Chapter Fifteen

Dean Fredericks

It has been a stressful few days with trying to narrow down who Sinclair was or is still working for and Kelia trying to fight me on being together, but she finally gave in yesterday and we ended up having a nice dinner. She actually wanted to try Fredericks, and it was funny seeing the look on her face when the host called me Mr. Fredericks then walked us to my booth that's a bit smaller for when I'm not with my brothers. We would've ended the night at my place or the club, but I had an early flight to see my little man play tonight and I be damned if I missed it for anybody or seeing my Lil Dove. Pulling up to the airstrip where our jet is housed, I notice Jax, Bree, and Chase are already waiting and per usual we are all waiting on Meech and Marsh.

"What's up awon arakunrin?" I greet him in our native language. Jax had us all do an African ancestry test a few years back and we learned our lineage traces back to Nigeria to a tribe called Yoruba, so we all started learning the language and speak it to each other from time to time.

"Waiting on ya slow ass lil brothers." Jax jest dapping me up then I move to give Bree a hug and dap Chase.

"Well let's be real the only thing those two are eva on time for are dinner and the club." Chase chuckles.

"Yea that's about right." I shake my head and then notice the bags being loaded into the plane.

"Um y'all do know we're only gone for the weekend, right?"

"Oh, those are the things we bought for the kids don't tell me you didn't get them anything?" Bree asks, looking at me sideways.

"You do realize I've known them for years now. I've been putting money on the kids cash app for years besides I've already made sure my lil man was decked out with the best for his football season." I tell her giving my duffel bag to the flight attendant.

"Lucky you, ya could've introduced us all a long time ago." Jax says heading for the plane's stairs after the pilot says we'll be taking off in fifteen minutes.

"Why the hell would I have done that then I wouldn't have had them all to myself. It's bad enough I have to share them with y'all now." I frowned and took my usual seat across from him. "

Well rude much." Bree says, plopping down next to me and pushing me. Meech and Marsh finally show up a few minutes later just in time for us to take off on time. Our flight was quiet and quick. Once we landed, we hopped into the Tahoe's we ordered and headed right to my Lil Dove's home which was a thirty-minute drive from the airstrip we had to fly into. We arrived at her place about nine thirty and clearly just in time to hear the two freaks going at but clearly, they kept themselves contained in the room with the door open as I scope out the living room after letting myself in with my key and putting in the alarm code.

"Shit Mon... Monta...Montavius fuck baby I'm cumming." I hear her screaming out, feeling a bit of jealousy and I could tell Jax did too when he sat to the left of me from the look in his eyes which he hides quickly but not quick enough from me.

"Hmm shit baby me too. Wait was that the alarm?"

"Fuck that alarm you better not stop." She curses him.

"Umm fuck not a chance baby give me that nut." A few minutes later he grunts I guess cumming after she does. I hear running water for a couple minutes then it goes off.

"Babe my brothers are here." I hear him tell her then it sounds like him kissing her. These two are making me miss my Kelia something bad but there was no way she could get off in such short notice. About ten minutes later in walks my brother.

"Awon arakunrin I see y'all made it but how the hell did you get into the house?"

"Sir I've had a key since she moved in, and she told me the code she was going to use the day I told her they were coming to install it."

"I'mma need yo ass to not talk to my wife so much nigga." He says punching me in the arm as he approaches the sectional, we were all sitting on. Then Jax stands giving him a one-armed hug and Chase, Meech, and Marsh do the same. Bree jumps up giving him a tight hug. After a couple more minutes in walks my Lil Dove looking as beautiful as ever and sexy as fuck with those tie die tights on all the chicks be wearing to make their butts look bigger but my Lil Dove didn't need it with that big juicy ass she has. I swear she just has this natural sun-kissed glow and effortless command of attention when she walks in the room. She damn sure has commanded the attention of all my brothers who are staring her down right now and they are hard to please. I stand and go right to my girl wrapping my arms around her then picking her up. She wraps her arms around my neck squealing my name.

"Hi Lil Dove, I missed you." I say putting her down.

"I can't tell, I haven't heard from you in days you damn jerk." She punches me in the chest and that shit hurt a bit.

"I'm sorry Lil Dove you know I didn't do it on purpose. Tracking down these damn traffickers and fighting with Kelia had my brain drained plus I figured you'd be preoccupied with that jerk face over there." I apologize to her placing my finger under her chin to make her look at me because I truly was sorry. She's my peace always even when she's calling me out on my bullshit.

"Don't let it happen again, or I'll tie ya dick and balls in a knot. You're the only best friend I have left." She says lightly hitting me in the chest and I really feel like a fucking idiot now. She just fully opened up to me and I ghost her. She's always been guarded when it comes to letting people in but she's always there for others.

"Shit Lil Dove, hey y'all give us a few minutes." I tell the crew grabbing her hand to walk outside on the patio. Sitting in the first chair I see I pull her onto my lap sitting her horizontal to me with her legs hanging over the arms of the chair, kissing her forehead and wrapping my arms around her.

"You know I love you Lil Dove, I really didn't mean to ghost you. I really wasn't expecting Kelia to be so difficult, but she reminds me of another woman in my life." She lays her head on my shoulder, and I hug her tighter.

"Oh, who ever could that be besides if she was easy, you wouldn't want her now would you?" She says rubbing circles on my chest with her fingertip.

"You're probably right but she finally came around and we had a great dinner yesterday at Fredericks which I can't wait for you to come try."

"That's good, I hope she's the one but if she hurts you, I'm dropping ha ass in some battery acid slowly."

"She is Baby and I'm glad to hear you'll still have my back." I say kissing her on the forehead hearing the sliding patio door open and I know who was coming.

"Ok that's long enough get cha grummy hands off my wife nigga." Monty says, grabbing her hand but gently pulling her from the chair and right into his arms. I hear everyone else start to come outside admiring the view her backyard gives like I am now.

"Aww Big Daddy don't be jealous." She giggles getting on her tippy toes and pouting her lips for a kiss that he quickly obliges her leaning down giving her three pecks before deepening their kiss.

"Mmm babe stop before you start something, and I end up giving ya brothers a show on their first day meeting me." She moans trying to break the kiss.

"Well clearly, she is going to fit in this dysfunctional ass family with ease. Hi I'm Briana but everyone calls me Bree."

"Nice to meet you Bree, everybody calls me Meira for short." She introduces herself to Bree as she pulls her in for a hug and she tenses up.

"Forgot to warn you Bree's a hugger." Monty says chuckling at the shocked expression La'Meira has on her face. The two of them were pretty much the same height and thickness now that I look at them together, but Meira is a bit thicker. La'Meira was maybe a shade lighter, rarely ever wore makeup skin is always glowing and usually wears her natural long hair whether it's curly or straight or braids while Bree usually has some long weave in her head and the occasional braided style plus makeup is always done to perfection.

"Ok Bree let her go she's not use to that." I tap her on the shoulder about to pull her off my Dove.

"It's ok D besides she's soft and smells good."

"Oh, damn I didn't get to mention to ya Bree watch out my wife is into women." Monty says with a serious face with a twinkle of arousal in his eyes as he looks at the two them still embracing each other then slowly pulling apart but stopping with Bree's right arm around Meira's waist and I see what has that look in his eye, Bree's not bothered by what he says but looks intrigued.

"Well damn did y'all forget the rest of us were here. Hi beautiful I'm Jax." He introduces himself gently grabbing her hand and kissing the backside of it.

"Wait a damn minute." She looks from him to Monty. It was the usual reaction when people see the two of them together because they look so much alike, everyone thinks they are twins.

"Wait I see the differences between the two of you now but damn it I'm going to need pre warning when yo ass is in the vicinity." She says slipping her hand away from Jax's walking over to stand in front of Monty and he places is arms around her waist.

"Deal beautiful." He winks at her, and I notice her biting her bottom lip for a second.

"Hey keep that smooth shit to ya self nigga not at my wife." Monty introduces her to Chase, Meech, and Marsh next.

"Nice to meet ya Meira but can you feed a brother." Meech asks rubbing his stomach.

"Nigga didn't you eat on the flight here, my wife is not our chef?" Monty grabs her hand to walk back into the house and everyone follows behind them. I stay out for a few minutes to call Kelia.

"My sweetness." I say as soon as she picks up.

"Hi babe, I take it you guys made it."

"Yea I wish you could have come with me, I really wanted you to meet my best friend and my babies."

"I know I promise I'll come next time. I actually put in time off for his next game."

"For real woman you just made my day that much better."

"You two are really close huh?"

"Don't sound like that. There is nothin romantic there and trust my brother would kill me if there were, but we are really close. She bought me peace without even trying at a time there was none insight no matter what I did. Do I love her yes am I in love with her no that's reserved just for you even if you're not ready to accept that yet."

"I will give me time Dean."

"I know look go ahead and get back to work I'm about to head inside and see what these fools getting into."

"Ok talk to you later love."

"Yea later." I say hanging up the call and hoping she gets La'Meira and I relationship because it won't change hell there's no need to. I walk in the house and its full of laughter and food.

"Well damn woman what you in here cookin up?" I ask sitting at the big ass island she and her uncle installed when they remodeled her kitchen. This thing was in rough shape when she bought it, but it has come a long way.

"Some French toast, scrambled eggs, sausage links, and since we're all chillin plus it's more brunch time mimosas." She gives me the menu turning to hand me a glass she already made for me.

"Well shit spoil us please." Meech states holding his glass in the air making us all laugh.

"Don't get used to it nigga." Monty chimes in. She turns on some India Arie on low and we all vibed out switching between rapping or singing whatever song came on next to enjoying the good ass food she cooked. Before I know it, we were all sitting on the sectional in the living room just talking about any and everything, the guys getting to know her and the same for her getting to know them. I sit to the right of here, Jax was to her left, Bree next to him then Chase next to her, with Meech and Marsh next to me and Monty on the floor leaning his head on her lap looking like he was about to nod off. After a while though everyone does start to nod, and I was waking up to Meira head on my shoulder making me smile but hearing the door open has me grabbing at my hip until I hear my girl's voice coming down the foyer hall.

"Mom who's black Tahoe's outside?" Za'Mara shouts coming around the corner first.

"Uncle Dean!!" She yells running to the couch then proceeds to wrap her arms around my neck from behind and soon Mariah comes running too when she hears her scream my name.

"How my girl's doing?"

"Great now that you're here, who are all these people?" Mariah asks first, looking at everyone starting to wake up.

"Hi my babies." Meira says and the girls kiss her on either side of her cheek.

"Well baby girls next to your mom is my other big brother Jax, that's Bree next to him, my little brother Chase, Meech, and Marsh." I point to each one of them.

"Wow you have a lot of siblings; it had to be fun growing up in your house." Za'Mara says waving at everyone.

"It was interesting to say the least." I laugh cause we definitely had some wild moments in our house with nothing but boys. I still remember Jax hanging Marsh from the tree branch outside our treehouse by his belt loop on his jeans using a rope with his mouth tapped because he wouldn't stop one summer. He lasted out there for a good thirty minutes surprisingly the loop finally broke when he wouldn't stop trying to wiggle free but luckily for Jax he wasn't to far off the ground and only had some scrapes as well as bruises on his legs and arms.

"I see the resemblance between all of you now, but I didn't know Mr. Montavius was a twin." Mariah says and we all chuckle.

"Oooh girls we have some things for you, I hope that's ok Meira?" Bree says looking over at her.

"It's fine and that was sweet of y'all."

"Lil Dove you think I had them spoiled you haven't seen anything yet."

"Guys can y'all go get the stuff out the trunk?" Bree request of all of us. We all get up to head out Monty stopping to kiss Meira and give the girls hugs on his way out the door. We grab all those damn bags, and the girls went crazy looking through all the stuff Bree, Jax, Chase and even Meech and Marsh, all got them and the things they bought Za'Meir we put on his bed for him to check out after the game. The girls went to their room for a bit to get their homework done while my brothers and I head to the patio leaving the women in the kitchen.

"Aight so catch me up on this drug and trafficking mess we are dealing wit." Monty says the moment he takes his seat, and we all do the same.

"I'm still trying to break the code on these other names from the info Meira pulled off his laptop, but I did pull one ya not go like at all." Jax is looking at him with his eyebrows bunched together.

"What's the name Jax?"

"Justin's brother Bradley but as a customer."

"You gotta be kiddin me right now and ain't no way he doesn't know what his brother into." I groan.

"Ugh fuck that's way to close to home. Message Jace and Jude to keep an eye on that nigga as well as his weird ass brother but let them know to not be seen." He instructs me as I'm sending the message through the app he created for our secure communication.

"Well, the customer from Jax's club pointed us towards this wanna be corner boy that sold it to him, but that corner boy took some persuading." Meech says.

"Yea that niggas version of persuasion was him pumping him up with some truth cocktail that after about twenty minutes had that nigga bleeding from his damn eyes, nose and even his ears." Chase says with a disgusted look on his face but a smirk at the same time.

"What it needs a lil tweaking, at least he gave up the person supplying him but not the big dog unfortunately." Meech shrugs.

"So, his supplier was some dude that calls himself Gunna, but his government is Steven Mitchell from St. Louis. His mama and siblings still there apparently, he got into it with his old supplier and was ran out the city. He moved to

KC about a year ago and worked his way up the ranks quickly now he's the main supplier in his zone." Chase informs us.

"Let me guess Money." Monty says not really asking because any time we need some street information its always Money and as much as Monty hates Chase still being friends with him, the dude has helped us on quite a few occasions with the information needed.

"Don't start Monty."

"I'm not." He says putting his hands up in surrender.

"So how are we going to out who his supplier is? Clearly, he's not trying to cross another one"

"He likes your sex club Jax, he pays yearly for his membership. I was thinking Monty could get one of his female agents to visit the club try to get close to him. Dope boys like him have two weakness women and money and I rather the cheap route first." Meech says.

"I'll do it. I'm sure he's seen me around the club he won't look at me suspicious." Bree chimes in from the door.

"How long has your nosy ass been standing there?" I ask.

"She's been there for about three to four minutes." Monty says not even turning around taking a hit of the blunt he pulled out.

"Look I can do it, drug dealers aren't keen to new faces and mines is well known. I can just have him catch my eye one night and see where his interest lies. None of you have had any issues with drugs since then so we have time to figure out what's going on." She instructs us sauntering back in the house as the doorbell rings.

"I hate to say it but she's right."

"Ok fuck it let her handle that and until she comes back with anything actionable, or something happens everyone is working on these damn traffickers." Monty concludes as Meira comes outside.

"Jax did you have a delivery sent here?"

"Oh, yea just in time, come Mama bear." Jax says standing from his seat putting his hand on her waist and leaning down to kiss her on the forehead. Monty and I both give a look to each other agreeing to whip his ass later. We all head in the house when we hear clapping then yelling of Jax's name and we walk into her jumping in his arms then kissing him on the cheek.

"Jax you about to be a one hand bandit I catch your hands on my wife again."

"Babe stop it. Look what he bought for each of us." She holds up the jersey with the kids school name, mascot and Za'Meirs number on the front then on the back his name at the top and mom on the bottom. The rest had uncle, auntie, sister and Monty's said dad. Now that earned Jax a hug instead of the punch he was going to get a few minutes ago. Everybody goes their separate ways to shower and get ready for the game. We arrive to the game just as Za'Meir's team is lining up on home team side. La'Meira spots him then yells his name, we all point to his number and then turn around. He takes off his helmet and runs to his mom picking her up and spinning her around. He lets her go then looks at Monty and reaches to shake his hand, but Monty pulls him in for a hug instead. The smile that spread across his face made me wish for a son of my own soon and happy for them being happy. They won their game thirty-two to six with my boy making the winning touchdown as the starting running back. That night was one of the best nights of my life, but one thing bothered me, and I noticed the moment Monty as well as Jax saw the same problem I did. Monty flew back with us the next night to handle some meetings for the week and we just left dinner after one of those long meetings. We've been gone almost two weeks since things have been so busy but thankfully tomorrow is Friday and we will be flying back in the morning.

"Arakunrin how the hell did you break ya damn phone?" I question him as we pull up to his home. I never understood why he has to have such a big place to begin with, but he likes his space.

"Man, my last client pissed me off. She had the audacity to get mad after flirting with me and I turned her down. So, to keep my hands from being around her neck after she told me she expected a discount for my rudeness otherwise she would claim sexual harassment or some mess like that, I threw my phone at the door after she left." He was still fuming from the balls on this woman threating someone who protects people for a living.

"Did you tell Meira about this, or you broke the phone before doing so?"

"Mannn, I haven't been able to talk to my woman all day that has further soured my damn mood." He explains as we walk into his mud room off the four-car garage. As we walk out into the open floor plan kitchen, dining room, and family room he stops in his tracks.

"What the hell Mon-." I start to fuss until I see what caused him to stop in his tracks so abruptly and it's a pissed off La'Meira sitting on his living room couch in all black with her elbows rested on her thighs, head down with her hair pulled back in a low bun, and a switch blade she's flicking open and close.

"Ife mi did something happen? What's-." I grab him by his arm as he's about to rush up to her since he's oblivious to the fact she's not fully here. She stops flicking the blade open and close leaving it open then finally she looks up at us and leans back in the chair.

"So, you know who I am now Montavius?"

"What do you mean baby of course I do?" He breaks free from my hold on him rushing over to kneel in front of La'Meira who still has a blank look on her face and before he can say anything she raises the blade to his throat pressing it into his skin so hard I'm sure he's bleeding. This fool has the nerve to be smiling when I rush closer to them.

"Lil Dove baby his phone is broke, he wasn't ignoring you. Show her the phone Monty." He calmly reaches for the phone in his pocket turning it towards her. She doesn't look at it at first, but he touches her cheek then it's like a switch flicks on behind her eyes and she blinks a few times then looks over towards the phone.

"See Ife mi it's trashed. I'm picking up a new one in the morning. Dean just gave me your number so I could text you off my business phone since I forgot to put in that phone too." He informs her still rubbing her cheek with his thumb which seems to be calming her.

"So, you weren't ignoring me?" She pouts then puts her head down again finally lowering the knife.

"Don't you dare drop your head in front of me. You have nothing to be embarrassed about baby. I'm glad you're here a nigga was feeling empty without you near." He commands her by lifting her head with her chin then gives her a kiss. She wraps her arms around his neck deepening the kiss. Monty drops the phone grabbing her off the couch wrapping her legs around his waist as he walks towards the stairs leading to his master bedroom.

"Well later you two love birds." I chuckle and Monty raises his hand chucking me the deuces. I just shake my head and leave the house to head to Kelia.

Chapter Sixteen

Jax Fredericks

It's been about two months since we started visiting La'Meira and the kids in Alabama every other week for my brothers but Monty, Dean, and I have been there every week. It's been getting harder and harder to leave them for the whole family. Mom started visiting a few weeks ago and she clicked instantly with La'Meira and the kids hell they already call her glam ma. That woman has been showing those kids off to anyone who wants to hear about her new grandkids and how proud of them she is. She thought she was going to introduce them to her lil boyfriend but we all immediately shut that shit down and I don't think they're even together anymore. Za'Meir and I have been working regularly with all his work over video call when I'm not there and La'Meira has let me know his grades have improved significantly. Shit has been quiet on the drug front thus far, so we have been thinking maybe it was a coincidence, but we aren't taking any chances and letting Bree work Gunna for info. Monty's leaving tonight to go back to the fam so we're all having a late lunch or early dinner which ever you want to call at Fredericks.

"Hey arakunrin." I greet in our tribal tongue as I meet up with my brothers at our usual table. From the looks of it only Dean is missing. We sit for a few more minutes ordering our drinks then in walks Dean but he's on the phone.

"Wait Za'Meir what's going on Za'Meir answer me. Za'Meirrr." He stops just before our section yelling at the phone putting all of us on high alert especially Monty who's standing in the booth. He stands there for a few moments then something is said to Dean causing him to drop to his knees saying no... no... no. I can't believe the shit I see next, but tears are dropping from his eyes, and we all stand around him trying to figure out what the hell is going on.

"Dean what the fuck is going on? Why were you screaming Za'Meir's name like that? Dean!!!" Monty is yelling but then his phone rings with Za'Mara's number and picture on screen. He answers the call on speaker.

"Za'Mara baby what's going?"

"Dadddyyyyyy." She screams out crying hard and my heart completely drops.

"Baby breath talk to daddy please."

"Ma mommy was take taken and Za'Meir was he was shot daddy please come home pleaseee." I thought my heart dropped before, but I fell to my knees next, Chase and Meech fell back into the booth, Marsh is leaned over with his hands resting just above his knees, and Monty is just standing there with tears coming down his face.

"Baby daddy is on his way. I will call you as soon as my plane lands, ok."

"Ooh ok. Daddy aunt Myra wants to talk to you."

"Ok put her on the phone."

"Ughhh Montavius."

"Call me Monty, Myra. What's what the hell is going on?"

"Um it all just happened so damn fast. A group of men attacked La'Meira in the parking lot when she went to grab her sweater, and the boys saw it and ran right into it to get them away from her but before they could one of them jumped from the van shooting. He shot Za'Meir twice and… and my Darius once. The police were close by, so an ambulance was here quickly, but the van sped away with her so fast. They are getting the boys ready to head to the hospital now and some police are out chasing the van."

"Look I'm headed to the airstrip with my fam now keep my girls safe till I get there."

"Monty um shit I don't know how to say this." We just made it outside walking to our trucks when we hear the hesitation in her voice, I don't think things can get worse, but I have a feeling it is.

"Just say it, Myra." We all pause near him as he still has the phone on speaker.

"Monty La'Meira saw Za'Meir get shot and she um she lost it like I've never seen her that enraged. She um was able to knock out one of the men but they had to beat on her pretty bad to finally get her in the truck. The reason I'm telling you this is well Monty she um she found out she was pregnant a few days ago and was going to surprise you when you came tonight. I didn't want you to walk into the room to see the gift with the test and feel blindsided." She starts crying again the day catching up with her. Monty loses it after that punching his hand through the back window of his damn Range Rover dropping his phone. Chase picks up the phone telling Myra we are on our way and to text her number.

"Shit bru we gotta get this cleaned up."

"It's a first aid kit in the trunk. FUCCCKKKKKK." He screams out and we know that shit is not about his hand seeing as he has had a lot worse wounds. We all look at each other and the decision is made this shit is about to be full throttle we had our breaking moment, but somebody is about to be fucked. I call mom while Chase bandages Monty's hand. Dean is on the phone with Jace getting a read on what the Smith brothers are up to while Marsh and Meech hit up the club and restaurant managers letting them know they'd be gone for a while. Once I'm done talking to mom with her screaming and crying, I deal with Bree next, and I can't ask her to stay if I tried. I hear Dean talking to Kelia next and apparently, she's coming too. Chase let us know Kenya would be out tomorrow that was the earliest she could get someone to cover her cases at the community center.

"I should have never fuckin left them. I wasn't even supposed to be here, had I not let that fuck convince me to come back my family would be safe, my baby-" He breaks off staring into space and I see my brother's eyes turn the darkest I've ever seen. We get the window taped up and get on the road with me, Dean, and Monty in his Range Rover. He schedules for someone to pick it up at the airstrip.

"Wait what da hell do you mean you let Justin convince you to come back." Dean questions him.

"He was talking about some family emergency he needed to tend to and the meeting with one of our clients from overseas couldn't be pushed back and they wanted to meet in person which isn't unusual for this couple, but this meeting wasn't even anything important. I could have said what was needed through a video call."

"Wait a fucking minute I'm not liking the timing of this. He gets you to come back the same week La'Meira gets taken and Jace said Jude followed him to the airport with a damn flight to Georgia and Bradley's last device ping was in Tennessee." Dean starts putting shit together pissing me off further.

"And I never got any alerts that her hack was traced, so either she was taken for other reasons or someone snitched to him that it was her." Monty pauses for a moment.

"Naw... naw... naw I can't believe this shit. The only person could have known anything was Whitney she came in my office one day while I was on the phone with Meira telling her she can't do any more jobs for Dean. I'm sure in the divorce negotiation they had to list the company they used for information gathering."

"Oooh this bitch. Jax call Bree and have her stay behind to help Meech at the lab. I'm calling him now to let him know to handle that problem first then the jet will be here waiting for them both." Dean orders. I swear sometimes he forgets who's older, but I know why he's so pissed. I call Bree who wasn't entirely pleased but was ready to take care of our snitch. Once we make it to the airstrip Bree hops in Meech's truck and the rest of us hop on the jet including our mother and Kelia. The flight is spent consoling our mother and making every call we can for help in finding out where the hell La'Meira is as well as checking on the boys in surgery.

"I got ahold of an army brother who works in the FBI Birmingham office he will connect with the police in Dothan to see where they are in finding her and I got something I'm not sure you should see Monty but probably need to." I inform everyone while giving Monty a sympathetic look because what I am about to show him is bound to send him over the edge.

"Kelia baby take my mom to the back please." Dean says. The moment the door closes on the private room in the back of the jet we move further away, and I play the surveillance video I was sent. The instant it starts I want to through my damn laptop. Seeing La'Meira fight off those men the way they put hands on her then seeing the moment our lil man was shot and was still trying to make it to his mother. Myra was right Meira lost her damn mind screaming kicking she even grabbed one of their knives stabbing two of them, she's a total fucking bad ass. We see the moment they were able to get her in the van finally with the aid of someone who looks too fucking much like Justin. He literally stabs her in the back, and she loses the last bit of fight she has in her then they toss her in the back with one of their buddies.

Chapter Seventeen

La'Meira Jennings

Aww fuck my head man my entire damn body is killing me. God, I hope my baby is okay, please let him be okay. Monty wanted to come with us to the festival he asked me to wait till tomorrow why didn't I just listen to him fuck. Now I'm lying in the back of a van with a dead body my son and nephew have been shot clearly, I have been kidnapped by his fucking partner my side is killing me from where he stabbed me, and I think I'm miscarrying. The list of bullshit going on is too fucking long and I feel myself snapping.

"We just lost two fucking men. You said that woman was some damn computer store owner with kids, not some damn MMA fighter. What the fuck did you just get us into Justin?" Some man screams at Montavius's partner Justin. They clearly underestimated me and still are cause they either think I'm dead or still knocked out.

"How the hell was I supposed to know she could fight like that. You weren't supposed to shot fucking kids in the middle of the damn parking lot. We just had to run from the cops. Boss wanted her for some client that's into fat bitches, now he's going to be pissed if she dies or bring the authorities to his front door."

"Well, we both know you'd prefer if she died it would make your plan a lot easier and get you exactly what you want or should I say who."

"We were tight and so close to being together then he sees this fat bitch and all of a sudden, he's barely in the office let alone answering my calls. She can't do shit that I can."

"Do you hear yourself that man is straight and never wanted you. Now what are we going to do about the girl because getting her over to the boss still gets her out of your way for whatever fake relationship is in your head." This pussy ass white boy has the audacity to think my man will ever want him, oh I'm definitely killing that muthafucka the moment I get free, and I will get free. Oh, shit the watch the damn watch. Thank you Love bug. They have my hands tied behind my back thankfully so I'm able to reach the button and hold it down for the five seconds he told me to if I didn't feel safe and needed him. If I knew him this darn thing will probably sends out some type of signal to his stalking butt. Ughhh fuck a pain worse than being stabbed rips through my stomach, please not my baby. I hear the door to the truck opening, so I bite my bottom lip holding my scream.

"Shit I thought you stopped the bleeding from the stab wound, look at all this blood." The guy Justin is with says and I know that gut wrenching pain I feel is me miscarrying.

"I did this must be from something else, fuck. Call Doc and let him know we're on the way." They hop in the van pulling off apparently to Doc. The pain becomes too much at some point because the next thing I know I am waking up on a cold metal table in sterile room, maybe these fools had a conscience and took me to a hospital or clinic at least.

"Look Doc fix her so we can get going."

"Well, if you hadn't beat on her so bad you could but she has a deep stab wound to her left backside thankfully it missed all organs, and she just had a miscarriage she's not going anywhere for at least a few days."

"Good she lost that thing."

"Thing you mean baby you buffoon. We both work for the same man, and you know he doesn't sell damaged goods, so hopefully a few days she will be good to move. Now get out so I can finish tending to her wounds and get her cleaned up then into a room to rest."

"Fine I'll be back in a few days so we can move her. I guess we need to lay low for a while anyways. I'll send some men to guard the place just in case someone's dumb enough to come looking for her."

"She can talk right, we still need to figure out what she knows."

"She needs rest first. She lost over a pint of blood you idiots between the stab wound and the miscarriage."

"Fine but I'll be back tomorrow that should be long enough for her to talk." Justin states finally leaving me with this so-called doctor.

"You can stop acting like you're still unconscious child. Those idiots may not be able to tell the difference in your heart beats, but I can."

"So, you're really a doctor? I thought you people took an oath to do no harm."

"I am and did that's why I saved your life instead of letting you die."

"But you're patching me up to be sold off to sex traffickers and probably tortured for information some due no harm."

"Look we all have a debt to pay to the boss and as much as I don't agree with his business, I like my life and as long as I do my job my family is safe."

"Yea wateva you're a weak excuse for a man." I say sitting up not in as much pain as I was before.

"You don't hold your tongue, do you? That won't help you last long in the world you're about to be in and I gave you some medicine to help with the pain."

"I won't be in that world my Husband will come for me and all of you will be sorry." I tell him and it's the first time I called Montavius my husband out loud. I hope he really does come for me cause I don't know how much longer I can fight, especially with him sending guards.

"You think pretty highly of this husband of yours but even if he gets through the guards their sending, the big boss knows about you and won't stop until he has you. Look come on down the hall so you can get cleaned up." He directs me as he helps me off the table and down the hall to a room then into the attached bathroom, it is a small, but it would get the job done.

"I'll have some food for you when you get out." He lets me know then walks out the room. I turn the shower on step in scrubbing the blood off my body and crying for my baby gone and hopefully for my baby recovering in the hospital.

Chapter Eighteen

Montavius Fredericks

I still can't believe this shit is happening, well Justin I can slightly believe but him taking my wife and shooting my fucking son. I don't think I've learned a way to kill that will be slow or painful enough to make him pay for this shit. We landed about ten minutes ago and are heading straight for the hospital to see about my boy. We all park in the emergency entrance and run to the front desk.

"We're here for my son Za'Meir Jennings he was shot at the fall festival."

"I'm so sorry to hear that. He looks like he's been taken into surgery. I'll need your ID to print you a pass."

"Ok it's me my brothers, his aunt, and his grandmother." We all hand her our ID's and one by one she prints out our passes. She points us to the elevators to take to the third-floor emergency surgery wing and to where the family waiting room is. As soon as we get off the elevator my girls spot me and run right to me. You can't tell me that these kids aren't mines. It' has only been a few months but it's like they have been in my life for years.

"Dadddyyyyyy." They both scream jumping in my arms and I carry them over to the seats placing one of them on each of my legs while they rest their heads on my shoulders as I rub their backs.

"Myra what's going on with the boys?" I ask Meira's cousin while trying to console my girls.

"Darius is out of surgery the bullet hit him in the hip and logged in the bone thankfully it didn't hit any major vessels. Meir is um still in surgery one bullet went through his arm and the other hit one of his kidney's and they were having a hard time stopping the bleeding."

"My poor baby." My mother cries out.

"He's going to be ok right dad?" Za'Mara pleads with her big brown eyes filled with tears.

"He's strong like your mother and will fight through this. We just need to let the doctors do their jobs ok baby girl." I reassuringly rub circles on her back as she lays her head on my shoulder.

"What about mommy, who's going to find her." Mariah inquires next with her head on my other shoulder as she tries to hold her tears back.

"Now daddy and your uncles are going to go find mommy right after we make sure your brother is in recovery. Grandma and aunt Kelia will stay here with you all then take you home, okay?"

"Okay." They both sniffle out then they get up to hug my mother and all their uncles and aunt. I didn't realize my life was so empty till I met them and I'm going to do whatever I can to protect them. I order some food for all of us and go down to grab it, as much as I want to be out there looking for Ife mi, I know she'd want me to make sure the kids were good first. When I make it back upstairs Jax helps me give everyone their food. By the time everyone is really digging into their food the doctor comes in.

"Jennings family." The doctor walks into the waiting room calling for us.

"Yes, he's, my son." I stand up to greet her and shake her hand.

"I'm Dr. Fleming, your son pulled through surgery well, he is really a fighter. One of the bullets hit his kidney and for a moment we thought we would have to remove it, however we were able to repair the hole and stop the bleeding. The other bullet was a through and through to his left upper arm with some physical therapy he will make a full recovery."

"Thank you, God." My mother exclaims standing behind me with the girls.

"When can we see him?" I ask as I feel a partial weight lift off my shoulders. Most would think I was weird or setting myself up for failure getting attached to kids I've only known for a few months, but I feel it deep down within me these kids couldn't be more mines if I was the one who helped create them.

"He's still coming down off the anesthesia so he won't be able to talk just yet, but I will have a nurse come get you in about thirty minutes only two at a time when he does wake, we don't want to overwhelm him. He really needs to rest with the trauma his body has been through."

"Ok but he has two young sister's and is he in a private room?" Dean comes to stand next to me and starts questioning the doctor.

"Ok they can both go in with their dad, but he is in our recovery wing with other patients, that is the other reason why only two can go at a time."

"No, he needs to be moved to a private room with his cousin Darius Moore. I don't care what the cost are move my nephews now." Dean demands the doctor.

"It doesn't work like that."

"Listen I have your director Mr. Charles Furman and two of your board members on speed dial, I will gladly give them a call if need be. I will be announced as the newest board member next week I'm sure you've already heard the name Chase Fredericks."

"I will let the nurses know to move them to the private wing Mr. Fredericks." She is shocked but schools her face quickly. We're used to that look at this point being black men on the board of major hospitals. This will be the third hospital that one of us has been added as a board member.

"Thank You Dr. Fleming you can let my mother know when he's moved my brothers, and I need to go find out about my wife but I will go see my son now." I say and she leaves to let the nurses know to prep the private room and start to move the boys. After about thirty minutes a nurse comes back to let me know I can see Za'Meir before they move him. The girls decide they will go once they move him so Dean, Jax, and I go see him instead. Seeing him bandaged up but breathing on his own but still connected to an IV was hard but eased my mind still knowing he would be okay. He actually stirs awake.

"Dad uncle Dean, uncle Jax." His voice raspy due to his throat being dry. Dean hands him a cup of ice water.

"Slow big fella, we don't need you choking." I lean him forward to sit him up straight and hand the cup of water to Dean.

"Dad, they got mom I tried to get to her even Darius tried but they just started shooting." He rushes out as his throat starts feeling better and tears up.

"Hey... hey it's ok son. Y'all did the best you could baby boy let us handle things now. They are going to move you and Darius to a private room together. Grandma and

Aunt Kelia along with your sisters will be staying with you. Your Uncles and I will be going to find your mother okay."

"Okay please come back." He grabs my arm pulling me down towards him and I can feel his body tremble from holding back his tears, but I let him know to let them go if that's how he is feeling then he does. After a few minutes of letting his tears run, I kiss him on the forehead, Dean, and Jax follow suit then we leave.

"Hey, I just got a text from Meech they have Whitney at the lab. He wants to video call in about thirty minutes." Jax reveals looking up from his phone.

"Ok well let's get to Meira's place I secured everything in that home even outside of what she did." We headed back to the waiting room hugging the women and letting them know we would be back, but my mother stops us in the hall.

"Listen I know what you six are about to be up to. All I need is for you all to come back with my daughter safe and sound and make those bastards pay for trying to take her from this family, understand?" No words are needed after hearing our mom condone our methods, but we all nod our heads, give her a kiss, and leave. Once we make it to the house, I connect my phone to the TV just as Meech is calling.

"Yo Meech what's going on?"

"You wanna tell him Whitney?" He says stepping from in front of the camera revealing Whitney strapped to an operating table then Meech hits a button moving the table in an upright position and we see how bug eyed crazy she looks.

"Monty, I never meant for it to come to this. I just wanted you to see me but six years as your assistant and that's all you ever saw. I took care of everything for you and still you wouldn't give me the time of day. Then you come around acting all in love with that fat broke bitch with all those damn kids like she's the best thing walking. So, when Justin came to me with the opportunity to get rid of ha, I jumped on it. She's not good enough for you."

"Why would Justin come to you and why does he want to get rid of her so bad?" Dean questions her.

"Justin knew about Sinclair being a part of the sex trafficking ring. It was his idea for him to become a client so his devices could be protected and then here she comes ruining that too. Sinclair's import/ export business is how they move everything around and he knows I've been trying to get him to finally see me." She tells us shaking her head probably trying to fight off the effects of the drug.

"How long have you known about all this?"

"The past year. I caught him deleting files about Sinclair that showed on the saved client hard drive or just hiding them not sure, but he accidently clicked on one of the folders showing a bunch of women dressed like whores and they looked high. So, I told him I'd tell you what he was hiding because of the clause I knew you didn't know so he read me in and started paying me to keep my mouth shut."

"You roger rabbit two meals away from anorexia looking bitch there would never be a world in where I would be with a woman like you. My wife helps people yo stupid ass saw this fool removing photos of women held against their will and saw a way to make money. She is better than you in every way and you lucky you are so far away talking crazy about my kids, or I'd kill you myself." I shout getting more pissed off by the second. Now it made sense why he never moved money around in the business. His family cut him off years ago but somehow, he was still living the high life even though he only owned ten percent of the company to our ninety percent. Something else is just not adding up for me though something else is off.

"Anything else Whitney?"

"All he was supposed to do was take her and hand her over to the guy he's working for, apparently, he has some client that likes fat bitches, and he sold her off once I told him she was working for your brother possibly seeing something she shouldn't have with their trafficking business."

"He DID WHATTTTT." I roar losing my control at hearing he's sold my wife like a piece of clothing or something.

"Meech deal with that bitch then you and Bree get here asap."

"Done." Bree says walking up next to her aiming the gun at the side of her head then she shoots Whitney and Meech proceeds to release her straps throwing her over his shoulder to get rid of her. Knowing him he's probably created a new concoction to dissolve her body in.

"See you in about an hour or so brother." He ends the call. I start pacing the floor because if they get her off to some freak only God knows how I will ever get her back.

"Yo chill ya go pace a hole in the floor. They can't take her to him, yet they stabbed her, and she was pretty beaten up too." Jax tries reassuring me as he stands to put his hand on my shoulder.

"He's right, so they would have to take her somewhere to get fixed first. One thing about these pricks they don't like physically damaged goods. They won't get all of their money." Chase has the look on his face when the wheels are turning on overdrive to map out what type of place they would need to keep someone alive off the grid.

"Wait a fucking minute." Dean pops up out of nowhere looking down at his phone.

"What Dean?"

"Yes, that's my Lil Dove fuckin yes."

"Will you fill us all in on what has you so excited." I get a bit of snark in my tone.

"My bad, I bought Lil Dove a watch when she first moved here being on her own. The watch is a smaller version of ours with the emergency button and tracker in it. Justin's dumb ass must have thought it was just a regular watch and left it on her because she activated the emergency beacon."

"Wait you have a tracker on my damn wife, and you just now want to tell us this?"

"Chill Monty you know all of our watches are the same way, you can't track us unless we press the button." Jax pushes my shoulder.

"So where is she?" I walk up next to him to see what he's still looking at on the screen.

"Some town called Dawson in Georgia. It's about an hour or hour and a half away from here. She hasn't been there long. I probably didn't get the alert sooner because of being in the hospital."

"We need to suit up and get there. We can't wait on Meech and Bree, they could move her by then especially if they somehow discover the watch, she has on is no regular watch."

"He's right they will definitely move quicker if they discover that watch, but we need to come up with a plan first." Marsh speaks up.

"Wait this may help us even further." Chase is tapping away on his phone with a smirk on his face.

"What?"

"Disconnect your phone. Jace sent me a live link to a bug he put in Bradley's car." He starts connecting his phone to the TV and up pops a video of Bradley in his car making a call then we hear Justin answering the call on his end.

THE CALL

"Justin what in the actual fuck were you thinking? All you were supposed to do was grab the broad, see what she knows, and then drop her ass to Calder to be sold and also not be seen doing any of it."

"Look I didn't plan on it going that way either, how the fuck was I supposed to know she could fight like that, and the shooting part had nothin to do with me that was Phil's dumb ass panicking."

"We both know you would rather kill the bitch anyway so don't think it's lost on me you were hoping she died from her wounds. Where is she anyways?"

"She's with Doc getting patched up, he says she needs to rest for a few days apparently the fat bitch was pregnant.

I'm glad it's gone she had no business having a baby from the man that should be mines."

"This shit again. Montavius never showed you that type of interest and the dumb ass broad you sent to get close to him in his club never reported any gay behavior from him, hell he barely fucked with her, so get the shit out of your head before you get us both killed." Bradley shouts at Justin making my damn stomach turn. This fool thinks I'd really be with him. He has me running moments together in my head to see if I ever gave him any sign, I liked men and I come up with none.

"Don't worry about my relationship with Montavius he will come around or I'll just destroy everything he has. I already have his girl and part of his men betraying him from his lil security business."

"Yea but you're already down two and you said it yourself most of them are either loyal to him or his brothers. But anyway, how long exactly before you move with the girl Calder wants an update cause his customer is getting antsy?" "Doc says a few days so maybe about four before we actually reach Calder. I'm waiting for couple more of them to arrive within the next two hours since I only have the two with me. I still can't believe ha ass killed one of my men and knocked out the other we had to leave him behind."

"Well, if you would have did your homework on her you would know the damn woman was raised around nothing but boys being the only girl in her family for years and was in both Jiu Jitsu as well as Boxing growing up and still attends classes occasionally till this day. She'd probably beat your ass if you got too close." I can't help but beam with a bit of pride at my baby's ability to handle herself when I'm not around but knowing she lost our baby his killing me right now. Jax and Dean place their hands on my shoulders as I lean over placing my head in my hands letting out a guttural scream.

"Well let's see how all that helps her when she becomes Calder's client sex slave before he kills her, or sells her back into the trade, they never last long. I wonder if Montavius will want her so badly when she's on drugs and been ran through." Justin says full of anger and resentment.

"Just make sure she's well protected so she makes it to her destination. You can't afford anymore fuck ups Dad has already said he won't keep protecting you, you're already cut off financially don't make it worse. So, get this shit wrapped up they have a load coming in tomorrow that I need to get ready for, I expect an update tomorrow when you talk to her about what she discovered."

"Ughhh ok Brad." Justin groans out loud and disconnects the call.

Chapter Nineteen

Dean Fredericks

"FUUUCCKKKK." Monty screams out again and jumps from his seat pacing the floor about to tear shit up, but Jax and I get to him first wrapping our arms around him. He's the biggest of us all pushing almost three hundred pounds but pure fucking muscle. First Za'Meir being shot, La'Meira being taken, and now finding out she lost the baby I don't know how much more he's going to be able to take and still come back from it. I can see his dark side taking over more and more as the shit goes on.

"We're going to get her back Monty and y'all can make all the babies y'all want." Jax is standing in front of him squeezing his shoulders trying to get him to focus.

"He's right Monty, we know where she is now, we know for sure that they won't be moving for a few days at least and no one will be there watching her for a few hours at least. I messaged Meech and they will be landing in about forty five minutes and he will be coming straight here while Bree goes to mom and the girls. I gave him the location to meet us there." I explain to him trying to keep him focused and sit down so we can get on the task at hand.

"Ok so we need to take our bikes that will be the quickest transportation since it's about an hour away, but we can make it in at least forty-five minutes." We were all in agreement on that part with our custom bikes we can get there quick and quietly.

"We won't have company there for at least another two hours. That gives us time to get there and get out since they're coming from the airport maybe a bit longer." Chase chimes in.

"Ok I have the drones in the RV we can use them to check the area before we go in and watch our backs while we're inside." Monty starts walking to the door, and we all get the hint and move with him to head to his trailer down the street. We make it in a couple of minutes walking in silence as all of our brains are in over drive running scenarios and just sheer disbelief from everything that's happened today. Monty starts opening all these hidden compartments once we enter the large RV he bought revealing weapons, military style bullet proof vest, surveillance equipment and more to aid on us getting my Lil Dove back.

"Ok Meech just texted me they will land in about in ten minutes." We suit up in all black and grab our favorite mask because it's time for Jagun Jagun"s to go hunting.

"Wait something just clicked in my head of all the crazy shit that's happened." Marsh says adding his blades to his vest and one in his shoe.

"What?" I ask.

"Did no one else catch this white boy being mad cause Monty don't want to fuck him as to why he fucking with La'Meira well besides what she knows."

"Mannnnn I was trying to block that shit out so shut up." Monty says with a disgusted look on his face.

"I feel you, but did you catch him saying the bitch you been fucking the same one you snapped on recently was sent by him." Marsh adds.

"Yea that shit had me looking up ha info and banning her ass from my damn club." Jax states clearly sick of the intrusions into his club.

"Naw don't do that yet. Once we get my wife back, I want to find out how deep she's in with him." Monty says looking up from checking his gun.

"Ok bet I'll send the notice to security." Jax is typing away on his phone.

"We also have to deal with whoever decided to cross us at the security firm too." I remind him running all my interactions with our agents at the firm trying to figure out which ones decided to be bitches. Once we all we're geared up we head outside to the garage we had added about a month ago to hold all our bikes. Monty wasn't wrong when he said riding on the roads out here were peaceful.

"Hey Meech and Bree landed." I say hoping on my all-black Ducati Panigale V4. Jax hops on his black and blue Yamaha MT-10. I'm sure Bree wanted to help bring Meira home, but we need all our women safe, and Bree is good with a gun so if anything does pop off, she can help protect them till we get back. Thankfully the roads are clear since it's pretty late at this point and with the watches we're all wearing now, we know the roads to avoid with state troopers we don't want any police presence with what we're about to do. Once we get close to where La'Meira's being held Monty motions for us to pull over at an empty lot about a quarter mile away. He takes the drones from his backpack laying them on the ground and types a few things on his watch causing them to lift off into the air. Soon we get a visual on all our watches of the area surrounding the old two-story colonial style home. It's about four acres of nothing but woods surrounding the home on either side and maybe an acre of cleared land, a long driveway leading to the road we just turned off.

"I think we should leave the bikes here and go in on foot, so he doesn't have time to alert anyone." Monty suggests looking at the watch showing us it's clear all around and has only two cameras, one on the front and other on the back door. We're leaning against our bikes when Meech pulls up about fifteen minutes later that boy must have been flying to get here. He parks next to Chase and hops off his bike as we huddle up.

"Aight Me, Jax, Dean, and Meech are going inside. Marsh and Chase be our defense outside just in case we get company early. One at the front the other at the back. The thermal shows it's four people inside. Two upstairs, one headed downstairs and one in a room downstairs and I think that's my woman." Monty says while we look at the thermal footage on the tablet he pulls out.

"Bet I just put the cameras on repeat, but I still think we go in silent. Two at the back door and two at the front door." I say typing commands on my watch.

"Let's move." We all nod and head into the tree line sliding on our mask. Of course I have my Ghost face mask this one is silver, Jax has his black and white purge mask with the X's for the eyes, Monty with his black Phantom of the Opera mask, Chase has his white Vendetta hacker mask, Meech has Jason hockey mask, and Marsh in Ghost skull mask. It takes us about ten minutes to reach the house and separate to our designated spots.

"In position, go." Monty says next to me as I pick the lock, and I hear the telltale click. We go in the back closes to where we think La'Meira is being kept. We hear movement coming from somewhere upfront, but we know it's not our brothers because it sounds like it's in a kitchen with pots banging. Monty confirms through his earpiece that Jax and Meech have entered and have eyes on an older woman in the kitchen. There are about three doors down this hall.

"That's definitely La'Meira she's chained to the bed arguing with someone." He whispers to me and she's behind the second door on the right. We hear in our earpiece from Jax that they detained the woman in the kitchen. We approach the door but then hear someone coming down the stairs off the back door we just entered. Monty turns towards the stairs gun raised as I pick the bedroom door lock.

"Get the fuck away from me you piece of shit." I hear La'Meira scream making me hurry this pick process. Behind me I hear a thud and turn to see Monty has dropped some old guy on the ground then zip ties him up. I hear the click sound I'm looking for and slowly open the door.

"Stop moving you fuckin cunt. Justin's stupid ass thinks Montavius is the fucking prize but you and this fat pussy I saw earlier are." Phil's bitch ass is trying to pin La'Meira to the bed as Monty sneaks up behind him lifting Phil up in a chokehold off La'Meira as I dig in his pocket for the key to her chain.

"Montavius Dean?" She looks at us in disbelief and I pull off my mask so she can see it's me as I get the chain unlocked. The moment I get it off her ankle she jumps in my arms crying.

"Let me go you son of a bitch." Phil struggles to get out of Monty's death grip.

"I got you Lil Dove. Fuck they hurt you so bad baby." I run my hands up and down her back. Soon Jax and

Meech enter the room after doing a sweep of the house to make sure no one else is truly here. Meech goes to help Monty with Phil who is slowly losing the fight anyway and Jax comes to stand next to us as we sit on the bed.

"Aww my Lil Phoenix I'm going to let you take them to the Lodge and feed them to the wolves for what they've done to you." Jax declares as he's kneeling in front of us while she sits on my lap with her head on my shoulder stroking the side of her face. She turns to hug him and then we hear a loud thud as Monty drops Phil on the ground and walks over to us. La'Meira pulls away from him when he reaches for her causing all of us to scrunch our faces up in confusion.

"Baby you don't want me to touch you?" He inquires as he squats down in front of me. She buries her head in my shoulder wrapping her arms around my neck tight. She won't even look at him and I see the moment his heartbreaks further in his eyes.

"We need to get on the move before we have company even though I'm good with a lil fun." Meech reminds us from the doorway.

"Give me a minute I need to talk to my wife. I saw a pickup truck coming in go get it and load these two on it along with ya bike Meech. Jax help him." Monty directs our brothers. I'm sure he wants to figure out what the hell is going on with Lil Dove as much as I do. Meech leaves to grab the truck as Jax grabs Phil by his arm dragging his unconscious body out the room like he's a rag doll.

"Ok Lil Dove what's going on, why won't you go to Monty and don't play with me woman."

"He's not going to want me anymore once he finds out so I might as well save myself now." She explains with her face still pushed into my neck.

"What the hell do you mean I won't want you anymore. It has felt like my ribs breaking one by one every moment I didn't know if you or our son was going to be ok, my mind slowly slipping into the darkness with all the ways I'm going to obliterate everyone involved but thanks to my brothers I'm able to be kneeling waiting for you to come to me." Monty conveys how hard things have been to her.

"I lost the baby." She cries out and it starts making sense why she thinks he may not want her now.

"Baby I know but you're still here and that means more to me as crazy as it may sound." He affirms and she finally turns to him jumping in his outstretched arms, but she winces in pain then he lifts her off her feet.

"Za'Meir?" She sounds almost afraid to ask how he is doing.

"He's awake and asking for you at the hospital now let's go home baby." Monty says turning her bridle style in his arms walking towards the door and I'm right behind him. Meech has the men zipped tied and gagged in the bed of the pickup which I'm sure he has given them something to stay knocked out for a while. He has his bike securely tied to the bed of the truck.

"Aight Meech head out we will be right behind you." Jax orders him hitting the back of the truck and he starts down the long driveway. We check the drones as we walk through the woods to our bikes noticing things are still clear as he turns on the road and we see him ride past us. We hop on our bikes and Monty straps La'Meira to his back because she has started to look a bit woozy. Once he's sure she's safe we pull off into the night. There are maybe two car spaces between us and the truck Meech is in when we notice cars coming in towards us in the other lane then they pass. My line rings and I answer through my helmet headphone.

"Yo I think that was them if they so much as slow down alert Jax and the others then let them have it. Don't let them even get out their cars, understand?" Monty explains picking up speed and alerting Meech with his headlights to do the same after we notice them making a turn assuming it's the spot, we just left but can't fully tell as were about a mile away now. I nod to Jax next to me and then he swirls his hand in the air then forward and we all take off faster. We've probably been driving for another twenty minutes and not seeing any headlights as of yet but that isn't a surprise as we didn't even take the same way we took here. My phone rings again with a call from Monty.

"Somethings wrong bru, I'm taking her straight to the hospital the boys are at. Drop ya bikes off at the house then meet me there." He says ending the call and I call Jax as I notice him speeding off even going around Meech causing me to worry for real now. Jax answers on the second ring.

"Yo what happened, why he take off like that?"

"He says somethings wrong with her and to drop our bikes off and meet him at the hospital."

"Why doesn't he just take her to a hospital here if he thinks something wrong the hell?"

"Don't panic bru I know trust me I'm feeling it too, but we don't want her at a hospital here and she would want to be at the same hospital as Za'Meir."

"Fucckk you're right. I just want her to be ok. Hmm we seem to have company behind us." I look in my mirror and notice car headlights. I look forward to see that Meech has turned off up ahead and I can't even see Monty's taillight any longer so if it is them at least our girl is off to get help. One car speeds up and goes around us reveling another car right behind it but then slows down. The car in front suddenly speeds up then whips the car to the left blocking the road and the one behind us does the same causing us to all slam on breaks doing back wheelies then turning our bikes to the side. Without even waiting for a word or window to roll down we pull our weapons and open fire in both directions because even if it's not them whomever was asshole enough to do what they just did deserves to get shot. I hear glass shattering then doors open on the other side of the vehicles clearly trying to avoid any more shots.

"Just give us back the girl and we will let y'all go." A man shouts who sounds oddly like Drew one of the agents from the firm which pisses me off since I told Monty it was cool to hire his dumb ass, now I'm going to make his death slow. I drop down shooting at the two sets of legs I see and hearing them both scream in pain. I hear a fuck behind me that's way to close for my comfort as bullets continue to ring out from behind me.

Chapter Twenty

Jax Fredericks

I hear the fuck from behind finding Marsh holding his arm which just pissed me off further. He was still shooting with his other hand, so it wasn't too bad but it's time to end this shit. Using the same move Dean has I drop down shooting at the three sets of legs I see and hearing them all go down. I wave to my brothers to move in Marsh and Chase on their side and Dean and I on our side.

"Is it me or these two look familiar." I ask Dean.

"They should that's Drew and Anthony bitch asses. Monty hired them about a year ago, I even vouched for his goofy ass." Dean shoots Drew in the knee then the other and I laugh, my brothers are so petty. I hear Chase and Marsh walk up behind us after a round of shots on their side goes off.

"Look I'll tell you whatever you need to know just don't shoot me again, fuck." Drew pleads out not knowing which knee to grab for.

"Now what the hell do you think you can tell us that we don't already know." I question him as I squat down in front of a bleeding Drew.

"You know why he took the chick but what you don't know is he always planned to kill her; she was never going it make to Calder. He hates that chick vigorously; he acts like some scorned woman or something. He's not going to let up until she's dead. He was even willing to pay Calder the half a mill his client paid for her to give back to him with interest. The client refused though, he wants her bad he was willing to pay double for her and pick her up himself after they told him she had a miscarriage. Man, I needed the money child support amongst other things have been screwing me up and he was paying cash up front." He rushes out as he rolls on the ground in pain and switches between the knee he's holding.

"Nigga I don't wanna hear that shit. If you were having troubles you could've went to me or my brother, I vouched for you bitch." A surge of anger runs through Dean causing him to shoot Drew in his hand then in his kidney and I know that from target practice the boys aim is lethal.

"You got about fifteen minutes before you bleed out without applying pressure to any those wounds. Ya buddies over there are already dead, you may get to live. So, tell me is there anything else we need to know?" I request as I tap on his knee with my gun hearing Dean scoff next to me.

"Calder he's some type of government official. I heard Justin ask him sarcastically how his constituents would feel about how he makes his extra money, which seemed to piss him off because he returned with ask, ya father he taught me." These sons of bitches are fucking sick, and they just don't know the bear they've poked. I looked over at my brothers and we all made a silent agreement.

"Well you may have actually been useful. So, here's what's going to happen, you are going to hop back in ya car head back to the house and let Justin know the Jagun Jagun are coming for him we will destroy everything he holds dear before he becomes one of Monty's wax figures." I inform him standing up nodding towards the other car and my brothers. They moved to put the bodies in the other car then I hear it crash into a nearby tree and burst into flames.

"Well better get a move on then." I nod my head towards the car riddled with bullets. Anthony only being shot in his leg helps Drew in the passenger seat and hops over to the driver's seat. We stand there and watch as they drive off.

"You placed the bomb in the car?" I question Dean. "Of course, I did they will be in for a surprise but let's go Lil Dove is not doing good. Monty just texted to say they made it there and he's worried." Dean says as we bump fist, and we all hop on our bikes to head to the beauty that has captured our hearts in one way or another. We pull up to the hospital after dropping off our heavy equipment at the house and check on the girls who were fast asleep. Walking through the emergency room the same guard that was here last night is still here and let us right up. We see Monty sitting in the family waiting room for surgery patients and we all sit around him.

"Hey bru what happened with her?" I ask as he notices Marsh's bandage arm.

"What the fuck happened to you?" He jumps from his seat before Marsh can sit grabbing his arm to look it over.

"I'm ok Dad it's just a graze." Marsh tries to joke with him even if he did actually look to him as a father figure since he never really got the chance to meet our real father.

"Look can nobody else please get hurt I'm not sure how much more I can take tonight." He groans out looking more stressed than I have ever seen my big brother.

"Meira was still bleeding when we got here, she lost over three pints of blood. They have her in surgery trying to stop the bleeding from the miscarriage and the stab wound. I almost killed her doctor when he said I may need to prepare our family." He explains to us plopping back in his seat and I understand even further why he looks so defeated. I was sitting here feeling defeated my damn self after hearing that and looking at my brothers faces, they felt the same. Dean looks like he is physically sick and clearly is as he rushes over to the garbage can in the corner and throughs up then squats down in front of it. I walk over to him and rub his back.

"Bru I can't lose her I just can't." He leans his head back staring at the ceiling. Our brothers come and surround us on the floor all hanging our arms over each other's shoulders with our heads down.

"Mr. Fredericks?" The doctor walks in about twenty minutes later. We all stand greeting him.

"We spoke before her surgery, and I told you to prepare your family-" Before he could finish Monty steps back and we all surround him to brace him for whatever comes next.

"No Mr. Fredericks let me finish I told you that, but I didn't know the strong woman that was laying on my table. She pulled through the surgery with no complications, whomever tried to sew her back up after her miscarriage was just incompetent, but I was made aware that she was kidnapped, and I am just glad God bought her through it all. I won't say that she will not have a hard recovery ahead of her though her body has been through a lot of trauma." He rushes to tell us since we were about to flip out when he first started and it's like we all were holding our breath because we all let out a heavy sigh at the same time.

"When can we see her doc and did you move her to the private suites next to her son and nephew?" Dean questions him.

"She has been moved to the suites about seeing her even though she made it through the surgery with no complications we had to place her in a medically induced coma due to all of her trauma so she can really rest and start her bodies healing. So please prepare yourself she is hooked to quite a few machines to take as much of the work off her especially because she had three cracked ribs that were causing breathing problems. I will have a nurse come to get you in about thirty minutes." He explains then turns to leave us in our thoughts.

"I can't believe all the wounds she has what the fuck man!" Chase shouts getting pissed and walking off to sit down. I am right there with him though cause what type of man puts his hands on a woman like that. She has three broken ribs, bruises all over her body including her face which one of her fucking eyes was swollen shut, stab wound, and she miscarried on top of all that shit if they didn't keep her sedated through all that pain, I was going to kill the doctor myself.

"I'm just glad she made it through wounds can heal with time and whatever she needs after I got." Monty declares going to sit down and we all follow suit to sit in silence until the nurse comes to get us not even bothering to argue that we all couldn't go back at the same time. I know the doctor told us to prepare ourselves, but nothing could prepare us for seeing her laying in the bed like this a machine breathing for her, the visible bruises becoming more prominent, handprints on her arms, her swollen face that is already turning purple and black and just man fuck I don't think I can do this shit. Monty drops to his knees in front of her bed, Chase is leaned over the chair next to her bed taking deep breaths, Meech and Marsh barely enter the room before turning around and sliding down the wall next to the door, Dean squats next to her bed with tears sliding down his face for the second time since he's been alive that I have ever seen, and I'm leaned against the door with my arms crossed over my chest with my head leaning back trying to hold back my own tears. One thing I know for sure is I'm ready to go state to state burning every city to the ground till we find everybody involved and I don't give a shit if I get caught, I'll smile in my mugshot. All of our thoughts are interrupted by the nurse entering the room and walking right past me.

"Guys I promise she looks in worse shape than she truly is in. All of this is to help her body not have to do so much work to heal." She explains pointing to the machines as she checks everything is running smoothly.

"I'm Nurse Brett and I will be here to take care of your sister while she recovers."

"She's not our damn sister that's my wife." Monty finally speaks standing to go over to the other side of her bed sitting in one of the chairs near her grabbing her hand and kissing it gently before placing it back down but still holding it.

"I'm sorry." She says finishing her work and leaving.

"I'm moving here." Monty expresses out of nowhere.

"We figured you would be." I say finally entering the room fully taking a seat on the couch on the back wall to the right of the room.

"No, I mean I'm moving now not eventually. While I waited on y'all, I spoke to Jace, Jude, and Rex promoting them to run the KC office. I'll be going back in a week or so to fully announce the transition. I sent out an email announcing the departure of Justin and Whitney from the company, cancelled all their access, and put security on alert for his presence. I just can't be apart from her and the kids." He informs us staring at her lightly running his hand over her face.

"I am too and already spoke to Kelia. She's been wanting a change of pace from working for the mayor anyways." Dean adds in.

"Damn I don't think we've all ever lived apart from each other except when we were in the military but even then, we came home after deployment." I say looking at my brothers.

"Well y'all can all move here and open second locations. Meira once told me she wanted a family compound." Dean suggests shrugging and I look at him actually contemplating what he was saying.

"Wait a family compound, what's that?" Marsh asks genuinely curious.

"Basically, a big plot of land for an entire family some have farms and live off the land but in different homes or one large depending on how big the family is. Meira talked about having hundreds of acres of land with a bunch of homes for her family even the kids when they grow up with a fully functional farm, different animals and huge garden." Dean paints us a picture of what she told him she wanted as he leans over to kiss the side of her face.

"Damn that sounds pretty cool. I'd be down for that; weed is not legal, but they have CBD and that's still profitable." Meech chimes in finally coming into the room but still having a tough time looking at Meira.

"I'll talk to Kenya, but Meech is right that does sound cool, and I'd be down too, I can do reality and construction from anywhere." Chase expresses.

"Well, I just checked they don't allow sex clubs or stores unless it's for educational purposes and I can for sure find a way to make that work. Yup count me in too." We all look at Marsh who's standing at the foot of her bed.

"I'd move to Iceland for those damn kids if I had too besides you know I go where y'all go any damn ways." He says chuckling lightly and we all join in.

"You hear that baby, you need to go ahead and heal up we will have your compound started soon." He says placing a light kiss to her forehead. We all sit in silence for a while even nodding off for a bit well until Monty's phone rings and I know it can't be anybody but the kids or our mom.

"Hi mama, yea we got her she's in bad shape, but she is healing. No, they have her in a medically induced coma so her body can rest. I know ma. We will be home in a bit the kids are on fall break, so they don't have school anyways. Ok Love you too." He says ending the call. I look at my watch noticing its almost nine in the morning. Everybody starts waking up slowly.

"I just thought about something. Meech where the hell did you put the Doc and Phil bitch asses?" I question him the moment I become more alert.

"Oh, them niggas sleep still hanging from some hooks I found in the shed. The concoction I gave them won't let them wake up till I wake them up."

"Bet, I'm going to go check on the boys then we should head there. There's a lot of shit we need to fill Monty in from last night."

"Damn he's right might as well get up now then." Dean leans over to kiss Meira on the forehead saying he loves her then walks towards the door. We all take our turn doing the same and head to Meir's room to find him asleep but wakes the moment he hears Monty voice.

"Dad?"

"Yea my man I'm here, we all are." He says pointing back at us as he walks to the side of his bed kissing him on the forehead.

"Mom?" He looks almost too scared to ask.

"We found your mom just like I told we would. She is not in good shape but she's right next door healing up to be better than ever." He explains running his hands over Meir's dreads. You would swear he was his biological son with the amount of similarities between him and us in general with his identical almond shaped eyes chocolate brown skin tone, large build for fourteen, long dreads and hazel eyes with specks of grey.

"Can I see her?"

"Not yet lil dude mama is going to be sleeping for a bit to recover from her injuries but just like your dad says she's going to be good, ok?" I tell him rubbing his shoulder looking him right in the eyes and he nods his head.

"We are going to go handle some business, but we will be back in a few hours, grandma will be here with aunt Bree and Myra." Monty rubs his head starting to look better the more he sees that he is ok then kisses his forehead again then we all file out running into Bree in the hallway.

"You big dummies scared me." She groans, hitting, then hugging us all in the same movement.

"We're okay woman. Things got a bit sketchy there for a moment but all in one piece." I say rubbing the top of her head and I notice she's alone making me shake my head because she clearly left before mom woke up with her impatient ass.

"Is our girl really in that bad of shape. Ma called me while I was on my way."

"Unfortunately, she is but she's here and healing that's all that matters right now." Monty says putting is hands in his pockets taking a deep breath.

"Well let me get in here and see her and our boys. Your packages are still out by the way." We all nod and walk off not needing an explanation. We all arrive at the garage, and we fill Monty in on the shit we were told while Meech does his thing with the traitor as well as the Doc.

Chapter Twenty-One

Montavius Fredericks

It's been a month two days six hours and twenty minutes since La'Meira was put in a medically induced coma which they tried to take her out of it a few days after, but she never woke up. They ran so many test trying to figure out why she wasn't waking up but concluded her body just wasn't ready to. She was taken off the breathing machine about a week after and she was breathing on her own, so that was a good sign. Meir has been home for the past few weeks and has even went back to school with his sisters. Mom has pretty much moved here because the only time she has left is to pack more clothes and usually stays in the RV if I'm at the house. I never made it back to KC and just did a video call from the office establishing Jace as the IT Director, Jude as our Ops Director, and Rex as Client Relations & Acquisition Director building their teams who will basically handle all clients' needs, so I don't need to be there. Even before these changes we had a good HR department but expanded it due to all the hiring that is going to be needed with new positions opening. During the call though my brothers all walked in standing next to Jace, Jude, and Rex outing the few that were left that were on Justin side, it almost turned into a fight because those loyal to us wanted their heads after they explained what happened. Chase acquired his Alabama real estate license the week after we discussed moving surprisingly Kenya was on board instantly getting her license as well so they can work together, and they found us a one hundred- and eighty-six-acre lot more than enough for all of us. We all picked out our spots with everyone designing their own homes and me just waiting for my wife to get up so we can do the same. Chase found Marsh a place for a night club easily since they were sparse in Dothan. Jax wasn't in a rush to get the BDSM club opened up so he's been chilling with the kids after giving Bree full rain of the club and hiring another manager to help run the club back in KC. Dean and Kelia have been at their rental home not far from La'Meira's or his new office getting things together or he's here when I go home to the kids for a bit. Meech has his CBD shop underway. Today is wash day for my baby which with the help of some videos and our girls I have gotten good at doing her hair for her. I pull her to the back of the bed to hang her hair off the end of the top part of the bed careful not to move the feeding tube she has in as I sit my bucket filled with warm water down. Using the cup, I've been using since I started this wetting her hair then applying the shampoo to her hair massaging it in for a few minutes repeating it at least one more time then applying her conditioner using the detangle brush to make sure it's distributed evenly. I decided to blow dry it out so I can smooth it into a ponytail then plait the end. Once I finish up, I wash her body down after changing the water yet again then dress her in one of her silk colorful moomoo's, it was actually really nice with a dark background but vibrant geometric shapes all over. I shaved her legs and underarms yesterday so I'm sure this feels good on her skin.

The nurse thought I was weird for using this all natural charcoal hair remover cream I found in our bathroom to remove the hair on her pussy as well. I know my woman and if I left her looking crazy, she'd kick my ass. Her regular nurse Brett comes through the door.

"Hi Mr. Fredericks, how is the Mrs. today? Oh, I really like this one she is going to have to let me know where she gets these." She says doing her normal routine.

"She's doing the same I just finished washing her hair and bathing her. I thought I felt her jerk away from me and squeeze my hand while I was."

"You are such a good husband I hope God blesses me with a man like you. The physical therapist will be in at one forty-five to work her muscles out again." She tells me side eyeing me and if my baby was awake, she'd probably knock her ass out. This damn woman flirts every time she comes in here whether it was with me or one of my brothers. Once she leaves, I massage the body butter scent I chose for today, a pumpkin spice gingerbread scent the kids said she liked, I would have done it as soon as I finished bathing her, but I knew the nurse was coming. I was holding her hand while I text Chase, who was out gathering his construction crew to build out our compound. We showed the kids the property last week and they were too excited, and both my girls want horses, but Za'Meir wants some chickens and dog kennel along with a big gym. I have been working on getting all those things bought with the help of Dean and Jax. Chase already had a plumbing company come out to map the property for each home, turns out it has it's on fresh water well and a pond on the far right end of it. Once I am done massaging her body down, I clean my hands. I slide one of my hands under her dress rubbing slow circles on her clit sliding my fingers through her wet lips, moving towards her entrance rubbing circles around it then sliding one finger inside, for my girl to be in a coma her pussy is always wet when I do this and I swear she squirms a little when I do it too.

"Mhm." I know damn well I just heard that. I move my hand up pinching her clit just enough to cause slight pain but more pleasure and she fucking moans again nobody can tell me I didn't hear that. I keep pleasing my baby looking at her face for signs she is waking up and then it happens she opens her eyes slowly still moaning squirming in the bed.

"Meira baby, are you really back?" I look at her pausing for a moment when she fully opens her eyes and looks over at me smiling.

"D don... don't stop babe." She moans with a raspy voice from not talking for so long and I do exactly what my baby wants a minute later she is coming all over my fingers. I push in and out a few more times curving my fingers rubbing that spot she loves until she stops spasming around my fingers. I take them out and pop them right in my mouth savoring the taste of her then kissing her lips. I move to grab her some water and clean her up.

"Slow baby." I instruct her taking the cup from her ready to call the doctor, but she stops me.

"Don't call that nurse in here yet. That bitch is going to catch my blades when I get out of here." She informs me slowly still finding her voice again. I have never been so damn happy in my life. She coughs a bit, and I know it's because of that feeding tube.

"Baby I don't want her ass in here either, but she needs to come take that feeding tube out. Warning you've lost about twenty pounds since you've been out." I explain pressing the call button and letting them know she's awake. She gives me a side eye like I knew she would about that woman, and something tells me she really could hear everything going on around her like the doctors told me she probably could. The next few hours are a blur of doctors and nurses checking her vitals, taking blood, and asking her questions. I'm right next to her the whole time. I make a video call to our family group chat showing them she is awake and talking. Everyone flips out saying they are on their way, mom even went to pick the kids up from school. My poor babies for the past month have been coming here to lay with their mom talk to her the girls helped with her hair and Kelia or Kenya came to make sure her eyebrows were good sometimes changing whatever hairstyle we manage to get in. Once they are done poking and prodding my poor wife, they let the family back and they all file in one at a time filling up the large suite she's in.

"Mommyyyyy." The girls yell hoping in the bed with her kissing all over her face and she does the same to them. Za'Meir stands at the door with his head down, he's been feeling guilty about not being able to stop them from taking his mom. I have tried to reassure him he did everything he could, so have my brothers and he has gotten better. Once the girls climb out the bed and give everyone a turn to hug and kiss on her she looks at him.

"Za'Meir come here now." She commands with a stern voice making him move at once.

"Hold your head up and look at me Papa. Don't you ever in your life scare me like that again dammit." She says grabbing him in her arms hugging him tight kissing all over his face and he laughs trying to get away.

"Maaaa stop ok... ok." He whines and we all break out laughing.

"Look at me I protect you I save you not the other way around please don't ever do that again." She demands getting stern with him again.

"I couldn't just watch you be taken away and not do anything. You're my favorite person on this earth well besides the rest of them you're at the top." He says getting emotional hugging his mom again after waving his hand around to the rest of us. I feel no type of way about it because I feel the exact same way. My brothers give me the look letting me know we need to talk.

"Baby me and the guys are going to step out for a bit, I'll be right back, ok?" I assure her kissing her forehead then walking out the room. We make our way to the roof top as we've done plenty times before since she's been in here. Once we make sure it is clear to talk Jax starts.

"So, we all know it's going to get out sooner or later that she's awake and we all know the only reason we haven't caught a peep from any of them is because they figured she wasn't going to wake up right?" He says looking at all of us and we nod.

"The plan is still the same one of us will be here with her at all times. The nurses know we don't leave the room when they come in and no medicine is given unless looked over by us and told what it is for from the doctor himself. Once she's out Jude has already put together a team for the house and one as her driver unless one of us are with her."

"Well, it's not like we have been totally silent since she was in the coma anyway." Marsh says with a grin on his face.

"What do you mean you haven't been silent Marsh?" I ask.

"Dumb ass, he wasn't supposed to know." Chase says slapping him in the back of the head.

"Oops." He says rubbing the back of his head.

"Talk NOW!" I convey calmly but they hear the venom in my voice.

"Look we wanted to make sure you focused on Meira big bro. So, we kinda been hittin up their so call shipments. Also looking into who the hell Calder could be." Jax explains placing his hand on my shoulder.

"We've been sending the women and men to our fam over in Texas to get rehabilitated and either sent back to their families or setup for school or whatever else they want." Dean adds in.

"We been talking about buying some land here to setup for them as well. Kinda like our compound we are building." Chase chimes in.

"So y'all just been making moves without me huh."

"Not without you for you. Bru, you didn't even cry at our own father's funeral hell none of us did but the look I saw in your eyes when it looked like we would lose Meira or our lil dude we knew you needed to be here and only here." Jax tells me.

"Facts Bru we had to take care of you for once and if I didn't let that rage out killing their men, I don't even think Meira would've been able to bring me back." Dean says hanging his head down running his hand over his waves.

"Trust, I know what you mean the only thing that kept the darkness back was taking care of her and the kids this past month." I express turning my head up looking to the sky.

"One other thing I know Meira quite well and um she's going to be pissed if we don't let her in on taking down Justin and his people, so before we make any moves, we need to talk with her." Dean tells me and I know he's right, but I can't help but to argue.

"Nigga I think I know my wife well enough; she will be ok with staying out of it for the sake of the kids." I let my pride take over and puff out my chest.

"Now we both know you wrong about that, and ya don't know her as well as you think. Hell, I'm starting to think I don't either." He says looking away from me.

"What the fuck does that mean Dean." I question stepping close to him with my head tilted to the side.

"It means... It... Fuck man it means I found out La'Meira is *The Queen* and I mean *The Queen*." He explains to me, and we all get the bug eyed dumb founded look on our faces especially me.

"Wait how to you know that for sure?" Jax asks.

"Because I checked her computer about a week ago just making sure it wasn't a file, she may have overlooked that she collected since I have her passwords, and I found a folder labeled *The Queen's Work* and sure enough was all the info she shared with us to help take down our previous targets along with the one we actually met her on." He says turning to look at Jax who turns around.

"Wait when the fuck did that happen?" I ask looking at them both.

"A year ago, you were away meeting that model chick in Paris. She sent us the info and Jax was flirting with her then told her we were a person down and if she wanted to have some fun, she agreed and met us there with her gold and black renaissance mask with a crown attached." Dean explains.

"There was a close call while we were there, and she saved my ass cutting a nigga head off with one of her swords that crept up on me while untying some of the kids we found." Jax reveals and I see the feelings the memory cause playing in his eyes.

"Why do I feel like that's not all." I say looking at him.

"Things got heated once we got outside. I grabbed her by her neck stopping her on the side of the building and we kissed and well fucked. She never took the mask completely off and neither did I, so we never saw each other's face." He finishes finally.

"So, you fucked my wife before me, I mean-"

"Before you get all worked up let's be real you would eventually bring her to The Stage or The Woods so it would have happened eventually." Chase jumps in before I can finish.

"Nigga I wasn't going to get worked up so shut the hell up."

"But you said there was a connection there how did you not realize it was Meira?" Chase questions.

"I guess my body kinda knew my eyes and brain just never caught up till now." Jax says shaking his head and then this look comes across is eye only for a second, but I caught that shit, he's sad. I rub my hand in my beard frustrated with something else I'll have to deal with and soon.

"Bru I'm not-" I hold my hand up cutting Jax off before he can finish.

"Jax I'm not worried about that she's my wife and we will figure the rest out later we got bigger shit to deal with. Let's get back." I walk off. When we get back the kids are getting ready to leave with their grandmother. We'd apparently been on the roof for a couple hours talking and we hadn't even noticed. I give each of them a kiss on the forehead and hug letting them know I'll call them before bed then we all walk into my wife's room ready for some answers and to come up with a plan.

"Well welcome back babes, where'd you guys go?"
She asks when we enter the room.

"First you have some explaining to do *The Queen*." I
say and she gets this shocked look and quickly fixes her face
ready to deny it.

"Before you try to lie or deflect, I saw the files on
your computer double checking if you may have missed any
files from the Sinclair case." Dean mentions stepping to the
other side of her bed opposite of me.

"Ummm." She starts.

"Don't even think about it my Lil Phoenix we fucked
a year ago and it's very easy to prove." Jax stands at the foot
of her bed and winks at her. The shocked looked gets stuck
on her face this time.

"Oh, shit babe I didn't know I swear shit... shit...
shit."

"Calm down babe it's ok about you sleeping with
that numb nut at least but hiding you being *The Queen* from
me is a different story."

"Well technically I wasn't hiding it from you. It's
been over a year since I been out so about a month before we
moved here."

"Yes, but you never told me and there will be a punishment for that later but for now we have to figure out our next move." Dean says.

"He's right about both parts." Jax then explains everything that's been going on since she's been asleep. She thinks I didn't notice her squeezing her thighs together when he called her his Lil Phoenix. I'm hoping it doesn't become a problem otherwise I will have to shoot my damn brother.

"Look I'm going to be honest with you after this shit the only part I will be involved in is any hacking that needs to be done then I want Justin in my wood chipper." She explains and I let out a deep sigh thanking God I didn't have to fight with her about it because I really don't want her out with us hunting.

"I'm glad you're choosing to stay behind. You will have security with you and the fam at all times including a driver until all this mess is over." I lean down to kiss her on the forehead then she puckers her lips for a kiss, and I happily oblige her and will always.

"I'm shocked you gave in so easily Lil Dove talk to us."

"Look I haven't been out in a while not just for the kids but for me as well. I love helping those kids, but it's been taking a toll on my body and my mental for that matter. I just want to be able to enjoy my life with my family and damn near dying has pretty much solidified that for me. I know it's selfish but." She says and we all grab a part of her stopping her and reassuring her.

"That's not selfish at all you don't owe anyone anything Ife mi." I say wrapping my hand on the back of her neck and squeezing slightly and she leans her head back closing her eyes letting a small moan out as her muscles relax.

"Ok so it's settled Lil Phoenix stays here; I'll bring your laptop and the secured satellite hotspot we use, so you can track down the asshole quicker for us and watch our backs. We will gladly bring Justin back to you for his punishment." Jax states rubbing the side of her calf and she seems to calm down even further. I am starting to notice they really do have a connection and a part of me wants to dead that shit, but something also tells me not to.

"Well, there is one more thing. We purchased the land for your compound Lil Dove so you can be busy designing that with Kenya and Kelia while we hunt."

"Really?" She says getting excited looking up at me and I nod my head yes then she starts dancing in the bed smiling from ear to ear puckering her lips again for another kiss.

"I know you've found the perfect spot Chase."

"Of course, love." He says and she reaches her arms out for him to give her a hug which he gladly accepts.

"Alright we need to get going, Jax stay with Meira, I'll be back after while ok baby?" I state and she pouts but nods her head. I lean down grabbing the back of her neck pecking her lips then kissing her again deepening the kiss the second time sliding my tongue against her lips before she welcomes me in. She lets out a moan placing her hands on either side of my face, but I break the kiss pecking her lips again for a quick kiss. I lean closer to her ear letting her know I didn't care what she did with Jax past, present, or future as long as she remembers who the fuck her husband is.

"I love you Ife mi."

"I love you too hurry back." She expresses with a pout again and I shake my head at her. Dapping Jax up letting him know to take care of my girl till I get back before we all head out.

Chapter Twenty-Two

La'Meira Jennings

I can't believe I've slept with my man's brother and he's ok with me sleeping with him in the future. What the hell did I get myself into and why am I turned on by this.

"Get out of your head Lil Phoenix." Jax says placing his big ass hand firmly around my neck using his thumb to push my head back to look up at him then rubs it back and forth. Damn he looks so much like Montavius but those greenish brown specks, just a hint lighter chocolate muscular and I mean big muscles are covered everywhere in tattoos well at least where I could see plus his dreads are at the middle of his back with dark red tips. Fuck he is truly one of God's favorite children.

"So, you guys normally share your women?" I question looking him in those hypnotic eyes and he has the nerve to smile with his pearly whites.

"We have talked about poly relationships if our women are ok wit, it before but none of us well except Chase of course but now Monty and Dean were in relationships. We aren't like most men even if we share with each other, we will still annihilate any man that touches what's ours, you understand?" He says still holding my neck rubbing his thumb up and down my neck slowly. I can't help but squeeze my legs cause this man is turning me on something fierce.

"Mhm." Is all I can muster up pulling my bottom lip between my teeth trying to contain myself.

"You like that don't you? I've heard about your lil kinks too Lil Phoenix. You like to be tied up, spanked, blindfolded, chased, among other things?" He questions me sliding his other hand over my breast then down my sides. I can't find my words so I just nod.

"Use your words baby." He commands as he squeezes my hip.

"Yes." I say barely above a whisper. Damn the shit this man is doing to my body should be illegal.

"I bet you're wet as fuck just thinking about all the things we may do to you? Can I check Lil Phoenix and remember use your words."

"Yes Jax." I whimper damn near moaning as he slides his hand down further to glide it up my leg reaching under my dress to my pussy then sliding a finger between my wet lips dipping his long large finger inside my entrance making circles causing a moan to fully escape me.

"Fuck Lil Phoenix you're so wet and tight. Is that for me?" He leans down ghosting his lips across mine.

"Ye..yes Jax." I manage to get out moaning his name as he adds another finger then quickly connecting his lips against mine in a heated kiss forcing his thick warm tongue into mouth making another moan escape my lips and he practically swallows it. He starts moving his fingers in and out then curving his fingers adding a third making me feel so stretched as it's been over a month since Monty has been inside me.

"FUUCCKKKK Jax." I moan over his lips that are gliding across mines as his fingers continue their assault on my pussy making squishy noises the faster, they go.

"I wanna taste her Lil Phoenix. Can I taste this fat pussy baby?" He asks for permission as he glides his tongue across my lips like he's not in complete control of my body at this point just that quick.

"Yes." I say breathlessly as he let's the rail on the side of the bed down with the hand that was around my neck. He pushes my dress up, putting my left leg over the side of the bed as he slows his hand movement then completely removing his fingers licking my juices from each of his fingers moaning out loud as he enjoys the taste of my juices.

"Shit Lil Phoenix you taste so fucking delicious, you better not give this shit to anybody outside of us you understand me?" He growls out with his baritone voice placing his hand back around my neck squeezing.

"I won't I promise." I tell him biting my bottom lip as he gives me a quick kiss then moves down my body, dropping to his knees placing my leg over his shoulder then lining his face up with my pussy rubbing his nose against my clit making me twitch from being sensitive.

"Oooh fu… fuck." I moan out as he flattens his tongue licking me from my entrance to my clit making circles around it then sucking it between his lips and biting down on it causing me to arch my back off the bed and pushing his face into her even more. Going from pain to pleasure when he quickly flicks his tongue up and down then causing a suction with his mouth around my clit.

"Jax shit I'm cumming."

"Cum on this tongue baby." He says sliding his thick long tongue inside me and smacking my clit making my pussy cream and clinch around his tongue while squirting at the same time.

"Jaxxxx." I practically scream out holding his head in place still pulsing around his tongue. As my heart rate slows, I release his head, and he comes up for air just as the nurse knocks and rushes into the room.

"Ma'am are you ok your heart rate was through the roof a moment ago." Nurse Brett asks looking from me to Jax then where his hand rest on my right leg and the other holding my left leg as well as my juices covering his beard. He slowly puts my leg down smirking at her then leaning over giving me a sloppy kiss as my juices drop from his glistening beard. I enjoy the taste of myself on his tongue.

"Is there a reason you're still standing there when you can see she's fine better then fine if you ask me." He winks at me and she finally turns to leave.

"Probably should've locked the door Mr. Hurricane tongue."

"Hmm I like that name and you're right let's get that rectified now." He says with a wicked smile walking to the door locking it and stalking back towards me like I'm his prey.

"Let's take this off too. I'm sure she will know why." He says plucking my pulse monitor off my finger. He lifts me up like I weigh nothing, and I instinctively wrap my legs around his waist and arms around his neck as he walks over to the small pull-out bed on the far end of the room. Looking at that thing has me wondering how my big ass man spent a month laying on that thing. Jax sits down in the middle of the bed laying back with his hands still on my hips and he covers just as much of the bed as I would imagine Monty did. These are seriously some huge fuckin men and so damn sexy.

"Pull my dick out and sit on it Lil Phoenix." He commands and I comply at once lifting up on my knees reaching my hand under his sweatpants then his boxer briefs pulling them both down just enough to release that monster he calls a penis.

"Shit." I say as it pops out just under the width of a soda can but damn near as long as a damn pringle can. I wrap my hand around it as much as I can. It is so pretty I know that's crazy but it is. So smooth blemish free he clearly waxes or shaves as he is completely hairless, the veins protruding around leading up to his fat mushroom head has me contemplating how he is going to fit in either of my damn holes. I stand up stepping off the bed squatting down between his legs then on my knees as my legs feel a little weak putting me eye level with his monster and do exactly what I was thinking, I'll sit on it afterwards. Licking the slit on his head then swirling my tongue around it licking up his pre-cum.

"Ssshit Meira baby." I love how responsive he is already. I push his dick forward flattening my tongue to lick from the top of his nutsack along his deep dorsal vein curving the sides of my tongue up to the tip sucking his head in for a moment then releasing it. I gather spit in my mouth dripping it down on his dick then using my hand to smooth it across his length doing it again until I know it's fully coated then opening my mouth as wide as I can flattening my tongue then taking him to the back of my throat. I relax my jaw taking him in deeper and swallowing around him.

"Shi... shit... shit baby what you trying to do to me." He moans grabbing the back of my head and I chuckle causing a different vibration as he's still in the back of my throat and he bucks his hips upward moaning. That just made my pussy even wetter, and I go harder. I bob my head up and down his length in quick deep bobs using my hand to squeeze twist the length I can't fit. I feel his hand tighten in my hair almost painful but enough to egg me on because I love how he's squirming and bucking under me. I stop at the head with my tongue still flattened then hollow out my cheeks creating a vacuum suction around his head slurping away.

"Fu... fuc... fucckk Lil Phoenix I'm about to cum baby." I grab his balls massaging them still working him in the vacuum suction I created and when I feel his balls tighten up and his dick twitch, I take him to the back of my throat swallowing around his dick as his thick creamy cum shoots down my throat. I pause there until he twitches the last time then I stand whipping the sides of my mouth placing my knees in either side of him on the bed and he snatches me down to him tongue kissing my breath away. I reach back grabbing his dick lining it up with my entrance and he bucks forward entering me partially stretching the shit out of me.

"Fuck this shit tight." He groans against my lips holding me by my neck as I lean back to ease down more of his length and that shit takes my breath away.

"Breathe baby." He commands me and I take a deep breath starting to slowly rise then coming back down seating him completely inside me. I swear this man is touching my cervix. I start rocking back and forth then circling my hips. That man was hitting every fucking crevice in my pussy, and he has the nerve to start using his thumb to rub circles around my clit as I rock making my nut sneak up on me and take over within seconds.

"Aaah." I moan looking down at him trying to catch my breath. Once I do, I plant my feet flat on the bed bouncing up and down on his wood like a damn pogo stick. I lean forward just enough to reach his neck with my hand wrapping it around as far as it would go and squeezing as I look him right in his eyes my walls still pulsing around him. That man growls at me like really fucking growls and that shit had my clit jumping while I'm still bouncing up and down. I release his neck just a bit then squeeze as tight as I can doing the same thing with my pussy as I come up and that man snaps grabbing me by the waist flipping us laying me on my back without even leaving the confines of my walls.

"Damn woman that's the shit you on huh?" He says looking down at me then down at where we meet, and I look as well as my essence covers his third leg. He pulls out to the tip grabbing me by the back of my thighs pushing my knees to my chest spreading me wide and slamming into me filling me to the hilt repeatedly at a slow murderous pace.

"Rub that clit baby." He commands still giving me deep slow strokes and I do as he tells me like he has some type of spell over me.

"Jax mhm shit you feel so good."

"Whose pussy is this Lil Phoenix." He asks me but I can't find my voice as I cum again arching my back off the bed making him go deeper as if that is even possible.

"Hold them shits there since you don't like following directions." He says as he releases my legs and smacks me on my clit hard twice as I grab my feet.

"Shittt Jax." I scream squirting all over his dick.

"Who. Pussy. Is. THIS?" He demands I answer as he smacks my clit with each word keeping his dick still deep inside me.

"Yo.. yours." I moan.

"Say it again."

"It's yours Jax fuck I'm cumming." I moan as he leans forward grabbing me by the neck as I let my legs go wrapping them around him and he kisses me so passionately I don't want to even come up for air while he's thrusting deep our pelvic hitting each other, his balls smacking my ass and my pussy so wet its sounding like extra cheesy mac and cheese. He speeds up and I feel his balls tighten letting me know he's about to cum right along with me.

"Cum baby." I demand placing my hands on either side of his face reconnecting our lips and he does just that deep in my pussy as I come with him. He removes his hand from my neck resting his forehead on mines while his dick is still twitching in me.

"Hmmm shit woman you don't know how bad I've been waiting to do that again. I hope you know you really can't leave me ever again. Let's get you cleaned up." He expresses breathless smacking me on the side of my ass and giving me a quick kiss. He slides out of me making me feel empty missing him already then picks me up bridal style and walks us to the full attached bathroom sitting me on the toilet.

"I wouldn't dream of it." I assure him as I relieve myself and he gets the shower going. I don't even remember when he snatches my dress or his shirt off shit. Next thing I know I'm waking up wrapped in his arms as my head rest on his chest hearing him answer the phone on speaker.

"What's up bru?" He answers.

"Shit we made some headway, and I got the kids settled. I just had to check on wifey, how is she?" I hear Montavius ask.

"She's good. She laying on my chest asleep."

"Sounds like you were sleep ya damn self."

"Nigga I was cause somebody could've warned me how dangerous she was."

"Now why the hell would I do that?" He laughs.

"That shit not funny this woman feels like she just took my damn soul. Ha ass go need a plan b since you think shit funny."

"Aight nigga let that be the last time otherwise I'll have to hurt ya fuckin feelings cause it would be mines no matter what."

"Yea… yea nigga dat shit don't phase me I can easily change that shit. I already have three set for Meir, Mara, and Mariah."

"Really nigga." He laughs out loud. I'm laying here thinking I was fucking crazy these fools are on a whole other level.

"But for real though bru I'm shocked you let me still have her I know how obsessed over her you are. I've never seen you in love with a woman before."

"I'm very obsessed with her she's everything to me but I lost her for a month I can't imagine not having her for a whole year and I see the way you look at her vice versus. As long as you remember she's my fucking wife above all we won't have any problems."

"I felt love for her even before we found out she was *The Queen* but I'd never come between y'all if you changed your mind about any of us being in a poly relationship."

"Trust, I saw your feelings in your eyes at the family arts and crafts day a couple months ago, but I haven't decided yet. She's become everything to me so quick." I know the moment he's talking about at our family fun day because I felt it when he was looking at me. Jax was being silly trying to paint a sunset beach scene and I went over to help him with his brush strokes. I stood in front of him since he was standing then grabbed his hand to guide his brush across the canvas and he placed his hand on my hip. I could feel him staring down at me and chills ran up my back when he started rubbing my side up and down with his thumb. I quickly removed myself not wanting to disrespect Montavius even though my feelings were starting to build, and I didn't know how to stop them.

"I know and that day was fun as hell, but I was trying to hide it and clearly did a bad job of it. I was just in the zone, and she felt right standing so close to me." It was a really fun day and damn did that man hand feel good against my skin. Leave it to Montavius though to take Za'Mara wanting to have a family arts day and deciding to rent out a huge studio then fill it with everything we needed to paint or draw. He even had a couple pottery and sewing stations setup. Him and I created a large fruit bowl together even though it was supposed to be a vase, but we painted it our colors emerald green for me burgundy for him and it came out nice. Even though I felt his eyes on me though I didn't think it was that deep or that Monty may actually be cool with it but I am happy that in some capacity he is, especially now that I know

Jax is the man that ruined me on the side of a building over a year ago.

"I know Jax we good. I don't know if she actually loves you but I can tell she has feelings for you that she was trying to fight but either way we can figure all that out later I'll be there in about an hour." Montavius states as a knock comes at the door and Jax tightens his arm around me for a moment then kisses the top of my head.

"Ight bru let me go I guess the nurse or doctor here." He says ending the call yelling for them to enter, he must have unlocked the door before we laid back down. Sure, enough it was the doctor and bitch ass nurse Brett letting us know all my scans and blood work came back clear so I could be going home as early as tomorrow then the doctor leaves. Jax carries me back to the bed letting the nurse check my vitals for the last time tonight. Nurse Brett is still working, she has the nerve to call me a slut under her breath and I snap pulling her down on the bed by her hair.

"Excuse you bitch. You have something you want to say to me you don't have to mumble under ya breath."

"Lil Phoenix as funny as you whoopin her ass would be let nurse thirsty go baby, now." He commands me in an even tone voice, but I hear the force in it anyway.

"Ya lucky bitch." I curse tossing her ass away from me.

"I'm telling my supervisor and the police about this you stupid slut." She screams at me making me laugh.

"Look I saved you from an ass whoopin once I won't do it again. Stop being so disrespectful, shut ya mouf and you won't get ya head snatched from ya shoulder." Jax informs her with a sneer on his face clearly getting annoyed with her theatrics now. Seconds later Montavius walks in smiling at me.

"Ife mi you look even better than when I left earlier." He says winking at me, and I blush. He walks up slapping hands with Jax and they switch spots. Montavius next to me and Jax lifts my legs sitting in the bed at the foot of it and resting my leg in his lap still keeping his eye on nurse Brett.

"What's going on here?" Montavius asks looking between the three of us.

"What's happening is your slut of a wife is sleeping with ya so call brother and she just put her hands on me." She feels so confident explaining to my husband like he's going to rush to her side or something. This bitch is going to get dealt with as soon as I'm better.

"Ife mi did you sleep with Jax?" He asks me placing his fingers under my chin to tilt my head back so I can look up into his eyes.

"Yes."

"Did you enjoy it?"

"Yes."

"That's good I'd hate to jack my brother up for not pleasing my wife while I'm away." He smiles then leans down giving me a deep passionate kiss taking my breath away for a moment. When he let's go, I bite my bottom lip still looking in his beautiful eyes, I swear these men have ruined me and I love it. I hear nurse thirsty as Jax likes to call her gasp and I look at her grasping for her imaginary pearls making me laugh again.

"Freaking weirdos, I'm so glad you're checking out tomorrow." She says leaving the room.

"Wait you get to go home tomorrow baby?"

"Yup doc said all my test came back normal and you guys kept my body in such good shape physical therapy is not really needed but recommended." I say smiling from ear to ear. I'm so happy I don't have to spend much time in this damn place. I've always hated hospitals.

Chapter Twenty-Three

Dean Fredericks

"Aight y'all let's keep this quiet we're only here for recon." I instruct them looking at everyone through the rearview mirror and they nod their heads. Before we can get out the truck my phone rings with a call from Monty.

"Hey we made it what's up." I answer through the car speakers.

"Love bug get here now somethings not right." I hear Meira say sending me on an instant high alert.

"Are you ok Lil Dove what's wrong?"

"I'm fine but something doesn't feel right can you please leave now." She pleads with me and I'm already throwing the truck in reverse and speeding down the block without any further questions.

"I'm leaving now Lil Dove I'm on my way to you now."

"Can somebody tell me what's going on?" Monty comes through on the call next.

"Meira has a sixth sense about things, and I've learned to listen to hear when she does." I tell him remembering the one time I didn't and had a client from hell that I went through a whole lawsuit with. She was on my phone and heard the damn woman's voice when she walked in my office and immediately felt something off about her. Could've saved me a lot of money had I listened.

"Hmm so we have our very own empath." I hear Jax say in the background. We suddenly hear a loud boom behind us as we get about six blocks away from the building we were going to enter, and I slam on breaks to look back.

"What the hell was that?" Monty and Jax shout through the phone.

"A fucking bomb just went off around the building we were just at. Fuck Lil Dove I'm going to kiss you when I get there." I declare shaking my head and putting the truck back in drive racing to my Lil Dove. Can't believe this woman saved my life again.

"Somebody had to know you were coming to do that. Hurry and get y'all asses here." Monty demands.

"Bet." I say ending the call. The drive to the hospital was about forty five minutes seeing as we were close to Georgia state line. We rush up to her room and the first thing I do is rush to her side grab her face and kiss her right on the lips sucking her bottom lip in before letting it go kissing her quick once again.

"Dammit I love you woman." I express and she smiles against my lips as I rest my forehead on hers.

"Love you too. I'm glad you guys are ok." She says looking over to Chase, Meech, and Marsh. I finally let her go and look over at my brothers.

"So how the hell could somebody know we'd be there? We just decided we'd check it out an hour ago." Chase says next to me as he reaches for Meira's hand squeezing it and smiling down at her.

"Do either of you have your laptop?" Meira asks.

"Oh, baby here is yours and the Hotspot." Monty says handing her the laptop and she quickly goes to work setting up on the Wi-Fi then opening the secured section.

"OK how did you guys find out about the spot to begin with." She questions and we break down everything to her then she starts typing away on her laptop. I see multiple screens pop up and disappear this woman on a computer is just as lethal as her in person.

"Ok so that property wasn't on my original list I pulled from Sinclair's computer someone added it about a week ago probably after all the lil raids you five have been up to lately." She says looking at each of us.

"Wait but doesn't that mean someone hacked our devices to be able to update the file?" Meech asks standing at the foot of her bed.

"No cause the file was shared with Sinclair it wasn't originally his so the owner of the file can still update it anytime. Actually, they forgot about something." She states with a light chuckle blanking out as her fingers fly across the keyboard again.

"Damn how did I miss that." Monty says in frustration.

"You're not La'Meira bru don't beat yourself up." I just shrug my shoulders even though we all went to some of the best schools the military would pay for and college funds our parents setup for the others Meira is just talented as hell with a computer. She went to college, but she is more self-taught then anything.

"Gotcho bitch ass!" She shouts out of nowhere causing all of us to look at her sideways.

"Who you got Lil Phoenix? Jax asks rubbing the leg that's in his lap I've clearly missed out on something.

"Justin's bitch ass that's who and here's where you can find him." She turns the laptop for us all to see.

"He thought he was so smart piggy backing off a public Wi-Fi then bouncing the signal around but he's using a basic VPN. Anyway, I tracked his ass to some small as town in Texas it's about ten miles outside Houston. I also found the property he's at and it's owned by his crooked as father well one of his many shell Corps."

"Well damn Meira." Meech says.

"Don't ever underestimate Lil Dove." I say leaning down to kiss her on the forehead and she smiles up at me.

"Well, how do you want to get at him?" Marsh asks.

"Y'all aren't going to do a damn thing until I say it's safe to do so. I set a bug in the Wi-Fi source he connected to since he's used it more than once and I am sure he will again. When he does the bug will take over his computer allowing me to access everything on it and y'all can put together a plan from there." Meira affirms with a stern look on her face and that mother energy radiating off her in waves.

"She's right let's get all the info we can before we make our next move but heads on a swivel. Jude sent Greg, Mike, Chauncey, Murch, and Von for security they will be here just in time for this one to go home in the morning." Monty agrees with her as he squeezes his hand that's on the back of Meira's neck making her calm and bite her bottom lip. I shake my head cause those two are nasty.

"Alright well I'm headed home then. Glad you'll be outta this place finally Meira." Chase says rubbing his thumb over the top of her hand smiling at her.

"Aww you guys are all going home." She pouts.

"Wait Lil Dove where do you think home is?"

"Kansas City duh."

"Baby we don't live there anymore. We all moved here even the girls except Bree but she's on the fence. Jax can deal with that once he gets the club here situated." Monty explains to her, and she gets so gitty we all laugh.

"You actually thought I'd be able to live thousands of miles away from the kids after how close we've become then on top of that being away while you're laid up in a damn coma Lil Dove."

"I mean you have Kelia now I wasn't going to get in-between that what if she didn't want to move?"

"Wouldn't have mattered I would still be here and either way she was happy as hell to move."

"Kenya was too after visiting a few times. We stay around the corner from your store." Chase adds in.

"Besides woman you gave us all a bigger family to love on and I need that cookin more often." Meech chimes in rubbing his stomach and laughing.

"I gotcha Munchie." She says winking at him.

"Wait a damn minute you over here passing out nicknames and I'm your husband where's my nickname?" Monty says fake mad, and I chuckle.

"Your nicknames are hubby, babe, Big Daddy and chocolate bar when I'm horny so stop ya mess." She assures looking up at him with a sly smirk on her face.

"Wait chocolate bar!?" Marsh says laughing.

"Yes, nigga chocolate bar." He says pointing at his dick making it jump while winking at Meira and we all shake our heads rubbing our hands down our face at this fool and his antics.

"Don't start shit Monty I have no problem pulling out my chocolate bar and have your knees give out in front of ya brothers."

"Ya better chill out cause I will laugh since you didn't warn me." Jax states smirking at Monty and now I'm really curious at what the fuck is going on between these two.

"Warn you about what?" I ask.

"Lil Phoenix are you ok with me saying?" He asks her.

"Yes, it's ok chocolate Bear." She says winking at him, and I swear that big ass nigga just blushed.

"We slept together again ok but don't think any y'all asses are touching her, it's bad enough I gotta share ha with Monty."

"What the actual fuck Monty you shared Meira with Jax like for real for real, hmm." Meech says shocked.

"Don't act like that chocolate bear." She takes her foot and rubs it against his dick making that brother bite his bottom lip cutting his eyes at her.

"Yes, he's been with her before ya forgot. I couldn't imagine not having her for over a year and besides having one of y'all just as obsessed as I am over her works in my favor and that nigga knows who at the top of the food chain." Monty says coolly and I'm glad no one else is around because they'd think we all were crazy for having this conversation.

"So, you just forgot allllll about your love bug I feel like an old chew toy."

"Really, don't act like that. Besides you have Kelia, have y'all talked about that cause she almost got ha ass bent over the counter with the way she likes to rub my ass?"

"Now wait a minute I'd love to see that." Monty jumps in smiling down a Meira. I almost forgot her ass was bi sexual.

"No, I haven't but I plan on it since we met at the club, she knows some of what we're into, we haven't gotten a chance to explore on The Stage as I've mentioned anything goes." I say smirking at her, and she catches my drift biting on her bottom lip the way she does when she's feeling horny.

"Shit Kenya was asking were you into women and if Monty was willing to share." Chase chimes in and I'm not surprised because Kenya is bi as well.

"Idk why she asking now I've caught her multiple times rubbing on Meira's ass or squeezing it. Hell, she made Meira hym her ass up in the hallway and tongue kissed the hell out of her then left her just standing there stupefied. I laughed I told her stop playing with fire, my wife is freaky as fuck." He says laughing and I remember that night Meira had come outside to cool off sitting on my lap and her pussy was wet as hell telling me Kenya keep playing with her.

"Yea she told me about that but said she got scared she wasn't expecting you to jump on her like that. I laughed at ha ass cause I told ha don't play with you... you give off that fuck ya whole life up sex energy." He says laughing and we all join in because that fool is right, she damn sure as hell does.

"Man, if you only knew." Jax states shaking his head but smiling.

"Hey I'm good as long as she's good and y'all remember ya fuckin place I'd hate to have to fuck up one of my siblings or their women about my wife." He explains with deadpan look on his face letting us know he is dead fucking serious and I don't blame him cause I'm the same way about Kelia.

"We know nigga calm down." I reach over pushing his shoulder and Jax laughs.

"All this damn sex talk I'm out my new sneaky link just texted. These country girls are something else." Marsh says chucking the deuces and heading out. Meech leaves shortly after with Chase in tow.

"Well Lil Dove I'm going to head out but don't think you're off the hook for your punishment or leaving me out either lil woman." I affirm leaning down close to her ear and squeezing her right thigh. She bites her lip and nods. I give her a kiss on the lips and dap my brothers up before leaving. I pull up to the house I'm renting with Kelia, and she meets me at the door jumping in my arms. I happily pick her up as she wraps her legs around my waist.

"Hi to you too baby." I chuckle out at how excited she is to see me not that I'm complaining.

"I missed you but honestly, I'm also really happy about Meira finally waking up I missed her, and I know how much she means to you. She texted me a few minutes ago letting me know she's coming home tomorrow." I walk us through the foyer to the living room that's right off the kitchen when I sit, she stays put straddling me.

"I'm glad you're so excited and I don't have to defend or explain our relationship which brings me to something I should've talked to you about before we even left KC." I see the look on her face as I say that, and I hope she's not thinking what I think she is.

"Before your brain goes there it's nothin bad. You got a glimpse of some of the stuff I'm into sexually well all of us are into the same thing and in a roundabout way something we agreed to a while back came up. You asked what happens on The Stage at the club and it's anything goes meaning we could possibly sleep with each other's partners and we're into poly relationships. Hell Jax, and Meira already slept together." I explain to her as she slides off my lap causing panic to rise in my chest.

"So are you telling me you want to be in a poly or open relationship or some weird shit with your brothers."

"Look I'm not telling you that you have to be a part of anything but there are some sexual things that we are into that being with me will possibly put you in the same room with especially if you want to go on *The Stage.*"

"So, Monty is cool with Jax sleeping with his woman and let me guess you want me to be ok with you sleeping with her cause you're ok with me sleeping with your brothers."

"Look you do what you're comfortable with just like they do. Us sleeping with each other is not the only thing we're into. We like watching others have sex or people watching us and there are toys that we play with outside of the ones we've already tried. Forget it I'm going to bed good night." I start feeling like I'm defending myself, so I get up and head to our bedroom to actually get ready for bed. I'm not going to defend my sexual preferences to anyone if she doesn't like my lifestyle, she's not the one. I hear her come into the room as I get the shower ready.

"Look I'm not judging y'all I promise I'm not. I just don't know about being a part of something like that. I told you when I met you at the club everything, we did was a first for me and I was just starting to explore my sexual bounds. Just be patient with me you are exposing me to an entirely different life style and some feelings I've had have scared me." She confesses from the door and now I feel like a dick. I'm just so use to people judging us for how we are, but I think I know what scared her.

"The feeling that scared you let me guess is it how turned on you get around Meira like when she hugs you extra tight or when you accidentally on purpose touch her ass." I say slowly stalking over to her noticing as her breath gets ragged the more, I talk about her and Meira.

"Yes, I kissed a girl in college on a dare, but I've never been turned on by a woman." Once I get closer, I run my hand up her thigh till I get to her panty line moving them to the side and rubbing two of my fingers across her soaked pussy lips.

"Shit my sweetness your wet as fuck just thinking about it." I say letting out a groan. I slip two fingers in her wetness, and she moans placing a hand on my chest.

"Take this shit off and get in the shower." I demand reaching around and smacking her ass. I step back taking off my clothes, grab her hand once she does as well and lead her to the shower. As soon as we are I snatch her up pushing her back against the wall and she wraps her legs around my waist. I enter her slowly and fill her to the hilt welcoming the tight wetness of her pussy then go to work.

Chapter Twenty-Four

La'Meira Jennings

So, Monty stayed with me last night while Jax went home even though he looked like he wanted to stay too. It feels good to wake up in my man's arms cause of course I pouted till he got in the hospital bed with me. Soon I hear a knock at the door and we both say come in at the same time.

"Good morning Ms. Jennings I'm nurse Styles I came to give you your discharge papers. I know you're happy to go home today." She says with a bright smile on her face.

"Yes I am." I sit up and we go over all the paperwork as I sit cross-legged in the bed with Monty behind me rubbing my back listening intently. I'm sure he will have me on practical bed rest for a week even though they're giving me a clean bill of health. I wish it was winter break already so my babies could've been home when I got there but I will surprise them when they get home. Monty packed all my things last night so once she was done going over things we are on our way home and of course he has to carry me into the house.

"Awww my daughter is finally home." I hear Montavius's mother semi shouting walking towards the door with her arms wide to pull me into a hug the moment he puts me on my feet.

"Hi mama Fredericks, how are you?"

"Much better now that you're home and good. I made the kids breakfast today before they left, and I left you and Monty a plate in the oven. Go warm that up for her boy my girl has lost so much weight we gotta feed her." She instructs him making me laugh at how quickly Monty moves at his mom commands.

"Thanks Ma I really appreciate it, but I think I just want to hit my bed for a nap."

"We can eat in the room, but you have to eat something baby. Tonight is your welcome home party, so you'll definitely need a nap." Monty explains taking the plates out the oven and grabbing some juice.

"OK babies I'll leave you two to it and see ya tonight." She says kissing me on the cheek then Monty and leaves.

"Go lay down I'll be in there in a minute." He tells me smacking my ass and I tip toe pout my lips for a kiss as usual he obliges. He says get comfortable, so I do taking off my tie dye colored maxi dress and my panties. Before getting in the bed, I notice my intimacy blanket in the closet, so I grab it snatching my comforter off the bed covering the sheets with it perfectly then putting my comforter back in place and getting comfortable under it. A few minutes later Montavius walks in with a tray that has two plates of delicious smelling breakfast. The bacon is calling my name well so are the pancakes, ok maybe I am a little hungry. When Montavius pulls back the blanket to get in a smirk appears on his face.

"I will gladly take care of that but first put some real food on your stomach baby." He confirms placing the tray on the bed then leaning over to kiss me on the neck right behind my ear and I hum that man knows that's my spot shit.

"So, this party tonight for me who's doing the cooking and who all will be there?"

"My mom and I and just family. Kids, brothers, Kelia, Bree, Kenya, and of course Myra." He's stuffing his face just as much as I am because these pancakes are almost as good as mines.

"We will also go over some of the plans for our family compound since everyone will be together. We waited on you since it's your idea to begin with." I smile at him telling me that because I never thought I'd have a family big enough for one let alone the money to do it. I already have design plans drawn up.

"You done baby?"

"Yea." I answer him leaning into the hand he's caressing my cheek with. He gathers our plates, trays, and drinks to take them to the kitchen, I even hear him loading the dishwasher. When he comes back in the room he strips at the door then gets in bed pulling me under him in the middle.

"Do you know how terrified I was when they told me someone took you from me then to hear about our son?" He lightly glides his hands over my cheek, down my neck, and over my collarbone.

"I know I should've waited for you to go with us and none of this would've happened." I turn my head away from him, but he turns it back towards him.

"That is nowhere near what I was going to say Ife mi. What I was going to say is you and the kids bring a side out of me I didn't know existed. I've never cried a day in my life but y'all actually pulled that outta me. I love you so fucking much baby, my soul is not at peace if you're not near, and I will burn every city in this godforsaken country to get you back every time." He wraps my legs around his waist lining his thick long dick with my entrance, but he grabs something from the nightstand on his side of the bed first.

"You're already my wife but it's time we make this shit official. Marry me Ife mi." He says almost as if telling me and not asking me as he slides the ring on my finger with one hand while using the other to rub his dick between my wet lips. I buck my hips forward, but he moves back grabbing my hand with the beautiful pear shaped emerald with the clearest diamonds around it and on the crisscross gold band. Of course, he got my ring size correct he wouldn't be him if he didn't.

"No dick until you answer me. I was told I should ask sooo?" He says as he looks at the ring then back between my legs where he's still rubbing his dick between my lips making me even wetter than I was before.

"Of course I will baby. There's already a marriage certificate on my computer." I moan out as he enters me with one hard thrust filling me to the hilt and staying there as he connects his lips with mines in a wet slow passionate kiss. He begins giving me these deep quick strokes that steal my breath away making me arch my back off the bed.

"Breathe baby you can take this dick, hmm fuck there you go, that's my good girl."

"Mon... Monty... Fucckk." I stutter out as he takes my legs from around his waist pushing them back to my damn ears by the back of my thighs as he pulls out to the tip and slams back into me doing that repeatedly until I scream then squirt all over his stomach.

"Fuck I love it when you do that baby. Do that shit for me again." He starts rubbing my clit giving me spine tingling to toe curling strokes.

"I'm cum... cumming." I look down where we meet at his dick covered in my creamy juices as I cum even more and I see my pussy spasm around his hard length. He smacks my clit, and I squirt again. He leans over taking one of my nipples in his mouth sucking it then swirling his tongue around it and nibbling on causing it to pebble even harder. I roll my hips meeting his thrust while I tighten my walls around his dick working every bit of cum out of him.

"Shit baby I missed my pussy. She's so fuckin tight warm and ooh fuck she's so wet." He moans in my ear with a deep growl. He suddenly pulls out flipping me over pushing my head into the bed entering me from the back now.

"Arch that back like I like baby." He demands smacking me twice on each ass cheek. I deepen my arch like he likes spreading my knees further apart then I start throwing it back meeting him thrust for thrust reaching between my legs to wrap my hand around his dick squeezing him with my hand and pussy each time he thrust forward.

"Oooh shit... shit... shit woman fuck. You about to make me cum doing that shit baby damn." He moans and I look back as he leans his head back biting his juicy bottom lip as he still holds on to my hips. Seeing his muscles flex with each thrust and his long dark brown locs cascading over his shoulders down to his hips. I let him go with my hand then spread my knees further apart allowing me to bounce my ass up and down milking him at the same time taking him deeper.

"Shittt baby." He moans grabbing a fist full of my long curly hair pounding into me as I feel his dick growing inside me as if that's even possible. I feel his warm cum painting my walls causing my orgasm to hit me so hard I cry out in pure ecstasy. His thrust slow causing my orgasm to keep washing over me like waves hitting a rocky shore.

"Shit." Is all I can get out as I fall flat on the bed with Montavius falling right with me, but he makes sure not to put all his weight on me.

"Come on baby let me get you cleaned up." He says kissing my shoulder then going to the bathroom to turn the shower on and coming back for me carrying me to the bathroom placing me on the seat in the shower as he walks out to fix the bed knowing him. He comes back a minute or so later grabbing the soap and my rag from the rack gesturing with his finger for me to come. That man washes every crevice of my body gently but thoroughly and I do the same for him even if he didn't want me to but before we could get out, he has me pinned against the shower wall for another round leaving me sated and definitely ready for a nap. I clearly took more than a nap because the next thing I know I'm being woken up by screams of mommy and ma from my kids. They soon find me in the room as Montavius walks in through the patio doors in my room as they launch themselves into my bed.

"Mommies home." They all scream in unison kissing all over my face and fighting to hug me.

"Hey… hey… hey I know you guys are happy your mom's home but give her a second she was asleep before you launched, ya silly butts on her."

"Oops sorry ma we're just excited your home." Za'Meir says as they all stand cause they know how I feel about them in my bed with outside clothes on.

"It's ok babies I'm happy to be home with you guys too." I says as I reach for each of them giving them hugs and kisses. They kneel on the floor next to the bed laying their heads on my stomach, hip and thigh.

"How was school?" He asks the kids sitting at the foot of the bed in front of us.

"It was cool, but coach has been acting weird towards me lately." Za'Meir answers first.

"What you mean acting weird Za'Meir?" I ask him sitting up further in the bed glad I decided to put one of my moomoo's on after we got out the shower.

"I don't know he been aggressive wit me yelling at me for no reason, football season over but he giving me extra workouts in weight room, maybe I'm just being sensitive it's nothing." He tries to dismiss the issue, but he looks kinda sad and I look at Montavius who looks pissed even if he has a blank look on his face as he's typing away on his phone, so I know some shit is about to go down. We talk with the kids a little bit more about their day and things I've missed.

"Ok ma we have to go decorate the living room for your welcome home party and help grandma with the food." Mariah says standing but giving me a kiss on the cheek first.

"You guys really don't have to do all that. I'm just glad to be home."

"You deserve it baby now lay back and relax I'll bring you something to snack on in a few minutes." Montavius commands me coming around to give me a quick kiss as the kids exit the room.

"Hey you guys don't do anything to crazy he actually likes him that's why it's bothering him, and I think I know why he's acting funny." I say grabbing his face before he can stand.

"I can't make any promises but why do you think he's acting up?"

"Ummm."

"Spit it out Ife mi." He says kneeling beside the bed now eye level with me.

"OK but don't get all murderous please." I say and he scoffs at that making me shake my head.

"Fine he asked me on a date maybe a few weeks before you showed up in my room and I turned him down saying I wasn't into dating right now then I showed up with you at every game after that. I noticed him looking at me funny a few times since then."

"Yea we noticed too. I hoped he wouldn't be a problem but seeing as he wants to make himself one, he will get dealt with appropriately. Like I said I can't make any promises you know how I feel about niggas thinking they can take you away from me and Jax feels the same way now plus Dean always felt that way plus he wants to fuck with my son sooo."

"Lawd just don't kill the man please and thank you. I know you already text the guys I'll be telling them the same."

"Um hmmm. Now relax I'll be back in a few minutes." He says giving me another kiss then using his pointer finger to push me down at my forehead and I laugh but lay down as he requests. Sure enough a few minutes later he comes back with a bowl of fruit, water, and my favorite yogurt. I lay there munching on my snacks laughing at text from Jax and Dean about Meir's coach as the TV pretty much watches me.

Jax: These zoning ppl are stressing me the fuck out I'm going to need some of my Lil Phoenix tonight to calm my nerves 😊 otherwise that coach is probably done for.

Me: You know I got you chocolate bear, but I can help you with the zoning dummies.

Jax: That's my girl and no I don't need you seeing shit else you shouldn't. I'll figure it out and push comes to shove I'll let you know if I need your magic fingers.

Me: OK fine I don't like ppl fucking with you 😣 tho.

Jax: I know my Lil Phoenix, but everything will be cool. You should be getting ready for tonight anyway baby. I can't wait to see what you wear 😊

Me: Maybe I'll send you preview.

Jax: Woman stop teasing me.

Before I could text him back Montavius walks in with Bree in tow who jumps in the bed with me kissing and hugging me making me laugh.

"Bree stop attacking my wife would ya. Baby it's time to start getting ready everyone will start to arrive within an hour or so." He informs me shaking his head at Bree's theatrics getting under the covers snuggling up under me.

"Ok get out I'll help her get ready." She waves him out the door as she lays her head on my chest. I just laugh at the two of them.

"So how are you feeling like really?"

"I'm feeling good Bree. I was a bit sad about the miscarriage, but I never really got a chance for it to sink in that I was pregnant so it's not as bad."

"I can understand that." She says getting up from the bed with a solemn look on her face heading to my closet and I wonder what's that all about, but she will tell me when she's ready.

"Sooo let's see what options we have."

"Something comfortable preferably a dress and not tight please." She continues rumbling through my closet and comes out a few minutes later with three different options: one being clingy but not tight with small blue flowers that ties at my shoulders, the other is one of my sundresses with blue and white horizontal stripes, and the other is a burgundy mid knee maxi dress but it was always tight and I rarely wore that one.

"Let me see how the burgundy one fits now it use to be tight but with these twenty pounds I dropped maybe it won't be so bad." She hands me the dress as I get out the bed taking off my moomoo noticing when she licks her lips when I get it fully off and I remember I have nothing under it and shrug my shoulders. I slip the dress on adjusting my boobs as it has a deep v cut noticing it fits better but I notice some saggy skin.

"Great something else I have to deal with." I mumble frustrated taking off the dress looking at my body in the mirror for the first time and not liking what I see. Yea I lost twenty pounds but this saggy skin looks weird. I walk off into the bathroom leaving Bree in the room knocking on the door.

"Meira hun what's wrong?"

"I look weird as shit that's what's wrong. Just leave me alone and tell them we're not having the fucking party." I scream at the door looking at myself in the bathroom mirror shaking my head.

"Meira get your ass out here there is nothing wrong with your body woman you still are one sexy ass fuckin milf dammit." Bree yells through the door twisting the knob trying to get in.

"I said no. Go the fuck away Bree."

"Fine I'm... I'm getting Montavius and I think I just heard Jax come in as well." I hear her run out the room screaming for Montavius and Jax to come.

"What's wrong woman?" I hear them ask her and she spills her guts getting on my last nerve.

"Ife mi get your ass out here or I'll kick this shit in."

"I'm going to fuck yo ass up later for this." I groan to Bree swinging the door open because I know my man he will definitely kick this door down to get to me.

"Don't threaten me with a good time Meira." She smirks at me walking back to my closet leaving me with Montavius and Jax staring at me with lust in their eyes.

"You guys could've told me I looked like a wrinkly fucking bull dog." I say bumping them on my way to my bed, but I am snatched back with a hand on my waist and the other around my neck pushing me into the bathroom door.

"Cut the fucking attitude Lil Phoenix you don't look like a fuckin wrinkly bull dog." He says with his hand around my neck using his thumb to push my head back to look up at the both of them.

"For real stop with the damn dramatics. You lost some weight but still are absolutely gorgeous and sexy as hell. If you want, we can start your workout tomorrow to help your muscle mass, but I never want to hear or even think you're thinking about yourself being unattractive ever again. Your beauty is so much deeper than your physical." Montavius demands squeezing my hip those beautiful hazel grey eyes commanding me and my heart feeling full from the love he gives me.

"I betta not either. You are beautiful inside and out. Every stretch mark, curve, and cellulite. You just spent a month in a damn coma you shouldn't even be here right now at all. By the way I like the burgundy dress."

"Shit me too. Well, see we made it easy for you. Now get dressed Ife mi." He smacks me on the side of my ass and gives me a quick kiss. He walks out leaving me with Jax and Bree who's hiding in the closet giggling.

"Get in the bathroom." He orders me finally releasing my neck and turning me towards the bathroom without me even answering him. We enter the bathroom and he immediately closes the door with his foot locks it then grabs me by the back of my neck turning me towards the mirror. He bends me over slightly putting one of my legs up on the counter and I hear him unzip his jeans as he leans over me placing kisses from my neck down to my hip biting my ass cheek causing me to moan and bite my bottom lip.

"Your skin is so fucking soft baby and this fat ass of yours is absolutely delicious." He leans forward speaking into my ear as he rubs his hand over where he just bit me then grips my ass. I feel him move his hand grabbing his dick then rubbing it against my lips that are becoming more and more slick as he rubs.

"Keep your eyes on that mirror and the beautiful faces you make as I fuck this pretty pussy of yours Lil Phoenix." He says biting me on the shoulder causing me to moan as he enters me stretching me so tight.

"Hmmm baby I missed this pussy."

"Ssshhh shit Jax you were just in it yesterday." I moan biting my lip and throwing my ass back at him deepening my arch as I do with my eyes glued on us.

"Any minute with your body not in my arms is too damn long. Now you better keep that moaning down or the rest of the house will hear us." He moans thrusting hard and deep making me bite my lip so hard the telltale metallic taste hits my tongue and my eyes close. He smacks my ass causing me to open them and he smiles.

"Good girl don't make me correct you again keep those beautiful brown eyes on us."

"Jaaaxxxx" I moan as low as I can, but this shit feels too good and the faces he and I are making looking at each other is taking my pleasure to a whole new level.

"Hmmm fuck look at your perfect body taking all this dick baby." He moans low in my ear as he wraps his massive arm around my chest and turning my head towards him to kiss me so deeply I feel everything he's trying to show me deep in my core. I moan against his lips as he licks the blood from my lip then sucking into his mouth.

"I love these pillow soft lips of yours." He lets go of my lip with a plop and moans giving me another quick peck.

"Fuck I'm... I'm cumming Jax." I moan as he turns me back to face the mirror.

"Look at the pretty faces you make coming undone for me baby." I cum so hard my vision goes black for a second and I slump forward with Jax still stroking me through my orgasm.

"Hmm come catch this nut baby." He demands letting me go and I turn to get on my knees moaning at the taste of me as I lick around his mushroomed head then down his long thick shaft down to his balls cleaning my juices off him with my tongue. Licking back up to his head I take him as deep as I can till he's hitting the back of my throat wrapping my hand around the rest squeezing then rotating as I swallow around his head. I feel his knees buckle for a second as he rest his hands on either side of me on the counter.

"Fuck woman. I swear everything about you is a turn on." He moans and I smile around his dick as I hollow out my cheeks creating suction as I still bob my head up and down. He grabs the back of my hair thrusting hard three times before I feel his warm cum hit the back of my throat and I swallow every drop. When I stand he pulls me by my neck into a deep kiss as we taste each other on my tongue.

"Your workouts start tomorrow. Now get ready so we can hurry up and get rid of all these damn people it's bad enough I have to share you with Monty bighead ass." He grunts with a sour look on his face making me laugh.

"You do realize chocolate bear you too are damn near identical right?" I say giggling as I grab for my toothbrush turning away from him. He fixes himself and grunts making me laugh harder as he heads out the door. As soon as I hear the room door close Bree rushes in with the burgundy dress some cute black and gold sandals and accessories with a wide grin looking like a Cheshire cat.

"Now when the hell did that start?" She starts to interrogate me crossing her arms with a pout on her face. I let out a huff at her dramatics and fill her in on everything as I get cleaned up then dressed.

"OK I'm a bit jelly you have two men, and I still haven't found my one." She whines standing behind me helping me fix my hair and clasp my necklace Montavius just bought me that's a gold chain with a diamond encrusted heart pendant that has a M made with emeralds in the middle. I smile in the mirror as I look myself over not feeling one hundred percent better but definitely not like I felt just twenty minutes ago. I lift my hand to run it through my hair and Bree notices my ring.

"Oh my gosh oh my gosh woman how could you not say anything." She says hitting my shoulder and grabbing my hand with my engagement ring.

"We're announcing it once I get out there woman relax." I reassure grabbing her shoulders to turn and head out the door. As soon as we exit, I'm shocked to see my mother and I tear up running to kneel in front of her walker chair to hug her.

"Ma what are you doing here? You shouldn't be out in the cold."

"I'm fine woman calm down. You really think I would miss the chance to welcome my precious girl back home after you leaving us for entire month. Not a chance in hell." She argues patting her hand on my right cheek. I give her a kiss then stand next to Montavius as he calls for everyone's attention. I notice Dean and Kelia coming in from the patio and she has this weird look on her face plus I feel her energy somethings not right, but I'll deal with it later. I also noticed Myra and the kids weren't here but uncle Tone is but he lets me know Myra was called into work this afternoon.

"So, as you all know some idiots tried to take my beautiful wife away from us a little over a month ago, but she fought her way back to us and thankfully stands in front of us with a clean bill of health. We both wanted to tell everyone thanks for stepping in to help with the kids and to my brothers most of all thanks for helping me bring her home. I know I don't say this often but I'm proud to call you all my brothers and appreciate you to the utmost." He announces holding up his champagne glass as he hands me mines then looks at me and I know what he wants me to say next.

"So, we have a surprise we'll probably not a surprise to those who are around us daily butttt. He officially popped the question were getting married." I announce swinging my hand up to show off my ring smiling and giggling as the ladies all rush me smiling and checking out my ring. Next to me the fellas slap him on the shoulder or shake his hand congratulating him and Za'Meir has a big smile on his face as he hugs Montavius.

"This is beautiful baby girl. You have a really great man on your hands." My mother tells me admiring my ring as the ladies go to rush him next. I swear you would not know that he's not a touchy feely person cause when it comes to the women in his life, he gives whatever they need.

"I know right."

"Him and his brothers showed up practically every day to spend time with me, update me on how you were doing, they brang the kids by, their mom and I have even gotten pretty close. I mean we played cards went for walks his twin even took me out to dinner and to get my nails done with the girls one visit." She informs me smiling at the memories they created with her and I'm in tears by the time she finishes. Montavius, Jax and Dean notice at the same time and rush over to where I'm sitting at the table with my mom.

"What's wrong Lil Dove." Dean questions making it next to me while Montavius is behind me handing me a tissue and Jax is next to him then before I know it everyone is around us.

"I'm fine guys it's happy tears. My mom just finished telling me how much time you all took out to spend with her while I was down. I can't thank any of you enough for what you've done between taking care of my babies to now finding out about my mom too. Ughhhh I really love all of you." I explain trying to stop myself from crying, but the tears just keep coming.

"I'll be honest with you. You did us a favor falling for our big brother and being friends with this knucklehead." Meech says from across the table.

"Straight facts. I mean we were happy but it always felt like something was missing." Marsh says next.

"Definitely something was missing but having you the kids, your mom, even Myra and her kids our family feels complete." Chase adds in shrugging his shoulders.

"He's right it does. So, if anything Lil Dove we owe you for bringing more love into this dysfunctional family of ours."

"Well, if that was an attempt to get me to stop crying it didn't help any at all." I say crying but laughing as everyone else starts to laugh too.

"You deserve all the love baby girl and I see God saw it fit to send it by way of two men instead of one." I look at her shocked then at Monty and Jax they have the same look.

"Girl I'm old not blind anyone can tell that you have a different connection with Dean then you have with Montavius and Jax but it's a connection none the less. Besides the smile that was on Jax's face when he came out the room only means one thing." Everybody has a shocked look on their faces now.

"Oh, please the women in our family have always been insatiable hell its why I never married ya father he was a weak ass man. Oops sorry kids. Matter of fact go to ya rooms y'all have heard enough." She commands and I almost fall out of my chair. They run off to their rooms calling us nasty and giggling on their way. "

Back to what I was saying ya father was weak and closed minded he thought me liking a lot of sex meant something was wrong with me. You however have seemed to have found the perfect man for you honey." She says patting me on the leg. I'm intrigued but also grossed out thinking about my mothers sex life.

"Well, that explains the other part of why she fits in so well with us and to think Dean you were going to keep my wife all to yourself." Montavius squeezes the back of my neck and bumps shoulders with Dean.

"Wait mom are you into women too at least sexually?"

"Girl yes you really thought aunt Lily was your aunt." She laughs.

"Maaaa I didn't need to know that much a yes or no would have sufficed." Everyone laughs thinking my embarrassment is hilarious.

"OK I'm officially traumatized call the kids back in here we need to go over the compound design and seeing as I have my very own architect in the family this going to come out amazing." I say getting excited just thinking about it and he just laughs shaking his head at me taking Dean's spot as he goes to grab the kids.

"Ok so y'all are done with the nasty grown folks talk." Mariah says coming back to the dining room and we all laugh.

"Yes, we're done with grown folks talk. We are going to go over how our family compound or community will be designed." I tell them and they get excited.

"OK Meira what you got for me first?" Chase questions pulling out a notebook from the bag Kenya passes him.

"OK so the design I had drawn out is this. A long concrete or paved entrance, gate or no gate I never thought much of it but the mailboxes to the right of the entrance. I wanted a long floral focal piece in the middle or maybe a koi pond with paved walk ways leading to each home. With the size lot you guys bought I'm not sure maybe six acres per house, houses evenly lining each side and the farm more towards the back with a stable for the kids horses, Za'Meir's gym a bit before that. My garden in the back has to be large I want all types of veggies and fruits. Mom loves to garden so maybe a green house." I describe my dream to him, and he starts drawing up a plan.

"Oh, definitely the koi pond and what about a hut or canopy over the mailboxes just in case it's raining or something." Kenya adds.

"What about a pool maybe one big one for all of us to use and we can all have Jacuzzis in the back of each of our homes instead." Meech gives another great idea.

"That would be nice but if we're going to have one big pool it has to be decked out, I mean grotto's, slides, maybe even a cool bridge, and fire pits." Jax and I say finishing each other's sentences and we smile at each other.

"What about lanterns or some type of lighting to light the walkways? One thing I noticed it gets dark as shit out here especially back up in there." Marsh adds in.

"OK so a long U or oval shape since we're going to have what at least ten homes?" Chase asks.

"Wait ten?" I question looking confused.

"Oh, yea surprise baby our moms are going to be in one house together, Myra and the kids in another, then your uncle in the other, and the last maybe a guest house or the place the kids go once they get old enough. I just know how you are about even numbers." I pout my lips for a kiss and Monty obliges which makes me smile even more. He walks off to check on the food, letting us know everything is done.

"Well, I guess that's enough of that. Any ideas put them in the family group chat. I'll meet with everyone individually if ya want to go over house specifics, but this is more than enough to get started." Chase says as everyone starts to take their seats at the dining table the breakfast table and the island after grabbing their plates.

"OK clearly large dining rooms and tables are in order as well." I say looking around at everyone seated all over the place. We say grace and it gets quiet for a while.

"Damn babe I knew you could cook and you too Mama Fredericks, but this is good as hell." I compliment them giving Montavius a kiss as he sits at the head of the table to my left.

"I taught my boys good." Mrs. Fredericks beams with pride looking at all of her sons. We all eat in silence for a bit more making small talk with each other here and there till everyone is all done. All the kids help clean up the dishes while Marsh and Meech take down the decorations then Kenya and Kelia clean the tables. They usher me and my moms towards the couch in the living room as they all sweep, mop the floor, and take out the trash.

"I'm going to stay over at Myra's tonight, I hardly get to spend time with her and the kids."

"You sure Ma, you can always stay here?"

"Yes, I'm sure baby. The twins and Mariah are coming too we're doing a whole sleepover party."

"Aww that's sweet but ok ma."

"Hey grandma you ready to head to aunties."

"Yup baby lets go before I get too tired to watch movies and eat popcorn with you guys." She laughs getting up using her walker chair. The kids all surround her as they walk out the house.

"Later ma." They yell as they get to the door.

"I'm out too my babies it will be too dark for me to drive soon."

"OK mama Fredericks. Thanks again." I say standing to give her a hug and she hugs everyone else then leaves.

"OK now that it's just us Kelia what's ya fuckin problem you been quiet and standoffish all night?" I question her as I walk into the kitchen.

"Lil Dove it's-"

"Dean shut it and have a seat I'm talking to Kelia."

"La'Meira it's not what you think."

"What do I think Kelia? You working my nerves and if you are about to hurt him please understand I will paralyze yo ass and cut ya eye lids off just so you can watch me cut ya damn head off then bury you apart from it so you'll wonder this god forsaken earth for eternity looking for it. So, I'd recommend you hurry up and speak." I cross my arms over my chest tilting my head to the left getting pissed but trying to calm down. I see the shocked and terrified look in her eyes as she grabs her neck.

"You'd really kill me over him?"

"Without a second thought. Are you insecure about our relationship or something cause I'd never purposely come between you two."

"NO it's not that I've just been conflicted with some feelings I have that I haven't had before."

"Oh, wait Kelia is it what I think it is?" I smile strutting over to the breakfast table she's sitting at. I see in her eyes the arousal as I walk towards her.

"Aww Kelia your attracted to me and don't know how to handle it." I run my hand through her soft long freshly silk pressed hair down the back of her neck then I pull her head back by the nape of her neck forcing her to look up at me.

"Get up Kelia." Commanding her to move and she listens right away. I have had my moments of being a Dom back in Florida, but I much rather be the submissive.

"Good girl now lay back on the table since I know you don't have any underwear on, I want to see something." She listens as if in a trance, staring into my eyes as I tell her what to do.

"Pull the dress up and spread those thick ass legs apart." Once again, she does as I tell her and her glistening pussy is staring back at me.

"Hmmm somebody's already wet." I stand in between her legs rubbing two of my fingers against her wet lips up to her clit and she moans. Everyone is standing around watching us. I look at Dean who's in a trance of his own watching us together and those joggers are doing a shitty job of hiding how hard he is right now. I look back at Kelia as I spread her lips using my thumb to rub her clit and she lays her head back on the table moaning.

"Eyes on me for this next part Kelia or you won't be cumming tonight." I demand. I sit in one of the chairs putting it right in front of her leaning forward flattening my tongue licking her pussy from her entrance to her clit moving it side to side on her clit. I look up to make sure she's still watching me, and she is, so I push her legs further apart flicking my tongue against her clit a few times before swirling it around then sucking her swollen bud in between my lip flicking it with my tongue again. She cries out at the suction I create around it squirming side to side.

"Stop moving." I say releasing her clit and smacking her on it. I hear moaning coming from my left and I look over to see Bree bent over part of the table with Marsh behind her eating her pussy while Jax stands on the other side with his dick in her mouth. I wink at him, and he smiles back mouthing you're next. I nod then dive right back in licking and sucking Kelia's pussy tills she's screaming out my name and cumming on my tongue. I lick a few more times as her breathing slows then I stand licking my lips. I grab her by the neck lifting her towards me and tongue kiss her, so she tastes her sweet juices on my tongue. I feel Dean standing next to us and he grabs me by neck turning me towards him to give me a kiss our tongues dancing with each other till he sucks on my tongue tasting her pussy on it and he moans.

"You don't know how long I've been wanting to kiss you like that Lil Dove." He leans down resting his forehead against mines.

"I'm sure I can guess." I say breathlessly while smiling as he kisses me again. I clock Montavius as he walk over to us grabbing my butt through my dress as he gets closer.

"This table is sturdy. Kelia get ya thick ass back on that table with your head on this side the opposite way." He instructs her and she does as she is told laying the opposite way she was.

"Now you Lil Dove ass over her head, face over that pussy." He points and I climb over the table as I watch Montavius struts around in front of me smiling. Thankfully this table is not too small but not big. It's just wide enough so poor Kelia's head isn't hanging off the table. All of a sudden, I feel two sets of lips and tongues on my pussy one on my clit the other over my entrance.

"Shit ooh shit." I buck against both of their mouths the feeling of them almost overwhelming but so damn euphoric I cum almost instantly.

"Hmm as good as I thought you'd taste Lil Dove." He sticks his tongue as far as it would go swirling it around in my pussy as it clinches his tongue and Kelia is still sucking the shit out my clit. Montavius kneels down in front of me and starts slurping on Kelia's already sensitive clit causing her to release mines moaning out fuck. When she gathers herself, I feel her slide her tongue in my pussy with Deans and I come again. She comes next all over Montavius's beard then he grabs me by the neck tongue kissing me and I taste her all over his tongue. I feel them stop attacking my pussy and I see they're kissing each other too as he lets me go for a moment. Montavius squeezes my throat, and I turn back to him.

"I love you so fuckin much Ife mi."

"I love you too hubby." He pulls me in for a quick kiss when I feel Kelia lick my clit and Dean's big fucking dick stretching my entrance. Montavius pulls out his beautiful chocolate dick rubbing it against my lips. I lick his precum from the tip then swirl my tongue around his mushroom head, but he pulls out before I get carried away and guides my head down toward Kelia's pussy as he enters her slowly.

"Fuuuccck." We both moan out at the same time the guys enter our pussy fully and shit this man is stretching me. You'd think after being with Jax earlier and my Montavius this morning my shit would be open but these men and their extra-large fucking penis's dammit.

"SHITTTT Lil Dove this pussy is tight and wet as fuck." He moans out thrusting deep and slow then picking up the pace. I latch on to Kelia's clit with my teeth causing her to buck and squirt on me and Montavius. I look up at him and he smiles at me giving her quick long strokes making her cream all over his dick and I lick where I can reach on his dick.

"Damn Kelia this some warm gushy shit baby girl." Montavius moans out slapping the side of her ass and she gushes again.

"Fuck love bug right there right… Oooh fucckk." I moan as I come undone and shaking as I feel myself squirt all over him and Kelia.

"Come suck this nut out baby." Montavius says pulling out of Kelia in shoving into my mouth fucking the back of my throat roughly as he holds my head in place by my hair. I feel Dean pull out of me as Montavius continues to fuck my mouth till saliva is sliding out the corners of my mouth and tears coming down my cheeks. I notice to the left of us Kenya riding Chase, who's sitting on a chair but Meech is squatting behind Kenya fucking her in the ass causing me to gasp around Montavius's dick taking it further down my throat. I reach for his balls looking up at him and start to massage them and he comes undone shooting his cum down my throat bracing himself on the table.

"Fuck woman some welcome home party." He chuckles pulling out of my mouth and grabbing a nearby napkin to whip my mouth and tear stained face. Before I can collapse down, he grabs me under my arms lifting me into his and I wrap my arms around his neck and legs around his waist. We share a brief kiss.

"Now how to do ya feel Kelia?" I turn my head to ask her.

"Ask me in the morning bitch my brain cells have been fucked loose at this point." We both giggle as Dean picks her up off the table and she does the same thing I did to Montavius to Dean. I notice Jax, Marsh, and Bree fixing themselves and they clearly enjoyed themselves as well and then Meech, Chase, and Kenya who looks thoroughly fucking pleased.

"Shit tonight was interesting." Meech says and we all break out into laughter.

"It's time to get you to bed Ife mi." Montavius announces kissing my forehead and all I can do is nod as I lay my head on his shoulder.

"Aight y'all clean up ya messes I need to get Meira to bed. Y'all welcome to stay here or at the RV since it's late no fuckin in my kids bed though." He states walking us to our bedroom which I'm still getting use to calling it that to shower and we jump right into bed.

"How are you feeling babe?" I question laying on his chest tracing the cross on his chest with my middle finger.

"I'm great baby and if you're worried about what we just did it just proves to me even further that you were made for me. I understand the freaky shit you like cause I like it too and I also know at the end of the day you don't love any of them the way you love me. I own your heart body and soul even in the afterlife." He tells me after pushing me head up by my chin to look him in the eyes as he says it.

"You truly do Montavius. If you said tonight was the last time I'd be perfectly fine with that as long as I have you and our kids. This might be crazy but what do you think about getting married at the court house next week?".

"Monday sounds good to me gives us the weekend to get these fools in there together."

"Wait really?"

"Yes, and forget the courthouse let's just do it in the backyard with the fam, I already have our marriage certificate from your computer in my email ready to print and sign. Chase can get officiant license online."

"Sounds like we're getting married next week then." I start inching up to give him a kiss then roll over on my side and he follows hanging his arm over my waist kissing the side of my head. Before I can think of anything else I fall into a deep peaceful sleep.

Chapter Twenty-Five

Montavius Fredericks

It's our wedding day. We end up pushing it back to Friday since the kids were out of school starting Winter break today. The girls went down to Florida to grab La'Meira's wedding dress, their bridesmaids, Mariah maid of honor dress and Za'Mara decided she wanted to be the flower girl over the weekend. I have Dean as my best man seeing as if it wasn't for him, I would've never found my beautiful wife or at least taken a lot longer to. Meira received a notification about Justin's bitch ass trying to find a hit squad, I still can't believe he actually used the exact same location to connect to Wi-Fi. She also was able to plant a bug on his computer so now she has access to it through any Wi-Fi source, my baby smart as hell man. I'm in Za'Meir room getting dressed with Jax, Dean and Chase. Marsh and Meech have been coming in and out since they are using the girls room. All the women are in the master bedroom with my bride.

"Lookin fly there big brother." Dean compliments coming up behind me in the mirror smiling just as big as me.

"Same to you Lil brother." I say fixing his bow tie. They all had on emerald green tuxes which are tailored to fit while mines is emerald green and black with a white shirt under. They had black bow ties, but Meira insisted I wear deep burgundy as it's my favorite color and it's sprinkled everywhere in the wedding décor. I have my hair two strand twisted in some type of intricate bun that my wife likes so who cares. We didn't hire a wedding planner because the girls insisted, they could get everything done with our help of course with any heavy lifting. Chase didn't end up needing to get his officiant license as mama Jennings was able to get her pastor to do the wedding instead. Meira's so excited about her uncle Tone walking her down the aisle. The old man broke out in tears when she told him over dinner Wednesday. A knock came at the door and in came the pastor.

"Alright young men it's time to take your places the bridesmaids are lining up." He announces as he leaves closing the door behind him and soon Meech and Marsh walks in. We all say a quick prayer then head out. Taking my place next to the pastor then "Let's Get Married" by Jagged Edge starts to play as my brothers walk out with their paired bridesmaids. Za'Meir stood next to me as the ring barrier looking as fly as his daddy. When baby girl came skipping down the aisle of white wooden chairs decorated with emerald green silk draped across them with burgundy bows in the middle I couldn't help but chuckle and smile my baby was so happy and carefree. When "Bound to You" by Christina Aguilera starts to play and Ife mi starts down the aisle with her uncle the tears start. Seeing her in that off white silk off the shoulder dress that hugs every curve perfectly then flares out at her knees creating a long train behind her. She's holding a beautiful bouquet of green, white, and red roses. The lace veil with crystals sewn into it just gave her an angelic look. Dean hands me and Za'Meir a tissue cause at this point we were all teary-eyed or actually crying in my case and I don't give a shit who sees me, I'm about to marry the woman that will be attached to soul for eternity.

"Well, hello handsome." She greets me as she stands across from me and I lift her veil.

"Damn baby you look absolutely stunning." I walk closer planting a kiss on her soft burgundy coated lips and I hear the pastor clear his throat next to me. If looks could kill he'd be dead for interrupting me kissing on my wife and I hear my brothers laughing behind me along with my mother. Our vowels are a blur and quick as I kept giving the pastor a death stare to hurry up. I zoned back in when it's time to say I do and place our rings on each other's finger. When I place her gold diamond encrusted wedding band with one emerald in the middle on her finger, I kiss it and when she pulls out my wedding band, I get the biggest grin on my face cause my woman knows me so damn well. She had my jeweler design a Titanium matte black ring with her name etched into it with diamonds. I pause the pastor before he announces us husband and wife.

"Just one more important thing. Za'Meir, Mariah, and Za'Mara come stand in front of us please." I request and when they do Dean steps up next to me placing a hand on my shoulder nodding. I kneel down on one knee in front of the kids smiling at them.

"Now I hope that y'all didn't think I forgot about you three in all this. I had almost given up hope in having a family of my own let alone this big of a family, but I wouldn't change it for the world. Za'Meir boy you seriously make the pride radiate in my chest on a daily with how determined, selfless, patient, and loving you are I hope you will do the official honor allowing me to be your dad?" I ask taking the gold link chain with the initial ZF pendant hanging from it covered in diamonds with the matching bracelet and I place both on him as he nods his head yes all choked up then rushes to hug me and stand next to Dean who's hugging him as he cries for a minute.

"Now my biggest girl Mariah to go through what you have to losing your birth mother at such a young age and still you get up every day smiling, loving, and helpful towards others you are so beautifully resilient but still soft when you need to be. It would be my absolute pleasure to officially be your dad if you'd have me?"

"Of course, daddy." She answers by wiping her tears with the back of her hand as I put her gold ring with two diamonds on either side of a pink rose her favorite color, then matching charm bracelet and necklace. She jumps in my arms kissing me on the cheek smiling from ear to ear with tears still in her eyes. I use the handkerchief I had earlier to wipe my tears.

"Now last but certainly not least my beautiful ball of energy bad ass Za'Mara. I knew seeing you pin or drop those lil punks in your karate class that you are tough as nails but understand this you will always be my baby girl, and I'll protect you till my last breath to make sure you keep that carefree and loving attitude. Will you give me the blessing of being your dad?" She nods her head holding back tears as I place her gold ring set the same way as Mariah except hers has a purple butterfly with matching necklace and charm bracelet as well. She nearly knocks me over jumping in my arms and I stand still holding her then I put her down to go stand with her sister and aunts. I walk back in front of my wife who's a mess of tears and I smile.

"Look I didn't sign up to do all this crying. I now pronounce you husband wife and big beautiful family now shoo something in my eye." The pastors announces and we all buss out laughing as I kiss my wife spinning her around in my arms.

"Damn I love you Montavius Ekon Fredericks." She declares kissing me again this one slow and passionate causing everyone around us to clear their throats. We laugh at them and finally part with our family in toe as we walk down the aisle and head over to our outdoor tents we set up for our reception. We are all flying out in the morning my baby wants a snowy mountain honeymoon with just us and the family. I rented out this ten bedroom eight and a half bath mountain cabin on bnb that has a guest house off in the back, it even has a room just for us grown-ups. Our reception is cool we just finished dancing and eating. The photographer is around taking a bunch of photos of the family, but we make sure none are to be posted well not yet at least. We are keeping a low profile until we're away and no locations are turned on for anybody. I have been dancing for hours with all of my women making sure none of them especially my wife misses one iota of my attention.

"I swear this was like a dream come true babe I really don't think anything could've made it any more perfect." She expresses as we sway to the music in our own little bubble, and she is so right. It's about midnight the kids turned in about an hour or so ago along with Myra, her kids and our parents. The only ones out at this point are us, Chase and Kenya, Dean and Kelia, and Marsh and Bree which those two have seemingly gotten closer since our mini orgy at Meira's welcome home party.

"It has definitely been one of the best nights of my life baby. Let's get inside the temperature is dropping and we do have an early flight for our winter mountain honeymoon." I rub her arms then pick her up bridal style to head into our home. Getting her undressed and cleaned up then right to bed after a much needed quickie in the shower we were off to sleep in no time.

"Fucckk good morning to you too Mrs. Fredericks." I moan out as I look down at my wife with my dick in the back of her throat smiling. Damn I swear this woman makes me feel like a bitch moaning the way I do when she's sucking my soul through my dick like she doesn't already own it. I look down again and she has her eyes on me I swear I can't look away from those big brown eyes. When she reaches to massage my balls applying pressure to that spot right behind it and then swallows around my dick sinking it deeper down her throat then fucking humming. My nut hits me so hard and quick I get lightheaded for a moment. My beautiful baby swallows every fucking drop.

"Damn baby what the hell!" I whisper yell still trying to compose myself. This woman just hit a new level of freak I didn't even think was possible.

"I would ask if you enjoyed it, but I think I have my answer already." She says trying to quickly peck my lips, but I grab her then roll on top trapping her in place not even needing to use my hand to guide my dick into its home. She clinches her walls as soon as I fill her to the hilt crashing my lips to hers working my hips in a circular motion.

"You thought you were just going to wake up give me mind numbing head and I wasn't going to get into my pussy wife?" I question thrusting deep and slow. She sucks my bottom lip in between her teeth biting down and moaning.

"I just wanted to give my husband a pleasurable first married morning mhmm." She moans after releasing my lip with a plop. I push her legs up to her ears leaning back to watch my dick stretch her fat pussy.

"Every morning waking up to your beautiful face and voice is pleasurable baby, but I appreciate the extra effort." I reach down gathering her juices on my thumb rubbing it over her back hole applying pressure then pushing it all the way in.

"Shit Mon...Monta... Montavius." She moans and I lean over her pushing so deep in my pussy I feel her cervix and hold there for a few heartbeats. She starts spasming around my dick telling me she's about to cum.

"Ife mi are you about to cum for daddy?" I ask pumping faster but still deep.

"Ye.. Yes daddy I'm cu cumming." She moans as I keep pumping into both holes and she starts rotating her hips.

"Fuuuccck." She screams cumming all over my dick milking my dick causing me to cum seconds later painting those already wet walls with my seed. I lean down and kiss her then hear a knock in the door.

"Come on you horny newlyweds our flight leaves in an hour and a half." Dean shouts through the door and we laugh.

"Come on baby let's get this honeymoon started." She says kissing my lips and I slide out of her getting off the bed first. I through her over my shoulder and smack her on the ass.

"You right let's move it." We quickly get ready tending to our hygiene and checking on the kids as they are coming in with their grandparents Myra and her kids along with Marsh and Bree. We make it to the airstrip with about ten minutes to spare. Most of us ride together the only person were waiting on is Jax and he's been acting funny lately. Right before takeoff he shows up not looking like himself. I look to Meira who's watching him too.

"It's ok baby."

"Huh?" She says snapping her eyes away then looking up at me.

"It's ok for you to want to check on Jax baby."

"You sure it's our honeymoon week."

"That's exactly why it's ok. I know you won't do anything I'm not comfortable with or disrespectful but it's Jax if I trust you with anyone it's him. Besides I know he's in love with you and it's ok." I express what I've noticed about my brother, and she looks shocked.

"NO, he's not wait, is he?" She asks and I shake my head yes.

"It's ok for you to love him too. I know who your soul is tied to baby. He needs you though something has been up with him and for once he's not talking to any of us about it. There's only one reason for him to do that."

"He doesn't want to start any problems with us." She says barely above a whisper, and I nod my head.

"Plus, even Marsh and Bree have gotten out their own way. So, I'm sure he's feeling alone even more. So go on I'm about to take a nap somebody didn't let me get any sleep." I kiss her on the cheek, and she giggles.

"Don't know who that could be but ok soulmate."

"In every timeline, universe, and even in the afterlife baby." I wink as I smack her on the ass while she gets up to go over to him and I adjust my seat to lay flat to take a much needed nap.

Chapter Twenty-Six

Jax Fredericks

I almost didn't get on this damn plane, but I know that would've stuck out like a sore thumb besides, I guess I might as well at least get to lay eyes on her. I get comfortable in my seat and feel her presence getting closer, but I don't open my eyes until she's sitting in my lap with her head on my shoulder and I instinctively wrap my arms around her.

"Why haven't you spoken to me or given me my bear hugs chocolate bear are you mad with me?"

"NO Lil Phoenix what I could possibly be mad at you for." I ask as she rubs her nose on my neck making my dick jump.

"Hmm chocolate bear then why have you been so distant lately cause I don't like it?"

"I'm in love with you Lil Phoenix and I don't know what to do with that when you're married to my brother. I know he's cool with the sexual, but I don't know about that part, and I'll never cross him even if I must torture myself." I rush to say before I punk out. Since I found out she was *The Queen* that I had a connection with all those months ago and the time spent with her before I knew I just couldn't lie to myself about how I feel.

"I love you too Jax and he knows you're in love with me and he's fine with it. He says he's willing to share me with you because he trusts you with me." She informs me shocking the shit out of me and I look over at him of course his intuitive ass knows and is looking at me. He nods his head confirming he's ok with us and just when I think I can't love or respect my brother more he surprises me again. I vow with my eyes to cherish his most prized possession, and he smiles closing his eyes to take a nap.

"See told you. Now don't ignore me again that hurt my feelings." She says sitting up to look me in my eyes and I see the sadness.

"I will not baby I put that on everything I won't." I declare giving her a kiss meaning for it to be quick, but she holds me in place with her soft hands on either side of my face pushing her tongue inside my mouth and they do their dance together before she pulls away taking my bottom lip with her then letting it go with a plop.

"Now what else is bothering you babe I can feel that wasn't all?"

"You two are too damn intuitive for my liking." I chuckle.

"That just means I'm right. No secrets babe." She demands snuggling into my neck again.

"No secrets. I'm still having trouble with the zoning officer for the club. I did the work for it to look more like a BDSM sex education club with member rooms on the top level that I have listed as practice areas which is within the guidelines. I even got the bar license, and everything started but he still won't approve the building there." I say blowing out a breath. It feels good talking to her again.

"I don't like him fuckin with you chocolate bear. I'm hacking his shit the moment we land. He's going to regret fuckin with you." She informs me getting upset wrapping her arms around me and I almost feel bad for the guy, almost.

"NO, you're not it's Monty and yours honeymoon and you will enjoy it."

"I will enjoy it once I ruin his life for messing with my chocolate bear." She says kissing me and rubbing my cheek placing her head back on my shoulder and I rub circles on her left arm. Just that damn fast I'm completely at peace. The more time I spend with her I definitely see what Dean was talking about just being around her calms me. I didn't even think it was possible but here I am on our family jet with this beauty in my lap her nuzzling her nose on my neck and rubbing my chest and I'm at the highest level of peace, I've ever been.

"Mmm baby if you keep sitting on my lap like this with your warm pussy on my dick I'm going to fuck the shit outta you on this plane."

"Well, I wouldn't mind becoming a member of the mile high club." She says and I stand up holding her in my arms heading for the room in the back closing the door with my foot. I lay her on the bed and kiss her on the forehead.

"You better be quiet or you're going to wake everyone up. Now take that dress off Lil Phoenix." I command her getting undressed and wishing we had more time, but I will gladly take what I can get. We get our quickie in but stay in the bed talking about everything and nothing until a knock comes at the door from the flight attendant letting us know we would be landing soon. We arrive at the cabin about an hour later and left the jet to refuel then head back for the rest of the family.

"Oh my gosh it's even more beautiful than the photo's eee." La'Meira is in complete awe of the large log cabin and the snow covered grounds and trees. She's so giddy she's bouncing on her tip toes and it's the cutest thing. I'm standing to her left as Monty stands to her right holding her hand as I hold the other, so she doesn't slip on the steps. We speak with our man in charge of our security while here for a moment then head inside.

"What the hell." She looks at us bug eyed when she sees how we paid the owners to decorate the place for Christmas leaving the ornaments and other small decorations out so we can do the tree and big fire place ourselves.

"You like it Lil Phoenix?" She lets our hands go to look at everything in this room.

"Aww Fredericks fami-." The chef starts to say.

"AAH WHO THE HELL ARE YOU?" La'Meira shouts pulling a blade out of some damn where and I swear this woman is dangerous and I fuckin love it.

"Baby… baby chill she's the chef for while we're here." Monty rushes to her side and I'm right behind him because she still looks like she wants to cut the chick.

"We're only here for a week. Why do we need a chef?" She asks putting her arm down but not putting the knife away.

"About that we thought since this is you and the kids first time experiencing snow why not stay here through New Year's." I tell her as she looks up at me smiling then at Monty and Dean.

"Plus, we figured after all that's been going and us being newly married and all we all deserved some real genuine time together with normal family problems cause I know it won't be all peaceful." Monty says laughing a little.

"UH yea a house filled with seven kids and thirteen adults sure it will be interesting to say the least."

"Exactly so chef is needed Lil Dove."

"Wait she doesn't think she's cooking Christmas dinner cause that shit not happening." She says and I look at Monty and laugh.

"Ife mi it's relaxing time for us she can handle all the food." He tries to convince her horribly.

"Montavius Ekon Fredericks if you think this woman is going to cook my families first Christmas dinner together you are out of yo damn mind." She shouts poking him in the chest and I laugh harder.

"Don't worry Lil Phoenix she will not be cooking our first dinner we can do it as a family." I assure her as I massage her shoulders, and she leans her head back smooching her lips for a kiss and I gladly oblige then make the I told you face at Montavius. He really thought she would be ok with that mess Dean and I both told him she wouldn't, but he was hell bent on her having to do nothing while we're here but have fun and lay around if she wants which I get but that's not our woman.

"Ok so I'm handling all breakfast which will be buffet style, I can make lunch when needed, and dinners but not Christmas dinner." The chef finally speaks up again after Meira scares her shit less.

"That's fine with me but I need warning if you're going to make any shellfish, and it can't be around my food I'm allergic." She informs the chef and all of us. We aren't huge seafood eaters, so we never noticed that she rarely cooked any.

"Well, no need for any shellfish to be made then I'm not taking any chances with that allergy baby." Monty declares and we all agree. None of us care about seafood that much to put Lil Phoenix health at risk and anybody who has a problem can get the fuck out.

"Seriously guys it's not that serious I just need to stay in the room or outside while it's being made, and it can't touch my food plus I packed two EpiPens just in case. I'm not going to make you guys not eat your favorite foods because of me."

"Ladies?" I look back at Kelia and Kenya to get their input.

"I'm with Monty and Jax Meira. No way we're risking you having an allergic reaction just to eat one damn food group. I've seen a girl damn near die from an allergic reaction to something just because her stupid boyfriend forgot she was allergic and kissed her after he ate it, hell no." Kelia says driving our damn point home.

"OK fine if y'all are genuinely good. Any other allergies she needs to know about though?" She questions everyone and we all agree we don't have any. The housekeeper we hired, and her team come in from the four-bedroom guest house out back.

"OK so brunch will be done within the hour oh by the way I'm chef Saundra. This will be your housekeeping team ran by Zara. We will all be available to you through an app you can message us through, and it will also show you the menu as well as remind you the serving time. If anything needs to be changed you can also do so through the app." Chef Saundra fills us in as the housekeeping staff gives us each a small card with a QR code on it. We all get it downloaded, and they head to do whatever they need to be doing.

"OK so our master bedroom is upstairs, our moms have the ones down here. I didn't quite know what to do with the kids though. It's actually ten bedrooms in here not including the staff quarters in the basement. There is also a surprise room only the adults will have the code to." Monty explains with a big smile on his face looking down at Meira then to the rest of us and we catch the hint.

"Well, the kids should go in the guest house for all of our sanity, and they aren't babies I'm sure they will love their own space to chill."

"True, so let's all get settled the rest of the fam should be here by dinner time."

"Jax you're next to us right." Meira looks up at me.

"Whatever you want Lil Phoenix." I say leaning down to kiss her on the forehead. We all walk up the winding staircase turning right for us to go to our rooms which are right next to the special room for the adults while Dean and Chase go to the left over the catwalk, but Meech is on our side. The place has six rooms upstairs three on each side then the four downstairs. The special room is not considered a bedroom. There is also a game room in the basement on the other side away from the staff quarters. My phone goes off with a text message from Monty summoning all brothers to his room as I am getting settled.

"What's up Monty brunch is smelling good downstairs." Chase says rubbing his stomach and Meech agrees.

"Babe." He says looking at Meira.

"So, I've been running a program on Justin's laptop and had alerts set for all our names. My program just alerted me that the hits he wants now are on all of us. $100k each he has also been hemorrhaging money between his colorful sexual habits and the drugs he pumps himself with he needs us out the way so Calder will continue to do business with him."

"You gotta be fuckin kidding me? Is the family safe coming here with us?" Chase questions going on guard.

"They are actually safer here with us seeing as Justin still thinks we are home. He might think that we are leaving for our honeymoon in a few days."

"Lil Dove what the fuck did you do?" Dean asks walking towards her with a pissed look on his face and she puts her head down stepping backwards. I instinctively step in front of her and so does Monty and he steps back putting his hands up.

"She's done something I know that look." Dean says.

"Lil Phoenix?"

"Fine I wasn't letting any of you get hurt I just got my damn family I wanted. So, I hit up some of my connects on the dark web other hackers, sex trafficking rescue camps, and some mercenaries that I feed Intel to sometimes and handed over access to Justin's computer as well as his cellphone. I also sent the files we had from Sinclair. I requested they bring me Justin and Calder but if it comes down to it just kill em and bring me their heads."

"Ife mi you didn't." Monty says running his hand through his beard and I pull at a few of my dreads frustrated.

"There may be a bit more." She says playing with her hands looking nervous.

"Spit it out Lil Phoenix."

"Don't give me that tone I'm helping protect our damn family I'm not some weak dumb woman who's ok with leaving everything on ha man's shoulders. The only reason Justin thinks we're leaving for our honeymoon in a few days is because I posted a picture saying can't wait to get away. He has his hit squad coming to the house to get rid of us, but he wants to be there to make sure I'm gone once and for all. So, I had the mercenaries one looking a lot like my hunk of husband here staying at the house armed to the tee along with a few at the RV just in case they hit there too."

"You gotta admit Meira's plan will help us get him stay out the way and protect those we'd be worried about the whole time anyways." Chase chimes in agreeing with Meira's method of madness.

"Ife mi I know you're smart and stronger than any woman I've ever met but we're a team you don't want me making unilateral decisions without you so don't do it for us either."

"You had this planned all along, didn't you? It's why you insisted on everyone being here and today to be exact." I inquire looking at her with one eyebrow raised and grin.

"Yes, when I got the first alert, I figured this was the best time to handle his ass, but I didn't want any of you doing it also because he's too close to home you'd actually be suspects."

"Fuck she has a point. The kids don't need that type of stress on them worried if one of us will be taken from them. You make it real hard to be mad with you Lil Phoenix." I say kissing her on the forehead and she smiles up at me then smooches for a kiss on the lips.

"Clearly were all good then but don't let your guards down when we're out and about. Chef just messaged brunch is done let's go enjoy our food." Monty announces and everyone starts leaving.

"You two stay." Meira demands and I hear the attitude in her voice.

"What's up baby?" Monty turns placing his hand on her hip.

"Really you two what was that with Dean?" We both look at each other and shrug.

"That was rude as hell. Dean would never hurt me. Why would y'all make him feel that way?"

"I didn't mean too. You put your head down and stepped back my instincts just kicked in and it will always be to protect you." Monty says and I agree with him.

"I stepped back because I know Dean can easily read me. The only thing I was worried about was him throwing me over his shoulder spanking me which probably would've turned me on or grabbing me and tickling the shit out of me cause he's the only person that knows where my tickle spot is."

"Look I'm not going to apologize for wanting to protect you at all times but where's this tickle spot?" I question stepping closer to her.

"You two will apologize to Dean that was rude as fuck or no pussy for either of you for the next few days and nope not telling you. Now go on."

"Fine." We both say turning to head downstairs.

Chapter Twenty-Seven

Dean Fredericks

It was pretty funny having my six foot six thirty-eight- & thirty-seven-year-old muscle-bound older brothers pout at the dining room table then apologize to me in front of everyone. Seeing them so domesticated and in love with La'Meira is weird but nice they both seem happy even if they have her in different respects. Brunch was amazing chef Saundra really did her big one. We all went outside to explore the grounds and check out the guest house which I'm sure the kids are going to love with their own living room as well as kitchen it even has a pool table that turns into an air hockey and ping pong table. We all cuddle up with blankets on the back covered patio around the fire pit. We don't even realize just how long we've been outside just talking about any and everything until the patio doors open and the kids rush out.

"Mom dad this place is so beautiful." Mariah announces sitting next to her mom.

"It really is. Can we go hiking tomorrow?" Za'Mara inquires sitting in between Meira and Monty but leaning on his shoulder.

"Yea of course we can." He will agree to damn near anything those kids ask him.

"So where are our rooms?" Za'Meir questions sitting between Jax and I dapping both of us.

"Hi everybody." Myra says stepping outside and her kids Darius, Denise, Myla, and Mercy all wave smiling.

"So, all you kids are back there. It's four bedrooms, three bathrooms and the living room has a pull-out queen size bed. Plus, two of the rooms have bunk beds." Meira explains pointing to the guest house behind us.

"Wait we have a whole house to ourselves." Mariah jumps from her seat excited. They all scream out thank you's running off to the guest house. Housekeeping already knows to take their bags back there and our moms to the rooms downstairs. Myra is upstairs with us and hopefully is cool with that. She gives Meira a funny look for a second but clears her face real quick. I look over at Meira who's laying her head on Monty shoulder while Jax is rubbing her hand that's on his lap and she doesn't even notice. I look down at Kelia and she notices too but she looks like she's ready to slap fire out her ass already making me chuckle.

"Relax baby we don't even know what the look was about." I whisper in her ear. Her and Meira have gotten even more close since our lil mini orgy but more so her being thankful to Meira for helping her come out of her shell and being ok with her sexual preferences which is just another reason I love that damn woman. Meira just has the biggest damn heart and is so affectionate if you didn't know her you wouldn't think she'd just as quickly slit ya throat though.

"I know that judgey jealous ass look anywhere. If she starts some shit I'm going to beat, her ass about my Meira." She says as Myra walks back in the house to find her room.

"So, you caught that shit too. I'm go deck that jealous bitch everything Meira does for ha and she lookin at her like that." Kenya announces next to Kelia and now I know it's about to be some shit. I really hope Myra gets her shit together and finds her some dick soon before one of these girls knocks her shit loose. Lawd I hope our moms don't catch on, shit. We get alerts through the apps that dinner will be ready in about forty-five minutes.

"Hey fellas let's go check out the game room before dinner." Marsh request coming outside with Bree who rushes to hug and kiss on Meira then Kelia and Kenya.

"Baby that's cool?" Monty looks at Meira for approval and we all turn to her.

"Of course, go on have ya men time I'll see y'all at dinner." She says smooching her lips for a kiss from him and Jax. I give Kelia a kiss then head downstairs with the boys.

"Nigga we got a problem." I inform them as soon as we get downstairs and close the door.

"Let me guess Myra." Chase says.

"What's up with Myra?" Monty questions.

"I hope she still not on that bs cause I'll hurt ha feelings." Jax says looking annoyed walking to the bar to grab a drink.

"So, you know what she on? Why didn't you say something to Meira bru?" I ask.

"No, I don't know exactly what she's on, but she came at me a while back flirting and I turned her down." He states taking a sip of his drink.

"Well ha dumb ass came in here looking at Meira crazy and Kelia and Kenya caught it. So, it's only a matter of time before they either say something to Meira or whoop ha ass themselves. Warning I'm not go stop em. I don't like that jealousy shit." I take a shot on the pool table landing my six-strip ball.

"Well, if that's what it is I'm not either because she better leave my baby the fuck alone." Monty states taking the next shot.

"So, you turned her down from sex now she sees you with Meira and knows she's the reason you didn't want her. Does she not know the type of lifestyle we're into?" I question him to see if they have had any type of conversation or if Meira might have maybe that will clear some of the tension.

"I don't think so but either way something about her I don't want any parts of. I'm surprised Meira doesn't feel something off."

"Honestly can't say she doesn't. Meira likes to feel people closes to her out. She gives family the chance to not cross her even if she feels like something is off with them. That's that big heart of hers but once you cross her that's it." I shake my head then take my next shot but missing it.

"Yea well we all know how ugly jealousy can get though." Monty says looking at Meech seeing as we had a problem back when he was in college some nigga, he thought was his friend did some wild shit and left him with scars. We play a few more rounds of pool joking and drinking. The alert comes through the app letting us know dinner is ready and we all head up. Luckily, the dining room is built for large families, and we definitely have turned into one and I am loving it.

"Served tonight for appetizers are bacon and chives potato skins and mozzarella cheese sticks. Dinner will be served in fifteen minutes." Chef Saundra announces as the staff sits the appetizers on the table. We all dig in chatting about activities we want to try tomorrow and soon out comes dinner.

"Now for dinner glazed lamb chops, mashed potatoes, and spinach, enjoy."

"Well, this is fancy. Boys this is sweet and all, but that woman doesn't think she's cookin Christmas dinner, does she?" Mama Jennings asks, and my mom makes a face agreeing.

"No ma'am ya daughter already scared the shit outta her about it when we got in." I tell her laughing.

"That's my girl." My mother says making Meira smile.

"So. I was looking at the menu on the app, but I didn't see her making any shrimp lobster or nothing seafood really but some fish. What's up with that?" Myra questions and we all look at her stupid because if anybody knows about Meira's allergy it's her.

"Um did you forget about Meira's allergy to shellfish Myra?" Kenya asks with a clear attitude.

"No but that means no one can have shellfish that makes no sense. She just doesn't need to be around when it's cooked or contact with her food."

"Well, we'd rather not risk an accident, so we told her no shellfish. Is that going to be a problem for you Myra?" Kelia jumps in and I know they are about to be on one any minute.

"She's fine girls chill she was simply curious. Hey Myra, I thought you were going to ask the dude you liked to be here with you what happened?" Meira jumps in trying to change the subject but doesn't realize she just hit a different hornet's nest. I shake my head and dig into my food.

"Well apparently he was fuckin family too." This bitch really just said that. I am so glad the kids are at the other table in their own little world.

"Damn that sucks but hey maybe you dodged a bullet. What family member was he messing with anyway?" Meira is clearly not paying attention to the tension radiating from her, well at least not at first because she feels it and looks up from her food.

"Wait you not talking about who I think you're talking about are you?"

"You already have a man you just had to be a hoe and screw his brother too. Did you know ya brothers screwing ya wife."

"Aww shit, hey kids y'all can take your food to the guest house we'll have them bring your dessert over." Jax instructs them and the kids all say ok getting their plates and rushing out the back door. I text in the app for their desserts to be delivered with some snacks for a movie or game night.

"Bitch what did you just say." Meira says tilting her head to the side and that's a telltale sign one of her other personalities is about to make an appearance. I just sit back in my seat cause the shady shit needs to stop.

"Of course, I know she's slept with my brother if you bothered to ask before just assuming you'd know we are all swingers and we are in a poly relationship but the only men or women she can sleep with are in this room." Monty informs her leaning forward interlocking his fingers on the table which means he was trying to control himself.

"Babe, you don't have to explain shit to her. What we do in our relationship ain't ha fuckin business, and you knew she liked you but didn't say anything to me?" She turns to Jax.

"Look Lil Phoenix it wasn't like that she flirted a few times and was being extra nice when you were in the coma but I told her I wasn't interested and that was that for me at least." He turns pleading with her not to be mad at him with his eyes and she concedes and smooches her lips for a kiss. He relaxes and gladly gives her a quick one.

"Wait so all y'all just fuckin each other that's nasty as hell. Auntie you see what they doing to Meira?"

"Bitch nobody doing nothing to me and just because you can't get one nigga to want to fuck you doesn't make my relationship nasty or weird it's what works for us."

"There is nothing wrong with how my babies are living it works for them, and I won't have you sitting at a table you wouldn't ever had the money to be at if not for them and disrespect them." Mama Jennings says getting upset and Meech instantly starts rubbing her back to calm her down.

"She's right I actually like that Meira is with Monty and Jax both my babies need that love from a woman and she's the sweetest girl and best daughter in law I could ask for well besides my Kenya and Kelia." Our mother adds in and hearing her accept our lifestyle and our women gives me comfort I didn't know I needed.

"Wait mama Fredericks what about me?" Bree is pouting next to Chase who is next to Kenya on our side of the table.

"You're my daughter girl not daughter in law."

"No ma she's your daughter in law too. We finally stopped fighting our attraction for each other well I stopped fighting it and She's my woman now." Marsh announces bringing their connected hands to his lips to kiss hers and she blushes.

"Aww really my babies all finding their women." She gets all emotional patting her teary eyes with her cloth napkin.

"You gotta be kiddin me you're both condoning the fuckery?" Myra shouts jumping from her seat.

"Bitch sit down before I put you down for trying my Meira. The only reason you up in arms is cause you thought

Jax would be your meal ticket taking care all dem damn kids you got." Bree shouts getting pissed too.

"Y'all are some weirdos I'm taking my kids and getting the hell outta here they don't need to be exposed to this shit and auntie you should be ashamed of yourself condoning this mess."

"Myra yo dumb ass not going nowhere with those damn kids. We both know you don't have money to go no damn where, well except the money we gave you to pay your bills up. So, you can either sit yo judgmental jealous ass down finish eating dinner or you can take yo ass to your room. I'm not going to repeat myself." Meira says way to damn calm for my liking.

"Dad, are you just go sit here and listen to all this mess and let her talk to me like this?"

"Myra sit yo ass down and shut up. I haven't said shit about you cheating on Marc and Denise nor Myla are his is the real reason he left yo ass not cause he cheated. Now you have the audacity to be judging your cousin who has found her well-deserved love finally because what you still in some imaginary competition with her. You can do as she said cause you not ruining my grandbabies first trip in years over some bullshit." Mr. Jennings drops a bombshell shocking all of us at the table cause this bitch went around telling us all her husband cheated on her and left her with four kids. She finally realizes she has no allies and sits down eating quietly for the rest of dinner then heads straight to her room. We almost forgot he was even coming and didn't know where he was going to sleep till, we found out earlier he was staying in the room with Mama Jennings due to her inability to get around all that good, he seems like a great little brother to mama Jennings.

Chapter Twenty-Eight

La'Meira Fredericks

"Well dinner last night was interesting to say the least. I want to do the tree decorations and game night tonight I hope that bitch keeps her emotions in check the rest of the trip." I'm laying between Monty's legs as he moisturizes my scalp for me making me even happier that I decided to get long minitwist in for our wedding.

"I think you should've let her leave but then the other side of me says we need to keep an eye on her. Someone as jealous as she seems to be can do some crazy shit baby and I have no problem killing ha ass if it comes to it. I just don't want you to hate me if I do."

"Never that Big Daddy."

"Alright you can get some more of Big Daddy if you want na Ife mi." He says stopping the scalp massage he is giving me but before we can start up for like the third time this morning a knock comes at the door.

"Hey y'all not coming down for breakfast?" Chase shouts through the door and we both look at each other.

"Yea we coming." I yell back.

"Yup might as well get up. Didn't you want to grab some board games and stuff in town anyway?"

"Yea me and all the ladies are going."

"Aight well the security will drive you and before you even think about it it's not even a damn option."

"Fine, what are you going to do while I'm gone anyway."

"You forgot the kids wanted to go on a hike. Me Dean Chase and Jax are going to take them. Meech and Marsh are not nature men even if they can handle their own out there, they prefer not to." He says getting up from the bed behind me looking for something good to hike in as I throw on some thick black sweater tights, emerald, green turtleneck, this cream-colored thick long cardigan sweater, and some black knee-high leather boots.

"Good morning babies." I kiss every last one of them including Myra's kids. I will never act differently with them just cause their mom is being an idiot.

"What's up kids y'all ready for our hike after breakfast." Monty asks them and they all get excited.

"But dad we don't have the shoes to hike." Za'Meir pops his head up from his plate packed with eggs, bacon, grits, and hashbrowns plus another bowl of fruit.

"You will when you get back to your rooms backpacks and all, it was just delivered about thirty minutes ago." He says looking at his smart watch and I swear that man thinks of every damn thing.

"Mom what are you doing today?" Za'Mara ask me as Myra looks up from her phone at me for the first time since I sat down.

"Well, me and the ladies are going into town to find us some cool family games to play and some more decorations for the tree so we can decorate it and the fireplace when we get back."

"Oh, yay I can't wait to do the tree." Mariah says getting excited.

"Me too can we have hot chocolate and play Christmas songs like we do at home." Za'Mara seems happier than I've seen her in awhile.

"Of course."

"We can stay up all night watching Christmas movies too if y'all want." Jax adds in squeezing my right thigh smiling at me and I kiss him on the cheek.

"This is about to be the best Christmas ever." Denise says bouncing in her seat and we all laugh except for her mother of course.

"You will not have my kids in your cult incest family mess, I refuse." She jumps up screaming at me and I loose my shit jumping across the table grabbing her by the neck and slamming her face into the table.

"Look bitch I've had enough of yo jealous judgmental bullshit you disrespect me and my family again I will gladly forget you're my cousin and make sure yo ass don't make it back to Alabama then adopt ya kids as mine."

"Hey, I wanted the kids." Kelia announces behind me.

"Wait really like not in a bad way. I wanted them too if she finally got rid of ha ass." Dean says next to her.

"Ugh auntie can you not kill my mother please and mom can you stop ruining everything for us dang." Darius her oldest pleads as he gets annoyed with his mother. He has unfortunately been a witness to his mom's stupidity for years and has had to grow up too quickly for my liking. The kids were texting me last night filling me in on all type of bullshit which further pissed me off cause I knew something was up with her but didn't think it was that deep.

"You lucky my baby is asking me to spare you but if you act up again God himself won't be able to save you from me." I let her know through gritted teeth digging my nails into her throat as I squeeze and slam her head against the table again then I let her go.

"Mhmm baby don't toot yo ass up in the air like that again I almost forgot the kids were in here." Monty says in my ear rubbing circles on my inner thigh after I sit back down.

"Shiddd you too bru. I started to bite that shit." Jax laughs next to me and these fools have the audacity to laugh more and bump fist behind my head. I can't do anything but smile and shake my head.

"Lawd what am I going to do with you two."

"Love us forever is all you can do we stuck like glue baby." Jax declares kissing me on the forehead.

"Alright ladies y'all ready to do some shopping?" Mama Fredericks says wiping her mouth and standing. The kids are already getting up to leave to get ready for their hike.

"I'm ready. You may want to go fix your face before we leave." I look at Myra.

"I wasn't going." Myra says looking scared but like she still wants to say something slick.

"You not staying here with our men so gone get ready heffa." Kenya says finally speaking.

"Wait a -." Myra starts to say but catches me giving her the death stare so instead shuts up and heads upstairs.

"Alright fellas we better go help the kids cause I bought jackets, boots, backpacks, and backpack survival kits." Monty tells his brothers along with Uncle Tone. They stand then he leans down to give me a kiss then Jax does the same as all the guys grab their winter coats heading out back. We all head outside as the guard is opening the sliding door to the bus, we are renting Myra comes out with her face beat probably covering the bruising. She is about two shades lighter than me and bruises easily. We have one other security guard inside the bus with us, I swear my men are overprotective. We all chat and take pictures of the beautiful scenery on the forty-five-minute ride. The downtown area is so pretty with all the Christmas decorations lining the streets as well as in store windows. We spent hours going through different shops buying everything from clothes to trinkets and more gifts for the family. By the time we make it back its almost dinner time.

"Well damn Lil Phoenix did you guys buy out all the stores." He helps me out the truck looking at how packed with bags the inside is, and I laugh after giving his soft juicy lips a quick kiss. He helps his mom and mines out as the rest of the men come out to help. We get everything settled inside and we make them put the gifts in Monty and I room so the kids won't snoop. Za'Meir starts the Christmas music, and we all start grabbing different ornaments to hang on the two big Christmas trees until I get an alert on my phone. I make eye contact with Monty and Jax they both grab their brothers as I walk off to the nearby office.

"So, Justin is caught he apparently decided to hit early but my people were already in place waiting on him." I announce leaning against the big Oakwood desk in the middle of the large office space.

"So what else Lil Dove, I know you?"

"One of the guards you had there was hit and it's not looking too good. Um they also kinda started a fire at your house love bug."

"Whatttt."

"The fire department was quick though, so it wasn't much damage one of my people is there acting as a family member getting everything dealt with."

"So, where's Justin babe?" Monty looks at me concerned because he knows I'm not saying something.

"Well, they currently have him drugged and tied to a tree somewhere on my property until they deal with all the damage to the house. We'll at least boarding up windows and doors." I am little sad about my house being messed up but glad we're one step closer to ending this shit show.

"Don't worry Meira I'm hitting up my construction manager now to hire five more men and to pay them double to fix any damage." Chase comes to rub my shoulder.

"Hey Chase come here real quick." Dean calls to him and I know he's up to something, but I won't worry about it now. I pull up the video on the office TV so they can see what happened.

"Tell them to take him to the compound property it's about hundred acres of trees they can tie him too and torture his ass uninterrupted at least till about eight am." Jax says over his shoulder watching the video on the TV and I do as he says.

"Enough of this shit let's get back in here with our family and enjoy this vacation." Jax says picking my head up by my chin giving me a deep slow kiss then giving me one of his bear hugs I love so much.

"The house will be fine, and so will the guard get out of your head Ife mi." Monty commands in my ear coming up behind me as I've moved from leaning on the desk and he massages my shoulders leaning down to kiss my neck.

"We got you Lil Phoenix let's go." He laces his fingers with mine and Monty does the same with my other hand. I take a deep breath, and we all walk out to the kids throwing popcorn instead of putting it on the strings. We all burst out laughing and join in. It takes us hours to finish the trees between stopping for dinner and everyone going to their rooms to change into their matching pajamas. We get through one Home Alone fully and part of Home Alone two before the kids are ready to call it a night.

"Meet us in the special room in ten minutes Lil Phoenix." Jax tells me picking up Za'Mara to take her to bed wrapped in her blanket and Monty takes Mariah. The only ones still actually up seem to be all the boys and Myla but she's about to doze off too so Dean and Meech grab Denise and Mercy. I head upstairs changing to something sexier and as I walk out, I notice Bree, Kelia, and Kenya entering the room in sexy lingerie and I already know this is a damn setup for some freaky shit. I get into the room filled with the scent of Love & Sex incense setting the mood and Kelia is on me instantly giving me a nasty wet kiss using her tongue like she has in my pussy.

"Hmm shit Kelia what was that all about?" I ask grabbing her by that juicy booty of hers bringing her closer to me.

"I've been wanting a kiss all day and you seem down since you and the men came from the office earlier, I was hoping it would cheer you up." She says biting her bottom lip looking off to the side. It's cute when her shy side kicks in with me.

"If you ever want a kiss, you let me know or just come get it, I don't care who's around, got it?" I say turning her head back to me bringing us eye to eye as we're pretty much the same height hell we all were give or take an inch on each of us. I give her another quick kiss as she rubs on my ass.

"What about my kiss?" Bree pouts.

"Bring yo ass here woman." I order her holding out my arm as Kelia moves to my side and I pull Bree into me connecting our lips, sucking on her bottom lip while rubbing on her thick ass through the thin lace lingerie body suit she has on. I slide my hand between her legs towards her pussy and she smiles as I realize the suit is crotch less and her juices are all over my fingers. She moans as I suck on her tongue and swirl my finger around her entrance. I let go of her tongue then give her a quick peck and pat on her ass and she moans again.

"Hmm you happy now woman?"

"I will be delighted when I get to taste that fat pussy of yours." She says licking her bottom lip.

"That can definitely be arranged after Lil Dove receives her punishment." Dean states fully walking into the room with the rest of the men with bare chest and different color silk pajama pants that are hanging low enough to show off their deep v cut. The four of us stand next to each other visibly turned on looking at our sexy ass men standing at the room door with looks of love and lust in their eyes. Monty and Jax have put their dreads back up in buns, Chase has his long thick plaits pulled back in a ponytail and Meech as well as Marsh have their loose hair pulled into men buns. Dean is our low boy with deep waves, and I love to rub my hands over them. The girls and I look at each other then they step away from me smiling and I know these bitches were distracting me until they all got here. I step back.

"Punishment for what exactly?" I step further back.

"Did you forget *The Queen*." Monty says stepping forward next to Dean. Shit I was hoping they'd let that go.

"But first there is something Monty and I want to give you." Jax steps forward and holds out his hand for me to come. As I get closer, he pulls me to him as he grabs my hand turning my back to his chest. Monty pulls out a gold link chain with an open heart on one end and a heart locket on the other. He unlocks the locket part placing the chain around my neck putting the other end through the open heart then using the small key to lock the locket on the other end. He pulls me toward him by the end of the chain pushing my head up with his other hand to look at him giving me a soul sucking passionate kiss then turns me towards Jax holding my chain from the back now lightly choking me. Jax pulls a beautiful gold bracelet from his pocket with some sort of tool placing the bracelet around my left wrist using the tool to clamp the piece together with a gold loop so I can't take it off. As I look at the bracelet, I notice it has a goddess knot on it, and I learned a while back that it means an unbreakable bond or eternal connection. It's beautiful the links on it are thick like my chain. He steps forward wrapping his hand around my neck caressing the side with his thumb. Monty apparently had it made with the choker after he decided he was cool about Jax and I having more than a sexual relationship.

"Forever my Phoenix." He declares kissing me so deeply it's hard to catch my breath when he releases me then kisses the bracelet on my wrist. These men have my pussy so damn wet already it's starting to run down my inner thigh. Once they turn me towards the room, I notice all the different toys and sex furniture in the room and I damn near cum on myself with excitement. Monty walks around pulling me by my chain leading me to this bench I've only seen online, and I look at him like a deer caught in headlights because I will definitely not be walking out of this room if this is how they're starting. I notice Dean to my right getting a damn flogger out a drawer and Jax has some damn nipple clamps. I turn to look at everyone else and they have taken seats on the California king size bed and two chairs facing us as we're on the far-left side of the room.

"What's wrong Lil Phoenix cat got your tongue?" I can't believe these men have officially stunned me into silence.

"This is sexy and all but too much fabric." Monty states pulling a big hunting knife from his pocket cutting the straps off my burgundy lace teddy then he cuts the thong off next leaving me completely bare to everyone in the room.

"Safe word." Dean says coming up behind me running the flogger against my bare back and ass.

"Emerald." I finally find my voice and I gasp in shock as Jax connects the nipple rings that have a chain in the middle connecting them both to my already hard nipples. Monty yanks the chain making me stumble a bit towards him. He pushes me into position on the punishing bench and I lay forward over the bar that sticks up in the middle to raise my hips and lean forward to place my forearms on the arm rest. Dean locks the ankle cuffs as Monty does one side of the arm and wrist restraints and Jax does the other.

"Damn that is one sexy fuckin sight." Monty steps back admiring me in such a vulnerable state, but I have never felt safer in my life.

"So Jax it's been a year since you met *The Queen*, right?" Dean questions him swinging the flogger side to side.

"Yup but to be exact eighteen months ago." He clarifies as his eyes roam over my naked body.

"Damn that's a long time she had to tell me she was *The Queen* and to come looking for you. So that's what -?" Dean says.

"Six hits each." Monty finishes his sentence. I look at the three men I love in diverse ways about to make my deepest sexual desires real even if they don't know it or maybe they do.

"Remember that safe word Ife mi you're going to need it." I squirm with anticipation.

◇◇◇◇◇◇◇

"Dean we think you should go first brother." Monty tells him and I see him smile before he disappears behind me then Monty appears in front of me pulling at my chain. Dean caresses my ass with the flogger for a second then I feel the tails slap against my ass giving a hot, sharp stinging sensation but makes my pussy wet at the same time. Monty wraps his hand around my chain at the same time Dean pops me with two quick hits then tickles me with the tails again. Monty kisses me as the next two hits come quick pulling my chain till my vision starts to go black but before I pass out, he lets it go just enough for me to breathe.

"Deep slow breathes baby you're taking your punishment so well." He directs me running his hands through my minitwist then I feel fingers rubbing my entrance sliding through my soaked lips.

"Shit she's wet as fuck like dripping wet." Jax is still rubbing his fingers through my lips then he stops, and I feel the flogger hit me again. I see Jax suck my juices from his fingers out the corner of my eye and I squirm again. I feel Dean fingers slide through my lips and dip into my entrance and I moan as he turns his fingers inside my pussy. I try to buck back needing to feel more but then feel the flogger tails hit my back.

"Hmm so anxious and responsive. Monty, I think our girl is a damn masochist." Jax says to him rubbing the flogger he now has across my back and over to my ass.

"Shit just when I thought you couldn't get any more perfect Ife mi." He pulls my choker and my nipple chain at the same time sending tingles all through my body making me even wetter.

"Fucckk." I moan. I hear more moaning from my left and notice Marsh has Bree in a sex swing alternating between fucking the shit out of her while she squirts everywhere and sucking on her pussy.

"Ummm you wanna go over there next." Monty asks still in front of me holding my chain.

"Maybe some other time you're going to be worn out by the time we get through with you."

"Brother?" Jax calls to Monty holding the flogger he's been dragging across my skin.

"No go ahead she went missing on you longer." Monty says shaking his head then turning back to me and smirking. I feel the flogger smack against my ass twice then against my pussy and I can't help myself and I squirt.

"Damn Lil Dove that was sexy as shit he says rubbing my clit with his fingers in a circular motion then I feel the flogger go against my ass again and I squirt all over his hand.

"Shit." I hear Kelia moan as she plays with herself on the bed and Dean smiles at her then and to Meech who kneels in front of her open legs moving her hand sucking her juices off her fingers then licks her from her entrance to her clit making her cry out in pleasure. Before I can focus back on us Monty is yanking my choker causing me to jerk forward sending pain through my body that turns to more pain as Jax hits me again with the flogger then turns to pleasure. I hear him groan as he disappears behind me, and I feel his lips latch on to my clit and I scream in pleasure my vision going black again as Monty pulls my choker tight. He releases me just as I feel Jax long thick tongue swirl inside my pussy sending me over the edge cumming all over his tongue and he licks every bit of it up.

"Fuck... fuck I don't think I can take much more babe." I moan.

"No chance Lil Phoenix we only stop when you use your safe word." Jax walks over in front of me as he hits me one last time handing the flogger over to Monty who let's go my chocker to walk around dragging the flogger tails against my back. I see Jax walk over to the shelf on the wall grabbing a bottle. Meech now has a spreader bar attached to Kelia ankles stretched to its max and has her knees touching her damn ears as he deep strokes the hell outta her pussy. Damn all their dicks are big as hell. Jax is walking over to me rubbing whatever oil or lube he had across his thick long dick smiling at me as I feel the flogger hit hard against my ass making me scream out.

"Hmm Lil Dove you really are taking your punishment so well, but we're not done with you yet." Dean says appearing outta nowhere grabbing my nipple chain causing a gasp to leave my throat. Another two quick hits from the flogger has me leaking again and I hear Monty moaning behind me.

"Stick ya tongue out and no teeth Lil Phoenix well maybe a lil." He says with a wicked look in his eyes as he shoves his dick into my mouth along my tongue till, he hits the back of my throat all while pulling my neck chain. He starts fucking my throat ruthlessly as Monty hits me again and I'm so overwhelmed with pleasure that tears run down my eyes. I feel Dean lick them making me moan around Jax's dick.

"Hmm that's my good Lil slut take your punishment baby." Jax moans still fuckin my mouth with quick short thrust never pulling that far out. I start to taste the oil Jax rubbed over his dick and its strawberries then I realize my throat is relaxing more than usual. Putting it together I figure he must have found some throat numbing oil and I moan around his dick, and he drops his head back moaning. So, I hollow out my jaw creating suction around his dick and his head shoots down quickly towards me with his mouth in a o shape. I feel Monty get his last two licks in making me so wet and before I can adjust, he slams into my pussy filling me to the hilt then pausing rotating his hips. I lose focus on my suction on Jax cumming instantly all over Monty's dick squirting again.

"Mhmm you two got this from here someone's begging for my attention." Dean says walking over to Kelia who Meech has in doggy style. He tells him to take the bar off and grab the lube and Meech smiles knowing what he wants, I guess. Jax makes me focus on him by pulling my neck chain as he still fucks my mouth so I look up at him creating suction again as Monty is fucking me so deep, I can't help but to cum again creaming all over him.

"Shit Ife mi this tight ass pussy is trying to milk the shit outta me. It's so pretty stretching to fit me crying all over my dick." He moans out speeding up his strokes smacking me on the ass with his hand this time and I'm so sensitive I buck back as much as the position allows me to.

"Dats my freaky lil bitch still trying to throw that ass back even in your position. Cum again for daddy." He demands and Jax pulls the chain tight cutting off my air as he hits the back of my throat, and I start to see black as he releases it while Monty is still stroking the shit outta me. I completely come undone screaming around Jax's dick as he cums down my throat and I cum harder than I ever have in my life. I feel like I'm floating. I swallow every drop of Jax's cum and he pulls out after thrusting a few more times dropping to his knees and kissing me passionately. Montavius keeps stroking me from behind causing my orgasm to keep going until he cums deep inside me leaning forward to kiss me on my back.

"Fuck that was amazing." Monty moans as he pulls out of me slowly and I miss the feeling already.

"She looks exhausted, let's get her to bed." Jax tells Monty as he is taking the straps off my wrist and arms. "I'll go run her a bath, she's going to need to at least munch on something too." Monty walks out the room not even bothering to pull on his pants. Jax finishes getting me untied walking out with us both stark naked and I catch a glimpse of Myra in the far end of the hall.

"She's going to need some cream for these rub burns from those straps. Damn baby I didn't mean to be so rough." Monty has a look of guilt in his eyes as he rubs lightly over the sensitive skin.

"Don't you dare ruin my fantasy. That was better than I could've ever imagined. They will heal. I have some of my unscented Shea & cocoa butter mix that will help with them put it on the bed and as far as food can you see if it's any leftovers, I'm hungry as hell." I order him still in Jax arms and I smooch my lips out to get a kiss and my baby gives me one as usual.

"Get her cleaned up I'll be back in a bit." Monty instructs Jax kissing my forehead then walking out thankfully he put on some damn pants, I'd kill Myra if she went after my husband. Jax gently cleanses me in the shower then himself then he lays me in the tub to soak for a few minutes. I hear the room door open, and Montavius comes to stand at the door then comes to rinse the bubbles off me as Jax unplugs the tub then goes to grab my towel as he wraps another around himself. Monty lifts me out the tub wrapping the towel around me. The two of them dry me off and rub me down as gently as they can with the Shea & cocoa butter moisturizer, I told them to grab with Monty up top behind me and Jax in front from the waist down.

"Jax you're staying tonight, right?" I ask him looking between him and Monty as he places me in the bed then gives me my food.

"Sure, Lil Phoenix I can stay with." He grabs a pair of Monty's sweatpants then gets in the bed on the other side of me. I rest my head on Monty's shoulder as I munch on some leftovers feeding some to each of them. Once I'm all done Jax takes the plate downstairs and by the time he gets back I am nodding off but once he gets in bed, I roll on my side facing him laying one of my hands on his chest as Monty spoons with me like we normally sleep then I am out like a light.

Chapter Twenty-Nine

Montavius Fredericks

I still can't believe the night we had a week ago with my wife. She has been so damn giddy, and the sex lately has been even more intense like what we did made us even closer than before. We've been doing game night every other night with the kids, we even did a grown-up's game night with some relationship game Meira found while out. It's Christmas eve and majority of us are out skiing or sledding except Meira, Kelia, Bree, and Kenya. I was shocked and skeptical of seeing Myra come out with us but so far, she's kept her distance hanging with the kids mostly. We're all sitting at a big lunch table with the family when my brothers and I phones all ding. We all look at each other just knowing our women are up to something so we excuse ourselves to go outside.

"What the hell are these four up to?" Chase questions grinning as we all make it outside.

"I don't know but I am definitely curious so on three." Meech says.

"Three." Dean says and we all open the text at the same time. A video of Kenya in the swing with La'Meira sucking her clit fingering her at the same time, while Meira is riding Bree's face and Kelia has a double-sided dildo with one end in Bree and the other in her and she is using her hand to move it back and forth plays. The video goes on for a good minute or two and we all have to turn the volume down cause their moans and slurping noises are getting loud. Another text comes through with a picture of La'Meira still riding Bree's face but now Kenya is tongue kissing her as Kelia is now sucking on Bree's pussy then another picture of Bree and Kenya in the sixty-nine position on the bed while Kelia has a vibrator fucking Meira with it as she sucks on her clit. The last message says don't rush home.

"Bru, are we dreaming cause this can't actually be our life, right?" Jax asks still looking at the messages like the rest of us completely dumbfounded and so turned the fuck on we have completely tuned out everything around us.

"Yup nigga this is our life like it's really our fucking life." Chase is grinning from ear to ear still looking at the pictures.

"Damn we actually found women that like the freaky shit we're into to the extent they like doing it with each other." I'm zooming in on the video turning it like I'm going to see a different angle still in pure disbelief and so turned on.

"But clearly like to keep us all involved when they do the freaky shit with videos and pictures. This shit is going in the vault for sure." Marsh announces.

"This is the sexiest shit I've ever seen like damn man." Meech says turning the video back on.

"Tell me about it." I say zooming in on the pictures now.

"Bru, I need to go lay in this damn snow for a minute." Dean states walking forward face planting in the snow and we all buss out laughing. The kids come out a minute later running to jump in the snow too thinking he's playing. It turns into a full-on snowball fight which I'm actually glad for to cause a nigga was brick hard. We spent a few more hours going down the mountain in sleds and tubes. When we get back it it's dark and the wives are in the kitchen prepping Christmas dinner.

"Damn it smells good in here baby." I walk up behind her wrapping my arms around her waist and lean down to kiss the top of her head and Jax stands next to us kissing her on the cheek.

"Hi Big Daddy and Chocolate bear how was the skiing? She asks leaning her head back for a kiss and I oblige as she seasons some oxtails in a large bowl.

"It was fun especially after Dean had to face plant into the snow to calm down after the lil display y'all put on for us." I recall looking down at her and the women standing around the island either chopping up vegetables, mixing ingredients for cakes or pies.

"Y'all in here doing the damn thing huh?" Chase says walking in kissing Kenya on the cheek.

"Where are the kids and our moms?" Meira asks.

"Baby they're all worn out. The kids went straight to the guest house to shower the staff will take them some snacks and moms and Uncle Tone went to their rooms too." I tell her kissing her exposed shoulder as all she has on is one of those tube dresses seeing as it is nice and cozy with the fireplace going in the living room.

"Y'all need any help?" Dean comes in next kissing Kelia with Marsh right behind him kissing Bree.

"No, we're good y'all can go get cleaned up and relax." Meira instructs us leaning her head back for another kiss this time I grab her throat kissing and sucking on her lips till she moans in my mouth.

"She's right y'all the ones been out with the kids all day." Kenya moans as Chase smacks her on the ass walking out the kitchen and we all head out cause they're right I really could go for a nice hot shower. The girls are still in the kitchen when I check my messages and all the guys are down in the basement shooting pool talking shit. We are probably in there for a good hour or two when we all get a text.

"Now what the hell are they up to this time?" Jax says picking up his phone.

"Well, I be damned." Dean says making me open up my messages quicker and as soon as I open the message up pops a picture of four fat asses kneeling at the door way of the sex room hairstyles pulled up in buns with nothing but G strings on and big satin bows tied around their breast. Then a message pops up telling us to come open our Christmas presents.

"Niggaaa I need to get me my own." Meech says and we all look at him remembering how he feels now.

"Now you know the ladies love you too." Marsh says bumping his shoulder.

"Yea but it's not the same. It's different for Jax, him and Meira have an actual connection but I don't have one with any of them like that. I'm going to sit this one out y'all." Meech goes to sit on the couch turning the TV on something to watch.

"Hey bru don't get down your time will come just like ours did. Hell might be one of the country girls when we get back home." I reassure him squeezing his shoulder and we all leave out. Suffice to say we had a great fucking Christmas and rang in New Years with a damn bang checking out the fireworks at the local park Jax and I each kissing Meira as the clock stroke twelve. The kids with their grandparents, Myra, and Meech headed out on Thursday, and we were making our way to the airport today.

"Babes is Meech ok he seemed down the last few days?" Meira asks me as we board the jet.

"He's feeling left out not in the sense of us doing anything –."

"But not having his own woman." She finishes my thought which we have seemed to start doing a lot lately

"Yea we told him his time would come like the rest of ours. None of us were out looking for our women all of you kinda found us in your own way." I tell her.

"Well maybe we all need to go out with him more and maybe he'll run into his girl. I don't want him sad babe." She says genuinely concerned about my little brother just adding to the many reasons I love this woman.

"We can try that, but you know we have some real-life shit to deal with once we get off this plane." I remind her as we take our seats. Jax sitting on the opposite side of her. People are going to start calling us her shadow after while the way you see her and see one or both of us at any given time now. I'm glad for that shit she will always be good and that's all my heart and sanity need. I lay back to take a nap because we took the special room for one last spin before we left late last night and had to be up for our seven am flight so to say I'm tired is an understatement.

"I told yo butt not to spend any of your honeymoon working on this mess Lil Phoenix." I hear Jax fussing with Meira about something she clearly wasn't suppose to do. I fake asleep to hear the rest of this mess she has gotten herself into again.

"Well, it's not like it took me much time babe don't be like that. There was no way in hell I was going to let him keep fuckin with you. So I handled it and you have your zoning for the club now besides his wife and job needed to know about his racist undercover cock loving panty wearing weirdo ass." She says and it takes all my self control to not burst out laughing, I swear my wife a damn fool but I want to know why the hell he didn't come to me if he was having problems.

"Ughhh woman what am I going to do with you but thank you baby for real." He tells her giving her a kiss.

"You're going to love me that's what and you're welcome I'd do anything for you.. you know that right?"

"Of course I do Lil Phoenix." I decide to reveal I'm awake because I don't like him hiding shit from me.

"So is there a reason you didn't tell me you were having problems with a zoning officer for the club."

"Shit I thought you were sleep." He says looking over to me shocked.

"I'm awake now that's outta the way answer me Jax." I order him calmly sitting up in my seat to look him in the eyes.

"Look Monty don't start. I specifically told her I would deal with the guy, but she decided not to listen but I'm thankful, nonetheless. I'll be out the two of your hair dealing with getting it up and running for a bit." He explains to me, but I'm not satisfied.

"That's cool and all but that doesn't explain why you never told me you had a problem."

"It's because he was trying to stay away from me. It was hurting him to think he couldn't have me at all. He was sad babes and felt alone after you proposed." She informs me putting her hand on his cheek rubbing it with her thumb and he leans into it then kisses the inside of her palm. I know how he felt about her, but I guess I never thought about how he was feeling after I proposed to her.

"Look Jax don't ever distance yourself from me like that you're my fuckin brother. If something or someone is bothering, you it bothers me too and knowing how you feel about La'Meira I wouldn't keep her from you especially if she feels the same about you and besides it's no coming between us." I tell him and we fist bump.

"Don't keep shit from again me Jax I'm not kidding." I give him a stern look as the flight attendant comes to tell us we will be landing soon. We all hop in our waiting SUV to head back home with Jax, Dean, and Kelia obviously with us.

"Oh, there's a surprise waiting for you when you get home Lil Dove and before you even think it when you see it nothing is too much for you and the kids." He says from the backseat laying across Kelia's lap.

"What did you do Dean?"

"Nothing you don't deserve." He says.

"He's right Lil Phoenix and it's just till y'all home on the compound is done which is the first on the list." When we pull up to the house she gets out looking at the house confused at first.

"It looks like nothing even happened."

"For the sake of the kids and cause we know you liked the paint job we kept that all the same just upgraded the windows to tempered glass, reinforced front door and garage door but still stylish." Dean describes some of what we had done for her and I'm grinning cause wait till she sees the inside. He enters the house which now has a code entry lock and that's when she looses it and I laugh.

"How the what the hell Deaannnnn." She screams jumping in his arms and I smile. We were able to get about eight guys over here since we're still waiting on plumbing to be fully done before they start on the house. We had all the drywall, paint, windows, and cabinets redone for the kitchen and living room. Bought new furniture for the living room and dining room plus new appliances. Upgraded the kids bathroom even found some space to make it bigger. Then had a ten by fourteen-foot deck built and screened it in with a built-in grill with prep area, bar area equipped with a stainless-steel mini fridge, new patio furniture, fire pit, and heating lamps.

"Now I know this was more than Dean because I only told you about the closed in porch the night we were sitting out talking and the mosquitoes tried to eat us alive." She says to me smooching her lips for a kiss.

"Well its only right you sacrificed your home to get the job done with Justin and you're my wife whatever you need or want I got you." I kiss her again.

"Where are the kids I haven't gotten a text and they're not in their beds?"

"They stayed at mom's place, and I checked the cameras they're fast asleep, see." I show her my phone of the kids knocked out on the couch in my mom's living room with her.

"Well, you wanna call Marsh so we can get this Justin mess dealt with now?"

"Yea might as well." I pull out my phone to call Marsh as she rolls our luggage to the room and the guys settle on the couch and Kelia says her goodbyes then leaves. A few minutes later she comes out the room in a black tank top with matching leather pleated skirt along with leather bustier, fish net stockings, black collar with matching cuff bracelets, hair pulled back in a ponytail, and black Timbs.

"I'm ready to go. Oh, and I had my friends drop a fun present off."

"Awww shit *The Queen* has arrived." Jax states standing from his seat on the couch.

"Huh?" I ask confused at first.

"That's what she wore when out kicking niggas asses well she's missing her mask and the knives she usually has strapped everywhere." He informs me walking over to her placing a hand on her cheek rubbing it with his thumb and I realize in this form of her is how they met.

"Hi my Queen." He leans down and gives her a slow heated kiss.

"Hi my favorite purger." She says referring to his favorite mask to wear.

"I better be your only one." He smacks her on the ass and wraps his arms around her waist.

"Aight Marsh will be meeting us there." I inform them after finally getting him on the phone. We all head out hopping into my truck. Pulling up to our property she tells us to head all the way to the back right before the tree line. I notice a yellow bulky looking machine come into view as we get closer, and I look over to my wife who is smiling from ear to ear.

"La'Meira what the hell is that and don't say I'll see either?" I demand looking at her from the corner of my eye keeping an eye on where were going even if it's a cleared field, I will never take any chances with her life.

"Fine you like taking the fun outta things it's my new model wood chipper. You can feed things in from the top instead the front makes torture less strain on the body and the blood goes up instead in ya damn face." She explains like she's talking about baking cookies for the kids. I park the truck a few feet back then Marsh with Meech pulls up next to me and Chase on the other side. We all get out walking around to the front of my truck.

"I see *The Queen* has joined us." Marsh says smirking when he sees Meira.

"Anybody wanna tell us why there is a big ass wood chipper sitting there?" Chase questions us looking confused.

"This one over here." I nod my head towards Meira. Then we here muffled screams and it must be Justin's bitch ass.

"So, they got some stuff out of him, but they felt like he was holding something back about who Calder truly is because they checked for politicians by that name and there aren't any. Oh and apparently my owner wants him dead if I'm not delivered within seventy two hours." She says not looking at any of us making me worry she always gives eye contact it's a thing for her once she gets close to you.

"Well come on let's see what this fuck boy has to say." She says pushing off the truck and skipping towards the wood chipper running her hands across it.

"I think we should be worried about her." Dean comments coming to stand next to me.

"You noticed that too huh?"

"I did too." Jax says standing next to me. We walk up to her and I place my hand on the back of her neck, Dean on her lower back, then Jax on her waist.

"You wanna tell us what's wrong Ife mi?"

"Not really." She says still not looking at any of us.

"I'll take that for now Lil Phoenix but when we're done here you will tell us." Jax says squeezing her waist and she just nods her head.

"Jax be a dear and get those ropes, Dean get the bitch from tied up on that tree about ten feet in, Montavius baby help me get my new toy started up would ya." She orders us all around and we do exactly as she ask. By the time Dean comes back with Justin thrown of his shoulder we have the machine started. It's pushed into the trees quite a bit but I'm sure that's on purpose as I look how it's positioned with trees on either side of it.

"Well hello Justin we meet again." She greets him squatting over his body where Dean threw him down. He twists on the ground in his binds screaming through the gag in his mouth. She removes his gag.

"You stupid bitch I'm going to kill you. You ruined everything." He shouts still wiggling in his restraints.

"You really think you're getting out of this don't you?" I question leaning over him kicking him in the side.

"You will never hurt her again." Jax declares leaning over the other side.

"Jax love string him up and hang him over the that hole. You may need to throw the rope over those two branches, so he hangs just right. Oh, and feet first babe." She instructs him and he does exactly as she tells him without even questioning her. Once he has him tied up like she wants he comes to stand next to her.

"So, Justin there are a few things I want to know one what's Calder's real name and two who's the buyer?"

"I'm not telling you shit you fat bitch. Monty this is really what you wanted over me seriously." He shouts at me.

"You really are delusional; I would've chosen any woman over you because I don't like men but especially this woman."

"Look I really want to get back to my bed so tells us what you know so I can get there."

"I'm not telling you shit you're going to kill me anyways." He spits.

"Fine I'd hoped you would want to go out with some form of dignity and trust me there are some things worse than death. Meech my favorite mad scientist would you please? She looks over to Meech.

"My pleasure Queen." He says pulling a syringe from his pocket with Marsh walking over with him to give him a boost and he sticks him right in the leg as he's been stripped down to his boxers and has clearly been bitten up everywhere by bugs. We wait a few minutes and then she starts again.

"So, Justin wanna tell me who Calder is now?"

"Calder's not his real name we call him that because of the street he grew up on. His... his... his real name is Steven Flemington, ughh." He groans trying to fight the serum but its no use Meech has that formula down packed but my blood damn near runs boiling hot to hear the name of a former ADA now Governor back in KC.

"Babe, do you have a blanket in the trunk?"

"Yes, you need it Ife mi?" I ask and she nods her head. I head to get the blanket coming back to spread it on the ground for her.

"Sit babe and pull my chocolate bar out." She demands turning to face where Justin is hanging over the wood chipper and I do as she request. I swear it's like this woman has mind control over us. She backs up dropping to her knees pulling up the back of her skirt revealing to me she has on no panties on under her fish nets that have a hole in the crouch area and I get hard instantly. She reaches behind her grabbing my dick then lowering herself on to it partially leaning forward as I fill her to the hilt. I lean back a little moaning as her walls squeeze around me.

"Now Justin one last questions who is the buyer." She slowly slides up and down my dick then grinds her hips against mines with my dick deep inside her walls.

"Ugghhh."

"Come on you know you want to tell me so just let it out."

"Fuuuckkk." I moan as she's bouncing harder.

"Artemis Troy you fat slut and I can't wait till he finds you. You'll never be able to touch Monty again."

"And you'll never get to touch what's mine. Jax my love." She leans forward on her hands and knees throwing her ass back fucking the shit out of me.

"Say less baby." Jax walks over to the rope untying it and lowers it slowly until the blades are shredding Justin's feet. He screams out in agony begging for us to stop but he's soon drowned out by babies moans of my name and the feeling of her contracting pussy begging me to paint her walls. My brothers stand on either side of us not knowing whether they want to look at us or at Justin being shredded. Blood splatters all over the trees behind the woodchipper and as he lets out his final scream Meira and I cum together.

"Fuck baby that's how you feel." I say smacking her on the ass then she leans back giving me a quick kiss. She slides forward and I slowly slide out of her already missing my home. Luckily, I thought to grab some napkins from the truck when I grabbed the blanket, so I clean us up a little then go to turn the machine off as it's nothing left of Justin but super small, shredded pieces all over the woods behind us. We hop in the truck leaving Meech, Chase, and Marsh behind. She tells them to set a fire but make sure they get buckets of water from the pond or well to put it out once it burns enough and its customary practice out here so no one will bother them they just nod their heads and get to work.

Chapter Thirty

Dean Fredericks

We make it back to the house and Meira runs off to the bathroom. Moments later we hear the shower running.

"What the actual fuck just happened?" I ask as we sit at the kitchen island.

"Bru I'm still processing this shit myself, that was sexy as hell." Monty smiles next to me.

"Did our baby just get off on one being petty, torturing that nigga, and then killing his ass with a wood chipper?" Jax asks grabbing some orange juice from the fridge pouring it in a glass.

"Yes... yes, that's exactly what just happened? Is it crazy that -." I start to say then the bedroom door opens and out walks Meira in a dark green silk robe.

"Let me guess am I crazy as shit for getting off on dropping that prick into my new toy?" She sasses walking around us rolling her eyes.

"We did not say that and don't come out here giving us fuckin attitude when you're still not looking any of us in the eye Lil Phoenix." Jax grabs her by the back of the neck pulling her back towards the island and closing the fridge door with his foot.

"He's right spill La'Meira." Monty states picking her up by the waist and sitting her on the island. I walk around standing on her right with Monty in the middle and Jax to her left.

"Now Lil Dove." I grab her by the jaw pulling her head from looking up to look at us.

"Fine I wasn't looking at you guys because I didn't want you to see the worry in my eyes after I learned the buyer was still coming for me if Justin didn't show up with me himself." She tells us turning away from us pissing me off because she left that part out earlier. This piece of shit thinks he's taking her from us he got us fucked up.

"You conveniently left that part out Lil Dove that's not good. We don't do secrets remember." I say pulling her head back towards me.

"What else aren't you telling us Ife mi don't lie to me I see it in your eyes?"

"I'm scared as hell that he will actually get me this time or come after the girls, and I can't have that shit I'd rather give myself up before he takes my girls." She expresses and tears start to fall from her eyes breaking my heart. She really doesn't seem to understand the lengths we will go to protect our family.

"There's no fuckin way he's taking you or our daughters over my dead fuckin corpse." Monty declares wiping her tears away with his thumb.

"I think that's the other problem isn't it Lil Phoenix?"

"Yes, if something happens to any of you, I'm going to lose my shit ok. I seriously don't know what the fuck is the right move with this one. I looked him up in the bathroom he's a hedge fund mix breed that gets off on buying black women to make him babies then tortures or sell them off he rarely keeps them. He seems to have a serious hard on for me. He wouldn't even let Justin pay him his money back." She finally gets diarrhea of the mouth and tells us everything with tears streaming down her face. I get a text that Chase and the boys are on their way home. I fill them in on what Meira just told us, and my phone instantly starts to ring, and I put it on speaker.

"Meira there is no way in hell he is taking you or our damn girls get that shit outta yo head. Meech is talking to Money right now and I text True from the Texas sanctuary you remember him, don't you? They all are coming." Chase says and I look at my Lil Dove face looking shocked.

"See Lil Phoenix we got you baby. Let us take care of this shit. Let's tackle the problem one step at a time."

"Right starting with when will these niggas be here?" Monty inquires looking annoyed with so many people being around as Chase comes through the front door hanging up the phone.

"Money three days since they're driving and two for True." He answers.

"Bet so three days total to get all the info we can on Governor Flemington and Artemis Troy." I say.

"Might be time to rope our FBI buddy in. Give him some damning evidence on the Governor, they'll handle him for us, and we take care Artemis ourselves. If we must leak the damn info, then take his ass out make it look like a suicide either is fine with me." Jax declares pulling out his phone leaning to kiss Meira on the forehead then walking out the back door.

"See what's going on around you Lil Dove."

"Exactly feel the fear it's cool but don't let that shit overtake you let it fuel that genius brain and magic fingers to get everything we need to end this shit Ife mi." Monty encourages her looking her in the eyes, so she finally gets it.

"One condition." She says with a smirk.

"Anything."

"What does Ife mi actually mean?"

"It means my love in our native language Yoruba." He tells her chuckling and glad she's coming out of it even if it's only a little bit.

"That's beautiful, so you've been walking around calling me your love this whole time." She says giggling then hopping off the counter her robe opening a bit.

"Lil Dove I'm going to need for you to go put on some clothes before you get bent over this counter." I tell her smacking that fat ass of hers and she has the nerve to have a smirk on her face telling me she's with the shits.

"Nope not now get yo ass in there." Monty smacks her on the ass too and nods his head towards the room for her to get a move on it.

"No fun." She says sticking her tongue out at him pouting then stumping off and I can't help but laugh.

"She is such a fuckin brat sometimes I swear." He shakes his head.

"Don't worry Kelia do the same shit." I tell him shaking my head at the thought of the monster I've created in her, and I love it. Meira comes back in the room as we're setting the laptops up on the island.

"We need to tell the girls and before y'all even think about saying no I've already texted them and told Ma to keep the kids for tonight. I'm about to prep dinner and make a light lunch since I'll be making catfish, mac and cheese, collard greens, with cornbread but lunch is just some wings and fries." She says while moving effortlessly around the kitchen pulling out things she needs for both. I wanna be pissed but I know she's right ugh fuck she's always right and I'm not telling her ass that. Jax comes back in from making that call to our FBI friend and stands right next to Meira pulling her into his arms she simply wraps her arms around him rubbing her face against the top part of his stomach, barely reaching his chest. He kisses her on the top of the head and pats her ass then she goes back to prepping the food.

"Alright seems like the FBI already have the Governor on their radar for a missing assistant presumed dead after some late nights with the boss. This will just make things worse for him. So, I would say that problem is solved." Jax fills us in sitting at the island watching Meira work her magic. Soon Kelia, Kenya, and Bree come through the door heading straight to us like we all weren't on a flight together just four hours ago.

"Hi baby Meira said it was something urgent we all needed to talk about. What's going on?" Kelia asks giving me a kiss but looking worried.

"We will tell everyone in a bit." I tell her patting her on the big ass I love so much. Meira has started frying the chicken and has the fries in the air fryer. She turns around looking at Monty and Jax and they both stand to go on either side of her grabbing one of her hands and kissing it.

"OK let's get this talk over with. Marsh y'all come into the kitchen." She shouts and they all come in.

"Look ladies the fellas already know all this, and you guys know about the kidnapping the guys rescuing me." She pauses looking at each of us.

"You want me to tell them Lil Phoenix?" She nods her head in response turning to deal with lunch as Jax tells the women with full detail the shit that's been going on. By the time he's done detailing everything Meira is plating out the food and we all head to the dinner table.

"Damn all this from a routine divorce case and a nigga who wanted a nigga that didn't want him. Ain't this some bullshit." Kenya says popping a fry in her mouth.

"So y'all are handling this shit right because they can't have our Meira?" Bree questions reaching across the table squeezing her hand. These women will go to war for each other, and it makes our job protecting them that much easier.

"Of course, we are but Meira felt like it was time to tell y'all since shit about to get hectic. With trying to get the dude who thinks he has the ability to buy her and the asshole with the audacity to think he can sell her." I tell them.

"We also need you ladies to stay aware of your surroundings more because we never know what they may try if they can't get her before we get them." Chase lets them know because it is paramount that they understand. We want to be around them twenty-four seven, but we can't smother our women like that, and we'd feel like shit taking away their independence.

"We have two teams coming over to help protect everyone that will split between you three and help deal with these pussies to add to the ones already here for Meira." Monty states adding some ketchup to his fries one by one like he us to do when we were kids and all I can do is shake my head with my brother's weird eating habits.

"Look we're all going to have our own guards, but I'd feel better if y'all would let me show you a few of my jiu-jitsu moves and Jax or Meech will show you how to use a gun. We will however continue our businesses and getting this compound built for our family." She looks at the ladies giving them that mother stare she pulls off so well to let them know she is serious.

"Sounds fine with me. Ladies?" Bree looks over at Kenya and Kelia. "I'm down. I get to learn how to protect myself better, get a good workout in, and spend more time with y'all." Kelia says shrugging then popping a fry in her mouth.

"Facts I'm all in they better stay the fuck away from us." Kenya adds in. I look around the table at my family and realize they couldn't have all come out better if I created them myself.

Chapter Thirty-One

Steven "Calder" Flemington

I can't believe I'm in this stupid ass situation. I didn't even kill this dumb bitch and I'm sure it was her boyfriend who was mad after finding out we were fucking around. FUUCCKKK! My phone rings and I can easily guess who it is since it's my damn burner.

"What!"

"Oomph I guess that white privilege isn't working out so well for you Calder?"

"Art I'm not in the mood for your shit."

"Not my problem I paid you for a product and haven't received it now it's been almost a week since your boy Justin fell off the face of the earth."

"Art, I told your ass a month ago when she was in that damn coma you need to just cut your losses. The more you try to go after this chick the more my business gets fucked and I can't have that."

"Well, I paid for her, and I want her dammit."

"What the hell is so special about this damn woman? I mean she's a beautiful woman cause I can't call her a girl at her age and even that I've offered you a younger one."

"She's beyond beautiful she's fucking perfect. Plus, she has twins in her DNA I can finally get a chance at having my boy or even two. All these sluts seem to make are ugly girls and I'm going to permanently keep her to raise my children she can nurture them the way I need. You saw how her son tried to defend her that's some strong love and that mixed with my genes and money would be perfect."

"Do you know how stupid and crazy you sound the woman is MARRIED. Not just married to any run of the mill man either the man owns one of the top security firms in his state and getting bigger. Plus, the man and his brothers are Marines and Navy fucking seals they got her back once and will gladly try again clearly."

"Fuck that and them I get what I want."

"Well do it on your own I'm washing my hands of you as my client permanently for this mess. I'm sure Justin is really dead, and I have a feeling they've been the ones hitting my damn shipments. You are costing me more money than you bring. So, consider your membership revoked and that includes all protection. Goodbye Art." I groan hanging up the call as a knock comes at my home office door.

"Come in." I shout.

"Boss we have a problem." My personal assistant on paperwork but my right hand says walking in locking the door behind him which tells me all I need to know.

"What happened?"

"A shipment was intercepted at the docks."

"Fuck." I shout slamming my fist into my desk.

"It gets worse it wasn't those vigilante people it was the FEDS."

"You gotta be fucking Ughhh." I stand up pacing the floor.

"They apparently got a tip about it. We don't know everyone they spoke to because of your missing assistant but clearly someone talked."

"Shit my whole operation is under the microscope because of a bitch I had nothing to do with going missing."

"There was no trace of us at the docks I made sure of it we just gotta hope people stay loyal. Even if the ones there never saw you, they could lead to those who have."

"True, fuck. If Artemis could've taken the loss, we wouldn't have so many missing shipments. Justin's dad isn't going to be so happy about all this."

"We need to close shop for a while on our end let him keep the auctions going."

"He put me here for a reason there is no closing shop for us. Fuck. Get out I need to think."

"OK boss." He says leaving my office. The smart thing would be to step back and let things around me calm down but I'm sure he won't go for it. Shit I must ask anyways but this is a conversation for in person. I contact his secretary to put me on his schedule for as soon as possible.

Chapter Thirty-Two

Jax Fredericks

Thankfully, it's been quiet these past three weeks.
The buyer either got spooked after the FEDS started raiding
Calder's deliveries and stash houses or he's waiting for the
right opportunity to come so he can grab her but either way
we are ready. Construction is moving along with the clubs
mine and Marsh's. Meech found a restaurant spot and
Montavius finally started hiring people for the security firm's
office here. I just left the compound checking in on the
contractor's Chase has there since he's at an open house and
Kenya is at one of their flips. They finally finished the
plumbing and bringing the electricity in from the street as the
internet lines have already been done too, so now they're
starting on the base of Monty and Meira's home which will
probably be the biggest at over six thousand square feet.
Money and his men have either bought or rented homes
from Chase while True and his team headed to KC after a
week. Pulling up to my Lil Phoenix home for lunch together
a nigga cheesing I will admit. It has been the best damn
feeling being able to be with her, no hiding how we feel,
having someone who truly understands me and all my crazy
shit.

"Lil Phoenix what's burning baby." I ask walking in
the door getting hit by a cloud of smoke. "Meirrraaa." I
scream running through the house trying to put out

whatever she had on the stove as panic sets in. This woman is very meticulous about her kitchen and food she would never leave it unattended to burn. Once I get the fire out, I start opening windows and the patio doors to let the smoke out. "La'Meiraaa." I shout again through the house heading towards the bedroom to find her laid out on the floor not moving. I turn her over slowly checking her for wounds but don't see any except for a slight bruise on her forehead. "Lil Phoenix baby wake up you scaring me." I slowly lift her up to place her on the bed then kneel next lightly shaking her. I pull out my phone to call nine one one as she starts to wake up moaning. "Baby I'm here talk to me." I say gently moving her hair from her face.

"Ouch what the heck happen Jax?"

"I'm wondering the same thing. I came into the kitchen full of smoke and found you in here on the floor." I fill her in on what I know when the operator comes through on the phone and I tell them what they need to know. I send a text to the family group chat and put the phone down.

"Baby you don't remember anything?"

"I remember putting the food on for lunch then running to use the bathroom really quick and, on my way, out I felt dizzy and that's it." She says trying to sit up, but I hold her down.

"Stop moving baby you hit your head when you fell." My phone starts ringing and I already know who's calling.

"Yea Monty."

"The EMT's are on the way. She woke up just a minute or two ago."

"What the hell happened to her?"

"She said she was coming from the bathroom and felt dizzy. No one was here so I doubt it was any type of attack."

"How far out are the EMT's."

"They just got here Monty relax bro she's sitting up and talking. I'm letting them in now to check on her."

"Ok I'll be there in a few minutes."

"Nigga I thought you were interviewing someone?"

"I was but Meira is more important and you of all people should know that."

"Yea I do see ya in a few minutes." I say hanging up feeling like a hypocrite knowing I would've dropped anything too. It's crazy the dynamic the three of us have but it works for us.

"How is she?" I ask standing up from leaning on the door frame.

"Her vitals are stable. I recommended going to check out the hit she took to her head, but she refused. Ma'am could you be pregnant?" He asks while still kneeling next to her on the bed.

"Oh, shit babe get my phone off the counter in the kitchen." She tells me and I rush out to grab it as Monty comes through the door. I shake my head because I know this fool broke the speed limit to get here that damn quick.

"What they say?"

"She's stable but they asked if she was pregnant, and she had me come get her phone." We walk back in the room, and I sit at the foot of the bed handing her the phone as he goes around getting in the bed.

"Oh, shit oh shit... shit... shit."

"Ife mi what's wrong, talk to me?"

"Well, if not having my period since before our honeymoon is something wrong then there you have it." Monty and I eyes both bug out when it hits us what she means.

"Well sounds like congratulations may be in order but if you're getting dizzy you want to get checked out for sure." The EMT informs her as he's packing his bag.

"Thank you."

"You're welcome and feel better." He says as they both leave. I scoot closer putting her feet in my lap and massaging them.

"Baby our honeymoon was what over a month ago now."

"So that means she's what five or six weeks?"

"I haven't even taken a test yet to confirm guys chill." She says doing the no eye contact thing again.

"Don't start Lil Phoenix tell us what's going through the big brain of yours."

"What if I lose this one too?"

"Baby we will worry about that if it happens and, in all honesty, I don't think it will. You only had the first miscarriage because of what happened to you." Monty reassures her squeezing the back of her neck and kissing her forehead.

"He's right and what do we do?"

"One step at a time."

"That's it baby. Now I'm going to go grab us some food and you a few pregnancy test. Anything special you want?"

"Oooh some Zaxby hot wings and fries." She says doing her happy food dance making me chuckle and glad she's feeling OK.

"Zaxby it is baby. I'll be back in a bit just lay back and relax please I'll clean the kitchen when I get back." I tell her giving her a quick kiss on the lips then standing to leave.

"Don't worry about the kitchen bru I'll clean it while she lays here and relaxes." He says kissing her on the forehead and standing to walk out the room with me then closing the door.

"So, do you wanna know if it's biologically yours?" He turns to ask me as I head for the front door.

"Doesn't matter I'll treat them like I do our other kids but if you want to be sure that's cool." I tell him leaving and now it's stuck on my mind whether or not it could be mine. Would it even matter Monty would claim it as his, but I'd easily change the birth certificate, so in all reality it doesn't matter. I grab our food and the test heading back to the house. When I pull in the whole damn family is there minus the kids. Bree is in the kitchen taking out something to cook for dinner apparently, the guys are all in the living room watching basketball except for Monty and Dean of course, and I assume Kenya and Kelia are in the room too. I'm glad I decided to go with getting the big family platter. I plate off her some food and grab the bag with the pregnancy test.

"What's up y'all? Here you go baby. I'll go grab your drink." I hand her the tray with the plate.

"Hold off let me go take these test before I get good full and comfortable." I give her the bag and she head straight to the bathroom coming out a few minutes later.

"The results already done Ife me?"

"I didn't want to look but they should be done in about five or six minutes." She starts stuffing her mouth with food to distract herself and I kneel next to the bed rubbing her leg to calm her.

"Deep breaths baby it's going to be ok no matter what." I reassure her and she starts to calm down. Monty slides over in the bed behind her rubbing up and down her arms kissing her shoulder as she sits up in the bed. She leans her head back on his chest and we stay like that for a few minutes as she takes her breathes and slowly but surely calms down with us both there.

"You want me to check for you Meira." Kelia ask and she nods her head. Kenya is sitting on the bed next to her and Monty while Dean kneels next to me.

"Um Monty you're about to be a Dadddyyyyyy." She squeals running to hug them both kissing Meira on the cheek but she's still in shock and hasn't said anything yet.

"I'm going to be a dad again like actually through baby stages and all." I see as he gets increasingly excited kissing her on the cheek and neck.

"Nope don't let your fears ruin your happiness Lil Dove. Aren't you happy?"

"Yes, and I'm trying not to let them it's just."

"Remember your breathing baby. Your feelings are valid we just don't want you to get stuck in them." I remind her.

"Hey y'all give us a minute." Monty announces looking at the ladies mostly, but Dean leaves too.

"I'm really not trying to ruin the moment for you babe I just don't wanna mess this up. I haven't felt insecure about something in years."

"Ife mi you're not ruining anything. I just want to make sure you're OK with this cause I am overjoyed baby."

"I am too actually. Doesn't matter if it's mines or Monty's I'm happy for another part of you running around here." I tell her tapping her nose and she smiles at me.

"So, you guys wanna find out which of you it is even though Jax has been pulling out since the slip up at hospital."

"True but it doesn't matter either way this baby just like our other kids will have us both always." Monty says and we fist bump. I swear my respect and love for my brother knows no bounds.

"So, I guess we should go out and tell everyone if the girls haven't already." We chuckle and shake our heads because knowing those two they probably did.

"If you're ready we can." She nods her head yes and we help her out the bed. Everyone is sitting in the kitchen and dining room including my mother who's smiling from ear to ear.

"OK so big mouth one and two probably already said it but we're having a baby." The room erupts in cheers, and I knew it's.

"I'm so happy we will be having a new addition or additions to the family. I promise I won't love our other three any less." My mother says hugging Meira and I'm glad to hear her say that cause as much as I love her, I'd cut her off about my kids.

"I know you won't, and I also know this will still be a bit different for all of you as this will be your actual blood. I just hope to carry full term healthy babies." I hear her say and I zone in on the fact that she said babies not baby. We all sit in the living room talking and the girls shopping apparently. Our other babies soon come through the door.

"What's all the hype about in here." Za'Meir asks entering the kitchen giving me dap, hugging Monty, his grandma, and then his mom. The girls come in hugging everyone till they get to their mom and doing the same.

"Well kids we have something to tell y'all." I say walking over next to Meira as she stands between Monty and me.

"You guys aren't leaving us, are you?" Za'Mara asks starting to pout.

"No... no... no baby girl we aren't going anywhere." I reach for her to come to me, and she does happily. I kiss the top of her head, and she snuggles into my side.

"Ever baby." Monty adds in reaching over to rub her cheek.

"What we want to tell you is that mommy is pregnant." Meira says rubbing her belly.

"Really that's cool is it Daddy Monty's or Papi Jax's?" Za'Mara asks and the three of us look dumbfounded cause I didn't know they called me that and two that they realized Meira and I were together.

"Well does it really matter sis?" Mariah asks her.

"Nope you're right it doesn't we will still get to have another sister or brother." She says as they have a whole conversation like we're not even there.

"Wait what if it's both like us Mara?" Za'Meir ask her and they high five each other getting excited.

"What made you think it could be Papi Jax and when did y'all start calling him that?" Meira interrupts their celebration still looking just as confused as us.

"Cause of how you two look at each other." Mara says.

"That and the way he cares for you like daddy Monty does." Meir adds in.

"Right like uncle Dean is there for you and protective of you but not like daddy and Papi are. They move like your shadows, and they'd step in front of a bullet for you without hesitation at that. It's intense but it's sweet." Mariah says looking between Monty and me.

"We always called him Papi between each other but didn't want daddy to feel any kinda of way about it, but Papi Jax has been a dad to us too and let's be real they are practically twins." Meir says and we all bust out laughing at the last part because we have been hearing that our whole lives it's why my dreads are colored at the end besides the fact, I just like the color.

"Well Monty you cool with me being called Papi?" I ask him and he gives me a really nigga look making me laugh.

"I guess I'm already sharing my wife with ya why not the kids too." He crosses his arms over his chest letting out a huff like he's mad about it, but I see the smile in his eyes.

"Hey it's not like I don't already have a birth certificate with me listed as their dad, so." I add in ducking the sponge he just threw at my head as I laugh.

"Wait we both can't have birth certificates drawn up for them doofus. Well, it would still be the same last name but do y'all want that?" He looks at the three of them.

"So, like changing our last name to yours?" Mara asks looking excited but trying to control it.

"Yes, all three of you would have our last name. Do you want to?" They all look at each other having a silent sibling conversation.

"Two conditions." Mara says.

"Name it" I say.

"Can we have a two Cane Corso's?" Meir request.

"And a really big fish tank at the new house since it's nowhere to put it here?" Mariah adds in. We both look down at Meira as she smiles at both of us.

"Deal." We both say and they immediately jump us. Everyone busts out into cheers and laughter again.

Chapter Thirty-Three

La'Meira Fredericks

I'm sitting at the island as Monty rubs my back as I munch on some more of the food Jax bought us while I watch Bree cook dinner. I notice Jax has disappeared, and I see him standing outside talking to one of the guards, so I hop off the bar stool kissing Monty's cheek before heading out to him.

"Babe everything ok?" I ask as I get close to him leaning my head on his arm.

"Get in the house now La'Meira." He demands looking forward into the woods.

"Now!" He calmly but still with a stern voice and I turn around going into the house.

"Somethings up with Jax babe." As I say that all the men stand up pulling out their weapons, they always have on their hip heading out the front and back doors. I know something is wrong instantly and I rush mom with the kids into the bedroom then grab my gun from the closet. I hear shouting out front, and I cock my gun checking the magazine then head for the front door as Bree does the same with hers standing at the back while Kelia and Kenya grab the biggest knives they can find. They both go stand in the hall where mom is with the kids as I go into my office to look out the window and see what's going on. When I do my blood runs cold at the sight of Artemis Troy standing in the road in front of my home.

"Artemis, right? Look I'm not sure what gave you the idea it was smart to come here but it wasn't, and I advise you to leave while you still have the chance to." I hear Monty advise him and I swear that man speaking in such a calm tone is scarier than him yelling.

"I came here for what belongs to me that I paid for." He states with an air of arrogance about him, and you can tell he's used to getting his way, but he won't this time.

"Well, you should get your money back nothing here is for sell now last warning back away from my property." Monty says and I swear that man radiates control and power off him. I hear motorcycles coming from both sides of the road stopping in front of the house and I recognize them as Money and his gang.

"You have two options either send her out now while you all are still breathing, or I can step over your dead body to get her but either way I will get what I want." I hear the first shot ring off from Monty's gun only missing Artemis because one of his men takes the bullet for him after pushing him out the way. Artemis has about fifteen guys with him, but Money came with at least twenty by himself before Monty and his brothers join in along with us ladies in the house. I hear more shots ring off and some coming from the back, but we know not to come out unless we have to so as to not distract the men. Bullets start flying into the window but do not penetrate them and I want to kiss them all over again. I peak out the window and notice Artemis and his men retreating into the woods across the street and he looks wounded. I hear the back door bust open, but I don't hear any gun shots, so it has to be one of the guys and then Monty and the others come through the front door. I almost panic when I see blood on Dean's side but I rush to my cabinet in my office and grab my big medical bag and rush into the kitchen where the guys have gone, and my stomach drops when I see Jax on the floor and Meech applying pressure to his side while Chase applies pressure to his leg.

"What the fuck happened?" I scream dropping the med kit next to him pushing Meech out the way pulling up his shirt while throwing Chase a tourniquet for his leg. I roll him once it's on glad that the bullet was a through and through then I get to work patching as well as cleaning him up first then Dean since his turned out to be a graze and everyone else is okay. I have them take him to our bed as I set up an IV bag for him and give him pain pills.

"Thank you, baby." He says trying to give me a kiss and I give one to him through tears.

"You better be ok I can't lose you dammit."

"Don't cry I'm ok baby even better now that you've patched me up. We'll talk about how you learned how to do all this later."

"Fine but I'm going to go check on the others and I will be right back." I give him another quick kiss then head out.

"Mommy." The kids all scream and come running to me.

"I'm ok babies it's not my blood."

"How is Jax?" Monty walks up behind me wrapping his arms around my waist rubbing his thumb over my stomach.

"He's ok both shots were a through and through with no major organs or blood vessels hit as far as I can see. The blood slowed quite a bit after cleaning out his wound." I fill him in leaning my head back on chest taking a deep breath. Pissed at how a happy day just goes to shit cause some asshole doesn't understand the word no.

"Kids everything is ok go to your rooms and chill out I'll be in there in a bit ok." He directs them and they nod their heads then go to their rooms mama Fredericks follows behind them.

"Money and part of his crew are tracking them through the woods the others are around the house cleaning up the bodies. Some of them were wounded so they're taking them to the RV for interrogation."

"Ugghhh ok." I let out a deep breath as he rubs up and down my arms.

"Baby go lay down with Jax. I'll make sure dinner gets finished, and the kids are straight."

"Yea Lil Dove you look exhausted. We will make sure everything is cleaned up outside and inside. Don't worry we got you."

"I'm just sick of this shit why won't they leave me alone." I sigh frustrated beyond reason walking off to hop in the shower.

"Come here woman." Jax commands me but his deep baritone Dom voice of his is not working this time. I am not in the mood.

"Not now Jax I really just want to shower and come cuddle up under you ok." I express taking off my bloody moomoo and he nods his head as I walk into the bathroom getting my hygiene together. I throw on one of my night dresses and hop into bed with Jax after checking his wounds.

"Lil Phoenix I'm ok baby. You did a really good job patching me up and the pain meds were just enough." He tries reassuring me as he wraps his arm around my shoulder pulling me closer and kissing the top of my head.

"I just hate that you actually got shot because of me."

"I'd do it all over again if it means you're still safe."
He says as Dean and the others come in.

"Papi Jax are you ok?" Mara asks rushing to his side.

"Yes, baby I'm good. I'm not even in pain thanks to mommy baby girl." He rubs his thumb over her cheek.

"OK Papi well dinner will be done in a few minutes. We all finished our homework and helped clean up." Mariah says getting in bed with us on my side and I can tell she's worried about hurting Jax. He takes his hand that's on my shoulder and rubs her cheek. I'm sure she's having a flash back of her mother and I know I'm going to have to call her therapist tomorrow. The kids stay in for a few more minutes before kissing us both and heading to eat dinner. The guys stay behind after letting their mom get some time with him.

"So, what's the word?" He asks as soon as she's gone.

"Unfortunately, he got away, but they know for sure he's wounded at least twice. Only a few of his men were able to get away with him and the ones still alive are held up at the RV being questioned on where he'd go." Meech gives us the run down standing next to the door. I can tell he's worried about Jax but the man has venegeance in his eyes and that worries me a little.

"We did learn that Calder has cut him off and that seemed to set him off into desperation since he doesn't have his protection anymore." Dean adds in sitting at the foot of the bed as Monty comes around to lay next to me and I grab his hand wrapping it around my waist needing him close too.

"Money has instructed six of his men to stick around they will be alternating in the RV with your regular guards to eat and rest up through the night."

"Can we just buy a bunch of RVs and stay on the compound?" I say out of nowhere feeling like they've ruined my safety home feeling at this point.

"I know why you're saying that Lil Dove but don't let them ruin your first home. I'll order your sage from your favorite place, and you can do your prayer over the home again." Dean says squeezing my foot trying to reassure me and I nod my head.

"Alright y'all get out they need to eat and rest." Bree demands coming in the room with Kelia carrying trays of food that they sit in front of Jax and I as we both sit up. Monty goes to slide out the bed and I grab his hand.

"You want me to stay Ife mi?" I just nod my head leaning my head on his shoulder as he lays back down in the bed with us.

"Arakunrin how are you feeling really? I just called him brother by the way." Monty ask Jax and explaining his native language to me which I love, it sounds so sexy when they speak. They have been teaching the kids and talking about doing a test for us to see what tribe we maybe from.

"Honestly, I'm pissed I could take that muthafucka head off but I'm sure you're talking about me being shot and I really am fine Lil Phoenix did an excellent job patching me up. Between her thoroughly cleaning out my wounds, stitching them up, combined with the pain meds and IV right away saved me." He says looking down at me smiling and kissing the top of my head wincing from the pain.

"Yea she really did a great job with that med kit bag she has. Where did you learn to do all that anyway babe?" He asks me raising his left eyebrow at me in an inquisitive look.

"I was with my best friend when she was murdered, and the ambulance took forever to get to her and I punished myself for a while that I didn't know how to help her till, they got there so I took EMT classes which came in handy when I needed to patch myself up. I started buying medical supplies and leaving full size as well as mini ones throughout our homes just in case something happens." I explain the last part low filling my mouth with my perfectly grilled steak.

"As if I didn't think I could love you anymore but saving Jax the way you did that shit solidified us even further baby." Monty expresses turning my head towards him by my chin then kissing my lips with those juicy soft skin toned lips I love so much. I love how he never ceases to let me know how much he loves me. We sit there in silence for a while Jax and I eating with me feeding Monty occasionally as we watch a movie. The kids come to say good night as Kenya comes to get our food trays before they all head out.

"Come on Jax you need to shower before I change your bandages." I stand from the bed coming to his side unhooking his IV holding out my hand to help his big ass up from the bed. Monty's out checking on the guards and securing the house before we all go to bed with Dean as he decided to stay with Kelia on the pull-out bed.

"I got it baby I'm not leaning on you."

"Fine don't move I have crutches in my closet that adjust and don't ask." I tell him as I go to grab the crutches and hand them to him. We get them adjusted to a better height for him and head to the bathroom. I get undressed with him after getting the shower at a good temperature making him sit on the shower seat as I bath him.

"You know how fucking sexy it is watching you take care of me right now Lil Phoenix." He says grabbing me by the waist bringing me to his lap after washing him off with the shower head.

"Babe don't start we can't buss your stitches." I try to push back but he lifts me sitting me on his unwounded leg.

"Fuck these stitches wrap your legs around me and sit on your dick Meira." He grabs my leg pulling up then around him then grabbing the other placing it around his waist all while turning me towards him, thank God for our workouts lately and my stretches.

"Ba -." I start to say as he pulls my face towards him pressing our lips together for a soul shaking kiss that has tingles going down to my core.

"OK… ok babe but if I feel like you doing too much, I'm stopping do you understand I'm in control?" I say grabbing him by his thick neck looking into his eyes and he nods his head yes as he bites his bottom lip. I lift up positioning my entrance over his dick slowly sliding down as he slouches down on the shower bench, and I wind my hips with him seated to the hilt.

"Shit Lil Phoenix just like that." He moans out as I bounce using my hands on his chest to steady myself. He grabs my waist on both sides guiding me up and down. I grab as much of his neck as my small hands allow and squeeze then lean forward kissing him while I rock back and forth hitting that back wall of my pussy. I start gushing and spasming around his thick long length.

"Fuck Jax don't ever scare me like that again fuck I can't lose you." I moan out feeling myself cum again. He smacks me on the ass, and I start milking his dick bouncing harder but careful to watch his stitches.

"I'm not going anywhere baby shit you fucking me so good." He moans in my ear moving down my shoulder biting hard and I scream out in pleasure and a bit of pain since this fool has some sharp ass fangs.

"Cum for me Jax." I say in that low sweet but demanding voice he loves.

"Fucckk Lil Phoenixxxxx." He growls out making another wave of pleasure course through my body. I lay my head on his shoulder as we both try to catch our breath.

"Hmm now I have to clean you up again." I lick his neck then stand on my wobbly legs grabbing the rag to clean off his cum covered dick. I clean myself up, we handle our hygiene then head to bed after I apply his new bandages. Give him a proper dose of the pain meds I have on hand he slowly drifts off to sleep as I lay my head on his chest. Before I doze off the door opens with Monty entering the room looking so tired. I ease out of Jax's arms going to the bathroom to run him a bath as he undresses in the closet. He comes in a few minutes later smiling at me bent over the tub as I look at him over my shoulder.

"Ife mi what are you doing you should be in bed?"

"I will once I get you cleaned up. Now get in." I demand turning in his arms that are wrapped around my waist to give him a quick kiss. He gets in with no arguments taking a deep breath to inhale the lavender and jasmine scented bubbles I put in the tub along with the Epsom salt I added to relax his muscles. I sit on the stool outside the tub behind him grabbing one of the rags then his favorite soap I make that's scented with sandalwood and vanilla.

"Babe please lay back and relax." I say kissing his shoulder as I lean over to dip the rag wrapped around the soap in the water then rubbing them together.

"I'm trying baby shit is just so crazy. That fuck nigga really thought he could come here, and we'd just hand you over. Then his pussy ass boys just gave him up I didn't even get to have any fun with them first." He lets out a sigh as I wash his neck and chest. Looking at his huge frame in our tub I'm so glad they went with the large garden size tub when thy fixed the place. I sit the rag down for a moment to massage his tight shoulders using my hands and elbows to get some of the kinks out.

"So apparently this fool bought land over in Birmingham for the two of you to live on for a bit before taking you back to California. Shit baby that feels amazing." He moans out as I hit a particularly tight knot under his shoulder blade. I rinse his upper half off then go to grab his long loc's bonnet with some grease then taking his loc's out of the bun he had them in and massaged the grease into his scalp.

"Hmm baby that feels so damn good. Baby I will never let him take you from me I promise." He moans out.

"I know you won't Montavius now let's stop talking about this I need you to relax so you can think clearly please." I beg him still massaging his scalp and he leans further back into me. I put his bonnet on and continue to wash him then start to let the water out using the tub handle to rinse all the soap off and handing him his towel.

"Ife mi I needed that so damn bad I didn't even realize it." He grabs me by the waist kissing me on the shoulder from behind.

"Well, that's why you have me." I lean my head back to look up at him and smooch for a kiss.

"I do need one more thing from you Ife mi."

"Anything baby."

"Bend yo ass over and put ya right leg up on the counter Ife mi." He instructs me dropping his towel as I do as he request.

"So damn smart, sexy and strong. I love you so much La'Meira." He leans over to speak into my ear as he rubs his dick against my slick lips.

"Mhmm." I moan as he slides into me slowly and feeling the stretch, I feel every time he enters his home.

"Fuck baby you're always so wet and ready for me and you mold around me like you were designed for me like I know you are." He moans giving me slow deep strokes as he keeps talking right at my ear and I can't help but throw it back at him.

"That's my good girl throw that ass back." He moans in my ear making me even wetter than I was before. He stands up pulling my head back by my hair then pulling out to the tip slamming into me to the hilt. He reaches under me to rub on my clit as he pulls out to the head and slams into me again causing me to squirt all over his hand.

"Fuck baby you're so responsive. Do it again baby." He commands pressing harder on my clit as he rubs fucking me with fast long strokes as I arch my back further and he sinks deeper. I give him exactly what he's looking for as I cream all over his dick squirting at the same time.

"Shit Ife mi you about to make me cum." He growls and my walls clinch around his hard thick length. He keeps stroking me deep and then I feel his hot cum shoot into me causing me to cum again.

"Mhmm fuck Monttyyy." I moan. He strokes me through our orgasm a few more times than wraps his arms around my chest lifting me up. He kisses my shoulder, neck, cheek, then tilts my head back planting his warm soft juicy lips on mines.

"Let's get in bed. This nigga better be glad he my brother and this bed so damn big otherwise he'd be on the couch." He states taking a warm rag cleaning me and then himself.

Chapter Thirty-Four

Montavius Fredericks

It's been a few days since that piece of shit decided it was a good idea to try and take my wife from me. There have been spotting's since he was shot. I just came home from the office since it's still some work to do on the building plus I'm still looking for a few more employees before offering our services.

"Babe. What are all of you doing here? Something happen?" I ask looking at each of them noticing Jax and Meira weren't in here but then they come out of the room.

"Hi babe." She greets walking over to me and I naturally wrap my arms around her waist then lean down for a kiss which she eagerly complies.

"So, what's going on Ife mi?" I question sitting at the island grabbing her into my arms with my front against her back.

"Umm I want you guys to hear me out and please... please don't jump to conclusions."

"Lil Dove you better spit it out cause now I know something is up."

"Fine I think the only way to end this bullshit once and for all is to let him have me." I damn near throw her across the room when I jump up out my seat.

"You're out of your fuckin mind La'Meira. There is no way in hell I'm giving you to that sick son of a bitch."

"I'm with Monty what the fuck were you even thinking saying some shit like that." Jax says next to me as she stands in front of us now.

"Don't you take the damn tone with me Montavius Ekon Fredericks." She says poking me in my chest and I sit down trying to calm myself. I notice Kelia trying to hold Dean back.

"If you all would shut up and chill and let me, explain." She says looking at all of us pissed off and I take a deep breath trying to calm myself.

"Ok Ife mi we're all listening."

"When I said let him take me, I didn't mean without all of you close by. You still have some of his men. I think if y'all have them call him and tell him they escaped with me he will gladly give his location or at least somewhere he's willing to meet up to take me. I know that can track me the entire way then when we're wherever he has this land at y'all swoop in." She rushes to tell us while we're still listening. I share a look with my brothers and know they won't let me talk myself outta this because in all honesty it's a great plan to flush him out.

"Look." I start to say but Meech interrupts me.

"Big bru I know you don't want to lose her, and I'll make sure of it, but she is making sense. It's time to end this shit wit this dumb ass."

"Fuck as much as I don't want to admit it, they're both making sense and it's not a half bad plan." Dean says and Kelia finally moves so he can come over to Meira to wrap her up in a hug.

"Well before I was so rudely interrupted, which I'm getting real sick of y'all doing, I was going to say as much as I hate to say it the plan does make sense." I say rubbing my hands through my beard.

"Bottom line he is obsessed with Meira and won't miss a chance at getting her finally. So, let's come up with a more detailed plan because there is no chance in hell he gets her for real." Jax chimes in standing up reaching for Meira and she goes to him falling into his arms as he kisses the top of her head. We spend the next few hours going over a plan and decide to put it in motion later tonight. Once the kids get home, we spend some time with them and let them know we may be gone for a day or two to finally end this for the last time. Once they are in bed and all the women including my mother are secure at the house with guards, we all leave heading towards the RV.

"Aight ya piece of shits it's time to serve a purpose." I say kicking them awake as they're tied up on the floor and they mumble through the duct tape. I lean down to rip it off.

"We told you crazy bastards all we know let us go or kill us already!" One the men named Jared shouts, and I kick his ass in his wounded leg making him scream out in pain.

"Fuck ok what do you want now."

"We want you to reach out to your boss and tell him that you were able to get the girl and need to meet up or bring her to him."

"How do you suggest we do that?" He asks and I nod for Dean to untie them both taking a burner from his pocket handing it to him.

"Now don't think you're slick we will have eyes and ears on you the whole time. There is a car outside waiting for you. You are going to drive a mile up the road and call him on speaker. Betray us and I'll show you there is a fate worse than death." I tell them squatting on the floor in front of him. We get them up and outside in the car.

"Ife mi if only you grasped how hard this is for me well us." I say looking at Jax standing next to me as I put the zip ties loosely around her wrist. That man refused to sit this one out.

"I can feel it and you know why I'm not scared this time?" She asks me looking at us both and I shake my head.

"It's because I know you both will move heaven and hell to find me not to mention Dean along with you. So don't worry I trust you and you." She says giving each of us a kiss. She sits in the backseat of the car, and we put the zip ties around her ankles then the tape across her mouth. Watching her scoot across the backseat to lay down like she is knocked out has this sickening feeling in the pit of my stomach as I close the door. I am trying to remember what my mother taught me but everything in me is screaming to snatch her out of this car, grab my kids, and charter our jet to a secluded island till this mess is dealt with.

"Remember what I told you. I'd love to have new live wax figures in my museum." I reiterate leaning in the window to look him in the eye as he realizes what I mean then shock and fear appears. I stand hitting the roof of the car signaling for them to pull off. I watch as they drive down the road while my brothers and Money's men stand to my sides and behind me.

"We got her bru." Chase says hitting my shoulder. I look down at my ops watch as the red dot symbolizing my wife goes down the road. Dean pulls out his tablet as the bug in the car plays them making the call.

"Mr. Troy, we have your girl. We were able to get free and they were dumb enough to let her come in alone to give us food. You still want her, right?"

"Don't play with me Jared of course I want her, but I need proof you actually have her and are alone." The other must record a video of the inside of the car and Meira laying in the backseat.

"Damn I can't believe I'll finally have my woman. Look I'm sending you my address hurry and get your asses here with her unharmed. Keep your fucking hands to yourself."

"Yes sir." They both say ending the call and when they get the text we get it too. Everyone heads to their respective cars and bikes heading out.

"Jax are you sure you're good? You were literally shot three days ago."

"I promise I'm good now let's go make sure our woman comes back home." He says putting his helmet then gloves on and we bump fists together then all take off. We decide to split up into groups of four coming in at different directions of the property. It was a four and a half hour drive there. We all parked in the woods surrounding the property on all four sides. Jax, Dean, Chase, and I hopped off our bikes as some of Money men walk up from where they parked their cars.

"Aight everyone's in place I'm sending up the drone." Dean steps out to find a patch of area where the tree line is open above us.

"Ok there is the car they are getting out now. This place seems to be well secured. I see at least five or six guards patrolling the front and west side of the property with two standing at the door." Dean sums up what we all are looking at on the tablet as the drone continues over the property quietly. We see two more guards in the back side and east. The property must be at least two acres of cleared land. I tap my earpiece we all have in to talk to Meech, Marsh, and Money.

"Aight I think it's best to hit simultaneously from all sides, silencers on, and Jax out here in the tree line with his sniper rifle." I direct everyone looking at him knowing he's pissed he won't be inside, but I know he knows it's best to put his sniper skills to use as we clear this much land.

"I'll take that but the moment the perimeter is clear I'm coming in."

"That's fine with me."

"Fuck we got company." Dean informs us as we all go to see what's going on and we hear two trucks pull up.

"Wait isn't that Calder? I thought he disowned this muthafucka." Chase says through gritted teeth.

"Doesn't change a thing. I'll get to have some fun tonight after all." We all agree to still move in. Jax grabs his climbing equipment and rifle heading up the largest tree. You would never think a man as large as him could move as quickly or quiet. Once he's fully in position I let the others know and we move as one guns raised even with Money's men. We take out the six in front as the others take out their targets and we converge on the large clearly renovated farmhouse.

"Ten stay outside surrounding the property and the rest enter quietly." I instruct through my earpiece. I already hacked the security system, so the cameras are on a loop and the doors all unlocked. We entered a large open space front to back and hear arguing off to the left where we can see light coming from a room door. I signal for the others to spread out and search the house as Jax joins us to my right as usual.

"So, you finally got what you wanted but you're still cut off Art. You've cost me a lot of money plus the FEDS are sniffing around my businesses now."

"That's fine I have the only woman I'll need now." I hear Artemis declare as I look through a crack in the door and he signals for one of his men to go do something. He walks into an adjourning room and comes back with a fighting Meira.

"Get your filthy fuckin hands off me."

"Now... now my future wife shall not have such a foul mouth." He says rubbing his hand over her cheek and she turns her head away.

"I will never be your wife ya pathetic waste of skin." She spits getting him riled up and he slaps her snapping her head to the left. It took everything in me to not rush in I even had to hold Jax back cause even though he couldn't see everyone could hear that slap.

"You are mines, and you will learn to love or tolerate doesn't matter to me either way. You will find I am very good at taming even the strongest willed women."

"Now Calder for the reason you're hear. I will handle your FBI problem the best I can and here's a gift for your troubles." Another door opens from the opposite side and out walks a guard with a drugged up Myra.

"Fuck he has Myra." I whisper to everyone. That explains why we haven't seen her in a while or the kids. I hear Meech come through my earpiece that they found the kids upstairs tied up. I just pray he didn't touch those kids. It also makes even more sense as to how he found Meira in the first place now.

"Hmm she's pretty, not as thick as this one but I know she will go for a good amount of money. Well maybe you have made up for your bullshit after all."

"She has three young girls and a boy upstairs I have them as well if you want them."

"You sick son of bitch if you touch a hair on those kids heads, I'll cut your ass into pieces and make you watch." Meira screams fighting the guard, but her hands are tied. I see Meech take the kids out the back door with the others and I know it's time to enter before they hurt my babies.

"You won't be making my wife yours ever you sorry sack of shit." I announce entering with my brothers right behind me taking out the four guards inside. Meira falls to the ground out of the way, and I see her grab a blade from her shoe to cut her restraints. I can't help but smile cause that's my girl.

"What the fuck how did you even get in here?" Artemis shouts looking around for a weapon probably but the problem with arrogant men is they get too damn comfortable.

"Fuck I should've known your dumb ass wouldn't be smart about getting her ass."

"Don't fuckin move." I point my gun at Calder's head as Meira gets up running to Jax and I. We both pull her between us then push her behind us.

"All this shit could've been avoided had you left MY wife the fuck alone." I say shooting Artemis in the left knee, and he falls over screaming in pain.

"You son of a bitch my father will have your heads for this, and she is MINNNESSS." He screams still holding his knee groaning in pain.

"And you. We were just going to let the FEDS handle your wafer cookie ass but the most high saw it fit to deliver you to us here." Jax states walking up on Calder hitting him across the head with the butt of his gun and he drops like a sack of potatoes to the floor. I inform through the earpiece to bring all vehicles around and we are burning this shit down in five minutes.

"Well Artemis I guess we will find out soon enough just how much daddy loves you." I kneel next to him then knock him out with my gun next.

"Y'all do realize I have things to do that for you right?" Meech inquires looking at Jax and I like we're tripping.

"Yup but that was more fun besides, they will probably still need it. Grab all electronics and check the safe." Jax orders as he goes back to check on Meira as do I.

"I am ok guys the slap was the only time he touched me I promise. I can't believe Myra told them where I was my own damn cousin." She looks around us at one of the guys carrying Myra out the door with disbelief and disgust in her eyes.

"Well Lil Phoenix it looks like they have her pretty drugged up and they had the kids upstairs I doubt she had much choice."

"No y'all aren't hearing me she gave them my location willingly the drugging didn't happen till afterwards when she realized it was only me, he wanted and was sending her as well as the kids with Calder. The dumb bitch ran into him I'm sure not by accident weeks ago."

"You gotta be fuckin kidding me. Ok we will deal with this shit later this place is about to go up in flames in a couple minutes." I declare bending down to pick her up bridal style then walking out the house to our bikes. By the time we reach them the house is going up in flames. Giving Meira her navy-blue helmet that says Mrs. Fredericks on the back and hoping on the bike myself I tell everyone to be safe and meet them back at the RV then slide my helmet on and pull off. The four-and-a-half-hour drive back was peaceful having my wife back where she belongs.

"That was such a peaceful ride babe." She says as we park my bike in the garage.

"Yea we need to do that more often Ife mi." I grab her in my arms leaning down to connect our lips in a slow heated kiss.

"Mhmm babe you're going to get something started in this garage with all these men around." She moans as I deepen our kiss picking her up and placing her back on the bike.

"Fuck them niggas they better look elsewhere."

"Hey Monty, we have a problem. Calder got away. He woke up and somehow got the trunk open then bailed off into the damn woods. They are out looking for him but he's a damn governor this shit can go bad." Chase rushes to fill us in as he's walking up to us and I get an instant headache.

"Why the fuck wasn't he drugged like Artemis ass and who the fuck was he riding with?" I request turning from my wife to look my brother in the eye because he knows how we operate.

"He was riding with one of Money's group of men and they drove off with him before Meech had the chance to since we had Artemis on the other side of the house with the kids."

"Where's Money?" I ask as I help Meira off the bike still holding her hand as we walk behind Chase leading us to Money.

"So just to be clear Money your men were dumb enough to let a sitting governor escape them." I ask for clarification purposes with a deadpan look on my face.

"Look they will find him they noticed almost right away that he was gone and started tracking him and if they don't, they know it's on them if he goes to the authorities only help, they will get is bail if they get it." He says coolly.

"Aight this shit better not come back to us that was y'all fuck up. Why the hell didn't they wait for Meech to do what he did to Artemis?" I inquire tilting my head to the right.

"I really can't tell you that was some real dumb shit and they should know better by now. These young niggas give me headaches I fucking swear." He groans rubbing the sides of his head and it clicks these some young ass dumb niggas he had on a damn governor.

"I'm not sure what is dumber you entrusting some young ass niggas on such an important person or them not tying this nigga up or anything in the damn trunk not even sedated." Jax adds looking like he wants to knock Money's head off and I chuckle.

"Money can you even trust these fools? How do we know he just got out and not they let him convince them to let him go?" I ask as Meech, and the rest join us.

"Look I wasn't in the car with them and being honest they've only been with me a little over six months but bottom line they will be dealt with accordingly my right hand and a few I know I can trust are headed back to check and see what's what."

"Aight bet. Meech let's go wake that nigga up and then we need to deal with Myra's bitch ass." I let out a groan running my hand through my beard cause just when I thought we were all solid here comes this bitch.

"Aww shit what did she do now?" We all head to the back of the garage which is bigger than the RV itself. It houses all our bikes and cars along with a newly built room for Meech and his damn projects.

"That bitch is who gave me up to Artemis and not because she was drugged, she was fucking him and thought he was going to be her rich savior or some shit. They bumped into each other in Dothan. She caught on to what he was really doing when he came back shot and she heard him shouting at one of his guards that they better go back and get his wife." She fills us in on what she discovered while there which aided in elevating my anger.

"This stupid bitch. I've seen jealousy do some fucked up shit but sell out ya own flesh and blood that helps ya dumb ass to a nigga you think either about to kill or worse that's fucked up on a whole other level." Meech states talking to himself more than us as he's probably reliving his brush with betraysl back in college.

"I'm sorry Meira you don't deserve this shit." He reassures her stopping to give her a hug and I flinch a bit. This fool gives me the side eye then shakes his head at me. I'm sure if Meira noticed I'll be apologizing for that shit later.

Meech sticks a needle into Artemis pushing in some clear substance.

"Give him a few minutes to wake up. So, what are you thinking about doing with Myra?" We all look at her to see what she wants to cause no matter what we got her.

"Honestly, I don't know. I've given her chance after chance. She literally has beef with me for nothing. Like my life has been one fucked up situation after another. She had the perfect fucking husband she didn't have to deal with him beating her ass because she got pregnant from his dumb ass. Her father didn't abandon her for a woman who beat on her for no damn reason but just cause she could, she didn't have to hold her best fucking friend as she bled to death cause some Lil dick prick couldn't take no for answer. Was she raped left for fuckin dead at thirteen no she's had every fucking thing, but I never acted jealous or resented her. Ahhhhhh." She screams out and I just grab her in my arms kissing the top of her head as my brother's surround us placing their hands on both our shoulders while she cries and screams in my arms. I can't believe the fucked-up shit she's dealt with, and her cousin acts as if she's done something to her. I understand now why she killed the twin's father but I wish he was alive so I could kill him myself but now It's going to take a lot to not kill that bitch myself. We hear Artemis stirring awake and before I can say or do anything she snatches my serrated hunting knife from my side then slices Artemis throat from ear to ear and blood sprays everywhere.

"I'm sick of this shit bring that stupid bitch in here let's get this over with this baby is giving me heartburn."

"Babe, we can handle her let me take you back to the house to rest, please." Jax pleads grabbing her bloody hands pulling her towards him to look him in the eyes.

"Jax." She starts but both Dean and I interrupt but I let him try to talk her down.

"Lil Dove please go back to the house with Jax we will deal with Myra. You don't need her blood on your hands or conscience anyway with the baby." He pleads with her.

"Fine but make it hurt." She demands taking a deep breath holding Jax's hand and smooching her lips for me to kiss her and I do blood on her face and all.

"I'll be home in a bit Ife me. Send Bree over here she will enjoy this for you."

"Hey, take her in my room there are some clothes in the bottom drawer for her to change into they maybe baggy, but she won't scare the shit outta the kids with all the blood." Meech instructs and I finally compute what that would've been like for the kids thinking it was hers.

"Shit quick thinking Meech I wasn't even thinking about that shit."

"Bru you are thinking about enough shit with what Meira just spilled out. You can tell she's had some shit go on in her life but that shit and now her own cousin crossing her like this and she's pregnant. Dat bitch is foul man." He says as I watch her be carried out in Jax's arms. I know she's emotionally being taken care of while I handle this shit for her physically.

"Damn your wife is lethal with a blade Monty." Money looks at Artemis open neck admiring her work, and I smile with pride.

"She's lethal with a lot of shit. Don't let her shortness or thickness fool you that woman knows about twenty ways to kill you with no weapon."

"Damnnnn she doesn't have a twin or sister that's not a backstabbing bitch like her cousin?"

"Nope only girl and her only friends are their women. She's not all that friendly and we all can see why but she is the best when she allows you close to her."

"And sis can cook like a muthafucka." Meech loves to add that in with his greedy ass rubbing his stomach and I laugh because he's not lying. My woman puts her heart and soul in her food.

"Man, y'all don't need another person in y'all poly relationship shit. Trying to find a woman like that is hard as hell." Before I can think straight my hand is around his throat and I have him pinned to the wall behind him.

"Shit Monty snap outta it he was just joking. Damn you strong as fuck. Help here." Meech ask trying to pry my hand from Money's neck.

"AH fuck fine Montavius let that boy go before I go get La'Meira." Dean threatens me and I immediately snap out of it.

"My bad Money."

"That's the one and only time you get to do that without me fucking you up Montavius." Money groans rubbing his throat.

"Nigga look you were talking reckless don't threaten my brother." Dean steps up in Money's face as he stands up fully.

"Fine I am sorry about that for real. I did get a lil outta pocket. I probably would've put my hands on anybody that sounded like he was fantasizing about my wife too." He apologizes rubbing his hand down his face partly not wanting beef with us and the other I can tell he genuinely gets it.

Chapter Thirty-Five

Dean Fredericks

If this dumb ass nigga doesn't stop talking about my Lil Dove like he wants her, I'm going to put a bullet in between eyes. Marsh has put Artemis to the side as Chase comes in with Myra and sits her in a chair that has more plastic under it in the same spot Artemis was just hung over and cuffs her to the chair. He gives her something to flush the drugs out her system but she's still a little out of it but that's fine we're still waiting on Bree who I'm sure is fussing over our pregnant girl before she comes.

"Dean you can stop looking at me like you want to kill me. I said I was good I'll go find my own country girl. I'm not going to try and dip into y'all tight family."

"Ok." I say looking at him with a blank look on my face not giving off the fact that I'm still watching his ass.

"Why am I tied to a chair? What the fuck is going on?" Myra shouts in a panic as she is fully coming aware of her surroundings and rocking in the chair side to side trying to release herself.

"Ah Myra you're finally fully with us?" I look over at her just as Bree comes in the garage door then Meech's back room.

"Well, well... well the bitch who thought it was a smart idea to hurt my best fuckin friend by giving her up to some sick pervert because she has insecurities no one caused but herself." Bree slaps the piss out of her after she finishes her rant.

"That bitch deserved it she always gets everything and what do I get fuckin scraps. She walks around like she misses perfect. Oh, she's so noble cause she's took in her dead best friend's baby and takes care of her mom boo fuck hoo." Before any of us can move Bree has punched her twice in the face then pulls a blade out stabbing her in the thigh purposely missing any major arteries and I chuckle.

"Listen you bottom feeding fish mouth seven eleven cum bucket don't you dare speak bad about a woman you couldn't hold a candle to, and you know one of the main reasons she is better than you? It's simple instead of her being jealous or spiteful of you having a better husband while she had one that beat on her she left his ass while you cheated on yours. Now this can be quick, or you can keep talking shit and I'll make it slow, which do you prefer?" She provides her with a choice I wouldn't have and Marsh just simply goes to stand next to her with his hand on her shoulder.

"Do what? What are you going to do to me?" Myra looks at us still confused for some odd reason.

"Kill you of course. Did you think you would set my Ife mi my wife to be taken from me and our family and there not be any consequences." Monty says stepping up behind Bree.

"I'm her cousin she'd never kill me or let you do it either. Just let me the fuck go and maybe I won't tell her of this betrayal and get me to a doctor." She shouts wiggling in her seat. It's funny she thinks she's getting out of this.

"Oh, you pathetic bitch who do think said it was time for you to go. You have crossed her too many times at this point so it's over for you." I inform her and watch as reality sets in.

"What about my kids they will hate her forever for taking me from them and I know how much she likes to play savior to them." I laugh at her statement and pull the papers in my back pocket out.

"Those are my kids now and they will be perfectly fine. I even have therapy set up for them already to help get over you." I throw the copy of adoption paperwork at her and laugh.

"What the hell you can't do that. They still have a father. You people are crazy."

"Yea you should've thought about that before you crossed my wife, ya simple minded bitch and regarding their father he's a non-factor did you forget he signed over rights once he found out three of them weren't his anyways."

Monty states calmly getting tired of talking with her ass just as I am.

"How did?"

"Look that's enough Bree can you hurry this along just a bit I wanna get back to Meira." Monty instructs her getting separation anxiety clearly and I just chuckle because I know the feeling.

"Not a problem Monty bear." She confirms taking her blade and slowly slicing Myra's throat so deep she hits the bone then blood sprays everywhere and spills to the floor.

"I swear you're the younger version of my wife Bree." Monty laughs and I do too.

"She killed Artemis the same way." I add as she looks at him curiously then smiles looking back at a now dead Myra with pride filling her eyes.

"You two and ya blades." Meech adds shaking his head walking towards the side of the chair uncuffing her as Chase goes to lift her out of the chair dropping her onto the plastic underneath. I move the chair out the way as they roll her up.

"Sooo shall I tell Meira you're using her favorite toy again I might add?" Monty asks Chase and Marsh. They have gotten just as attached to her woodchipper as she is.

"I mean the damn thing is so efficient." Chase states.

"And let's be real it is kinda cool to see the human body turned into tiny shreds like that." Marsh smiles and shakes his head like he's picturing it as we speak.

"Ya actually right. No more extra arm day." I tell them and we all laugh as they load Myra and Artemis into the back of Monty's pickup truck.

"Meech, you going with them?" Monty asks him and I know why. Little brother has been disappearing a lot lately at night and I'm sure I know why but we will wait till he wants to tell us.

"No, I'm going to clean up here then I have somewhere to be."

"I'll go with them I want to check out this woodchipper. I may need to get me one." Money volunteers leaning on the truck and we all nod our heads walking off to our women with one in tow who thankfully cleaned the blood off her face and hands at least. I go to peak in on Meira and she's fast asleep in Jax's arms who is watching us at the door. We nod our heads at each other as Monty walks in leaning over the bed to kiss Meira on the cheek then heads to the bathroom. I nod and smile at them both then I head out thankful our family is good and now, I can tell my baby we got our kids which means it's time to get married.

Chapter Thirty-Six

Jax Fredericks

It's been three months since we finally got rid of Artemis and had to end Myra at the same time. It turned out not to be so hard of a transition for her kids who apparently were sick of her shit, they have their moments where they miss her, but they love being with Dean and Kelia. They both seem to be happy to have a house full of kids especially Kelia who has turned into a stay-at-home mom happily. Everyone's businesses are fully up and running. Bree handles the day to day of the club/sex education school here and I go in a few days out the week. Monty has gone back to traveling a few times a month meeting with clients and visiting the KC location. Meira had to make him see the logic in doing it now rather than when she gets closer to her due date. We found out at her first doctor's appointment she was six weeks by the time of the appointment so now she's four and a half months and we will be finding out what we're having next week. All of us have been pitching in trying to get the main house in the compound done quicker as we all have backgrounds in a trade because of Monty. I am the electrician and carpenter, Monty is the HVAC, Dean is the plumber and carpenter as well, Chase is an architect, Meech is an electrician as well, while Marsh is building construction. The home outside walls are made from cinder block with extra deep footings since apparently, they get the occasional tornadoes. We finally have all the outer walls, windows, and doors in and roof on. Thanks to some bribing with free lessons at the club along with a few construction favors we were able to get permits pushed through quickly plus all the pre-ordering we did had things sitting in the huge, air-conditioned warehouse on the property ready and waiting. Today I'm heading there to help Dean and Chase with putting up the framework with my baby in tow.

"You sure you have enough food Lil Phoenix?" I check with her reaching over to rub her baby bump which has become one of my favorite things to do lately.

"Yes babe. Bree and Kenya came over last night like I couldn't cook for my damn self and made some fried chicken wings, mac and cheese and collard greens with some cornbread, so I brought all that plus my yogurt and chips. If anything, I'll ride into town to grab something else, and you made us a big breakfast that we just ate." She says rubbing my hand as we drive down the asphalt driveway that turns into a paved driveway.

"Don't be like that babe they're just trying to make your pregnancy as comfortable as possible as you would do for them. We are going to be out here for a while putting up walls for the first floor then hopefully make it to stairs for the second." I fill her in as we park next to everybody else's trucks.

"I know Lovie it's just an adjustment having so many people in my life now that are there to really help. I can't wait to see all the walls put up though, everything is just coming together so nicely and each of you having a hand in making our home is really sweet." She says giving me a quick peck as I help her out my truck. She walks over to the golf cart we use to ride around the property, and I head into the house.

"What's up awon arakunrin?" I greet dapping up my brothers.

"So, the paperwork is all done for tomorrow." Dean lets me know and I smile.

"Perfect lets get to work so I can get my pregnant woman out that stuffy warehouse."

"I haven't been over in a couple days, how is Lil Dove doing?"

"Tired of being waited on apparently." I inform him with a chuckle.

"Sounds about right." He laughs a bit as well then, we get to work putting up four thousand square feet of internal walls the extra thousand square feet per floor a wedding gift but thankfully it's ten of us inside putting them up and four outside cutting the necessary wood. Chase has grown the team here quickly and back in KC to keep up with all the projects he has in motion. We work mostly through lunch but of course my Lil Phoenix was not having it and came over with lunch making us all sit down for at least fifteen minutes to eat. I give her a kiss as she hops back on the golf cart to head back to the warehouse and before I can start work again my phone rings of course its Monty.

"Yes arakunrin?" I answer.

"Where's the wife? I called her phone, and she didn't answer."

"We just had lunch with the crew. She left her phone on the warehouse bench. Apparently, pregnancy brain is real." I chuckle.

"Trust I've noticed. I've been having Bree and Kelia make her salmon and any leafy green she will keep down when I'm not home. That damn heartburn has kicked in overdrive."

"Tell me about it. I figured out though the regular milk doesn't work but the lactose milk works wonders." I lean on the front door frame.

"Damn that's perfect. I was getting worried for a minute. Those babies must have a lot of hair according to mom which I can see with that thick pretty hair she has hell we all have a lot of hair."

"Very true I had to help her wash and put all that hair in a ponytail last night felt like a damn arm day to blow it out."

"That's about right." He laughs and I do too.

"Well let me get back to putting your walls up big bro."

"Bet see ya tomorrow." He says ending the call. We worked for a few hours then Marsh as well as Meech showed up to continue the work as the construction workers head home as it is well after nine p.m. The ladies came about an hour ago to grab Meira even though she didn't want to leave yet.

"Aight I think we got as much work done here that we can tonight the team will be back in the morning to finish this first floor off and start on the second." Chase basically gives us stop orders putting the nail gun on the worktable taking off his work gloves and belt.

"Yea you're right I need get home and check on Kelia anyways, she hasn't been feeling good." Dean states doing the same. We all either put our tools on the table or in our trucks after heading out making sure everything is locked up.

"Lil Phoenix my babies." I say walking in the house to see her and the kids snuggled up in one of her huge fluffy blankets with popcorn between them on the couch watching a movie like they do every Friday. I dap up my boy kissing my girls on the cheeks and kissing her on the forehead.

"Papi we aren't babies ya know." Mara says smiling up at me.

"Y'all will always be my babies. What are y'all watching anyways?" I ask rubbing the top of her head.

"Some action movie Meir found on Netflix. It's not that far in you going to come watch it with us?"

"Yea let me shower real quick princess."

"I'll go warm up your plate. Kenya made smothered pork chops, white rice, and string beans with bacon and onions." Meira says slowly standing up grabbing that round belly of hers with one hand and the other on her back as my stomach growls at the thought of that dinner. One of the many talents of our women is they can throw down in the kitchen. I rub her back as she walks in front of me towards the kitchen.

"You feeling OK baby?" I ask rubbing circles on her lower back then leaning down to kiss her exposed shoulder.

"Yes, I'm fine I just feel big as a damn house already." According to her she wasn't even this big with the twins at almost five months. I think she is pregnant with twins, but they are heavier and plus like she said she's nowhere near as stressed as she was the last time.

"You're probably carrying two babies again and you look good as hell to me, but I understand where you're coming from. We can go to that pregnancy workout class you found if that will help you feel better." I assure her kissing her shoulder again and she smiles nodding her head yes. I tell her I will get the class schedule as I head to take a quick shower. I use the new winter scent scrub and soap she made for me. I swear I feel like a new person every time I use one of her creations and that put's the thought in my head to get with Monty about a workstation for her outside of the house so she can work in peace. I head out to the living room smiling as I see my family snuggled back on the couch my plate and drink sitting on the coffee table in front of them. I sit down on the navy-blue plush rug in between La' Meira's legs grabbing my plate and digging into my food while we all watched the movie. Monty was checking in on Meira as I hear her giggle and then tell the kids he'd be home tomorrow morning. Made sense her appointment is bright and early Monday morning. I finish my food and drink then lean back against her baby bump. She leans down kissing my forehead then starts rubbing her hands through my locs lulling me to sleep. When I wake the movie is long over with another playing, the kids are gone off to their rooms, and my plate as well as cup are gone.

"Well, hello sleepy head." She says rubbing my shoulder and neck.

"Dang how long was I asleep?" I stretch my body feeling a bit stiff sitting on the floor.

"About an hour and a half. The kids started nodding and went to bed about an hour ago."

"I guess I was more tired than I thought. Come on baby let's go to bed." I stand and reach my hand out for hers as she stands turning the TV off at the same time. She strips while I pull the covers back getting in with just my boxer briefs on. I pull her close into my side the moment she gets in the bed good wrapping my arm behind her neck and shoulder while my hand rest on her breast. She places one hand on my chest while I place mine over her belly under the cover rubbing circles with my thumb. We lay like that till she grabs my hand placing it between her legs then pushing them between her slick lips.

"Mhmm." She moans. I thought she was insatiable before but now it's at an all-time high. I push my fingers into her fat wet pussy curling them to hit that spot I know drives her crazy and find a rhythm. I turn towards her kissing on her shoulder then her neck finally reaching her lips sucking the bottom one into my mouth as she moans louder and rotates her hips. Our tongues find their way to each other gliding over the other in a passionate dance. She rubs her hands up and down my arms reaching for the back of my neck pulling me closer.

"Mhmm mo. more." She moans over my lips.

"You need more baby. You want ya dick. Tell me you want it." She nods her head yes.

"Use your words Lil Phoenix."

"Yes, I need you in me." She moans.

"Good girl." I slide my fingers out of her slowly bringing them to mouth and licking them clean of her essence. I slide my boxer briefs off then get up on my knees.

"On your side baby." That position feels even better since she's been pregnant. I take her left leg in my left arm holding it up slightly as I line my rock-hard dick up with her entrance pushing deep inside her in one quick motion.

"Fuuuccck." She moans and I start stroking her slowly and deep.

"Fuck baby this pussy feels sooooo damn good." I moan squeezing her ass cheek as I thrust into her quicker pulling out to the tip and slamming back in repeatedly until she's gushing all over my dick.

"Ja… Ja Jaxxxx." She moans as I feel her juices running down my legs.

"So responsive Lil Phoenix mhmm you're cum is sliding down my legs." I say smacking her twice on the ass and I feel her clench her walls around my dick gripping me so tight trying to drain me of every bit of nut I have.

"Breath baby." Her walls pulsing now as she comes down from her orgasm. I push deep into her pussy feeling her cervix and I rotate my hips in a circular motion to hit some of her favorite spots and she comes undone so beautifully for me.

"Oooh fuck I'm... I'm cummingggg." She moans and I feel the moment she starts to.

"That's right baby cum all over your dick. Give me every drop of that nut." I command her thrusting deep and exactly right to make her orgasm last longer as she milks my dick at the same time.

"Damn baby uuggh fuck." I growl releasing my seed deep inside her walls knowing if she wasn't already pregnant a plan B wouldn't help this time.

"Shit baby I'm sorry." I apologize leaning over making sure not to put too much of my weight on her as I rest my head on her shoulder slowly coming down from my nut.

"Sorry for what babe?" She asks confused rubbing my arm then turning her head to kiss me.

"I came to damn quick. I swear this pussy was dangerous before, but your pregnant pussy is freaking lethal dammit. Got a nigga toes curling and shit." I chuckle nuzzling her neck with my nose.

"Hahaha sir I came twice before you did and I'm still feeling the tingles from the last one. You are more than good."

"As long as you're pleased my love. Now let's get you cleaned up." I slide out of her slowly hopping out the bed then picking her up to head to the bathroom. While she's relieving herself, I turn the shower on then head back to change the sheets since somebody is always a waterpark and forgot our intimacy blanket. By the time I get that swapped out she's sitting in the shower with her head leaning against the glass.

"You ok Lil Phoenix?"

"I'm ok the babies were just moving around a bit and took my breath away." I can't rush into the shower fast enough to sit next to her picking her up to place her on my lap rubbing her back with one hand and the other on her belly.

"Stop worrying Lovie I'm ok babies can do that sometimes when they get active it will probably get a bit worse depending on how big they get." She educates me rubbing her finger between my brows.

"I can't help it you and kids are the most important people to me. I thought I loved my brothers, but you have given me a love I couldn't even imagine possible. It's like that secret ingredient in a family recipe without it taste good but with it... it makes everything right." I express and she smiles pushing her long, thick, curly hair behind her ear.

"Aww Lovie, I love you so much." She says placing a hand on either side of my face and connecting our lips in a slow sensual kiss.

"Come on let's get you to bed. You're going to need your rest if you plan on going into the store for a few hours." She nods her head, and we get cleaned up then head to bed. The next morning all the fam is gathered in the living room and kitchen but we're still waiting on Monty.

"Morning everybody." Meira greets the family as we enter the kitchen. I dap up my brothers as Monty comes through the front door.

"Daddy's home." Mara screams running to jump in his arms and he drops his suitcase and briefcase to catch her then swings her around. I sometimes forget she's a teen because she acts like a little girl, and I take it that's due to not having the chance with her bio father but I am happy to give her whatever she needs so is Monty.

"OK now that Monty is here. Dean you have the papers?" I ask walking next to Meira in the kitchen and Monty joins us giving her a quick kiss then wraps his arms around her.

"Ladies come." Dean calls out taking a stack of papers out of his book bag placing them on the island as our women stand around it.

"What's all this Love bug?" Meira looks over the island as I grab the ones for Monty and I placing them in front of her. Marsh does the same for Bree standing behind her and so does Chase behind Kenya, Dean behind Kelia as Monty and I stand on either side of Meira.

"What these are... are our last will and testament along with our estate and trust fund paperwork to add all of you to it as well as the kids." I announce looking down at her as the shock look covers her face and the rest of the women.

"These are the new birth certificates for all the kids listing me as the twins and Mariah's dad. Then Dean as you fours dad. With all your last names changed to Fredericks." Monty adds in looking at all the kids as they get excited jumping on their dads.

"Everything I have goes to you and the kids Lil Phoenix, all of them." I say turning her head towards me and she tears up then tip toes to give me a kiss. She does the same to Monty when he lets her know that she will get a monthly check from our businesses as she is now part owner of them.

"This is too much." She shakes her head sliding the papers away from her, but Monty moves them back.

"For real guys we love you we don't need all this, and we aren't even married yet Dean." Kelia says looking over the papers in front of her.

"Same here hell we're not even engaged Marsh. Are you guys really sure about all this?" Bree has tears running down her face. Marsh turns her around leaning down to give her a kiss.

"Deadly sure." He says placing a big ass princess cut diamond ring on top of her papers and she loses it then jumps on him.

"Yes, yes… yes." She screams kissing him all over the face as we all laugh with his untraditional ass.

"I know it's nothing fancy, but you've had all of me woman from the day we rescued you. It just took me a while to see it and I'm sorry it took so long." He expresses his feelings the best he knows how then grabs the ring sliding it on her finger as he still holds her in his arms.

"It's perfect for us and we both needed that time to grow before starting all this." She says giving him another kiss.

"Well damn all my babies getting engaged and married." Our mother says wiping the tears from her eyes.

"Wait so this means we are all one family now." Myla questions from the other end of the island next to Kelia who's signing all the papers like Kenya, Meira, and now Bree are.

"Yes, it does. Everything we have will one day belong to all of you and you all never have to worry about anything again, we got you. You have your bank accounts setup for your monthly allowances as well." Dean announces kissing the top of her head as she smiles at all of us. The women finish signing all their papers as Monty and I start breakfast, and the rest of the guys take the kids outside to play. We enjoy a peaceful Saturday just hanging out on the back patio and in the yard. I notice Meech leave like he has been doing regularly and it's almost time to get on him.

Chapter Thirty-Seven

La'Meira Fredericks

Waking up to my men taking care of me just gives me the warm and fuzzy. I may act like a brat sometimes with the rest of the family, but I love them all and how they're here for the kids and me. Today is no different Kelia hasn't been feeling good, so Bree is here cooking breakfast for the family while I get ready for my doctor's appointment. I am so excited to find out what we're having and to see if the other baby decides to show their face this time cause I know it's more than one in there.

"How you are feeling Ife mi." Monty walks up behind me wrapping his arms around my waist and I lean back on his chest with a huge smile on my face. Everyone deserves to feel this happy with their partner or partners.

"I am mind blowingly happy my handsome husband."

"That's good to hear Mrs. Fredericks. Come let me moisturize this sexy glowing body of yours." He rubs his hands over my arms as I stand in front of the sink in the bathroom just finishing up my hygiene. Once we're both ready we head to the living room.

"Kelia boobie how are you feeling?" I inquire rushing to wrap my arms around her in a tight hug and she hugs me back just as tight then lets me go to rub my belly.

"I'm feeling a bit better. You ready to find out what we're having?" I just shake my head cause every last one of them says they're baby or their kids.

"Yes, I am but I have something to tell you, and I hope you're happy about it. I meant to say something the other day, but the guys had us wrapped up the whole weekend." She gives me this worried but curious look.

"Can you tell me now? I'm ok with everybody knowing it's not like we hide much in this family." She chuckles nervously.

"Trust, I know what you mean and the only one seems to be hiding anything is Demetrius." I say giving him the death glare and he puts his head down.

"Well, boobie your pregnant probably about two months." I say tapping my chin with my pointer finger and I laugh when Dean rushes over to her wrapping his arms around her waist.

"Wait how do you?"

"Did you forget Lil Dove is our empath. She senses and sees things we don't."

"Well, I did take a pregnancy test that was positive I was hoping it was a false positive."

"Wait why would you want it to be false, I thought you wanted kids?" Dean questions walking around her to stand next to me.

"I do it's just we adopted four kids that I love by the way, and I didn't think you would want another so soon and I didn't want you to think I was laying it on thick after signing all those papers the other day." She rushes out trying to look away, but he turns her head back to him by her chin.

"Woman I wouldn't give a damn if we had ten kids, I'd still be happy about you being pregnant with our child and I already know you're not with me for my money woman. Hell you didn't find out just how well off I am until Saturday." He explains leaning down kissing the tears that start to stream down her face.

"Eeeh more babies in the family." I bounce on my tiptoes and the whole family bust out in laughter.

"Well, I was going to do this more romantically then my -."

"Oop let me get over here." I say stepping in between Monty and Jax grabbing both of their hands rubbing circles with my thumb.

"What's going on?" She asks looking around confused. Then Dean drops to one knee pulling out this beautiful canary yellow cushion cut diamond with white diamonds around the band. She loses it bursting into tears screaming as he tells her how much he loves her and how she compliments as well as bring out the best parts of him. All the women in the room are in tears by the time he finishes sliding the ring on her finger as she nods yes.

"OK you got us all in tears and the kids have missed their bus." I say as Monty hands me a napkin to wipe my tears and I'm even more glad I don't wear make-up.

"Don't worry I know you guys have your doc appointment to get to we will drop the kids off and give the two love birds here a moment too." Marsh announces as Bree wipes her eyes too. All of us head out after congratulating our second newly engaged couple again. Sitting in the waiting room I am beyond nervous and part of me knows why, and the other is screaming at me to chill the hell out.

"Ife mi relax." He grabs the back of my neck squeezing then rubbing small circles around my neck and I slowly calm down. We are called back for my check-up about five minutes later.

"Good morning Mrs. Fredericks and Mr. Fredericks." The ultrasound tech greets us and the three of us answer in unison then she makes a face but quickly fixes it. Monty steps in front holding the room door open for us all to enter.

"OK Mrs. Fredericks looks like we're just doing an ultrasound today to check your baby's growth then hopefully get gender. Go ahead and hop up on the table then roll your shirt up for me." She instructs and Jax lifts me up onto the table then they both stand next to me Monty holding my hand as Jax rubs my thigh. I lay back rolling up my shirt glad I decided to wear my comfy tights and loose-fitting maternity shirt with my Uggs.

"Um ok I warmed the gel up so it shouldn't be too cold." She has the look I've come accustomed to when out with both my men at the same time and I ignore her if she acts right though. She starts rubbing the wand over my stomach and we start to hear our baby's heartbeat then we see her as I notice the absence of the penis when she goes towards that area.

"OK so you are definitely having a girl but if you look right there it is a second head behind her and um. Wait here I need to get the doctor."

"Is something wrong? Why do you need the doctor?" Monty inquires clearly getting worried and so I am.

"I just need to confirm something with the doctor I will be right back." She says rushing out the door.

"It's going to be fine Ife mi." He tries reassuring me by kissing my forehead and rubbing the back of my neck then running his fingers against my new gold black collar that has both his and Jax's initials in an open heart.

"He is right Lil Phoenix. She probably just needs help trying to see the other babies gender." He adds in rubbing the sides of my belly with his thumb.

"You're probably right." I say relaxing back on the bed then pouting my lips for a kiss from Monty. We sit there for about ten more minutes than the doctor finally comes in with the ultrasound tech.

"Good morning Mr. and Mrs. Fredericks nice to see you all again. It's nothing to worry about I just need to confirm a few things in the ultrasound." We all nod our heads as she picks up the wand moving it across my belly and then I notice what she's looking at.

"Wait is that what I think it is?" I say leaning up some to see the screen better.

"What is it baby, wait a minute." Jax stops then leans forward slightly with his face in pure shock and excitement.

"You are joking right?" Monty whisper yells looking just as shocked as Jax and excited.

"Nope I am not as you can see here, here, and here. You guys are expecting triplets and from the looks of it one girl and two boys. I will get you a few pictures." Doctor Trent my obgyn informs us and it makes so much more sense now.

"Wow just damn." Is all Monty can seem to get out as he falls back into the chair next to my bed and then leans forward dropping his head into his hands rubbing them through his locs.

"Damn three babies. We getting a set of boys and another girl, bruuu." Jax squeezes Monty's shoulder shaking him slightly with a big grin on his face.

"I swear Ife mi just when I think I can't love you more." He expresses getting up giving me a kiss right on the lips in front of the doctor as well as the tech and I smile as he lays his forehead against mine.

"I couldn't agree with him more Lil Phoenix. This is crazy we need to put even more of a rush on our homes." He rubs his hand over my infinity bracelet, and I smile at him as Monty stands up right then moves to the side grabbing his phone out of his pocket. Jax stands where he was giving me a quick peck and rubbing my cheek.

"OK you are all good to go Mrs. Fredericks just wait for the tech to give you the pictures and I will see you in two weeks. I just want to make sure you and these three beauties are healthy as well as growing nicely as well as run some extra test. I like to keep a closer eye on my ladies' carrying multiples. The nurse up front will make your appointment." She lets me know standing to leave.

"Thanks doctor Trent."

"Ife mi we need to step out and take this call with Chase and Money. We will be right outside ok." He assures me putting his hand in mines and squeezing slightly. I nod my head ok and they leave.

"Must be nice possibly pregnant by twins." The ultrasound tech says whipping the gel off my stomach and I sit up pulling my shirt down.

"Excuse you."

"I mean you don't have to worry about who the baby looks like they are both handsome and you all are clearly in some weird poly relationship." She says turning to hand me the ultrasound pictures.

"Bitch." I shout grabbing her by the throat pulling her towards me. She clearly mistook me for some soft timid chick but only if this bitch knew. Before I can rip her ass a new one the door opens and in walks True.

"Queen let the dumb Lil girl go she clearly don't know any better." He demands walking in closing the door behind him.

"When did you get back?" I ask still holding her by the neck and squeezing as she claws at my hand.

"Few days. We wanted to come back and help with the compound but had to wrap some stuff up first."

"Oh, yay does that mean you will be setting up shop here with us." I ask smiling but making a pouty face because I like True, he has always been cool peoples. We met a few years back when I rescued his sister and delivered her to his survivors ranch.

"I'm thinking about it, but Queen, can you please let the pussy munching dick sucking pass around go cause if she hits yo belly I'm putting a bullet in her." I laugh and finally let her go reaching out to him for a hug and he obliges. She falls to the floor holding her neck and grasping for air.

"Wait how the hell you know she does all that?"

"Now you know those brothers don't play we know everything about anybody that will come in contact with y'all especially you and the kids." He states smirking at the ultrasound tech still on the floor. I shake my head because he is so right. The fellas do not play about us, and I have seen the files myself that they have on everyone from the damn mail carrier to the man that checks us out at the local grocery store.

"I'm going to have you kicked out of here and arrested you just assaulted me you nasty bitch." She finally speaks standing up to head for the door.

"Is that anyway to speak to your patients tsk… tsk… tsk. Let me go talk to your manager." True says beating her to the door and I notice the other guard standing at the door. All I can do is shake my head and slowly get off the table heading out the door as well. I smile and nod when I notice the guard is Murch one of my regulars, but he has been gone on maternity leave for the past two and a half months. I told this fool to stay longer but he swears no one else can protect me like he can, and I giggle at the thought. He is an old Marines buddy of Monty and Jax.

"Good to see you Murch how is the wife and baby boy?"

"They are great, and the wife really enjoyed that two-day spa you sent her on with her sister. You really didn't have to do all that."

"No, I didn't but I wanted to. Monty gives me more than enough money than I know what to do with and I would rather help someone else with it besides I remember my first, she needed it." I say waving him off as a commotion picks up between True and the head nurse on duty.

"That's why you're the best." He smiles at me but keeping an eye on True and the nurses that's now yelling at the tech asking her do she know who we are then telling her to meet her in her office. I just shake my head and start to walk off with Murch right next to me and I hear True as he walks up behind me. Once we exit the building the cool air hits me as it isn't quite warmed up yet.

"Hubby is everything ok?" I ask walking up behind him placing my hand on his back.

"We will talk about it at home. I wanna get to the compound to check on a few things. We will need to make changes to the babies' room to make sure all three will be comfortable."

"Wait did you just say babies like plural?" True asks looking shocked.

"Yes, plural as in Lil Phoenix is pregnant with triplets." He adds smiling like a proud papa causing me to smile too.

"Well, I'll be damned Queen, you just pulling out the big guns." True chuckles. The guys help me in the truck and True rides with Murch.

"Wait did you not tell him Jax?"

"Tell me what Ife mi."

"Well big bro we kinda added a thousand square feet to the first and second floor as a late wedding pre baby gift."

"You gotta be kidding me. Nigga for real?" Monty smiles and shakes his head as he drives us to the compound."

"You always look out for us so it's only right we do the same now that you have a family of your own."

"You mean we have a family arakunrin. I appreciate it though." He tells him reaching his hand back to fist bump him.

"Well, I guess now is a good time as any to tell him babe?" I ask Monty and he nods his head yes.

"Well, Jax I was thinking, and I talked to Monty about it already but how would you feel about having the master next to ours. Meaning you live with us instead of having your own place unless you absolutely need to."

"For real I figured you two would want some space eventually, but I'd love to baby. I'll just leave my house for the kids to hang out next door or something." He says and I turn around doing a happy dance in my seat.

"Yay. I was thinking about putting a door between our rooms then another entrance in the closet to our love nest."

"Sounds good to me." Monty says lifting my hand that he always holds while he drives to kiss it, and I see Jax nod the same from the back. We ride for about twenty minutes in silence while I order more baby stuff seeing as we have three to worry about now and now know two are boys plus, I get another princess to spoil. We pull up to the compound and I am amazed at how much they have gotten done over the weekend. I notice some of True's men walking the center of the property helping finish the walkways to each home and we decided to go with a koi pond in the middle with a fountain and different plants surrounding it as well as the walkways. I see all the colorful plants I ordered as well as the pond but they haven't added the fish yet. Each one has a purpose like the ones that repels mosquitoes, some do the same for snakes and other bugs. That took me and the girls hours to research the right combination since the kids want pets and a few of us have allergies. Before I can reach for my door as we park in front Jax is at my door helping me out the truck.

"So, you guys have started painting the outside, it's exactly as I envisioned it." I bounce on my tip toes in excitement.

"I thought the dark blue trim would look too much like black but seeing it on I like it. That dark grey metal roof definitely saved time even if it was a bit pricey." Monty lets me know wrapping his arm around my neck and I figured it would be a bit pricey but they last so much longer.

"See I told you so." I say looking up sticking my tongue at him and he laughs pinching my titty.

"That front porch was a good add too. Having it go across the entire front of the house makes it look cozy." Jax comes up standing next to me.

"Wait are they putting up a swing you didn't tell me you got the swing."

"You like it?" Jax asks.

"It's perfect babe." I tip toe for him to give me a kiss and he does. We walk closer to the house as Chase, Dean, Meech, and Marsh come out one by one.

"So, what we are having, I'm not waiting till tonight, Lil Dove?" I giggle shaking my head at Dean as he grabs me from Monty into a hug and I look back at them both and they nod.

"Well, how do you feel about a girl?"

"Yes, another princess." He shouts in excitement.

"Wait but what about the two boys?"

"What you talking about La'Meira?" I see the curious look on the rest of their face and laugh.

"Lil brother we're having triplets a girl and two boys." Monty shouts not able to contain himself and I laugh even more as they all burst out in unison WHATTTT.

"Damn triplets like three Lil babies are growing in here for real?" Dean smiles gently grabbing my belly and rubbing on both sides. Chase and the rest follow suit as Dean goes to congratulate Monty and Jax too.

"So that's why we need to make some adjustments to the kids wing for the babies. It needs to be bigger."

"Well, the room is already about four hundred square feet with its own bathroom and walk in closet. We figured it would make things easier and besides Meira had already been hinting at thinking she was having twins." Chase says still rubbing my stomach as I lean on his side watching all the men move around working.

"OK I guess that will be enough room." Monty says behind me.

"What colors were you thinking so I can get the paint ordered Lil Dove? They will be done with the framing for the top floor by Thursday and drywall has already started downstairs."

"Ooh I wanna see."

"NO." They all yell at me unison and I cross my arms over my chest getting mad.

"I don't care about that bratty attitude Lil Phoenix. It's a bunch of men walking around with dangerous tools. We aren't risking you getting hurt."

"He's right I'll send you some videos later I promise." Chase says kissing the top of my head.

"Fine I want the walls a neutral light grayish blue color because Kenya says she's going to paint a safari mural on one of the walls for them with Mara."

"That will look nice. Our Lil Mara is quite the artist." Meech states standing next to me and I give him the side eye because I'm still mad with him.

"I will tell you but not yet Meira. I promise don't be mad at me. I'll come grill ya steaks like you like them tonight." He says leaning down kissing the side of my neck and I bite my lip.

"Hmm, I guess. You know how I feel about secrets. Don't make me stalk yo ass Meech."

"She will do it too. I never told y'all, but Dean knows but the first time she came to KC it wasn't because I went to get her. I didn't answer my damn phone all day because I broke it and came home that night with Dean to see her sitting on my couch flicking a damn switch blade. That's another reason ha ass has that tracker in ha now." Monty fills them in on one of my many antics and I look back at him smiling because I was not playing with his ass. That man put a tracker in me after they took me the first time but had a tracker in my phone and the new car, he bought me after that little fiasco.

"I promise I will tell all of you soon. I just need to figure some stuff out first." He explains leaning down to kiss the top of my head then rubs my belly. I swear I'm surrounded by giants. We chat for a bit more about different paint colors for the first floor and how they got the electricity and plumbing approved today to even start on the drywall. These men are efficient and resourceful as hell. They eventually tell me it's time to go home eat and put my feet up. I'm a bit tired so I don't argue.

"Jax get her cleaned up and in the bed, I'll make us some Salmon bits and broccoli." Monty instructs him once we're in the house and I smile because he knows how much I love salmon cooked just about anyway. Jax walks with me to the bathroom to shower then helps me get moisturized and back into bed to find something to watch.

"I still can't believe you have three beautiful lives growing in there. Women's bodies are freaking amazing." Jax expresses his gratitude and amazement as we lay in bed snuggled up against each other watching one of my favorite shark movies. We lay there a few more minutes before Monty comes in with one my long trays filled with our food. We have come so accustomed to Jax in the bed closes to the bedroom door and Monty on the side where the patio door is and of course I'm in the middle my favorite spot. He hands the tray to Jax as we untangle ourselves from each other then he goes back to the kitchen to grab our drinks and comes back getting on his side. I'm glad we upgraded to the king size bed after Jax started staying here more than his place otherwise this would be tight.

"What are we watching?" Monty asks as he helps me with my pillows to sit up.

"Deep Blue Sea." Jax answers him.

"Of course." He laughs and I do too. We have probably watched it ten times since being together and I've watched it a lot more than that.

"Mmm babe these are so good."

"She's right. You did ya big one with this. What did you add to them?"

"Just did a honey glaze on them this time and used that creole seasoning Meira has in there with the regular seasonings I use." We all eat and laugh at the movie like we never watched it before then Jax takes our dirty dishes away staying to clean the kitchen.

"I'll try to get back later tonight baby. I'm going to go help with the house. Go take you a walk in the backyard so your heartburn doesn't act up too much and take a nap, ok?"

"Ok but only if you make sure you get back before midnight. You have been working really hard lately, and ya need ya rest too."

"OK Lil Phoenix I promise. Give me kiss so I can go." He pulls me into a slow sweet kiss I swear I can feel every bit of his love through his kisses.

"I love you." I say as I lay back.

"I love you too. See ya later bru."

"See ya and she's right you need to rest." He nods his head. We get up to walk around the back yard for about ten minutes then I go lay down to take a nap while Monty goes into my office to work for a few hours.

Chapter Thirty-Eight

Montavius Fredericks

The past couple of months have flown by and I can't believe Meira is already a few days short of eight months. Today is our baby shower and the nerves are clearly getting the best of my woman. The news I had to tell her a few months back was that we finally found out what happened to Calder and Money's men. Turns out that prick bought their loyalty and convinced them to testify against us. They have been trying to build a case against us, but Meira was able to hack using our FBI connects access. She was able to find out that they barely have a case but are moving off the strength of Calder. I come out the bathroom and notice Meira standing in the floor length gold trim mirror in the corner of our room looking at herself in her floor length all white sundress that scrunches up around the breast making them look even more juicy than usual.

"Well, hello gorgeous." I say walking up behind her reaching around to lift her belly up relieving some of the weight.

"Damn I use to think this was a lie, but it really feels amazing when you do that." She exhales leaning her head back against my chest.

"I'm here to serve you, my love." She smiles and tilts her had back for a kiss that I happily oblige. I never get enough of touching and kissing on this woman. It's crazy how in less than a year's time I have went from not even wanting women to touch me even during sex to feeling off if she's not near.

"How are you feeling about today Ife mi?"

"About all of you possibly being arrested today not so good but I trust you."

"Please do baby cause the lawyers are here and they have a federal judge on speed dial."

"Fine I also I have the timer on the file to release everything about his crooked ass the minute y'all are booked. What about Money though?"

"We are doing our best to help with his case. His men gave them so damning info though. They didn't know a whole lot but knew enough for him to be arrested with us and possibly kept." She frowns but nods her head understanding the predicament he's in. His business is why I never wanted my brothers around him. He's smart but doesn't use his common sense enough but hopefully if we can get him out, he will cut the shit out and go legit with us.

"Let's get this over with." She says taking a deep breath.

"Don't be like that baby. You still need to enjoy our day." I say kissing her forehead then slowly releasing her stomach and smacking her on the ass getting the giggle I was looking for. The door opens before we exit, and it can only be one person cause everybody else knocks first.

"How's our woman doing?" Jax asks closing the door behind him and walking in front of Meira. "She's feeling better, but you know what's on her mind." I say kissing the top of her head and walking into the closet for my shoes.

"Lil Phoenix we will be good. I will watch his back and make sure he comes back to you I promise." He assures me as I walk back to sit on the bed shaking my head.

"Do you really think it's just him I'm worried about? Have these last seven months or so not shown you how much I love you ya big idiot. I can't imagine not having either of you dammit how can you not see that. I don't sleep right unless at least one of you is here and I know where the other is. I embedded a damn tracker in ya ass for the love of all things holy. Ughhh I gotta pee these babies are kicking my bladder loss." She says frustrated and walks off to the bathroom. I shake my head because I knew that was coming. My brother can be thick headed at times, and this is one of those times because my Ife mi loves his big ass just as much as she loves me. I actually don't feel bad or jealous about it like I thought I would. I like our dynamic most won't get it but hey who the fuck cares.

"Now you've upset our woman Jax. I should kick you in the balls for this shit. Get yo ass in there and fix it now. We will enjoy our day before these asses run up in here thinking they're big dogs."

"Shit I really messed up, fuck. I'm going." As he goes to fix our woman's mood, I head out to check on how things are going. All the ladies got together to put a fairytale zoo themed baby shower together because Meira never got a chance to have one with the twins. Everything outside looks beautiful and worthy of my wife and babies. I sit at my throne our stage set exactly how we sleep every night, and everything feels exactly right. About ten minutes later Meira and Jax come walking out the back of the house and her face drops in shock as everyone stands cheering. She knew that they were planning something special, but the entire back yard has white tents, cardboard cutouts of us, her with Jax even all of us with the kids. Tables decorated with white animals print tablecloths, black plates, with gold-colored/ utensils, and animal print napkins. Everything is green, tan, gold, and white. Emerald green silk ribbon bows on all chairs. There is a green runway rug leading to our thrones with white rose petals. Behind our thrones and food table are balloon arches with triplets on the way written in gold and black on another cutout. I have to admit the girls did their big one with this. Everybody continues to give her a hug as Jax leads her to our thrones.

"Oh my gosh y'all this is so beautiful." She says tearing up as I put her crown on her head after she sits pointing out something new, she notices.

"Only the best for you Ife mi." She smiles so big as I use my thumb to wipe the tears falling from her eyes. We take our seats after we place the long table in front of us. The ladies thought it was a good idea to eat first then play games to work off the food which turns out to be a good thing. They played all type of games even made Jax and I join in a few times. We have a diaper and dress contest which I win since I've been going to new parent classes with Jax. We can't remember the last time we were around a baby, so we wanted to be prepared. They play the guess the babies' weight which Kelia wins each baby is about five and a half pounds give or take a few pounds. The tie your shoe game was funny as hell and the chug a bottle. Jax and I step away for a bit while the girls present all the gifts.

"So, Blue just texted and said they will probably show up in about ten minutes or so." Jax tells me as we watch our woman smile at everything she and the kids received, a lot of which has been setup in the house already since the entire main floor is now finished and most of the rooms upstairs.

"OK bet at least Meira was able to enjoy her day with the fam before all hell breaks loose."

"True but hopefully we can do this peacefully I'd hate to actually get a charge but have no damn problem with it if they come in here crazy stressing my baby out."

"Facts." We head back to our thrones as the girls finish up the gifts and I lean over to whisper what Jax just told me, so she's prepared. She nods her head and goes back to opening the gifts.

"Dance with me Ife mi." I say standing placing her hand in mines as the music slows and I pull her from her seat. I turn her back to my chest wrapping my arms around her waist as we sway.

"They are about to pull up baby and I need you to stay calm for me. I do not plan on missing the birth of my babies and I'd hate to catch a charge if they do something stupid. I won't hesitate to put a bullet in all of their skulls where they stand." Jax walks up in front of us placing his hands on either side of her belly.

"I won't either so listen to him and be our calm, cool, collected Dove as Dean likes to call you and not my fiery phoenix." He leans forward putting his forehead against hers giving her a kiss as we hear the side gates open. I look over to our team of lawyers who notice and walk over to us along with the rest of my brothers.

"Ife mi this is Brinx our family lawyer and his team they are going to make sure we're good." I introduce her once they reach us and he reaches out to shake her hand.

"You better make sure they return to me the same way they left, or you'll find out how a pig feels over a hot fire but big difference you won't get the pleasure of being dead first but nice to meet you." I shake my head at my wife cause a part of me knows this wasn't going to go completely smooth plus I know she means every word.

"Yup perfect woman for you Mo." Brinx chuckles shaking his head then introducing her to the rest of his team as the agents approach us. My brothers and I surround La'Meira and Brinx stands in front of us. Uncle Tone takes our moms and all the kids in the house.

"I am agent Franklin we have an arrest warrant for the Fredericks Brothers and Blake Rue also known as Money for drug trafficking, kidnapping and attempted murder of a state governor." The agent recites our charges, and Brinx reaches out his hand for the warrant.

"Hold the hell up this warrant says none of this therefore you aren't taking my clients anywhere. By the way I am their lawyer, and this is the rest of my team."

"They will be leaving with us, and you are welcome to meet us there."

"Tamia get federal judge Berkeley on the line I am pretty sure she will be happy to hear about agents showing up with an improperly issued warrant and while she's doing that Genesis get Assistant Director Hudson on the line as well, I'm sure he would like to know what his agents are up to." He instructs his team and a few of the agents look over at agent Franklin wondering what the hell he just got them into, and I chuckle standing with my arms crossed over my chest. Soon they have both on the line and Brinx starts to explain what's going on to them.

"Hudson what are you allowing to go on in your office? Do I need to get the remaining judges up as well?" She inquires in a stern voice clearly annoyed with the whole situation.

"No Judge Berkeley I will get this situated. Franklin what the hell is going on?" He tells her. She says she will be checking back to make sure this mess is handled and ends the call.

"Sir we have it on good authority with a witness and now confidential informants who can corroborate the illegal activity they are all into."

"Besides their word what actual evidence do you have?"

"We are still gathering but these men are a flight risk, and we need to bring them in before they run off or kill someone else."

"Director Hudson my clients are not a flight risk two of them have a seven-month pregnant wife whose baby shower we are standing in right now. The others wife is inside pregnant, and he has four kids already. These men are devoted family and businessmen as well as retired Marines with one of them a Navy Seal who have not committed any of the crimes they are accused of."

"Look you can have them in for questioning in the morning with their lawyers that is all and when I get there, I better see a file with some actual evidence, or you are letting them go at once and will not contact them further." He yells and hangs up.

"My clients and I will meet you at your office in the morning and here's your paper back." Brinx informs the agent, and I try not to laugh in his face.

"Eight am sharp or we will be back with a warrant for their arrest, and nothing will stop us from taking them in." Agent Franklin states clearly pissed turning to stump off with the other agents in tow. The moment they close the gate we all bust out laughing.

"Yo it was hard as hell holding it together that long, his face was turning red as an apple." I busted into a fit of laughter and so did everyone else.

"Well, well... well Brinx you may be worth keeping alive after all along with your lil minions." Meira says walking around us clapping her hands. She may seem sarcastic, but my beauty is very much serious.

"Glad to be of service Meira." He says jokingly either not realizing she's serious or knows she is but not taking her seriously either way big fuck up on his part.

"It's Mrs. Fredericks to you we aren't friends, and I don't know you, but I will. Now I'm going to relax get out of these godforsaken clothes and take me a bubble bath y'all enjoy your night." She announces sass shaying away taking off her bra and throwing it over her shoulder as she does.

"Should I be worried about the misses?" Brinx asks.

"Very much so Lil Phoenix is *The Queen* nigga." I see the moment realization hits him and Money because we never told him.

"You fuckin kidding *The Queen* is your damn wife Monty, how the fuck did that happen?" Brinx questions spazzing on me. He helped in taking down some of the trafficking rings she gave us info on and wanted to meet her.

"Her skills with a knife and how she fights makes sooo much sense now. Thanks for tellin a nigga though damn." Money says actually looking bothered.

"Hey its noting against you Money it just wasn't relevant at the time." Dean says placing his hand on his shoulder.

"Yea and besides as you can see, she is out of the game. She decided she just wants to be a wife and mother along with whatever business or charity she wants to get into." Jax explains getting slightly on the defense.

"Only reason we're saying anything now is because he's our lawyer and now hers. You protect her with everything Brinx I don't give a shit if I must ever go down for anything so she stays out here that's what it will be."

"Bet." He says walking up to me shaking my hand. Brinx is another Marine buddy that got out early and went into law to protect our asses if shit ever hits the fan. I stand and talk with them a few more minutes before I head into the house to my beautiful wife. I find her standing outside the tub clearly just getting out the shower.

"Hi there beautiful."

"Hi to you too handsome you coming to join me in my bubble bath?"

"If you will have me, I would love to." I move from the door taking my clothes off as I walk over to her.

"Well go wash up and get in why don't ya." She sasses me lowering herself into the pearly white deep soaking tub, the one in our new home is even larger. Just another month or so before we can move in. All of us being so hands on have avoided major delays but we had a few minor ones. The HVAC company we contracted out thought they were going to play us doing half the project them requesting more money than we agreed to, I took off a week worked sunup to sundown finishing the work myself with some help from my brothers. I clean up quickly because I truly need this alone time with my wife. I didn't think we'd get off having to go tonight at all, but Brinx is worth the money.

"It's about time slow poke." She says leaning forward so I can slide in behind her then she leans back against my chest and just that fast I'm at peace.

"I was making sure I was clean Ife mi. You and all these bubbles." I say picking some up placing some on her nose.

"Really babe." She giggles turning to put some on my face and I laugh.

"How do you feel about tonight?"

"I loved it even seeing the FBI agents get their asses handed to them."

"I thought we were going to at least have to go with them tonight, but Brinx is worth every dollar."

"He knows who I am now doesn't he?"

"Yes, baby he's, our lawyer. I know you're not going out with us anymore, but you still need protection when you're behind that computer of yours. You don't trust 'em?"

"I'm not sure about who I trust anymore outside you guys."

"What about the girls?"

"Honestly I love them I really do but I know for sure Kelia is hiding something just not quite sure what it is yet, Bree I just worry about her going off the deep end she's not as in control as you guys think and Marsh is feeding into it, and Kenya is scared of something but it's not Chase."

"Woman I swear you never cease to amaze me. I thought only Jax, and I caught the Marsh and Bree thing, and Chase has been worried about Kenya since she has yet to set a wedding date, but Kelia we missed or more so chalked it up to pregnancy. But enough of them how are my babies in there?" I ask placing a hand on each side of her belly rubbing circles with my thumb as I feel them moving. The water is warm which is not her normal temperature, but she knows not to do that while carrying our babies.

"They are good as you can feel. I swear one of them likes to keep their damn foot up by my chest." She chuckles placing her hands on top of mines.

"Is that why the bra bothers you so bad?" She nods her head yes. I learn something crazy everyday about what her body goes through carrying our kids.

"Let's get out of this tub though hubby I need my chocolate bar to put me to sleep."

"Say less Ife mi." I use my foot to press the stopper letting the water out. I slide out the tub to grab our towels then help her out the tub and drying her off in the process. Skipping our usual moisturizing routine, I dry off as she walks to our closet in all her naked glory just glowing so damn beautifully grabbing the intimacy blanket and I know what that means. We went at it from every angle possible my favorite was me sitting on the edge of the bed for her to ride me. Fuck this woman has been sexy as hell to me since day one but seeing her carry our kids and riding my dick had me cumming like a teenage boy getting some for the first time. She has been religiously going to that pregnancy workout class twice a week and clearly, they have been doing a lot of leg days.

"Fuck woman you can't have me cumming like that." I tell her as I remove the intimacy blanket from the bed after cleaning her up.

"Oh, like you had me squirting while you ate my soul from my pussy or when you had me on my side with one of my legs on your shoulder?" She says getting under the covers and laying back with a smirk.

"Ight you keep talking like that I'm going to do it again." I wink at her before I turn to put the blanket in the dirty laundry basket. I cuddle up in the bed with her until I feel her fall asleep then I slip on my Pj pants and head out on the back patio.

"Damn y'all got all that cleaned up already?"

"Um nigga you been gone for like three or four hours. Everybody came back out once y'all went in and started packing everything up." Dean shakes his head sitting in one of the patio chairs smoking on a blunt that I grab from his annoying ass.

"Hey, the misses needed some extra attention and of course I had to oblige." I take a pull from the blunt and exhale out my nose.

"Yea we heard. I see she has you talking in your native tongue." Brinx chuckles and I notice the rest of his team is gone.

"She will have ya toes locking too but yo ass will never know now mind ya business." Jax says cutting his eyes at Brinx and I know it's only cause of Meira since otherwise he sees him as a brother.

"My bad I won't say shit else about that, but *The Queen* is she really retiring?"

"In a sense. She no longer wants to physically be out helping but as you know her hacking skills are even better than mines so that will be her only role." I let him know what's what then taking another hit, passing it to Jax.

"OK bet and with her hacking skills I doubt I'll ever have to defend her then so no throwing yourself on the sword sir." He states looking over at me and I know what he's thinking but I could care less if it came down to me or her, she will always take priority.

"Are you going to be able to keep Money out of jail?"

"Yea the boy is smart."

"When I left a few months back when the sorry ass niggas came up missing, I went home and dismantled my entire operation passing my connect over to my second in command since my right hand decided he was ready to get out too. Chase found us both homes and I opened a clothing and jewelry store that I've been running online for a while but never put forth that much into it."

"I always knew yo ass was smart as hell. You could've picked a lot in the compound unless you just wanted to be on, ya own." I tell him walking up to him placing my hand on his shoulder.

"Wait for real. I figured you didn't want a me around like that. It's no secret you don't really fuck wit me."

"Look I just didn't want what you had going on to blow back on my brothers they have always been my priority plus I felt like you were wasting that brain of yours on some shit that would get you jailed or killed."

"Besides after how you stepped in when we needed you for Meira you are a part of the family nigga." Jax says putting him in a head lock rubbing the top of his head with his knuckles like he use to do the rest of our lil brothers, and we all laugh.

"Hell, the wife has already told me to be nice to you she sees something in you and trust you so wants to keep you around."

"Oh well that settles it what Lil Dove wants she gets."

"Pretty much." I shrug and we all share a laugh.

"I'm not trying to be funny or anything but what's so special about her besides her being *The Queen* of course?" Money asks.

"I was going to ask the same cause I've never seen Monty like this, nor Jax over a woman." Brinx says looking at all of us. Dean explains first but stops and I see he's going to need some time with his best friend after bringing up those memories.

"Peace is definitely one of them, but she understands our lifestyle with no judgements. She accepted Kenya with open arms and helped her embrace a side of her she's been holding back. So, a nigga can get a bullet really quick about her." Chase says.

"Facts she got me and Bree together. Helped me realize I was acting like a lil boy trying to avoid falling for her when my dumb ass had already, and I've never been happier." Marsh says for the first time out loud to us even though we already knew.

"The peace understanding our lifestyle is all cool, but the woman is the easiest to talk to and can out cook damn near everyone we know." Meech says and we all say facts.

"I can't explain mines without sounding all mushy but bottom line the woman is my heart and soul in human form." Jax expresses.

"Agreed but she is so resilient, smart, and matches a nigga crazy. She is made for this family, for us and her blessing us with six damn kids is just icing on the cake for me." I relay to him how I feel the best I can as I bump fist with Jax.

"So, you and Jax are in an actual relationship with her not just sex cause I remember how y'all get down?" Brinx asks.

"Me and her are married but her and Jax are in a committed relationship. Before you ask no I'm not jealous in the least. I have to travel sometimes knowing Jax is here taking care of our family seeing as I can't always put them on a plane every time, I need to leave even though the cameras are ok makes me feel at ease." I tell 'em before they even ask.

"Crazy ass nigga per usual." Brinx says shaking his head.

"She loves it, and you think I'm crazy you should hear how she tagged Jax ass." I laugh.

"What you mean tagged Jax." Money asked looking confused.

"Mannnn she edged Jax so long one night when he finally came, he blacked out and in such a deep sleep she was able to stick a needle in the back of his thigh putting a chip in 'em." I laugh because he didn't know how she got it in him.

"Wait she did what and what the hell is edged? She crazy… crazy." Money says laughing now too.

"It's when you fuck your partner close to orgasm then stop and start over again repeating until you finally let them cum." Chase educates him.

"Damn bru she sex dazed you then chipped yo ass but to add to that you have to know the person well enough to know when they are cumming otherwise ya miss ya window." Dean says laughing.

"Nigga I know you not laughing she chipped yo ass back on our honeymoon and she used Kelia to do it." I laughed even harder cause these fools don't know the lengths my wife has went to chip all of our asses.

"Wait the damn threesome those sneaky ass women and Kelia knew what she was doing. I'm going to get her ass when I get home."

"Nigga please it was Kelia idea to use the threesome to distract you so Meira would show her how to use the app." Jax adds in laughing.

"Wait threesome with Dean and his girl hold up I'm missing a lot." Brinx says.

"Same." Money adds in.

"Shit clearly we are to cause I didn't know she was round here chipping niggas damn." Chase says.

"Ummm you realize she's chipped the three of you too. Different chip type from ours since she monitors our vitals plus location." Jax says and they all looked shocked.

"Wait she has different chips?"

"She made two types of chips the ones she put in Me, Jax, and Dean then the ones that are in y'all, ya women, and the kids plus our mothers."

"Damn she chipped ya mama too." Money asks.

"If she cares about you, she is chipping ya ass no if ands or buts about it. She did ask ma if she was OK with it before she did it. I had to explain to her that Meira is like us her brain doesn't process things like everybody else and she doesn't live by society's norms. What others see as crazy she only sees the logic or benefit of it." I explain shrugging cause I get her.

"I can get that. Wait does that mean she will end up chipping me too?" Money asks.

"If is not what you should be worried about it's the how cause she will chip you." Jax chuckles out.

"Brinx I'm not sure about you brother she doesn't seem to want to warm up to you." I tell him and Jax gets a worried look on his face and I nod my head at him. He puts his head down then stands dapping everyone then leaving to go lay with her, but I hope he remembers to shower first cause she will slap his ass.

"Wait something just happened, didn't it?" Brinx asks.

"Yea if she wants to explain it to you, she will but this is just another reason I'm happy with our arrangement I help her in one way and Jax does in a another."

"But back to you Money you moving on the compound, right? I don't have time to get cussed by my best friend for leaving you out."

"I mean yea why not I can rent my house out and make coins off it. I'm not go lie to y'all I'm glad y'all accepted me into the fam hell that's the only reason I started that stupid gang selling drugs shit to build a family, but we see how that shit turned out." He says rubbing his hand down his face reminding me of Chase.

"Well, you don't have to worry about that shit with us." Dean reassures him, getting up slapping his hand with his and pulling him in for a hug then we all do the same.

"Look enough of the kumbaya shit we have to be up early as fuck to drive an hour to meet these sorry ass FBI agents." Brinx says and I can tell he's a bit bothered but there isn't shit I can do about it unless wife becomes ok with him.

"About that. Meira kinda sent the rest of the files we had on Calder's sex trafficking involvement directly to the director and our connect in the FBI. Plus, she dug up a lil something on each agent that showed up tonight. I have a feeling we will be getting a call to not come in."

"What the fuck? Why am I even surprised Lil Dove is sweet but vicious when she needs to be." Dean says shaking his head chuckling.

"She passed vicious damn that woman is lethal, and I love it." Brinx stands to leave.

"That's my wife but I'm still going to bed I don't trust them niggas at all they may still try to pull a fast one. Oh, Money ya boys being dealt with too." I tell him stretching and he looks shocked.

"I told you my wife does not play about her family. They will be delivered to a spot she had set up for you. Leave ya phone when ha people come get you and take you to them." He's so out of it he just nods. It's going to take a minute for him to adjust to a family dynamic but that's cool. I walk off into the house and hear the rest of them saying their goodbyes. I walk into Meira wrapped in Jax's arms asleep and he clearly heard my thoughts because he bathed.

"Is it crazy I feel bad for not being able to fix the hurt she's still feeling?" He asks rubbing his hand over her silk scarf on her head.

"Nope unless we both crazy which is possible cause I feel the same, but I guess only time can fix this one as much as I hate it." I get in the bed.

"Fine not go stop me from trying though." I give him the same here look. I feel Meira wrap one of her legs around mines then she grabs my hand placing it on her stomach and that's all I need to drift off to sleep.

Chapter Thirty- Nine

Jax Fredericks

I wake up the next morning with Meira still on my chest and Monty outside fussing at somebody, so I get up slowly to check after giving my Phoenix a kiss on the head.

"Hey arakunrin what's going on?" I ask stepping out the door the damn sun almost blinding my ass.

"Oh, nothing major fussing with Jude ass about a client I told him needs to be band for a stunt he just pulled with one of our agents."

"Oh, anything from the FEDS?" I start stretching.

"Oh, them niggas called Brinx apologizing and saying we didn't need to come in. Wife did a number on their asses and I'm sure all the info she pulled on Calder from Justin's laptop sealed his fate."

"Sounds good to me. We'll probably see it in the news soon enough."

"MOONNNNTTYYYY JAAAXXXXXXX!!!" We hear Meira scream and we both take off running to the door and the kids are coming through the room door at the same time. I grab the kids to take them out the room while Monty checks to see what's wrong as Dean and the others walk in the front door.

"What's going on the kids look panicked?" He rushes over to them after making Kelia sit on the couch. He's just as bad as we are with Meira.

"She's in labor get the truck ready. Jax get in here." Monty demands peaking his head out the door. I kiss the kids on the head and rush in the room grabbing her baby bag handing it to Dean since he followed me in.

"It's ok Lil Phoenix remember your breathing baby. Have the contractions started to get bad or did her water just break?" I question following them into the bathroom going to turn on the shower while he does her breathing exercises with her.

"So far water broke and one contraction she said it wasn't too bad and that was three minutes ago and counting."

"Ok baby let's get you in the shower." I direct her reaching for her hand and helping her into the shower.

"Jax stay in the shower with her I'll get her clothes since Dean took her bags to bring around the truck."

"Oooohhhh shit... shit." She started screaming.

"OK that makes seven minutes between contractions." Monty announces before leaving out the bathroom.

"Alright Lil Phoenix let's get you cleaned up really quick." I instruct grabbing her washcloth and soap then cleaning her up.

"Baby, should you still be bleeding I mean it's not a lot."

"It should've stopped by now, but it could be leftover and it's different with every pregnancy."

"Ok I'm done let's rinse you off." I say as Monty walks in on the phone.

"Yea doc the last was three minutes ago and before that one it was seven minutes." He reads the doctor in on what's happening.

"Hey, let her know she's still bleeding." He turns giving me a worried look.

"Doc, you hear that is that normal? Ok we are getting ready to leave now." He hangs up the call.

"She says it could be her having multiple she's bleeding more than the last time. She's getting her room ready. They are just waiting on us." Before we could get her in her clothes she has another contraction.

"OK we down to five minutes we need to hurry." He says and that we do. When we get out mom is in the room with Bree changing the sheets.

"Go babies I'll get this cleaned up feed the kids and meet y'all there." We all nod walking out the room and head off to the hospital with Dean and Kelia in the front seat.

"Money said thanks for the present Lil Dove, and he will be to the hospital as soon as he gets done."

"Mhmm." She moans as another contraction hits.

"OK still at five minutes try your breathing baby were almost there." Monty instructs rubbing her belly while I rub her back as she sits in between us legs spread leaning forward a little. She starts taking her breaths and rocking back and forth. She has two more contractions before we reach the hospital and sure enough a nurse is waiting at the emergency door when we pull up. We get her checked in and head right to her private labor and delivery room.

"Hi mama looks like we have some triplets coming today. Don't worry we checked and their lungs and everything else have developed nicely. Now they will need to stay a few extra days but that's just a precaution. How are you feeling?"

"Epi.dur.al NOWWWW!" She yells as we get her in her hospital gown and in the bed. The doctor turns to tell the nurse to get the anesthesiologist to get it started.

"OK so before he gets here, we need to check how many centimeters you are dilated. I need you to scoot to the edge and place your feet in the holders." Doctor Trent instructs her, and we help her move into place.

"Alright mama you are going to feel some pressure just breath through it for me. Ok you are coming along nicely. You're about six or six and a half centimeters dilated, only four more to go." As she finishes up and we get her back another contraction hits her down to four minutes now.

"Ok I don't like that you're still bleeding even if it's just a little, but the anesthesiologist will be in a couple minutes and the nurses are going to get you hooked up to the monitors. You can listen to your babies heart beats till you're ready to push." I swear I've never been so excited in my life, and I see it in my brother he is too but there is a hint of worry in the room with her still bleeding. The anesthesiologist comes in just as another contraction hits her and this one seems to be worse than the others.

"UGGGHHHHH this shit hurts if either of you think I'm doing this shit again you can kiss my ass." She cursed.

"Ok Mrs. Fredericks I need you to sit up and hang your legs over the other side of the bed and be very still." The anesthesiologist instructs her setting up his tools as Monty helps her sit then turn her legs towards us. We give her a pillow as instructed and each of us take one of her hands rubbing her thigh to calm her with the other as he places a long ass needle into her back after sanitizing the area. He finishes with what looks like a large band aid then we help her lay back slowly.

"OK give it a few minutes and you will start to feel the pain subside. Congratulations on the new addition." He says leaving the room.

"I will never ask you to do this again. Why wouldn't you tell me they would put some crazy looking shit like that in your back Ife mi?"

"For real I was scared as shit he'd nick something. I looked up the changes but missed this part. I thought you were incredible before but damn Lil Phoenix." I express as I'm rubbing her leg with one hand and her stomach with the other.

"I'm starting to feel slightly better already guys relax but these contractions are getting quicker." Just as she fully settles laying down family comes in one by one.

"Ma the babies are ready to come?" Za'Meir inquires standing next to me leaning on my arm and I gladly wrap it around my big guys shoulder.

"Yes, they are hmmm." She confirms but moans a little clearly another contraction hitting her which means it won't be long now and as soon as I finish that thought in walks the nurse to check her again. Everyone leaves to go to the private family waiting area.

"OK mama it's time to call the doctor you have progressed three centimeters in about an hour. These babies are ready to meet their parents." She pulls her gown down then takes off her gloves smiling, heading out the door.

"Of course, our babies would be impatient like their fathers."

"I am not impatient that's him." I say pointing at Monty and he starts to say something but Doctor Trent walks in first.

"Alright mama let's deliver some babies. I am going to need you to slide back in position but come all the way to the edge and Mr. Fredericks I'm going to need one of you on either side." She finishes getting ready and giving out instructions to the nurses who walk in with three baby beds. Before I know it, the doctor is telling her to push, and we were seeing the first baby head come out and I never seen something so fucking amazing.

"You got this Lil Phoenix remember why I call you that baby A is almost out." I encourage her holding her hand as she pushes, and I rub her cheek with my other. In this moment I've become even more obsessed with this woman. A few seconds later she's pushing, and baby A is coming out completely which turns out to be one of our boys. His lungs are clearly working since he came out crying but calms the moment Monty speaks and that's clearly Montavius Akanni junior. The doctor hands out the scissors to cut his umbilical cord and I feel the pride radiating off my brother.

"Alright we have two more and I see the seconds head starting to crown." Doctor Trent says, and I can't believe they're coming so quick. Baby two is our little girl Ayomi which means my joy. Meira wanted our babies to have a part of our heritage. Ayomi took her time coming out though and she did with her eyes open looking around but not crying.

"Doc, she looks exhausted is baby three about ready to come out as well?" I ask cutting the umbilical cord for Ayomi Jameia then the nurse takes her to get cleaned up.

"I don't see him crowning yet." Just as she finishes her sentence Meira cries out in pain.

"Ife mi what's wrong?"

"I see the problem he's trying to come out butt first I have to turn him." Doctor Trent says then applies pressure to her stomach to adjust Jackson Djimon then he starts to come out the right way with his eyes wide open too but crying slightly. Once he's fully out Monty and I both hold the scissors to cut his umbilical cord then the nurse rushes him off to get cleaned up.

"OK mama last thing we need to get your placenta the company you requested sent over the storage container for it." She nods weakly and I can't help but worry about her.

She takes a few breaths then pushes slightly for it to come out and this big ball of what looks like a blood clot comes out. Doc transfers it to a temperature-controlled box and hands it off to a nurse. Meira wanted to do the same thing with the twins but couldn't afford it, so we made sure it was done this time around. We help her lay back as the nurses come back with the babies handing one to each of us.

"They're so small." Monty says holding Junior, while I have Ayomi, and Meira has Jackson.

"They are almost a month early, but they are an ok weight, but they need mommies' milk to give them the best nutrition."

"Hi my handsome boy you ready to eat?" She says talking to Jackson bouncing him just a bit and I mimic what she does to Ayomi and so does Monty. She pulls out her breast and he latches on instantly.

"Just like ya daddy." She laughs a bit then wines.

"OK Jax place Ayomi on my other breast."

"Really baby you look so tired you sure you have to do all this now?" I ask her.

"Doc should she be doing so much?" Monty questions Doctor Trent.

"I have learned that mother's know their bodies best and if she feels up to it let her but not too much you still need to eat something as well and get cleaned up." She just nods her head in response. I lean over reluctantly placing Ayomi on her other breast and she has no problem latching on either.

"OK take Jackson Lovie and Hubby put Junior on now since I'm still leaking." I pick up Jackson patting his back for him to burp like they taught us in class, and he does a few pats later. Junior has a bit of a problem latching on but gets it fine the second time.

"OK that's perfect the nurses are going to take the babies to the nursery to get their shots and blood taken for normal test but from the way they just ate without issue I think they are just fine. I will be around for a few more hours if you need anything." Doctor Trent announces leaving the room behind the nurses.

"That was amazing Ife me. I will go fill in the family on our babies and send them back to see you if you want, they can wait." Monty states leaning over to give Meira a kiss telling her he loves her.

"Not yet I want to at least shower first I look a mess and sweaty."

"You look beautiful to me but whatever you need." He kisses her again then leaves.

"He's right you look more beautiful than ever before. I'm truly in awe of what you just went through and the beautiful human beings that just came out of you. My soul has never felt so at peace thank you Lil Phoenix." I give her a slow kiss.

"Thank you, Lovie I am exhausted, though I think I'll take a shower later. I just need to close my eyes for a bit."

"OK I'll step out for a bit and let you rest baby." One of the nurses comes back to help her clean up, but I let her know she doesn't want to shower yet, so she just takes the baby monitor off her stomach and checks to make sure the epidural medicine is done and changing her IV bag then we leave together. I head down the hall to where everyone is looking at our babies.

"Damn they look exactly like you two." Meech states looking in the window at them.

"They're just perfect." Our mother admires them looking full of joy.

"I can't wait to hold them they're so tiny." Za'Mara says next to Monty who has his arm wrapped around her and the other around Mariah. Za'Meir comes next to me, and I wrap my arm around his shoulder.

"You happy about your lil brothers and sister?" I ask him.

"So happy Papi but they're so small are they ok?" He questions looking at them.

"They are fine. They were born a lil early so they will stay here a lil longer than usual but -." Before I can finish my sentence, an alarm goes off saying code blue in room two and I quickly realize it's Meira's room and take off with the fam right behind me.

To be continued...

Love Unapologetic

SNEEK PEAK

Steven "Calder" Flemmington

I have been hiding out in this damn cabin for about a week now. I still can't believe they had all those damn files on us. The moment we discovered all this mess started with Sinclair's incompetent ass I sent Julius my right hand to handle him as discreetly as possible. If I wasn't here hiding out from the FED's this place may actually be relaxing. Justin's father cut me off completely leaving me on my own but luckily my right hand stayed loyal and had this place under one of his aliases. He did threaten, however if I didn't find his son's killer, I would be next so of course I gave him the info I did have on them. My sulking is broken by the front cabin door opening then closing and I stand to go inside because it can only be one person.

"Julius."

"Yes, sir it's me."

"Is Sinclair handled?" He left a few days ago to find and get rid of him.

"Yes, I made it look like a suicide. I made him right a letter and all." He explains setting some grocery bags down on the table.

"Well, I'm surprised he didn't do it anyways with the divorce he went through then the investigation the FED's started on him." I blow out a hard breath and run my hands through my messy hair. I seriously need a haircut.

"I think he was going to work with them that is why he wasn't thrown in jail yet or already has but either way he's gone. What do you want to do next?" He questions putting away the groceries.

"Honestly it's not much we can do but I know we can't stay here much longer. I'm all over the damn news. We have to figure out a way to get out of the country."

"I reached out to some of my old CIA contacts as long as you can pay them, they may be able to find a way for us out of the country within a week." He turns from the fridge placing his hands on the dining table chair in front of him.

"I hope we have a week. Did you make sure you weren't followed?"

"Of course, I ditched the car I was using on the side of the road walked about five or six miles and stole another changing out the plates. I'm not new to this boss and you know that."

"I know ughhh. I never thought I would be in this shit. I followed all the rules Justin's dad gave me and still. FUUUCCKKK." I scream throwing one of the chairs across the small room and it shatters against the fireplace.

"Well, I won't have to cut any firewood tonight." Julius shakes his head and he's only partially kidding because up in these mountains it gets really frosty out. I'm hungry at this point so I make a sandwich which is the only thing I know how to make but luckily Julius can cook. I go out to take a walk before it gets dark trying to clear my thoughts. I damn near get lost but finally make it back to the cabin and I can already smell what Julius is cooking up.

"Damn Julius that smells amazing. We make it out of here I am definitely going to need you to teach me a few things." I walk into the small bathroom to wash up but when I head out the front door bust opens but it's not the FED's.

"Who the fuck are you?" I walk fully into the small open space, and I notice Julius gun aimed right at our intruder as well as his three partners who step in. They look familiar but I can't quite put my finger on why.

"You went after *The Queen* and that is unacceptable." The stranger speaks but still doesn't tell me who the hell he is then suddenly, the lights go out and the only thing I can see is the muzzle flashes from guns going off. I feel a hot burning sensation in my side then my chest and another in my shoulder. I fall to the ground as the realization that I have been shot not once but three damn times.

Everything starts to spin and the pain becomes excruciating. I start coughing up my blood then notice the shots have stopped and the lights come on. I roll over and see Julius on the ground with multiple bullet wounds to his body but the that lets me know he's dead is the one right between his eyes that is leaking his blood slowly. I start to smell whatever he was cooking burning.

"Well, you will be dead soon. If only you would have just stuck to serving your constituents and left my Queen alone, you would have lived a long life." The other stranger speaks standing over me.

"Time to go this place will be engulfed in minutes." Another voice comes from the doorway. Everything starts to go black, then the room gets hotter and hotter as the minute's past. I start coughing up more blood as my lungs fill with blood and smoke. I can't believe this is how my life ends on a dusty old wood floor.

About The Author

Lala B.

Lala B. is a new author finally pursuing her dreams of publishing her first book and many other stories she has spent years creating but keeping all to herself. She is still learning all the ins and outs of the literary world and welcomes all constructive criticism to help advance her into being a great author. She loves creating stories that create a safe space for others to dream and open up their minds to new experiences. She has been writing since she was middle school age starting out with short urban stories and has even dabbled in the paranormal realm. She plans on bringing all those books to life for you all to enjoy.

You can keep in touch by following us on social media:

www.facebook.com/AuthorLaLaB

Facebook Group:
https://www.facebook.com/groups/1624464475163982/?ref=share&mibextid=NSMWBT

IG: AuthorLalaB

Bluesky: AuthorLalaB

Website: www.sipngrabyouabook.com

Upcoming Releases

I Married My Dead Cousins Husband

Love Unapologetic: The Fredericks Family Series Book Two